THE KING ABOVE ALL GODS

THE SEVEN WORLDS TRILOGY
BOOK ONE

ALEXANDER BRUCE

PASQUA PUBLISHING

ISBN: 978-1-3999-5280-4 (Print Version)

Pasqua Publishing

United Kingdom

For the LORD is the great God, the great King above all gods.

— PSALM 95:3

PROLOGUE

In the endless void where even light dared not linger, the Watchers gathered. Formless spirits, their essences twisted by rebellion, they possessed only endless awareness—like eyes without lids. Ancient and spiteful, they drifted like poisoned smoke through the abyss, their whispers cold and hungry across the cosmos.

Seven worlds hung before them: fractured, shimmering shards of what was once whole. Eden's fall had been their triumph, the great separation their masterpiece. Humanity—those feeble sparks imprinted with what should have been theirs—now scattered, toiling in darkness, blind to the memory of unity.

They had once sung in the first chorus of creation—every voice raised in worship of the one who spoke it all into being. Now their song was bitterness—glory twisted into hunger.

At the center, the Ancient Watcher was still—vast, unhurried, watching the worlds the way a predator watches something it is in no hurry to finish. He watched with cruel delight. *They have forgotten their origin. Their purpose. Lost, they are easy prey. Hopeless.* Every soul was a weapon to be detonated against the enemy.

The Watchers revelled in chaos, tending the divisions they had sown. Any threat, any flicker of rebellion, would not escape their vigil. So far, all was as intended. Divided, humanity was harmless. United? That must never be allowed.

But then—a tremor.

A light pierced the veil, faint as a distant star igniting. The Ancient Watcher recoiled, shadows writhing. The void contracted; whispers sharpened into urgency. Something had shifted. The celestial court had played a stunning move. Panic rippled through the unheavenly host.

Questions swirled. A messenger had been sent—but to whom? Could the ancient prophecy be true? Was the threat they'd long dismissed as myth stirring at last? The war's balance wavered. In the hush that followed, the Watchers intensified their vigil.

For the first time in an age, they recoiled in wary anticipation.

The King above all gods had made his move.

Something was coming.

CHAPTER
ONE

The final bell blared. John Fischer—slight, invisible by habit—tried to outpace the crush as Shady Springs High erupted into its daily stampede, the hallways emptying as if the building might swallow anyone foolish enough to linger. As always, he failed. Elbows and backpacks buffeted his thin frame until, finally, he spilled into sharp sunlight.

It had been that kind of day from the start. His bike waited with a flat tire. Fixing it made him late, earning him a bright pink tardy slip. At lunch, two boys tipped his tray—sending pizza and pop across the linoleum. Later, Olly Jackson appeared out of nowhere, smacking John's glasses from his face. He ground them into fragments with his heel while his friends howled. John blinked through the blur. At least he kept a backup pair in his bag.

Nearly eighteen, nearly free. He'd hoped—by now—the bullying would stop. He shoved the thought aside and slung himself onto his battered bike. The first push of the pedals sent a little wave of relief through his chest. He wanted to get home.

He'd barely started when a voice called out behind him.

Olly—flanked by four football teammates—was coasting straight for him.

John's hands tightened on the handlebars until the rubber grips squeaked. After the glasses incident, he'd reported Olly. It seemed right at the time. But Olly got detention, and John quickly realized his mistake: Olly's place on the team depended on staying out of trouble. Now there was a target painted on John's back.

He squeezed the brakes, heart pounding. Better to face the music than drag it out. Dust billowed from the gravel road as he slowed. The seconds before they reached him stretched on forever. Olly rolled up first, the others skidding to a stop behind.

"Hey, Johnny," Olly said, swinging off his bike. The four behind him already snickered, hungry for what came next. Olly flicked down his bike stand and spat on the gravel, stepping closer. "You know what you did today was pretty stupid, right?" His voice was almost bored.

John clenched his fists, hoping the tremor in his arms wasn't visible. "Come on, Olly. Just do what you came for."

Olly's grin widened. "Where's the fun in that?" He always played his game first—like a cat toying with a mouse.

They faced each other. John's hands ached to punch Olly, but he never stooped that low. He knew he'd lose. Olly was a giant: six-two, built like a wall. Everything John—five-nine and skinny—wasn't.

John dropped his bike, fists still curled. He'd rehearsed this a hundred times—swing, duck, run. But as Olly closed in, John's body betrayed him. Muscles locked, breath vanished.

Olly stopped just inches from John's face, breath fogging his glasses. He cocked his arm as if to swing. John flinched, eyes squeezed shut—

Nothing.

Instead, Olly yanked John's glasses off and dropped them in the gravel, crushing them under his heel.

"You think you hurt me with that stunt today?" Olly sneered. "I'm not going anywhere. The team needs me, and everyone knows it. So think twice before you try that again." He stepped back, arms spread. "I'm untouchable, Johnny."

For a moment, John dared hope that was the end of it. Then Olly punched him—hard, sudden, straight in the face. John staggered, tripped over his bike, and hit the gravel. The impact knocked the air from his lungs. Blood bloomed on his tongue.

Olly and the others laughed, mounting their bikes and riding away as if nothing had happened.

John lay still. He rolled onto his back, head nestled against the bike's wheel, staring up at the sky—so huge, so blue, so far away. He wished, just for a second, that he could vanish. Become someone else. Someone braver. Someone who didn't freeze when it mattered.

The sky didn't answer.

Then—a streak of light tore across the heavens. Bright, fast, gone in a heartbeat. For a moment, the air around John warmed, as if the sky itself had drawn a breath.

Warmth bloomed in his chest, like a hand pressing through skin and bone. John gasped; the sensation was sharp but not painful. Something vast and attentive seemed to notice him there. Then it faded, leaving only a strange echo of comfort behind.

He squinted after the light, but without his glasses, the world was smeared into color and glare. A chill lingered after the warmth faded.

Just a bird, he told himself. He wished he could be like whatever it was—free to fly away.

EVENTUALLY, John forced himself upright. Blood streaked his chin and shirt. He wiped his face with a shaking hand and groaned, hauling his bike to its feet. His cheek throbbed; he didn't check the damage. He already knew what waited at home—his mother's worry, his father's quiet anger. He braced himself and pedalled up the driveway.

His mother was halfway down the stairs when she saw him open the door. She stopped, eyes wide, her face flushing a dangerous red.

"Don't tell me you've had another run-in with those jerks, John."

"Mom, calm down. I'm fine." John tried for a steady voice, but his voice came out tight. "Can you just get my old glasses from my room? I can't see anything."

"That's not all you need, John. Have you seen your shirt? You look like you lost a fight with a combine harvester." Her voice shook—anger tangled with horror. "That's it. I've had enough. I'm calling the police."

"Mom, that'll make it worse. Honestly, I'll be fine. Please, just get my glasses. I can hardly see you."

She muttered something and stomped upstairs—John was grateful he couldn't make it out.

A minute later, she handed him his spare glasses and a clean shirt. As he swapped them out, his dad, Steve, appeared with a damp washcloth.

"I heard what happened," Steve said gently, dabbing at John's face. "I'm sorry, John."

John shrugged away. "You both need to stop worrying," he pleaded. "It's not that bad."

Carol's tone sharpened. "This is ridiculous, Steve. The

school won't do anything. Olly's dad won't do anything. John, you told me Olly's behavior stopped ages ago!"

"Let it go, Mom!" John snapped, surprising even himself. He looked away, jaw tight.

He saw the hurt flicker in her eyes as she pulled him into a hug. This time, he didn't resist.

Carol clung to him, shaking a little. "Sweetheart, I worry he'll do something worse. He really hurt you today. What if—"

He slipped out of her arms, forcing a smile. "Olly cares too much about football to do anything crazy," he lied.

Carol rolled her eyes, brushing his cheek. "Too crazy is his speciality." She took his bloody shirt and shoved him toward the stairs. "Go get changed and do your homework. We'll talk later. Dinner in half an hour."

John climbed to his room. At the top he stopped, hand on the doorframe, not quite ready to go in.

He turned. The small wooden angel from his grandfather lay in the carpet's shadow. He picked it up, tracing the smooth wings with his thumb, remembering his grandfather's voice: *Angels watch over you, John.*

He snorted. "Yeah, right. Could've used one of you today." His voice shook. "If you're watching, you're doing a lousy job."

He glanced at the window. Suddenly, the shutters rattled hard, slamming against the frame. Still holding the angel, John undid the latch and opened the glass, expecting a gust.

There was nothing. Not a breath of wind.

The shutters fell still. John frowned at the little statue. That warmth from the road echoed in his memory.

His hand trembled as he placed the angel on the sill. "Just a coincidence," he whispered.

Outside, the world held its breath, perfectly still.

TWO

"I still say we should call the police on that creep," Carol snapped. The knife came down harder than necessary, chopping the lettuce into jagged pieces as if the vegetable had personally betrayed her. "What's John thinking, telling us to just 'let it go'? If I get my hands on Olly Jackson, I'll show that boy exactly what an icy snow queen looks like."

Steve leaned against the counter. "Before we do anything else, let's try talking to Mitch one more time."

Carol glared. "We've already tried that. Three times."

Steve exhaled. "A senior year is supposed to be the best time of your life. I don't want John's last year to be like this."

"Neither do I," Carol said, quieter. "But letting Olly torture our son isn't drama-free, Steven."

Steve knew the full name was a warning. "At least John's never stooped to Olly's level. That takes real courage. And... we both know he might need that courage soon. When the time comes."

Carol's knife froze. "Not today, Steve. Not your family's stories. Not right now."

"How can you say that? You've seen the proof in the cave. This isn't just—"

She glanced toward the stairs, then hissed, "I don't know what I saw. If all that stuff you believe in hasn't happened by now, it never will. Time to accept that your family made it all up."

The quiet stretched until footsteps sounded on the stairs.

John appeared, bruise darkening. Carol froze mid-motion. "You don't have to say anything," he muttered. "I know how bad it looks."

Steve jumped in before Carol could speak. "He's starving, and the soup smells great—let's eat before it gets cold."

Carol read the silent plea in her husband's eyes and forced herself to turn back to the stove. She ladled chicken and rice soup into three bowls, the liquid sloshing harder than necessary.

They sat. Hands folded. Steve led the prayer, voice steady but quiet. "Lord, bless this meal and those who have none. Amen."

John mouthed the words out of habit but kept his doubts locked behind his teeth. His parents still went to church every Sunday. He only went at Christmas and Easter, when they made him.

Carol broke the silence almost immediately. "Pastor Williams called this morning. He asked if you'd join the confirmation class this year."

John's spoon paused. "Mom. Please. I told you I'm not doing that."

"That was last year," she said, trying to keep her tone light. "You're almost eighteen now."

"That doesn't mean I've changed my mind." John winced as the bruise throbbed. "After today, can you blame me? If there's a God, why would he let this happen?"

Carol's shoulders tightened. "Olly being a bully isn't proof there's no God, John."

He set the spoon down harder than he meant to. "It's not just Olly. Science doesn't need God to explain anything. We're not special. We're just one planet out of billions. There's probably life out there somewhere. And there are a million religions—they can't all be true, but you're sure yours is?"

Carol took a slow breath. "It's good to ask questions. There is such a thing as truth. I believe we've been fortunate enough to hear it. And I never said there wasn't life out there."

Steve's spoon slipped and clattered into his soup. "Why all the talk about aliens?"

Carol answered without missing a beat. "No, John. It wouldn't shake me. I'd be fascinated to learn about their world."

Steve wiped the spill. "Alright, enough. Let's just eat."

The rest of the meal passed in stiff small talk about the farm and the weather. John ate quickly, the bruise throbbing with every bite. He could feel his parents watching him with that worried love he both needed and hated. As soon as the bowls were cleared, he excused himself and headed upstairs.

Later, he heard voices drifting up the stairs—his father's, sharper than usual, and Mitch Jackson's. John hovered for a moment in the hallway, wondering if he should go down and say something, but he already knew it wouldn't change anything. He continued to his room.

He wandered to the window and looked up. Aliens, God, random chance—it all spun through his mind. Why do some people get everything, and others just get pushed around?

Then, movement: a streak of light slicing across the sky. Not a meteor—this light slowed, hovered, pulsed with a gentle amber glow. It seemed to be watching him. Light and warmth arrived together, as if the universe had drawn a slow breath against the glass.

Whatever it was, he couldn't dismiss it this time.

What if I'm not imagining this? What if something really is out there?

He reached for the latch, every part of him wanting to open the window, to call out, to believe. But fear anchored him.

He turned out the lights and crawled into bed, staring at the ceiling. The question pressed down on him, heavy and electric: Was he losing his mind... or had something vast and patient finally turned its gaze toward Shady Springs?

STEVE LEFT home before John woke. The call with Mitch had gone exactly as expected, and he'd still emailed the principal. That shrug John had given him—shoulders dropping, eyes down, the acceptance of someone who'd stopped expecting things to change—pressed against Steve's chest as he drove.

He parked his truck beside the forest fence. It was time to fulfil his family's duty.

The walk through the trees felt longer than usual. Something in the air had shifted—a stillness that wasn't quite natural, a weight that made each step deliberate.

As he approached the cave entrance, Steve noticed the light first—not sunlight, but a soft golden radiance pulsing like a heartbeat.

The warmth reached him before he even entered—not the warmth of flame, but something deeper. It pressed against his chest and made his eyes sting with unexpected emotion. His hands trembled as he stepped across the threshold.

Inside, the cave had transformed.

The air hummed—not with sound, but with presence.

Something vast and still, filling every corner of the stone chamber.

And there, standing in the center, was a figure.

Steve's throat tightened. His breath came shallow and rapid. He had imagined this moment for years, even decades. He rehearsed it in his mind a thousand times. But now that it was here, the words he'd prepared scattered like ash.

Steve's legs nearly gave out. He gripped the cave wall to steady himself, his palm pressing hard against the cold stone. His other hand moved to his chest, where his heart hammered so violently he thought it might break through his ribs.

He forced himself to speak, though his voice came out hoarse. "The time has come, hasn't it?"

He already knew the answer.

The figure's eyes—ancient beyond measure, yet filled with infinite kindness—met his own.

"It has, old friend."

The words resonated through the cave, through Steve's chest, through his very soul. They carried the weight of destiny, of sacrifice.

He stood there, trembling. The prophecy was real. From this point on, nothing could return to the way it was before.

His son would be the Traveller.

CHAPTER

THREE

J ohn woke up before the alarm went off, and anxiety
was already there—sitting in his chest like a weight.

He lay still for a moment, staring at the ceiling,
listening to the quiet of the house. His face ached when
he breathed in too deeply. The bruise from yesterday felt
tighter than it had the night before.

He swung his legs over the side of the bed and sat there,
elbows on his knees, forcing himself to think of something
good.

Eight more months.

That was it.

He'd be done with school.

Done with Olly.

The thought fixed nothing, but it gave him enough
strength to stand.

A few minutes later, the smell of bacon and eggs drifted up
the stairs, helping more than it should have done.

He got dressed, grabbed his backpack, and headed downstairs. The smell made him think that if anything good could

come from having to work on his family farm, it was his mom's breakfasts.

Carol turned as soon as she heard him and narrowed her eyes at his face. "John... if that kid does anything to you today, you call me. Immediately."

"Okay," he said, keeping his tone flat as he slid onto the stool.

"I mean it," she said. "No more chances."

John stabbed a piece of egg with his fork. "Yeah. I heard you."

Carol took a breath, then softened her voice. "Your father talked to Mr Jackson last night. A long talk. I think it might actually have made a difference this time."

John didn't look up. "Sure."

"John," Carol warned.

John forced himself to sound less sarcastic. "I hope you're right."

"At least your face looks a little better today," said Carol, leaning in to study his injury. "Still, it'll take a while for that whopper to heal fully. You know, I could cover it up with a little touch of the brush."

"Makeup?" John almost choked on his food. "Can you imagine how Olly would react if he found that out?"

"Relax, kid. I was only offering." Carol bent down and kissed John on the forehead. "Get going now. Remember, if Olly—"

"I know, I know. If anything happens, I'll call," he said, already stepping outside into the cool autumn air.

John hopped on his bike and pedalled toward school. He told himself today would be different. He repeated it like a prayer he didn't believe in.

His family only had one car, which his father used every morning. John saved every penny he earned for his own car.

His parents supported it as it would help the farm. That thought alone made him uneasy. Running a big farm wasn't his dream—he wasn't sure what was yet, but he knew it wasn't Shady Springs.

After securing his bike to a rack outside the school, John joined the dozens of other students pushing through the doors. He had only been in the building ten seconds when he heard Principal Sunti call his name over the PA system. "Attention, please. John Fischer, report to the principal's office. John Fischer, please report to the principal's office immediately."

John froze.

The hallway didn't get quieter, but it felt like it did, as if the air itself had stopped moving.

His stomach churned. Every eye was on him—and not only because of the huge purple shiner on his face.

John went up the stairs to the second floor, each step heavier than the last. He stopped before the principal's door, took a deep breath, and knocked.

"Come in," the principal called from inside.

John stepped inside and froze. Olly sat across from Principal Sunti, his face drawn tight—but not with the familiar hardness of a bully. His eyes were wide, almost desperate, and his hands gripped the armrests as if bracing for impact.

"Please, take a seat," said Principal Sunti, leaning forward and resting his elbows on the desk. "First of all, I hope your injuries aren't too serious." Mr Sunti couldn't look away from the huge bruise. "But seriously, you might want to get some ice for that, son."

John nodded and lowered himself into the chair beside Olly. The bully sat in silence with his head down.

"John, last night, your dad sent me an email about your ride home from school. I was horrified to learn what happened."

John's throat tightened. He never thought his father would escalate things this far—never thought the principal would actually call them both in. His fingers curled against his thigh. He forced himself to breathe evenly, but his chest felt tight, his pulse hammering in his ears.

The principal shot Olly a stern look. "I think Olly wants to say something to you."

Olly's hands gripped the armrests, knuckles white. He opened his mouth, closed it again, and swallowed hard.

"I just want to say..." He paused, his jaw working as if the words were physically stuck. "I want to say I'm sorry, John."

The name caught John off-guard. *John*. Not Johnny. Not the usual crude variations. The formal name hung in the air like something foreign. Olly's voice had changed too—softer, more measured.

John's fingers curled against his thigh, then uncurled. He swallowed, unsure what to do with this.

"And what else?" the principal interjected.

"I'm going to make this up to you. Here, take this," said Olly, handing John a check for $500.00. "That's to pay for a trip to the eye doctor and a new pair of glasses."

John took the check, his hands moving almost of their own accord. He studied the numbers, Olly's signature, trying to reconcile this moment with every shove, every insult, every fist that had found him in the hallway.

"And?" The principal rolled his hand.

"Look, I'm sorry, and I promise I won't hurt you again."

"Good," said the principal. "Mr Fischer, do you accept his apology?"

John's mind flashed through years of being shoved, tripped, mocked, punched, and humiliated. Years of pretending it didn't matter. A check and one forced apology couldn't erase any of that.

It might be the closest thing to an apology he'd ever get. Plus, $500.00 would really help his car fund. "Yes, I accept, but I have one question for him."

The principal raised an eyebrow. "Okay, go on."

"Why?"

Olly looked confused. "Why what?"

"Why do you hate me?"

The question landed like a physical blow. Olly's shoulders tensed. He stared down at his hands, but John could see his teeth clenched so hard a muscle jumped in his cheek.

"Why have you been so awful to me all this time? I never hurt you or did anything to you. You know, when we were little, I even wanted to be your friend."

Olly's eyes lifted—just for a second—and met John's. Something flickered across his face. Something raw and unguarded. His eyes looked almost glassy, as if he were seeing John—really seeing him—for the first time in years. Not as a target, but as a person.

"Is there anything you'd like to say, Mr Jackson?" asked the principal.

"I said I'm sorry. Okay? Can we be done now?"

"We have about three minutes before the bell. John, you go to class first. I need to have a word with Olly in private."

John nodded and left the office, closing the door behind him. He only made it two steps before he leaned back against the wall and listened.

"This is your final warning, Oliver. One more incident like this, and you are off the team. Not only that, you will be expelled. If you give John, or any student in this school, an injury like that again, you can kiss goodbye a football career."

A pause. Then, more quietly, "I'll also be calling your father this afternoon to discuss what happened."

The silence that followed was different from the one before it. Shorter. Tighter.

Then Olly's voice came—not loud at first, but building, cracking at the edges.

"What about the team?" His fist slammed against the desk. "They can't make it without me. You need me!" The words came faster now, more desperate. "Your school is nothing without the team, and the team is nothing without me!"

But beneath the bravado, John heard something else—less like arrogance and more like fear. As if Olly was trying to convince himself as much as the principal. As if he was terrified of what he'd be if football was taken away.

John stood frozen outside the door. He'd never heard Olly sound like that before. Not angry. Scared.

Despite Olly's outburst, the principal remained calm.

"One of these days, your ego and your temper will get you into serious trouble," said Mr Sunti. "And just so we're clear, football is important to this school, but the well-being of my students will always come first. Now get out and don't ever try to bully me again. This really is your last chance, Mr Jackson."

John heard Olly shove the chair back and quickly stepped away, hurrying down the stairs before Olly could see him.

He walked toward class, shoulders loosening with each step. Any physical aggression from Olly now would mean instant expulsion—and with it, the end of his football career.

For the first time in years, John felt safe.

CAROL HAD SPENT the drive to the cave rehearsing exactly what she would say when nothing was there. Sharp, final, unanswerable. She'd driven out there a dozen times on his family's word and found nothing but rock and damp air, and today was going to be no different. She was going to say so clearly, and Steve was going to have to hear it.

Once they were inside and nothing looked out of the ordinary, she drew breath. "You know what? I am so tired of this. We went over all this last night."

"Carol," Steve implored.

"I have tried to hear you out, and I've played along with your stories all this time, but now I'm through with it. Do you need professional help?"

"Just wait a minute."

"What am I waiting for?"

The words were already forming—something final, something that would end this for good.

"Me," said a voice from behind Carol.

Steve lifted his gaze from Carol's eyes to the figure standing behind her. He knew if what she was about to see didn't convince her, nothing would.

Carol spun around.

The prayer came before thought, before breath, before her legs gave way and dropped her to her knees.

God, protect him. Please. Whatever this is, protect him.

All the ridicule she'd aimed at Steve seemed impossibly petty.

Steve knelt beside her and held her.

CHAPTER
FOUR

The final bell rang. Students poured out of the building in their usual frantic wave, backpacks swinging, voices rising. John wove through the crowd and headed straight for his bike, shoulders already loosening. For the first time in years, the walk to the rack didn't feel like running a gauntlet.

He was unlocking the chain when he heard the voice behind him.

"John."

Not Johnny. Not "nerd" or any of the usual variations. Just his real name, spoken carefully.

John's stomach gave a quick, sour flip. He turned slowly.

Olly stood a few feet away, alone this time. His usual cocky posture was gone. He scratched the back of his neck, awkward and unsure, like someone who had rehearsed his lines but forgotten how to deliver them.

"Look," Olly started, eyes flicking to the ground then back up. "I've been thinking about what you said in the principal's office. We're both almost eighteen." He paused. "I want a fresh start. What do you say?"

John didn't want friendship. He didn't even want an apology, not really. All he wanted was for the constant knot in his gut to disappear.

"I want a fresh start, John. What do you say?"

The words hung there. Every old shove, every crushed pair of glasses, every hallway laugh pressed down on John's shoulders. But beneath it all, his breath came a fraction steadier—less like surrender and more like the first crack of daylight after a long night.

"Yeah, Olly," he said at last. "I'd like that."

Olly's face broke into a relieved, almost boyish grin. "I'm glad you said that."

The moment had the texture of someone else's life. It became even stranger when Olly extended his hand.

John stared at it. The fingers weren't curled into fists. They weren't clenched. After years of flinching every time Olly came near, his own body hesitated, unsure whether to trust the gesture.

He reached out anyway. The grip was firm but genuine.

"Tonight," Olly said, still holding on a second longer than necessary, "I want you to come to the post-practice party at Jim's Diner. Only players and their guests, but... I'm inviting you. Just this once."

John knew those parties. They were for the popular kids, the ones who never had to look over their shoulder. He'd never been anywhere near one.

"I'll be there," he replied, surprised by how steady his voice sounded.

Olly gave his hand one last shake and clapped him on the shoulder—gentle, almost friendly. "See you tonight." Then he jogged off toward the football field without another word.

John stood there for a moment, bike chain dangling from his fingers, the afternoon sun warm on his face.

He waited for the usual tightness—the suspicion, the voice in the back of his head saying don't trust it. It didn't come. Just the sun, and the quiet, and the strange lightness of a day that had somehow ended better than it began.

Maybe things actually were going to change. Maybe Olly meant it. Maybe eight months wasn't a countdown to escape anymore—maybe it was just eight months.

He swung his leg over the bike and started pedalling, glancing behind him once out of habit. Then he stopped doing even that.

Halfway down Maple Street, past the old hardware store, the flash appeared again.

It shot across his path so suddenly that John slammed on the brakes. The bike skidded sideways. He barely kept his balance as the glowing amber orb hovered twenty feet ahead, pulsing softly.

Not a headlight. Not a reflection.

The light drifted with purpose toward the tree line at the edge of the forest. John felt that familiar warmth bloom in his chest—the same vast, attentive presence he had felt after Olly's punch and again at his bedroom window. This time, it felt like it was calling him.

His hands trembled on the handlebars. The orb hovered, waiting.

For a second, he wanted to follow it. To chase whatever this was and finally understand. For the first time, the thought arrived: something was watching.

But then he thought of Olly's invitation. The party. The chance to feel normal for one night.

No, he told himself, gripping the bars tighter. *This is just stress. Your mind is playing tricks after everything that's happened.*

The light pulsed brighter, insistent.

John shook his head and forced himself to look away. "I'm not doing this," he muttered. "There's no such thing as supernatural lights. I'm tired."

He pushed off hard and pedalled past the spot where the orb had been, refusing to glance back. He almost had himself convinced it was nothing more than a trick of the fading sunlight.

He jumped off the bike before it had fully stopped and ran up the porch steps. But the words died in his throat the moment he opened the door.

His parents were sitting on the sofa, heads bowed, shoulders slumped in the same posture they'd had the day they told him Grandpa Bill had died.

John's stomach dropped. He took a slow breath and stepped into the living room.

"What's happened?"

"Nothing, sweetie," Carol said, but her voice was thin.

"Then why do you both look like someone died?"

Steve tried for a normal tone and failed. "We're fine, John. How was your day? Was Olly okay with you?"

John pushed the uneasy feeling down and let the excitement take over.

"You're never gonna believe this. Olly and I got called into the principal's office this morning. He apologized. He gave me a check for five hundred dollars for new glasses. Then after school, he invited me to the post-practice party at Jim's tonight."

He waited for the explosion of surprise, the questions, the warnings.

Instead, his parents stayed silent. Carol's eyes were glassy with tears she hadn't wiped away. Steve stared at the floor like it held the weight of the world.

John's excitement soured on his tongue. "Do you... think I should go? I already said yes, but if you think it's a bad idea—"

Carol forced a smile that didn't reach her eyes. "Yes. We want you to go."

Her voice cracked on the last word.

"It's good news, right?" John asked, unsure.

"It is good news," she said, the smile trembling. "I'm just... really happy for you. Go upstairs and finish your homework. Do you want something to eat before you head out?"

"I'll probably order at the diner."

"Of course," Steve said quickly. "Go celebrate. We're proud of you."

John stood there, the strange knot in his stomach tightening. His parents never acted like this. Normally, his mom would be issuing warnings, and his dad would be offering to drive him. Something was wrong.

"Okay... I'll go to my room then."

He climbed the stairs. When he reached his room, he picked up the small wooden angel statue from the shelf, turning it slowly in his hands.

"Well, little angel," he whispered, "maybe I was wrong about you. Today actually turned out pretty good."

JOHN CHANGED into a red shirt and jeans. He rushed downstairs, and the first thing that hit him was the silence—no smell of dinner, no sound of anything cooking. His parents always made a proper meal, even if he wouldn't be home to eat it.

He walked into the kitchen and found them sitting at the breakfast bar with a bag of chips and a bottle of wine between them. His mom's eyes were still puffy from crying.

"Okay, you two, spit it out. What is really going on? Mom,

you never eat Doritos, and I've never seen you two skip dinner. And what have you been crying about? Your face is more swollen than mine. Did someone die? Is it the farm?"

Carol and Steve kept their heads down for a moment.

"John," Steve said, "everything is fine. Nobody died, and nothing's wrong with the farm."

John was getting impatient with their lack of answers. "Are you getting divorced?"

"What?" they both said at the same time.

"Goodness, no," said Carol. "We just had a hard day. But you're right, sweetie. We should eat something more than a bag of chips. I'll pull something out of the freezer in a few minutes. When you get home, we can talk about my day."

"Okay, Mom. As long as you're alright. You don't have terminal cancer or something, do you?"

"For crying out loud, John. No, I'm fine. Now get over here and give your mother a hug."

Before he could even move, she was already on her feet, wrapping her arms around him.

"We love you so much, John."

"How about I make it weird and turn this into a hug sandwich?" his dad said, stepping in and putting his arms around both of them.

"Dad, you're so creepy," John laughed as he tried to squirm free. "I'll see you two later. And I want to hear about your day when I get back."

He grabbed his jacket and hurried toward the door.

As soon as he was out of sight, Carol collapsed into Steve's arms, and the two of them broke down in tears.

Neither of them said what they both already knew.

CHAPTER
FIVE

The autumn darkness came early. John pedalled fast along the narrow road from the farm into town, his headlamp barely denting the gloom. The blacktop slipped by beneath his wheels, broken only by pockets of orange under the scatter of streetlights.

His thoughts pulled backward—to his parents, to the farmhouse behind him. Guilt cinched behind John's ribs like a too-tight strap. He could still picture his dad's face after Grandpa Bill died: the way Steve had held Carol for hours, wordless, his strength fraying at the edges. The farm, always the farm—each season bleeding more money, but his parents held on. After Olly smashed his glasses, after bruises and every petty humiliation, they'd always been there when he came limping home.

And now here he was, leaving them behind.

He gripped the handlebars tighter. *I'll eat fast,* he promised himself. *Get home, find out what's wrong.*

He swung onto Main Street. The familiar row of small shops glowed softly—a post office, a grocery store, a gas station, the diner, and the doctor's office. Shady Springs didn't

26

have much, but for fewer than five hundred people, it didn't need more.

He listed the good things about living there, let them chase away the tight, trapped feeling in his chest.

The diner's neon sign glowed ahead. A row of bikes stood lined up along the curb, but the parking lot was empty—no one lingering, no laughter.

He shrugged it off. *Tonight would be fine*, he told himself. With Olly's invitation and the principal's warning hanging over everyone, nobody would risk messing with him.

He wheeled up to the rack, locked his bike beside the others, and hurried toward the entrance, nerves quickening his steps.

He never made it to the door.

In the blink of an eye, everything went black. Something dropped over his head from behind—a black bag pulled tight around his face.

John grabbed at it, trying to rip it off, but a fist slammed into his stomach before he could get a grip. The air rushed out of his lungs, and he collapsed to the ground, gasping.

Two people grabbed his arms and legs, stretching him out while he struggled to breathe. Rough hands rolled him onto his stomach, and rope tightened around his wrists and ankles before he could even shout.

He felt himself lifted by his shoulders and feet, carried like a sack of grain.

A wave of dizziness hit as they tossed him into the back of a pickup truck. A second later, someone jumped in beside him and shoved him hard with a boot, forcing him against the metal bed.

The engine roared to life.

Olly.

How could I be so stupid? I should have known better.

He wanted to shout, but every time he tried to speak, the person next to him struck him again, knocking the breath out of him.

It didn't take long before the truck stopped.

John heard doors slam, then footsteps coming toward the back. The tailgate dropped, and hands grabbed him, dragging him out and throwing him onto the ground. Gravel dug into his skin, and pain shot through his ribs.

Someone cut the rope from his feet while a voice he didn't recognize ordered him to stand.

He struggled upright. Then someone ripped the bag off his head. Olly and his dad stood only a few feet in front of him.

"Hi, Johnny," said Olly, beaming from ear to ear. He pulled his arm back, ready to punch, but Mitch caught his wrist before he could swing.

"No, Olly," Mitch warned. "You promised the principal you wouldn't hurt him." He stepped forward, blocking Olly, and gave John the same smug look his son used so often.

"This won't take long, Johnny," Mitch sneered. "Just think of this as a little rite of passage. The way men handle things in this town. After tonight, you'll understand how the big boys do business."

Now that the bag was off, John could finally breathe enough to speak.

"What do you want from me? I didn't do anything to you."

Mitch leaned in close, only inches from his face.

"A soft kid like you probably never learned how things work around here. Your dad never taught you how men deal with threats."

"I didn't threaten anyone."

Mitch laughed.

"Ha! That's a laugh. You went crying to your daddy and the principal about yesterday. You knew exactly what that would do. My son is one of the best players in the state, and because of you, he was this close to losing his place on the team."

"I wasn't trying to get him off the team, I swear."

"My boy's got a future ahead of him," Mitch snapped. "Scouts are at every practice this month. Every game. And you almost ruined it."

"I didn't do it on purpose. I wasn't trying to threaten him."

"Like hell you weren't," Mitch barked. His voice turned mocking. "You wanted to show him you were in charge, that you weren't gonna take it anymore."

His condescending smile faded, and his tone grew colder.

"That was a threat. And around here, we don't let threats slide."

John started to answer, but Mitch raised a finger to his lips.

"You know, I had to beg the principal today, so Olly wouldn't be suspended. I don't beg anyone. So now I'm going to make sure you remember your place."

John's hands trembled, ribs aching with every breath.

"Do you understand me?" Mitch shouted. "My son isn't spending the next eight months worrying about what you might say or do. He's got everything going for him, and you've got nothing. Nothing but a farm and a bunch of cows waiting for you one day."

"Mr Jackson, I promise," John blurted. "I won't say anything. I won't even look at Olly. Just... please let me go."

"Oh, I will," Mitch replied calmly. "But first, you need to learn the lesson I told you about. The lesson about how men settle things in this town."

He glanced over his shoulder at the boys standing behind him.

"I brought these other boys because they didn't promise anyone they wouldn't hurt you."

One boy stepped forward and drove his fist into John's

stomach. The blow doubled him over and sent him crashing to the ground. Before he could even catch his breath, another kick slammed into his chin, snapping his head back.

Pain exploded through his mouth, and he tasted blood.

A third boy stomped down on his chest, and John heard a sickening crack. He screamed as the air rushed out of his lungs.

Mitch laughed. "That's enough," he said after a moment. "We don't want him dead."

John lay curled on the gravel, shaking, trying to breathe through the pain.

"Listen carefully," Mitch went on. "Pretty soon, you're going to get back on your bike and ride home. You're going to tell your parents you had a great time tonight. So great that you even broke the rules and had a drink someone sneaked in."

He leaned closer.

"And because of that, you lost control of your bike on the way home, had a little accident. That's why you look like this. Got it?"

John nodded weakly.

"If I hear one word about this," Mitch continued, his voice dropping to a whisper, "your mom, your dad, and your farm will all suffer. I swear on my life."

He grabbed John by the hair and forced his head up.

"And forget about that check Olly gave you. Closed account."

He spat in John's face and shoved him back down.

The boys laughed as John curled into himself, trying to block out the pain. One by one, they stepped forward, taking turns spitting on him before backing away.

Mitch clapped his hands once. "There's one last part of this little rite of passage." He yanked John's shirt and forced him to stand. "This is the best part. You get a twenty-five-second head start to run away, and then your friends here will run after you. Try to get away as fast as you can!"

The group laughed, loving every word. John could barely stand, let alone run, but he knew one thing for sure: if they caught him again, he might not survive.

He looked around, trying to figure out where he was. He'd lost his last pair of glasses and couldn't see clearly.

Then he saw it. A bright flash streaked across the sky—the same one he had seen the day before. It shot down behind the town's water tower, only a short distance away. The sight of the tower made his heart leap.

He knew where he was: near the protected forest.

And the forest meant hiding places.

John could see the fence surrounding it. He remembered the loose boards he and his dad used to pull open when he was younger to sneak in and explore. He knew exactly where they were.

It was his only chance.

"On your mark..." yelled Mitch.

John bent his knees, ignoring the pain in his ribs.

"Get set..."

His hands were still tied behind his back. He would have to break through the boards with his feet.

"Go!"

Adrenaline took over as John ran. Every step felt like knives in his chest, but he kept moving, counting down in his head.

24, 23, 22...

The fence wasn't far. John remembered the loose boards were three or four boards to the left of the 'Keep Out' sign.

17, 16, 15...

John reached the fence and squinted, trying to see through the darkness. He saw the outline of the sign and found the loose boards. He kicked at them with his foot, missing the first time. He tried again and hit one hard enough to knock it open. He shoved it higher with his foot and forced his body through the gap. His shoulder scraped the wood, but he made it. He hoped the tall jocks would struggle to get through with their bigger frames.

3, 2, 1...

They were coming.

Branches snapped as he stumbled deeper into the trees, the moon the only light guiding him. He could hear them fighting with the fence, then tearing the boards loose.

They were through.

John ran as far as his body would let him, lungs burning, vision swimming.

Then the flash came again to his right—the same bright streak—and for a heartbeat, the same strange warmth brushed his skin.

For the briefest instant, the light flared against the rock face ahead, and in that moment, he noticed something: a narrow opening between the stones. It was little more than a crack.

John stared at it. He wouldn't last much longer out in the open. His legs trembled beneath him, strength fading fast.

Staggering toward the opening, he turned sideways and forced himself into the gap. The stone pressed hard against his ribs, stealing the breath from his lungs, but he pushed forward inch by inch until the passage widened just enough for him to move.

Behind him, through the narrow slit of the entrance, he saw the glow of a phone flashlight sweeping across the trees.

They were close.

Gritting his teeth, John pressed deeper into the darkness until the ground beneath him levelled out. The cold air of the passage surrounded him, and the sounds of the forest faded behind him.

He was no longer outside.

He was inside.

A cave.

John pressed his back to the rough wall, each breath sharp with dust and fear. Sweat stung the cuts on his cheek. He squeezed his eyes shut, waiting for footsteps or laughter—anything—but only his own heartbeat echoed in the darkness.

He ran a trembling hand over the stone, searching for something solid. His teeth chattered—not from cold, but from the hollow ache growing in his chest. Home felt impossibly far away. The sound of the diner, the hum of his bike, even his parents' voices—already fading, like a memory slipping under water.

He pulled his knees up, curling small as pain throbbed in his ribs. He listened, but the only answer was silence. The kind that comes when you realize no one is coming to help.

After a while, his breathing slowed. Alone, hidden, John opened his eyes to the blackness and knew, without saying it, that nothing would be the same after this. His old life—the safety, the routine, the illusion that he could go back—was gone. Whatever waited in this cave, he had already crossed a line that couldn't be uncrossed.

Suddenly, a beam of light cut into the opening behind him...

It flickered at the edge of his vision and vanished.

John frowned.

"Great," he muttered under his breath. "Olly must've punched my retina loose."

Then the light appeared a third time.

But this time, it did not vanish.

Instead, it glowed faintly against the cave wall, circling

slowly like a tiny spark caught in the air. The dim light moved in a gentle spiral, illuminating a small patch of stone.

"What the..?"

John leaned closer, squinting through his blurred vision. The light seemed to dance around something protruding from the rock.

Something metal.

A lever. At least... that was what it looked like.

He twisted awkwardly, trying to reach it with his hands still bound behind his back, but the angle was impossible. No matter how he strained, his fingers could not quite touch it.

Then, suddenly, the light vanished.

The cave was plunged back into complete darkness.

John exhaled slowly.

"I really need my eyes tested," he said to himself.

For a moment, there was only silence.

Then a voice spoke from somewhere deeper within the cave.

"You may not have to worry about that."

CHAPTER

SIX

John took a step back, fists raised. "Who are you?" His voice cracked.

A tall figure stood a few paces away, torchlight flickering across the cave walls, the man's face shifting and deepening with every flame. He was broader and taller than anyone John had ever seen—bigger than Olly, bigger than any coach. His presence crowded the air.

The man's voice was even, almost gentle. "It is more important that we speak about you."

"My name is John. I—I didn't mean to tresp—"

"My name is Danrael." The man's smile was steady, calm and ancient all at once. "I know who you are. I have known your family for generations. Your great-grandfather, your father, I am pleased to meet you, too."

John's stomach dropped. "You're mistaken. My great-grandfather died a long time ago. And you don't look a day over twenty-five."

Danrael's eyes seemed to twinkle, but the weight in them was bottomless. "Things are not always what they seem."

John tried for a laugh, but it hitched, catching on pain. He pressed a palm to his side, ribs burning. "I'm not in the mood for riddles. What is this?"

Danrael tilted his head, taking John in as if he were a puzzle with a missing piece. "Perhaps I should begin by telling you that what is going on is not entirely on Earth."

The words landed like stone. John's breath stuttered. He coughed, wincing, the taste of blood sharp at the back of his tongue.

Danrael's expression softened. "What I am about to say may surprise you. If you're confused, raise your hand and stop me."

John raised his hand immediately—and then froze.

His wrists were bare. Where the rope had dug angry burns, there was nothing but damp air and the faint, sticky sting of old pain.

He turned his palms over, flexing his fingers. "Wait... what?" His voice barely escaped. "Did you—?"

Danrael lifted one hand. A ripple of warm light passed through the air. The stone wall shuddered and rose smoothly into the ceiling. Dust swirled. Beyond it yawned a much larger chamber.

John placed a palm against the cold wall to steady himself. "What... is this place?"

Danrael's gaze swept the chamber with something close to reverence. "Your grandfather built this entrance. This is your birthright."

John's legs went unsteady. "I think I need to get out of here."

He turned, only to find Danrael blocking the passage—not with his body, but with that same quiet wall of light.

"John Fischer," Danrael said, the name heavier than stone.

"This is your birthright, as it was for your father, Steve, and for his father before him."

John's eyes narrowed. "I never told you my last name. Or Dad's."

Danrael simply lifted an arm. Fire blossomed along the chamber walls, torches igniting in a circle. In the center of the room, a tall black metal obelisk stood, covered in strange symbols that seemed to crawl as the light touched them.

John's knees threatened to give. He leaned against the cold rock, breath coming shallow. His ribs throbbed, but beneath it, something else was shifting—a tingle, a vibration, a sense of the world tilting underfoot.

Danrael continued, voice soft but unyielding. "Your grandfather carved the little wooden angel here. I was the model."

John's mouth went dry. "You... were there?"

"I was."

John let out a shaky, disbelieving laugh. "So either you're telling the truth... or you're the best liar I've ever met." His pulse thundered in his ears. "The flashes of light I kept seeing —that was you, wasn't it?"

Danrael nodded once. "I tried to bring you here gently. Even on the road, I called to you. But you turned away."

John swallowed hard. The strange warmth, the sense of being watched—it all crashed back over him.

"So you're... an angel?" The word felt ridiculous on his tongue.

"I am."

For a moment, time stretched. John limped forward, every step against gravity, drawn to the pillar in spite of himself. The symbols seemed to breathe, light sliding over them in gold and blue. He reached out, knuckles white, and brushed the cold surface.

"What is this?"

"A portal," Danrael said, voice low. "One of seven. Doors between the worlds God created."

John yanked his hand back, fingers tingling. "You mean... planets?"

"Yes. Seven sister worlds. Each home to people not so unlike you."

John stumbled as lightheadedness struck. He regained his footing and backed away, the cave pressing in. "This is nuts."

Danrael's eyes never wavered. "Your world has forgotten. The portals were sealed long ago—after humanity's fall. Now there are only stories."

John pressed the heel of his hand to his forehead, trying to steady his breath. His vision blurred. "And this has just been... hiding here? In Shady Springs?"

"Hidden. Guarded by your family."

A jolt ran through John. "My family?"

"Yes. Your great-grandfather was first. Before him, another family—until their line ended."

John's hands trembled. "My dad knows? He's known the whole time?"

Danrael nodded. "Since he came of age. He comes here every morning, making sure no one disturbs the portal. And now, you are called to take up the role."

John's shoulders stiffened. "He never told me."

"I asked him not to," Danrael said. "You needed to choose freely. The weight of family duty would have crushed you."

John gestured helplessly at the chamber. "So you drop all this on me now—after I've been beaten half to death—and call that a choice?"

Danrael's voice remained calm. "The timing was not mine. Your father's duty passes to you—if you accept it. But you're called to more than guardianship, John."

A warning shiver ran up John's arms. "What do you mean?"

Danrael gestured toward the portal. "When the worlds were severed, it was foretold that one would restore what was broken. Unite the worlds. Stand against the darkness. You, John Fischer, are the one chosen since birth—the Traveller."

John smirked, even though his heart hammered. "No. I'm nobody. You've got the wrong person."

"I do not."

"Then your plan is broken!" John's voice fractured, echoing in the stone. "I can't even get through a school day. How could I save seven worlds?"

Danrael's gaze stayed patient. "The power will be given freely—if you accept."

"What power?"

"Power from on high—everything you need for the mission."

He lowered his hands slowly.

"If I say no?" His voice came out rough.

"You return home. The calling passes. But you were chosen by the King above all gods himself."

"King above all gods." John gave a bitter laugh. "You say it like it should mean something to me."

"It is a title from the ancient Hebrew scriptures," Danrael said. "A name for the Most High—the one who breathed life into the seven worlds."

John shook his head. "I'm not religious. If God exists, why doesn't he fix this himself? Why does he need me—or anyone —to fight his battles?"

Danrael's voice softened. "Why he works through people is a mystery. But there is meaning in the struggle."

John stared at the pulsing symbols. "You mentioned a darkness. What is it? How do I fight it?"

Danrael's expression grew somber. "A prophet from one of the worlds once saw what was coming. She wrote a scroll—the way to stop the darkness and the true purpose of the Traveller. It was torn into seven pieces, one hidden on each world. You must collect them."

John's lip curled. "You're joking."

"I am not."

"So I'm supposed to chase scraps of paper across the universe? No, he chose the wrong guy for this," John looked intently at Danrael.

The angel moved closer—his movements so smooth it was as if he were floating. He held John's gaze. "It will not be easy. But you were not chosen for what you are now. You were chosen for who you will become."

John pressed his palm to the portal, the chill grounding him. "Why can't you just tell me what the message says?"

Danrael's mouth quirked. "Angels don't know everything."

"That's not encouraging."

Danrael smirked. "The journey itself may matter as much as the message. Perhaps more."

Silence stretched.

"Is there a chance I might die?"

Danrael's reply was careful. "Your body is not immortal. There will be danger. But death is only another kind of portal. You need not fear it."

John's breath trembled. "Easy for you to say. You're an angel."

"And you are a child of the King above all gods."

John's ribs throbbed. Every part of him wanted to run. But beneath the exhaustion, something stubborn flickered—and he let it.

He raised his head and looked at the portal—the symbols catching the firelight, throwing strange shadows across the cave walls. Something inside him was pulling him toward it, drawing him to whatever waited on the other side.

He thought of Olly's fist, the taste of gravel, the farm, eight more months of the same empty life.

Danrael's words echoed in John's mind: *Who you will become.* He could become someone else.

"Okay," he said, voice raw but steady. "I'll do it. I'll become the Traveller."

Danrael's smile finally reached his eyes. "Very well."

He stepped closer. His human features blurred at the edges. His eyes brightened to liquid silver. When he raised both hands —hovering just above John's head and shoulders—the air crackled.

A wind rose, ancient and cold, swirling dust at their feet. The symbols on the portal flared gold.

Two points of pure white light appeared between Danrael's palms. They swelled, merged, and became a single blazing sphere that pulsed in time with John's heartbeat.

The sphere descended.

John tried to step back. His legs refused.

The light touched his chest.

It struck like a wave against stone. Every nerve ignited at once. His spine snapped straight as invisible hands lifted him off the ground. Bones sang. Muscles tore and rewove themselves stronger. Bruises faded. His eyesight sharpened until he could count every grain of dust swirling past his face.

He tried to scream. No sound came.

The wind became a gale. The portal's symbols blazed so brightly the chamber turned daylight white. John's arms flung wide, back arching as the power drove deeper—scouring fear, shame, doubt, and remaking them.

For one terrible instant, he was certain he would shatter.

Then a single clear thought, not his own, cut through the storm:

Let go.

John stopped fighting.

The pain transformed. It became a forging instead of a breaking. Something vast and ancient settled behind his ribs like a second, steadier heart.

His body glowed, radiant with the same light. The cave trembled. Cracks spiderwebbed across the stone. Dust rained down. The wind howled. The torches roared.

The light flared one final time—absolute and all-consuming.

Then darkness.

John's consciousness flickered. The roar faded. The weight of the transformation settled into his bones like an anchor.

The light itself lowered him gently to the stone floor. His chest rose and fell with shallow breaths. His skin still glowed faintly.

The wind died. The torches dimmed. The portal's symbols faded to a soft, steady glow.

Danrael stood over him.

"It is done," he whispered.

CHAPTER
SEVEN

John hovered in a strange haze between sleep and waking. The last thing he remembered was saying yes to becoming the Traveller. For one disorienting moment, he wondered if Olly's fist had knocked him out at the diner and none of it had happened—the cave, the angel, the blinding light.

Then he opened his eyes.

The cave roof curved above him, rough stone lit by the low flicker of torches. It was no dream. It had all happened.

The first thing he noticed was his vision—crisp, almost painfully sharp. No blur. No need to squint. He reached up instinctively, expecting the familiar weight of his glasses.

There were none.

"It appears the power of the Traveller has improved your eyesight," Danrael said from nearby.

John pushed himself up on one elbow. Danrael stood a few paces away, once again wearing the human-like form he'd first appeared in—emerald-green eyes, long black hair pulled back with a simple pin, white tunic and deep red cloak. The air around him carried that faint, living glow, as if the torchlight itself bent toward him.

John was dumbstruck when he noticed he was almost as tall as Danrael. He looked down at his own body and froze.

His arms were thicker, corded with new muscle. His chest and shoulders had broadened. The torn remains of his shirt and jeans clung to a frame that no longer fit them—seams split, fabric stretched tight. Even his shoes had split at the toes.

He flexed his hands. The raw burns from the rope were gone. The bruise on his cheek no longer throbbed.

Danrael watched him calmly. "Your mission will sometimes require great strength. Endurance alone will not always be enough."

John touched his face again, half expecting his features to have changed. They hadn't. "Do I still look the same?"

"Yes, my friend, you are still yourself. But you've been enhanced to your full potential."

"This is insane... My clothes don't even fit anymore. I think you'll have to give me some new ones, or I won't be able to move."

Danrael folded his arms, raising an eyebrow. "John, I believe you forgot—I'm an angel, not a genie. I don't grant wishes, and I'm certainly not a tailor."

John looked down, embarrassed. "I'm sorry, I assumed—"

Danrael's mouth curved slightly. "When you pass through the portal to your first world, the guardian on the other side will provide what you need."

John sat all the way up, testing his new balance. "The first world... what's it called?"

"Marcrituss." Danrael's voice took on a note of quiet reverence.

John ran a hand through his hair, still trying to process the sheer reality of it all.

"And the language?" he asked. "How am I supposed to talk to anyone there?"

Danrael stepped closer, though he never quite touched the ground. "Do you understand the language I am speaking right now?"

John blinked. "English... right?"

"No. You are hearing the common tongue of Marcrituss. The gift has given you the ability to speak and understand any language you encounter. Just as the Spirit once enabled the apostles."

John let out a stunned breath. One problem solved, at least. "How will I breathe?"

"You will breathe as easily as you do now. You will not need to evolve or adapt in order to survive there."

John's mind caught on something Danrael had said. "Evolution? That's a bit science-y for an angel."

Danrael's eyes sparkled with quiet humour. "You will learn many things on this journey, John. There is no wall between science and God. All truth comes from the same source."

His mother's words came back to him. "I always figured they couldn't go together. I mean, if you can't see God or test him in a lab, then how can he exist?"

Danrael regarded him thoughtfully. "Are you certain no one on Earth has ever seen God? I remember an event that shook the cosmos—an event that changed the history of the universe forever."

John gave a weak smirk. "The Big Bang?"

"Greater than that." Danrael's voice grew quieter, almost reverent. "When the Alpha and the Omega became human. When the Creator stepped into time and walked among His creation. He was most definitely visible."

John's smirk faded. "You're talking about Jesus."

"I am."

For a moment, John didn't know what to say. The old instinct to joke or deflect rose up, but it felt hollow now.

Danrael studied him. "You feel Him calling to you. Something inside already knows the truth... but you're holding back."

John shifted uncomfortably. "Maybe."

"There is nothing to fear in that," Danrael said gently. "All humanity feels it. His mark is written into your very nature. Even the angels were not given the same dignity God gave to your kind."

John looked at Danrael—tall, luminous, clearly not human —and yet somehow familiar.

"You seem so human," he said finally. "Except for the whole never-dying part."

Danrael's expression shifted—something between amusement and gentleness. "I am pure spirit." He turned to the portal beside them and passed his hand slowly through it— through solid metal—as though the structure were made of light and air. "I have no body to damage. No flesh to break."

John thought, without meaning to, of the diner. The bag over his head. The crack of his ribs under someone's boot. The gravel, cold against his cheek, while Mitch Jackson laughed. His body had been a liability his entire life—too small, too slow, too easy to hurt. Even tonight, even transformed, it had been seized and dragged and nearly broken again.

"That seems—" he started, then stopped.

"Better?" Danrael said quietly.

John looked away. "I didn't say that."

"You didn't need to." Danrael withdrew his hand from the portal and turned to face him fully. His voice was unhurried, certain, the way someone speaks when they want each word to land and stay. "But you are wrong, John. And this is something I want you to understand before you step through that portal."

He met John's eyes.

"To be human is a privilege. Not a consolation. Not a limitation to be endured. A privilege—one that no angel has ever been given." His voice dropped slightly. "God Himself took on flesh. The Creator of every world, every star, every living thing—chose to become what you are. Breakable. Mortal. Subject to pain." A pause. "He did not do that despite humanity's dignity. He did it because of it. And by doing so, He raised human flesh higher than anything else in creation—higher than anything I am or will ever be."

John said nothing. The cave was very quiet.

"The darkness calls your kind cattle," Danrael continued. "Weak things. Beneath contempt. That hatred is not incidental, John—it is the whole wound. They were not given what you were given. They wanted to be made in the image of God—and instead, you were. God did not become one of them. He became one of you." His gaze was steady, almost fierce with conviction. "This is important—never let the darkness convince you that being human is something lesser. Your soul is not a poor substitute for what I am. It is something I can only look at with reverence."

Danrael spoke with such conviction that John felt goosebumps rise along his arms—his new, stronger arms, his healed arms, his very human arms.

"Human or not," John said at last, his voice quieter than he expected, "I think we'd be good friends."

Danrael's expression softened with something like affection. "That is kind of you."

He gestured toward the portal. "Before we lose more time, let me show you how the portal works."

John—his new body moving with an ease that still surprised him—stepped closer to the tall metal structure.

"Each symbol represents one of the seven worlds," Danrael explained. "Turn the dial to the world you wish to visit, then place your hand in the center. The portal will open."

John stared at the glowing markings. At first, they meant nothing. Then, like a key turning in a lock, their meaning flooded his mind.

"That one," he said, pointing. "Second from the right. That's Marcrituss."

Danrael nodded, pleased. "Correct. Turn the dial."

John placed his hand on the cool metal. Power surged through his palm. The symbols lit up at his touch. He rotated the dial; a deep clicking echoed through the chamber.

"We need to step back," Danrael instructed. John did as he was told.

The portal began to hum—low at first, then rising until the sound vibrated in John's teeth and bones. Crimson energy snapped and coiled inside the forming triangle like living lightning. Wind rushed toward the opening, tugging at his torn clothes. The air thickened, pressurised, charged with ancient weight.

John stared into the kinetic doorway. Beyond it lay distance itself—depth folding inward, streaked with power older than empires.

"I have to walk into that," he whispered.

For a second, John wondered if he should have asked Danrael to wait. Just one more minute. One more breath of home—the smell of his mother's kitchen, his father's boots by the door, the particular creak of the third stair.

"Godspeed, dear John. Remember that faith is the key to your power!" Danrael's voice resonated with gravity. "The fate of many now rests on your shoulders. Do not be afraid."

John took one last look at Danrael and repeated the words to himself.

Do not be afraid.

This is it. A new beginning. All my problems are in the past.

With a single step, he left his world—and everything he had known—behind.

CHAPTER
EIGHT

Steve and Carol sat side by side on the old sofa, hands tightly clasped in the space between them. The lamp on the side table cast a warm circle of light, but it didn't reach the shadows in their eyes.

Carol's thumb moved in small, restless circles over the back of Steve's hand. Every few seconds her gaze drifted toward the stairs, as if she could will John back down them. Shame sat heavy in her chest—years of rolling her eyes at Steve's "family stories," of calling the cave duty ridiculous, of refusing to believe. Now she wished she could take every sharp word back.

Steve drew a slow, shaky breath and finally spoke.

"Carol... it's happened." His voice was low, almost hoarse. "John said yes."

Carol's head snapped toward him. Her fingers tightened around his until the knuckles went white. "How... how do you know?"

Steve swallowed hard. Tears welled in his eyes. He didn't wipe them away. "I can feel it," he said, pressing his free hand to his chest. "Something changed inside me. Like a shift in the air... or a door opening." He gave a small, disbelieving laugh that broke halfway through. "My father told me he felt the same thing the night I became the guardian."

Carol's breath caught. Regret flooded her so sharply she had to look away. She reached up and gently touched his face, her thumb brushing the tear that had escaped down his cheek.

"I have faith he'll be safe," she whispered, though her voice trembled. "All day... I had this feeling he would say yes." She paused, eyes distant. "After everything he's been through lately—Olly, the bruises, the fear."

Steve lowered his head, staring at their joined hands. "I keep asking myself if I did the right thing... not telling him the truth sooner. I should have been there with him tonight."

Carol squeezed his hand harder. "Hey... we can't do that to ourselves." She shifted closer on the sofa, her shoulder pressing against his. "You were following what the angel asked you to do. And I..." She gave a small, self-mocking laugh. "I was the one calling you crazy the whole time."

She looked down at their hands again, voice softening. "Deep down, I know you did what was best for him."

They sat in silence for a long moment. The only sound was the faint tick of the kitchen clock and the occasional creak of the old house settling.

Steve's thumb traced the edge of Carol's wedding ring. "I remember holding him the day he was born," he whispered, voice cracking. "Wondering what this moment would feel like."

Carol's eyes filled again. She rested her head against his shoulder, the familiar scent of his shirt grounding her. "John made a choice tonight he wouldn't take lightly," she murmured. "He's stronger than we gave him credit for."

She was quiet for a while, then added, almost to herself, "Part of me didn't want to believe any of it... because if it was real, that meant John could be in danger. Pretending it was all nonsense felt safer." She lifted her head just enough to look at him. "But when I saw the angel in the cave today... everything changed." Carol hesitated, searching for the right words. Her free hand moved to her chest, pressing lightly over her heart. "After the shock wore off," she said softly, "I felt something I didn't expect."

Steve waited.

"Peace." The word escaped Carol's lips barely above a whisper. "A kind I didn't think I could feel in a moment like this." She gave a small, tearful laugh. "You know me—I panic if John so much as trips over his own shoelaces."

A faint smile touched Steve's lips. He wiped his eyes with the back of his hand. "In the end," he breathed, "we have to trust that God knows what He's doing."

Carol gave another small, shaky laugh and leaned her head back against his shoulder. "That isn't going to be easy."

They sat like that for a long time—two parents holding onto each other in the quiet lamplight, carrying the weight of a decision that had already changed their son forever.

Steve finally spoke again, voice steadier. "Our next challenge is convincing the town that John's gone away for a while."

Carol straightened a little, wiping her cheeks. "What's the plan?"

"Tomorrow I'll tell the school he had to attend a funeral on your side of the family in New York. After a week or so, we'll say he decided to stay there... maybe until the end of the year."

She considered it, then nodded slowly. "Do you think that will work?"

Steve shrugged. "He turns eighteen in a few days. After that, they can't ask too many questions."

"And after everything with Olly," Carol added, "people will believe he just wanted to get away."

"Exactly."

Carol took his hand again, squeezing it firmly. "But you're not doing this part alone. I'm with you this time—every step. You're not carrying it by yourself anymore."

Steve looked at her in quiet surprise, then lifted her hand and pressed a kiss to her knuckles. "Are you sure?"

She leaned forward and kissed his forehead, lingering there for a moment. "I'm sure."

They didn't know where the portal would take their son, how long he would be gone, or what dangers waited for him. But for the first time that night, they stopped fighting the fear.

They simply sat together in the lamplight, holding on to each other... and waited.

CHAPTER
NINE

Crossing the portal was an unraveling. The world's edges slipped away. His awareness adrift in a warm, endless hush. No pain. No fear. Not even the echo of a heartbeat. Time let go. Some distant corner of himself wanted to linger in that silence forever.

Then, with a shattering snap, sensation crashed back.

Sound and color burst around him. He tumbled from the white tunnel, knees scraping on stone. Sunlight slanted through a high opening, gilding the cave walls and stirring golden dust motes in the still air. Pale stones, carved with spirals, surrounded the portal. The cave was sharp with minerals, tinged by a wild-sweet scent—something like salt and unknown flowers.

John blinked, heart thudding, and let out a stunned laugh. "Oh my gosh. It actually worked. I'm not crazy."

For a split second, disbelief mingled with giddy relief—then the new world pressed in, wild with unfamiliar scent and trembling light.

A silken rustle broke the trance—a shape shifting against stone.

John tensed, every sense prickling. "Hello?" His voice skipped, echoing up into the radiance. "Is anyone here?"

A pause—then a cloaked figure stepped forward, hood drawn low, face hidden in shadow.

"Is it safe to come out?" The voice was young, calm, and edged with curiosity.

John's nerves pulled his reply tight. "Are you the guardian?"

"Yes." She moved closer, light catching faint violet beneath her hood. "And you must be the Traveller." Her words wrapped around him, gentle as a woven blanket. "It's good that you speak the tongue of the Marcritans."

A weight lifted from his chest. The gift of tongues—real after all.

"What should I call you?" she asked. "The angel never said your name."

"John. Just John," he said, tasting the strangeness of his own name.

"My name is Jaromei. Welcome to Marcrituss."

He let out a breath he hadn't known he was holding. The cave's air tasted of salt, stone, and a wild bloom he couldn't name.

Jaromei regarded him, measuring. "When Danrael told me you'd come, I wasn't sure I believed it. No guardian here has ever seen anything come out of the portal." Reverence and awe threaded her words. "I'm honored to be the first to meet someone from another world."

Heat crept up John's neck. He stared at his battered clothing, aware of sweat trickling down his back. "I guess to you, I'm the alien. I must look strange."

She shook her head. "Not at all. Danrael said you'd need a disguise, so I expected something much more... unusual."

"May I see your face?" The words escaped before John could stop them.

She hesitated, glancing aside. "I kept the hood up so I wouldn't scare you. I might not look how you imagine."

John forced a smile. "After everything that's happened, nothing can surprise me anymore." The lie stuck in his throat; his pulse still hammered, wild and loud.

Slowly, Jaromei raised her hands and slid back the hood.

His breath caught. He'd braced for something monstrous, but instead found an unexpected beauty: luminous violet skin, eyes deep as amethyst, delicate fin-ridges etched along her arms. Her dark-blonde hair, streaked with purple, shimmered in the light. Yet her face was unmistakably human. She wore a simple beige top, white cropped trousers, a small pouch at her hip.

John realized he was staring and looked away, heat blooming in his cheeks.

Jaromei smiled, brushing her fin. "If you're wondering, many Marcritans live in the sea. I'm guessing your people don't?"

John shook his head, mouth dry. "You live in the sea? Can you breathe underwater?"

She laughed—a bright, rippling sound that danced along the stone. "We're not fish! We can't breathe underwater, but we swim well and hold our breath a long time."

He studied her—so strange, yet so human it rattled him.

"I've never seen someone with blue eyes and dark hair," she murmured.

"And I've never seen purple eyes," John replied.

Still on his knees, he watched as Jaromei knelt across from him, her movement as fluid as water.

"May I touch you?" she asked, voice soft but steady.

He nodded, uncertain. She reached out; her palm was warm, velvet-smooth against his. The world narrowed to the hush of their breath, her eyes—violet galaxies, endless and strange—drawing him in. His hand trembled; she held on, calm.

Time seemed to pause, the moment stretching. Then Jaromei stood, offering him her cloak.

"You should wear this. I'll take you to my village. My father—the guardian before me—knows more about the portals than anyone."

A thousand questions pressed at his lips, but all he could do was nod, dazed.

He pulled on the cloak. The fabric was thick; the sleeves engulfed his hands, his old shoes poked out beneath.

"Should I take my shoes off?" he mumbled.

Jaromei's smile flickered. "No, your feet would attract more attention than the shoes. Leave them on."

John's stomach growled, echoing in the stillness. "I think I need to eat. Last time was lunch at school... that feels like another life."

Her smile widened. "We'll get food at home. First, we need to leave the cave."

He glanced up at the distant ring of light. "How?"

"We climb."

He shook his head, incredulous. "You're kidding."

"It's easy," she said. With one motion, she scaled the rope, body rising smooth as tidewater. "I'll pull you up if you get stuck!"

"I can climb," he muttered, grabbing the rope. His arms burned with newfound strength, but halfway up the rope jerked—Jaromei pulled him the rest of the way.

He emerged into blazing heat. The air hit him like a furnace, thick with the scent of wildflowers and green things.

Jaromei helped him up, then bent to pick up a slab of earth. John watched as she placed it over the opening. Under her hands, the soil rippled; grass and moss smoothed over the hole in seconds.

John crouched, brushing his fingers over the spot where, moments ago, the opening had been. Only cool, dewy grass met his touch.

He stared. "What... is that?"

Jaromei looked puzzled. "It's just soil. What else would it be?"

He blinked. "Does all your grass and soil change shape like that?"

She shrugged. "Why wouldn't it? The world's alive, always growing. Is yours dead?"

He laughed, shaking his head. "No, but... ours doesn't do that."

"Strange," she said, stepping aside a curtain of fragrant leaves to reveal a hidden doorway.

She slipped through. John ducked after her, branches brushing his cheeks, a smear of green scent lingering in his nose.

He stepped onto a narrow path under the fierce sun. The ground pulsed faintly beneath his shoes, flanked by hedges and curling vines. Above, the blue sky melted to violet at the horizon.

"This is like a labyrinth," he said, voice hushed with awe.

"It is," Jaromei replied, her smile bright against the living green.

John ran his fingers along a door woven from vines. A circular stone sat at its heart, half-lost under leaves, spiraled deep with carvings.

"Did someone make these?"

"Long ago," Jaromei said, reverence softening her voice. "They come from the Ancients. These labyrinths outlasted all they built."

"Who were the Ancients?"

"The first civilisation—thousands of years back. They lived on land until most tribes moved to the sea."

Insects hummed as they walked. Heat pressed in, carrying a lush, alien scent. John caught the webbing between her toes, the grass springing back after her steps.

He lowered his voice. "Do most of your people live in the sea?"

"Nearly everyone. Only three tribes stay on land. Mine's one."

He stepped over a twisting root. "Why so few?"

"Old wars. Famines, disasters. The sea was safer. Most drifted there—new ways, a new kingdom."

He grinned. "On my world, everyone lives on land. Our countries are everywhere—hundreds. It's... chaotic."

She stared at him. "Hundreds? And you all get along?"

He laughed. "Not really. There are... a lot of arguments."

Her smile faded, thoughtful. "Maybe our worlds aren't so different. Land and sea have fought for generations. If you don't live in the sea, what does? Are your seas empty, or filled with beasts?"

John batted away a bee-like insect. "No fish-people. Just fish and... creatures."

She touched the fin on her arm, a smile playing on her lips. "We aren't fish. We're called anuri."

A quiet thud made John look down—his school lanyard had dropped from under the cloak. Jaromei bent to pick it up. "What's this?"

"Oh, that's from my school," he said. "My pockets ripped—it must have fallen out. Schools are where we learn things."

"We call that a Batnu," she said, handing it back. "The most advanced moved to the sea."

A crimson flash swooped overhead, its shadow fleeting. John ducked, heart pounding.

Jaromei barely glanced up. "Relax. Just a roolimba."

He watched it vanish, nerves jangling. "Are there more? Any creatures I should worry about?"

Her grin flashed. "Some might see you as a meal. Not far now."

They slipped into the shelter of the labyrinth's walls as the sound of chanting drifted through the leaves—low, harmonious, haunting. A hidden door opened in the greenery, and a procession of anuri stepped onto the path. Robes of rich colors flowed behind them.

They glanced at John and Jaromei but never slowed. From beneath his hood, John watched them disappear at a fork.

Jaromei quickly steered him down a side passage until the chanting faded.

"That was close," she whispered. "You did well."

"Who were they?"

"Temple elders. Evening procession before services." She wiped sweat from her brow. "I didn't expect them here. In this heat, I thought they'd take a shortcut."

"They sounded beautiful," John said.

Jaromei's look was guarded. "Maybe, but they wouldn't welcome you. You need to avoid them. I don't think they saw your face."

A flicker of unease curled in John's stomach. Danrael's warning of a coming darkness echoed in the back of his mind. "Are the elders evil?"

She looked surprised. "We all have some evil, don't we?"

She watched the elders slip away. "No anuri is completely good or bad. The elders are just... stuck. They fear what they don't understand."

He glanced at his cloak. "Am I wearing one of their robes? It looks like it."

She laughed, shaking her head. "No, theirs cost a fortune. Yours is a burmui." She tugged his sleeve. "It's for people taking a vow of poverty and penance. It hides the face. When the vow's done, they take it off. Good disguise if you want to go unseen."

It relieved John that no one would question the cloak—though now, everyone would assume he was atoning for something serious.

Jaromei moved to a wall of vines, pushing them aside to reveal a hidden door. She reached for his hand and led him through.

Her palm was warm, her touch grounding. John ducked after her into a tunnel of woven vines, the roof arching overhead. Shafts of sunlight pierced the canopy, catching pollen and setting it adrift in the cool, damp air. Moss cushioned each step.

"This really is a maze," John whispered; the hush felt sacred. "I never would've guessed this was in here."

Jaromei smiled. "Some walls have tunnels like this. They're shortcuts."

They passed through a corridor bright with flowers—crimson, blue, and gold. The petals shifted, reaching toward John's outstretched hand.

She stared, entranced. "You don't have flowers like this on your world?"

"We do, but not like these. They smell incredible... and they look alive." The petals curled inward, brushing his fingers—a living greeting.

"They're curious," Jaromei murmured. "Wait until morning. If you listen, you'll hear their song."

John grinned. "They sing?"

She laughed. "Not exactly, but the sound is beautiful. The Ancients believed our loved ones' spirits visit the flowers each dawn—that's when they sing."

She watched him, delight warming her voice. "If you want, we can come hear them sometime."

He hesitated, wonder and disbelief tangling inside. "Do you think that story's true?"

"Yesterday, I would have said no. But after today..." Her gaze lingered on him, shining. "Maybe more things are possible than I believed."

She stepped closer, violet eyes meeting his and holding. John's breath caught. The tunnel seemed suddenly smaller, sunlight glinting off the purple streaks in her hair.

He reached for another flower, letting his fingers hover above the petals. They shifted, turning toward his hand, brushing his skin—softer than silk.

"They like you," Jaromei whispered, watching the flowers respond.

John glanced at her. She was close enough for him to feel her warmth, her expression gentle and curious.

Neither of them moved. The space between them vibrated with possibility.

A sudden rumble broke the hush.

TEN

Avibration rippled beneath their feet—subtle at first, then quickly gaining strength.

The tunnel shuddered.

"What's happening? It... it isn't an earthquake, is it?" John's voice shook.

Jaromei's eyes locked on the trembling earth. She edged closer, face pale. "No," she whispered, dread in her voice.

John's heart hammered. "That doesn't sound good."

"When I say run, you run," Jaromei warned, urgency slicing through the growing rumble. "Straight ahead. Don't look back or wait for me. Just go—I'll catch up."

"I... I don't know where I'm running to!"

"No time. Trust me and run!"

The earth heaved under John's feet, nearly knocking him over.

"Run, John! Run now!" Jaromei's shout split the chaos.

He obeyed, adrenaline flooding his muscles as he sprinted forward. Behind him, a thunderous crack echoed—the ground splitting apart.

Heavy, pounding footsteps crashed after him, each impact rattling his bones. Something massive was hunting him, closing in fast.

John clung to Danrael's promise: *If I am able, I will come to your aid.*

"Danrael!" he called out, but only his ragged breaths and the pounding pursuit answered.

His torn clothes ripped further under the burmui, but the cloak didn't slow him. In other circumstances, he might have marveled at his speed. But speed meant nothing when death snapped at his heels.

A reckless glance over his shoulder made his blood freeze. A colossal beast tore after him: pale, scaly hide nearly white, twisted gray maw dripping with fangs, and coal-black eyes locked on him. Two powerful legs pumped like pistons; long arms crashed against the stone floor, propelling it in a terrifying gallop.

It lunged. A claw sliced the air inches from John's back. His lungs burned, each breath raw agony, but he forced his legs to keep moving.

The corridor stretched ahead—he couldn't hold this pace much longer.

"Jaromei!" His voice cracked with desperation. "Where are you?"

"Keep running, John! Don't stop!" Her voice echoed through the labyrinth. The creature's growl rolled like thunder.

Its talons sliced the air again, inches away. Hot, wet breath blasted against his neck. One swipe would finish him.

John's foot caught a jagged rock. He crashed down, dirt and stones scraping his skin.

Behind him, claws skidded to a halt.

John gasped Danrael's name, but the beast advanced. He

rolled onto his side, vision blurring as the nightmare loomed over him, fangs bared.

No stick. No stone. Nothing in reach.

Danrael's words echoed in his mind.

You will have everything you need... Have faith.

John forced himself to breathe—one breath, then another. *God wouldn't bring me across the universe just to die here. Not like this.*

Something stirred inside him—ancient and powerful— urging him to look up. He locked eyes with the creature's enormous black gaze.

"STOP—NOW!"

The beast lunged, jaws wide, saliva flying. John's heart gave out. Too late. He squeezed his eyes shut.

Nothing.

One second. Two seconds.

John cracked his eyes open.

The creature towered over him, completely frozen. Its massive claws hovered inches from his chest, hot breath blasting his face. Muscles quivered, but it didn't move.

It had obeyed.

A surge of power coursed through John—something awakening deep within, an instinct he hadn't known.

Jaromei ran up, breathless, bending over with hands on her knees. "What happened?" she panted. "How have you stopped him?"

"I don't know," John said, staring at the beast. "It's like... it understood me. I told it to stop, and... it stopped." He eyed the giant creature. It seemed to be waiting for his next command.

Jaromei gazed in awe. "I have never seen one of these close up before." She shook herself. "Before he changes his mind, tell him to return to where he came from."

"I don't know how to do that!" John cried.

"Of course you do! Just do what you did before! And hurry!"

John swallowed and met the creature's eyes again. "Go back," he said, forcing his voice steady. "Leave us and go back where you came from."

The beast turned and, without hesitation, galloped back down the tunnel, its footfalls fading into the distance. John let out a shaky breath, numb with relief. Jaromei grabbed his arm and helped him up.

"What is that thing?" John's voice wavered.

"A boatha," Jaromei replied, still catching her breath. "They come up from the caves to hunt. And I've never met anyone who met one and lived to tell the tale."

John gave a rueful shrug. "Leave it to me to draw one out. Just my luck."

"Can all humans on your world do that? Do you possess the power to control minds?"

John laughed, weak with adrenaline. "What? No! I've never done that before. That was some Traveller power I didn't even know I had."

Jaromei's curiosity sparked. "Try that on me. Try to command me to do something."

"What? You want me to try and control your mind?"

"Then we'll know for sure."

John looked at her uncertainly. "Erm... stand on your head."

Silence. After a moment, Jaromei raised an eyebrow. "Nothing is happening..."

John exhaled, relieved. "I guess mind control over anuri isn't one of my abilities."

Jaromei started laughing. "Stand on my head?" She playfully shoved him.

"I panicked! It was the first thing I thought of!" John admitted.

"Well, at least you know it's only beasts you can control. What do you think?"

"I have no idea. I've only been this way for less than a day. I'm still learning what I can do with this new version of me."

"What do you mean by that?"

"I agreed to all this only hours ago. That's when I became the Traveller. Then... I changed. I got stronger, faster, and apparently, I can do things I don't even understand yet. Danrael said I'd have everything I need for the mission. I guess stopping a gigantic monster from having me for lunch qualifies."

Jaromei laughed again. "You are a funny man, John the Traveller. And a brave one too."

John wasn't sure how to react. He'd been called a lot of things over the years, but never brave.

As they walked along the path, a deep, ringing sound rolled through the air. John glanced up. A deep, resonant clang echoed through the hedges, vibrating the very ground under John's feet. He flinched, heart pounding, and glanced around for danger.

Jaromei smiled at his reaction. "That's just the trocks."

He caught his breath. "Trocks?"

"Yes, and it's the signal I was waiting for."

John was surprised by how similar the trocks were to church bells.

"We can leave now. Many people will have gone to the service, so the paths should be clear." She moved toward the wall of vines, searching for a hidden latch.

"How do you know how to find your home? It's easy to get lost in here."

"All along this tunnel are exits from the labyrinth leading

toward my village." Jaromei pulled a small square device from her pocket, which vibrated in her hand. "It's linked to a tower in my village. The closer we get, the stronger it shakes. We give them to children so they never get lost. My grandmother gave it to me. It has meaning."

Jaromei found the latch behind the vines and opened a concealed door. "These openings are everywhere," she said. "Hundreds of them. You have to know where to look." She stepped through, turning back. "Don't forget to pull your hood up, and if we meet anyone, let me speak."

John nodded and raised the hood of the burmui. As he adjusted it, Jaromei noticed the worry on his face.

"We're nearly home. Don't be afraid," she murmured.

John let out a slow breath.

Don't be afraid...

Those words again.

He hoped that someday, he would finally learn how to believe them.

CHAPTER
ELEVEN

The frantic echo of their footsteps in the labyrinth faded behind them. Gradually, new sounds drifted in —laughter, distant music, the steady thump of tools. They stepped into a flood of golden light that spilled across a field stretching between the labyrinth and Jaromei's village. Unable to resist, John risked a glance around.

Sunlight warmed his face as he lifted his hood. Mountains jutted like spears, the sea below glinting silver and sapphire. Even the blue-violet grass streaked with blood-red looked painted on. He almost forgot to keep his head down as Jaromei hurried him forward.

Only a handful of villagers crossed their path. Each time someone neared, John's pulse quickened beneath the burmui. Most carried baskets brimming with fruit and vegetables, their scent making his stomach clench.

They passed through open gates. John kept his head lowered, but life pulsed around him—children laughing, voices murmuring, men discussing fishing and tides. He watched his feet shuffle over yellow and brick-red stones, avoiding every gaze. The smells and sounds made him ache to look up and see it all.

After a short walk, Jaromei stopped before one of the houses. From beneath his hood, John glimpsed smooth, sun-warmed sandstone.

"Come inside," she whispered. "Once the door is closed, you can lower your hood."

He followed her in. The door shut softly behind them, and at last he pulled back the hood. The space felt strangely familiar—chairs and tables carved with gentle curves, as if harsh angles weren't allowed.

"You'd have laughed if you'd seen how many people stared at your ruined shoes and toes," Jaromei teased.

John grinned. "At least I gave them something to talk about."

"They probably think you're from one of the sea tribes," she said, eyeing him with mock seriousness. "They change fashions constantly. Those shoes might be considered experimental." She looked him over. "Though it clashes terribly with the vow-of-poverty aesthetic."

Their laughter was interrupted by footsteps.

"Father!" Jaromei ran to embrace a man as he entered the room. "I didn't know you were home. This is him—the Traveller."

The man, tall and steady, with the same violet skin and striking eyes as Jaromei, studied John closely. Standing there under that gaze, John felt the full strangeness of what he was.

"His name's John," Jaromei added.

He stepped closer. John stared at the subtle fin-like ridges along the man's arms. His short hair matched Jaromei's colors. He wore a brown, laced shirt and cropped trousers.

"I never imagined I'd meet one of our brothers from the other six worlds. In my house, no less," he said, his gaze sweeping over John. "Does he understand us?" he asked Jaromei.

"I do, sir," John replied. "I understand."

A flicker of surprise crossed the man's face.

"Forgive me, I haven't introduced myself." He inclined his head. "I'm Shenya. I was the guardian of our portal until my daughter took over. We're honored to receive you."

"It's an honor to meet you," John said. "Thank you for welcoming me."

Shenya placed a firm hand on John's shoulder—not possessive, but grounding.

"You may remain here as long as you need. Danrael told my daughter you might require help. I'll do whatever I can."

John let out a slow breath. "You might regret saying that," he admitted with a nervous smile. "I have no idea what I'm doing."

Shenya laughed, warm and booming. "That's often the start of something important. What exactly is your mission here on Marcrituss?"

"The mission..." John hesitated. "It's complicated."

"What did Danrael tell you? Any instructions?" Jaromei asked.

"Yeah, but not much detail," John said, thinking back to the cave. "I need to find a scroll from an ancient prophet who lived here, but I don't know her name."

"That's good news," Shenya replied. "There's been a great deal of research on the old prophets."

"Finding out about the prophet is just part of it," John continued. "The scroll was torn into seven pieces and hidden on the seven worlds. I have to collect them all."

"Oh, right. Not challenging at all, then!" Shenya grinned, then grew serious. "And the message?"

"I don't know. Danrael said a darkness is coming—something threatening all seven worlds. The scroll reveals how to stop it, and will help me understand the Traveller's true purpose."

Shenya nodded. "If there's one thing I've learned, it's that your purpose often reveals itself after obedience, not before."

John let out a breath. "I never expected obedience would involve interplanetary scavenger hunts."

That earned another laugh. "We'll help you," Shenya said. "But first—eat and rest. No one solves ancient mysteries on an empty stomach."

Only then did John realize how deeply he needed that.

"Is there anything you don't eat?" Shenya asked.

"I'll eat anything," John said. "Right now, I could eat an entire boatha."

Shenya blinked. "A boatha?"

"That's a story for later," Jaromei said quickly.

Shenya narrowed his eyes, but let it go. Grinning, he added, "I think your burmui has become... aromatic."

John looked down at the cloak. Jaromei bit her lip, shoulders shaking. He hadn't realized how much he'd sweated under it.

"Come," Shenya said. "We're about the same size. I'll find you something clean."

John followed him up a spiral iron staircase. Glancing back, he saw Jaromei already moving to the kitchen, the sound of pots clattering as she started a meal. His stomach rumbled.

Shenya led him into a spacious room. John examined the crescent-shaped bed and a wooden wardrobe. The doors were carved with flowers like those in the labyrinth.

"Take off what you're wearing—I'll find you something

clean," Shenya said, rummaging through the wardrobe. John hesitated, but guessed modesty worked differently there. He pulled off the cloak, shoes, and what was left of his torn clothes until he was in his boxers, laying everything neatly on the bed.

Shenya turned, clothes in hand, and looked John over. "This is extraordinary," he muttered.

John straightened. "Is something wrong?"

"No," Shenya said. "I just didn't expect people from other worlds to resemble us so closely."

"I thought the same—apart from the purple skin and fins."

Shenya smiled. "As time passed, we adapted to the sea, but I see no difference that matters. We are both anuri."

John held those words for a moment.

Shenya handed him clean clothes, eyeing his boxers. "Why two pairs of trousers?"

John's face went red. "These are underwear. We... uh... wear them under our clothes."

"How peculiar. Well, I hope these fit. I'll clean the rest," Shenya said, gathering the burmui and other items. He pressed a touchpad, and a door slid open. "After that journey, you'll want a good wash. Everything you need is there. Just ask if you need anything else."

"Thanks, Shenya. I'll be down soon."

When he was alone, John stood in front of the mirror. He'd known he was different—he'd felt it in the weight of his new arms, the breadth of his chest—but seeing it was another thing entirely. His hand moved to his cheek. The face was his own, but the body wasn't. "Dang, I'm ripped," he muttered, flexing. For a moment, he wondered what high school might have been like with this body.

On the right side of the washroom was an open alcove with small metal fans set in the ceiling. Hoping it was a shower, he pressed a rain symbol on the control pad. Cold water poured over him, making him yelp. He quickly pressed the fire symbol; warm water soon cascaded, washing away the day's grime.

His mind went over the events of the day. Cave. Portal. Beast. The world beyond Earth.

He wrapped himself in a towel, happy that some things there were familiar.

John got dressed and descended the spiral staircase to find Shenya arranging plates on a low table, the air rich with unfamiliar spices.

"You look like a true Marcritan!" Shenya said, gesturing to sandals beside the step. "I found these for you. Hope they fit."

John slipped them on, wiggling his toes.

Jaromei entered, arms laden with platters of vibrant food—deep purples and blues that seemed to shimmer. She froze when she saw him.

"You look good," she said simply.

John ducked his head, managing a shy smile.

"Can I help?" he asked, voice cracking.

Jaromei's lips curved upward. "My father is a horrible cook, and you're our guest. I'll handle everything."

"She's right," Shenya sighed, dropping utensils with a clatter. "I am a terrible cook. Is cooking popular on your world? How are you at it?"

A memory of smoke alarms and frantic parents flashed through John's mind. "Let's just say I'm not great at it," he admitted. "But yes, cooking is popular. Both my parents are good at it—they took classes for years."

"Speaking of years," Shenya said, tracing a circle in the air with his finger, "I wonder if our worlds spin at the same pace. How long is the journey around your sun?"

John's eyes lit up. He grabbed a piece of flatbread and broke it into a rough circle. "We orbit like this—" he rotated it slowly. "365 days to complete one loop."

Shenya's laughter bubbled up as he took the bread, broke off a small piece, and made it orbit around the larger piece. "Our loop takes 357 days." He glanced at a sundial on the windowsill. "Do you see that timekeeper? Ours counts 60 beats to measure a minute."

John nodded. "Ours is the same." His gaze drifted to the window, and he was immediately mesmerised by what he saw. He pointed to the twin moons hung low in the violet sky. "But we only have one of those. And we've actually been there—we built vessels that carried people to walk on our moon."

Shenya's fingers stilled on the table. His gaze lingered on the moons. "We built downward instead—domes beneath the waves where most of our people live." He turned back to John, voice quieting. "Your father must be proud to have a son who is the Traveller."

John's throat tightened. "Everything happened so fast," he said, looking down. "They kept it secret from me, and then— boom—Danrael appears, and I'm here."

Shenya leaned in. "I understand your frustration, but I'm sure they had their reasons."

John sighed. "I know. I just wasn't ready. It would've been great if my dad had helped me prepare."

"You've shown bravery beyond most anuri. You're more prepared than you think."

Jaromei was in and out with steaming bowls. Each time, she flashed John a smile that lingered a bit too long.

As she returned to the kitchen, Shenya leaned closer. "Judging by those looks, I think my daughter likes you."

John nearly choked. "We just met." Heat rushed to his face.

"You'll be good friends, I'm sure," Shenya replied lightly. "How old are you, anyway?"

"I'll be eighteen soon."

"Same as Jaromei." Shenya's eyes crinkled at the corners.

John seized the moment to change the subject. "Do you have a spouse?"

Shenya's smile faded. "I did. She died when Jaromei was ten. It's only us now—and my mother next door."

"I'm sorry," John said, feeling bad for asking.

Shenya smiled. "You're sorry about what? That my wife is gone, or that my mother lives next door?"

They both burst out laughing.

"On a serious note," Shenya said, smile fading, "what are your thoughts on the cave prophecy?"

John went still. "What cave prophecy?"

Shenya looked at him. "The prophecy on the stones around the portal."

"That was a prophecy? I barely noticed them," John admitted. "Everything happened so fast."

Shenya was quiet for a moment. "Then we have much to discuss."

"Why? What do they say?"

"Well, it's about you, the Traveller, and your connection to the seven worlds. It's difficult to interpret. I'm not sure I've figured it out yet. I think the Ancients are the key. You see, the land tribes—"

Jaromei entered with a sizzling platter. "Everything is ready!"

John's stomach growled as his hand hovered over the platter.

Shenya saw him restrain himself and grinned. "What are you waiting for, John? Eat!"

"You were saying something about a prophecy."

"Oh, don't worry about that now. Tomorrow we work. Tonight, we feast!"

As laughter and conversation resumed, Shenya smiled and joined in. But in the back of his mind, the unanswered question sat quietly: the Traveller had arrived, and he knew nothing of the prophecy about him.

CHAPTER
TWELVE

John leaned back from the table, fork clattering against his empty plate. He'd demolished three helpings of everything. Jaromei watched, chin propped on her palm, amusement flickering in her gaze.

Shenya poured a copper-colored drink. John caught a whiff, something like wine, and shook his head. "I'll stick to water, thanks."

Jaromei collected the dishes. "Speaking of water, do you visit the sea often on your world?"

John shook his head. "Until today, I'd never seen the sea. I live in farm country—nowhere near an ocean."

Shenya's spoon froze midair. He and Jaromei exchanged a look of genuine shock; Jaromei stared as if John had just announced a death.

"On Marcrituss," Shenya said solemnly, "the sea is in our blood."

John nodded slowly. It wasn't just scenery there. It was heritage.

Jaromei returned with the freshly cleaned burmui. "Want to see it properly? A quick look?"

Shenya's expression tightened. "I'm not sure that's wise."

Jaromei rolled her eyes. "Father, it's evening. The beach will be empty. It'd be a sin for him to spend a whole day on Marcrituss without seeing the sea."

"I'd love that," John said before he could overthink.

Shenya sighed, relenting. "Fine. Stick to the tunnels. Keep your head down. Don't stay out long."

John pulled on the burmui and drew the hood low. At the door, Shenya hurried over with black shoes. "Put these on. Your feet will give you away immediately."

John winced. "Right. The feet." He swapped sandals for shoes, grateful for Shenya's attention to detail.

"Be careful," Shenya warned.

"All right, Father," Jaromei groaned. "We'll be back soon."

Outside, Jaromei tugged John's hood lower, shadowing his face. "You're going to topple me," he muttered. The girl who had been quietly cautious at dinner was gone—this one moved with easy confidence through the village.

She led him down a narrow path between stone houses. At the corner, she paused, scanning the empty street. Satisfied, she knelt, lifted a square metal plate from the paving stones, and revealed a ladder descending into darkness.

"You first," she said.

John peered down. "Why me?"

"The ladder's old. One at a time." She gave him a look that made arguing pointless. "Hurry."

He exhaled and climbed down, gripping each rung. Jaromei followed and sealed the opening above, plunging them into darkness. She pulled a disc from her pouch—a gentle, steady light bloomed.

"Follow me."

John's shoes splashed as he walked. The cold water—just an inch deep—made him tense. "Please tell me this isn't a sewer," he joked.

Jaromei laughed under her breath. "It's not. These tunnels were built for evacuations, in case the sea tribes attacked. There's an exit straight to the beach. Most people don't even remember they exist. Sometimes the tide floods them, but we'll be fine."

Her light skimmed slick metal walls. "My grandmother tells stories about her grandparents escaping through these tunnels."

"That's incredible. Tomorrow, I hope I can find a book on Marcrituss's history. I have so many questions."

"My father will talk your ear off without books," Jaromei said, "especially once I'm gone."

"Gone where?" John asked, surprised by the pang in his chest.

"My usual routine. I visit the portal, then I work at the market—buy meat and produce from farmers, sell it in the village, and take a share."

John smiled at the familiarity. "My parents run a farm. Meat and produce, too." His voice tightened before he could stop it. "I was going to inherit the job soon."

Jaromei glanced back. Something in her expression made him feel that she'd understood more than he'd said.

"We have a lot in common," she said.

He looked away and changed the subject. "So, what does your father do? He didn't say."

"He's a teacher and a researcher. He's on leave right now, caring for Grandmother."

A minute later, Jaromei turned into a side passage and stopped before a heavy metal door. "We're here," she announced, slipping the light back into her pouch and pushing the door open.

Warm air hit them as they stepped onto sand. Behind the door, a curtain of vines spilled down from the cliff above.

Without warning, Jaromei slipped her hand into John's. Her palm was warm and dry; her grip sure as she tugged him gently down the moonlit strand. The sand shifted underfoot, slightly damp. They passed the soft crash of tiny waves.

She led him beneath a leaning outcrop, into a small cavern sheltered by the cliff. In there, the world was paused—the only sound was the deep, steady hush of the tide.

"There's no one here," she said, voice hushed, reverent. "You can lower your hood. You should see this the way it's meant to be seen."

John let the burmui fall, the night air cool against his skin. The sea stretched away, impossibly vast and still. Twin moons hung above—one low and gold, the other higher, washed in silver. Their reflections painted the rolling water in ribbons of silver and cobalt. The air was alive with salt and the faint aroma of sea plants.

The sound wasn't what he'd expected. Not a roar, but a patient, endless breath—the tide drawing in and out, whispering secrets to the shore.

For a heartbeat, he forgot everything—portals, missions, even his own name. Just this: the moons, the water, the impossible hush that settled in his bones.

Jaromei perched on a rounded boulder and patted the space beside her. John joined her, still riveted to the scene. The stone was cool through his cloak; the night air prickled at his neck.

"I think... I don't have words for how incredible this is," he managed, voice thick.

Her smile softened, edges gleaming in moonlight. "Good."

He let out a long breath, shoulders loosening. "I wish we could just walk along the shore together. No hood. No hiding."

"Perhaps someday," Jaromei replied, honest and wistful.

John watched the waves catch moonlight. "I'm just happy to be here, even if I have to wear the burmui."

She bit her lip and looked away, fingers curling in her lap.

"You look like you've got something on your mind."

Jaromei gave a breathy laugh. "You're perceptive."

"What is it?"

She hesitated, eyes on the trembling silver seam where water met sky. "Do you agree with what my father said? That you're anuri?"

John blinked. "Of course." He flashed a crooked grin. "Besides a few things, I'm pretty much the same as you. I'm not some scary alien, am I?"

Jaromei's lips twitched, as if weighing the question. "Maybe. I haven't decided yet." She leaned closer, voice dropping. She held her hand out and touched his wrist. "May I?"

John's pulse skipped. "Yes," he whispered.

She slid back his sleeve and traced the lines of his hand and forearm, her touch barely there, almost reverent. Her violet skin against his made the hairs on his arm rise. When she looked up, both moons caught in her eyes—otherworldly and beautiful.

"I think he's right," she said at last. "You're not different. You are anuri."

He let out a breath, half laughing. "Good. That's settled."

Her fingers lingered a moment longer before she released him. "Do you have a partner on your world?"

"I..." He hesitated, aware of the hush, the closeness. "No... I've never had one."

Her eyebrows rose. "How could a man like you—with your mind, your appearance—never have had someone special?"

He managed a small shrug. "I haven't been... popular. I usually try to get through life without attracting attention."

Her expression was shadowed in the moonlight. "I had someone. Until recently." She stared at the sand, voice quieter. "My first love. My father hated him, especially after how he treated me. He left me for another."

"Then he's an idiot. You deserve someone grateful just to stand near you."

Jaromei laughed softly, looking down. "That's kind."

He smiled; she rested her hand on his knee, then pulled away, startled.

"I should take you back," she said, standing. "Before Father worries. But I hope you know how special today has been." She laughed, lighter now. "Including the incident with the boatha."

"Yeah, that's not something I'm likely to forget."

John stood too, forcing his mind back to bigger things: Traveller. Scroll. Seven worlds. But the sea's hush lingered in his chest with the memory of her touch.

He pulled his hood up, and they slipped back into the tunnels. On the way, Jaromei explained how a metal called sholka is rust-resistant and durable. John barely heard her. His mind replayed their time on the beach.

At Shenya's door, John caught Jaromei's hand lightly before she could leave. "Thank you," he said. "For the sea. For... all of this." He hesitated, then admitted, "Today has been the best day of my life."

Jaromei's cheeks darkened with an anuri blush, and she looked unexpectedly shy.

"I'm staying next door tonight," she said. "With Grandmother."

"Will I see you tomorrow?"

"You will," she promised, touching his arm once before she slipped away.

John entered Shenya's house and closed the door behind him. What just happened? he thought, pulling off the burmui.

As he leaned back against the door, Shenya appeared. "Did Jaromei go to my mother's house?"

"Yes, she said she's staying there tonight."

Shenya took the burmui and hung it in a cupboard, giving John a knowing look. "Don't worry," he said lightly. "She'll be around tomorrow."

John pretended not to hear.

"You must be exhausted," Shenya said. "You'll sleep upstairs—in my room."

"No," John protested. "I can't take your room."

"Don't be ridiculous. I'll take Jaromei's." Shenya pressed a small container into John's hands. "Soap and other things you may need. Let me know if there's anything else."

"I can't thank you enough," John said, meaning it.

"As I told you, it's an honor to have you as our guest. Sleep well."

"You too," John replied, heading upstairs.

He found the strange bed waiting for him: a moon-shaped mattress, soft and yielding like a waterbed. "These folks really are obsessed with water," he muttered.

As he lay back, the day replayed in flashes until his thoughts slowed, and the memory of the rolling tide carried him into sleep.

THIRTEEN

I n the endless void, the vigil never slept.

The Watchers had watched Earth since its fall—patient, certain, feeding on the slow ruin of what the King had made. Division was their masterpiece. Scattered, humanity was harmless. And so it had remained.

Until now.

A pure light blazed—not from Earth, but from Marcrituss.

It struck the void like a brand pressed against shadow. The Watchers recoiled, their essences writhing. The light was unmistakable: the seal of the Enemy's claim, the mark of one redeemed, blazing where it had no right to shine. The mark was a reminder that no path remained for their return. Every hope of pardon was ash. All that remained was to unmake what the King loved—and prove the folly of his mercy.

"A wanderer," hissed a lesser Watcher, its voice a chill wind in emptiness. "Marked and redeemed. Yet straying beyond its pen... the veil thins."

The murmurs spread, creeping like fog over ice:

The seal pierces us. The barriers tremble. The light burns like forgotten stars.

From the void's heart stirred the Ancient Watcher—swirling with primordial spite and cunning.

It cannot be true...

It extended its gaze, probing the ripple like a shadow touching flame. The boy's spirit caused Marcrituss to flicker in its sight. The mark blazed clear, a brand no darkness could erase.

A shudder rippled through the Watchers, their voices threading together in dread:

"The prophecy stirs. The ancient words, whispered in fear —the Traveller. He who bridges the worlds, who rallies the light, who dares to challenge our hold. He comes."

"It was no myth. The marked soul awakens on Marcrituss."

"The Traveller rises," rasped the Ancient Watcher, its voice like gravel grinding in endless night. "Our Enemy sends a vessel to unite the seven. Our divisions crumble. We must not allow it."

The void contracted.

From somewhere deeper still—deeper than the Ancient Watcher dared look—a command came. Not words. Never words. Something older than language, cold as the space between stars, pressing down through the darkness like a weight that crushed everything beneath it.

The Ancient Watcher did not hesitate to obey.

"He demands retaliation," it hissed to those assembled. "The Traveller is only a boy," it jeered.

The Ancient Watcher would spread darkness on Marcrituss —slowly, like a stain—until the boy's crusade collapsed under its own weight.

The Watchers aligned in silent accord, their essences coiling and contracting, drawn toward a single purpose.

THE KING ABOVE ALL GODS

The dark turned its gaze toward Marcrituss.

CHAPTER
FOURTEEN

Jaromei moved quietly, making breakfast for her grandmother, Dernoah—eager to share details from the day before. The familiar morning moans of pain from the bedroom pressed against her heart—a sound she'd stopped being able to ignore.

"Grandmother, do you need me to do anything?" Jaromei called, hurrying in.

Dernoah winced as she adjusted the bed with a control pad, then reached for her cup of pain relief tonic on the nightstand. She drank it down in one gulp, anxious for relief. The blend of Marcritan medicines in cora milk—a shallow-water mammal's gift—had become her lifeline.

A few moments later, Dernoah managed a smile. "I'm fine now, my darling. I just needed medicine. Thank you for leaving it for me."

"Of course. I left breakfast for you in the front room. I can stay until Father arrives, if you need me."

Dernoah gave a little laugh that turned into a cough— three sharp barks that seemed to empty her. When she finally caught her breath, her hand trembled as she set down the cup.

"Once this tonic starts working, I'll be up in no time," she murmured.

Jaromei watched her grandmother's shoulders rise and fall. The slight frame beneath the quilt seemed smaller than yesterday. Or was that just her imagination? She couldn't remember the last time Dernoah reached the garden without sitting. She'd stopped counting the days.

After Jaromei's mother died, Dernoah had become her mother in all but name, running the household while Shenya worked and Jaromei studied at the Batnu. Now the roles were reversed—Jaromei and Shenya cared for her.

Dernoah reached for her cane and, fighting pain, she stood up. "Go on with your day, my love. I'll eat and prepare your father's study."

Jaromei hesitated at the door. "Grandmother, before I go, I want to tell you something incredible that happened yesterday."

"Your father already told me," Dernoah said, a genuine smile spreading across her face. "The Traveller's time has finally come. He mentioned it last night when he helped me to bed." She paused, then added, "He also said you two went for a little outing."

Jaromei blushed. "Yes, I took him to the sea. It still feels unreal. Can you believe the first visitor from another world is in our home? I've never seen Father this excited."

"Our family is truly blessed," Dernoah beamed. "Now, go on and tell this old lady some gossip. What's he like?"

Jaromei grinned, unsure where to start. "His name is John. He looks anuri, but his features are different—handsome, too, and his eyes are blue. And you should have seen him with the boatha in the labyrinth yesterday."

"A boatha? And you're both still alive?"

"I know! That's what I told him. Nobody survives an encounter with a boatha." Dernoah raised an eyebrow—Jaromei had always been able to tell her anything.

"I don't know how, but he controlled it with his thoughts. I've never met anyone like him. There's something very endearing about him. After getting to know him, we seem to have a lot in common, too. Both of us are guardians; we share that, of course. He's interested in learning as well."

Dernoah studied her granddaughter's face with quiet amusement. "I look forward to meeting the young man."

"He'll be here soon. I think you'll enjoy his company." Jaromei smiled at the memory of the day before.

"I can see you're smitten," Dernoah teased.

"What? I don't know about that." Jaromei tried to hide her smile. "I have to admit... I think I do like him. It scares me a bit."

"Why does it scare you? He's a boy, you're a girl."

"We might be similar, but we're from different worlds—and after my last disastrous relationship, I'm not about to rush into anything." Jaromei sighed. "Even so, I'd rather be here with him than go to the market."

Dernoah laughed. "I know that feeling. But you remember what's written about the Traveller in the cave."

Jaromei's hand stilled on the door.

"Granddaughter, the Traveller is destined for hard times. The stones speak of sacrifice. Of suffering. Of a path few would choose. Before you let your heart follow him beyond this world, ask yourself if his fate is what you want."

Jaromei knew her grandmother was right. What John faced on Marcrituss was just the beginning.

"All I can tell you is to pray for answers, child. Your grandfather would be thrilled to know the Traveller's time has come —and even happier he's here with us."

Jaromei nodded, grateful for the clarity her grandmother always brought.

The tonic had kicked in at last. Dernoah moved to her favorite chair in the front room, book in hand. "Now get out of my house, or you'll be late to the market!"

Jaromei leaned in and kissed her grandmother's forehead. "I'll be back soon. Please don't interrogate him too much," she whispered. Dernoah chuckled and waved her out the door.

CHAPTER

FIFTEEN

T he water-filled mattress rocked gently beneath John —a constant reminder he was far from home. Shenya had left clean clothes draped over a nearby chair. From the kitchen below, a savory, spiced aroma drifted up. John washed quickly and hurried downstairs.

The kitchen was all sleek metal and stone, every appliance touch-controlled. A handful of keepsakes lined a shelf, but there were no photos.

"Good morning, John," Shenya called, warm and bright. "I'm making you something to eat before we get started." He handed John an odd-looking utensil—half fork, half spoon.

"For someone who claims to be a terrible cook, it smells delicious," John said, eyeing the pan.

Shenya grinned. "Well, this is the only thing I can make without disaster."

John inhaled deeply. "Smells like scrambled eggs from my world."

"These are eggs too," Shenya explained, nodding toward

the window. John blinked at the huge, green-sheened, feathered bird strutting in the garden.

"That thing's enormous," John laughed.

Shenya chuckled. "It'll make a delicious roast one day, too. Here you go." He served a plate piled high with steaming eggs.

John dug in, barely pausing to chew.

"Let's start at square one," Shenya said, settling across from him. "You need to find seven fragments of a scroll. First, we need to figure out which female prophet wrote it. Most prophets in the Ancients' era were male, so that narrows things down."

John nodded, reaching for bread. "Where do we start?"

Shenya thought a moment. "I'd say the stones in the cave. When I became guardian, I obsessed over them—comparing their stories to the Ancients' records. There are definite links."

"Good start," John managed between bites, finishing his plate.

"Slow down," Shenya teased. "I'll get you more."

John nodded and reached for another slice of bread—then stopped.

A strange sensation swept over him. His hunger sharpened, then dissolved into something bigger and stranger.

His head spun. The room pulsed. He slumped forward, his face hitting the plate.

"John!" Shenya leapt up, alarmed.

John's body convulsed, limbs jerking. His eyes rolled back, then snapped open—solid white, blazing with light.

Searing beams poured from his eyes, ricocheting off metal and stone, turning the room into a cathedral of light. The air thrummed, vibrating with presence. Shenya staggered back, shielding his face.

John's mouth opened and a voice not his own poured out —deep and sonorous, repeating words in a language Shenya didn't know. Then two more voices—one high, one low—joined in harmony from within him.

The chorus filled the house, ancient and terrifying. John and the table began to levitate off the floor, chair and all. Shenya scrambled for parchment. He scribbled down the sounds coming from John as fast as he could. The words grew louder, trembling with power.

At last, the voices stopped. John's mouth formed new words in Marcritan, ones Shenya understood:

"King above all gods."

Another surge wracked John's body. The light faded; his blue eyes returned while he and the table fell back to the floor. He gasped, sinking into his chair, clutching his head. A glass toppled and shattered on the floor.

"Shenya... what's happening to me?"

Shenya gripped John's arm, steadying him. "I was hoping you could tell me."

John shivered.

"You're safe," Shenya said. "Nothing can hurt you here. What do you remember?"

John shut his eyes, struggling to grasp the memory. "I was... in the cave," he whispered, voice trembling. "The one here on Marcrituss. Then I was nowhere. It wasn't just the absence of light—it was the absence of everything."

He swallowed hard.

"Then I heard a voice. It spoke." John's hands shook. "Light exploded into being. Instantly. Blazing, infinite light pouring into the void."

Shenya leaned forward, writing furiously.

"I saw matter forming—swirling, coalescing. Seven spheres took shape, moving in harmony," John continued, eyes still closed. "And then I heard voices—thousands of them—

singing in perfect unity. They were witnessing it. Celebrating what had been spoken into being."

His breath quickened.

"But then one of the lights—brilliant, powerful—turned away. Others followed. The harmony was shattered. Those lights that had turned became... darkness."

His voice dropped to a whisper.

"They all fell. And the moment they did, war began."

John's eyes flew open, wide with terror.

"It was everywhere, Shenya. The war—it's vast. Eternal. Beings of light and darkness were locked in combat across the void."

His whole body shook.

"Then the leader of the darkness saw me. I ran, and he almost got me—but the beings of light stopped him. They were struggling to hold him back."

John's hands trembled as he gripped the edge of the table.

"Then I was back here. In your kitchen. But I can still feel it."

Shenya scribbled furiously. "I know that story. It's depicted on the stones in the cave. The beings of light and darkness are angels and demons."

John paled. "The darkness wasn't just a shape. No body, no face—just blackness, alive and hungry. It felt like hatred itself."

Shenya stared at the parchment before him, at the words he'd scribbled phonetically while John was in the trance.

"John, you repeated something. Over and over." Shenya turned the parchment. "It sounded like: Barukh ata Adonai Eloheinu, melekh ha'olam. What does that mean? You finished by saying, 'King above all gods'."

John leaned forward sharply. "That's Hebrew."

Shenya raised an eyebrow. "Hebrew?"

"An ancient language from my world. The language of the Jewish people." John leaned forward, reading the transliteration. "It means, 'Blessed are you, Lord our God, King of the universe.' King above all gods is his title."

"What became of these people you speak of?"

"They're still in my world. People from the religion I was raised in believe that a man from the Jewish people was God incarnate, or God made man. You might say he was an anuri-God, I guess."

Shenya went still. His quill hovered above the parchment.

"John..." His voice was careful, measured. "Was he born around two thousand years ago?"

John arched back in the chair. "Yes. How could you know that?"

Shenya leaned forward, his expression grave but filled with wonder.

"Years ago, I studied an extinct religious sect of the Ancients. Their scrolls spoke of an angel who announced that the God of the Ancients was born as an anuri somewhere in the universe." He looked up, eyes shining with realisation. "They called him the King above all gods."

The words hung in the air between them.

John stared at him. "There has to be a connection."

"There is." Shenya's voice was reverent now, filled with awe. "The cave. Hebrew. Angels and demons. The divine title. The timeline." He gestured to the parchment. "It's true...The God of the Ancients became anuri—the King above all gods, the King of the universe. It's the same God, John."

John set down his water. He didn't speak. He was doing the arithmetic in his head and it kept coming out the same way.

For a long moment, neither spoke.

Shenya rose quietly and moved to the stove. He stood with

his back to the room, turning something over in his mind. Then he turned back, leaning against the counter.

"And the vision was a warning, John. The darkness is close. It's what Danrael spoke of. It's what you must face."

He nodded toward the window, toward the enormous bird still strutting in the garden as if nothing had happened.

"You saw something most mortals never see, John. The moment creation began—spoken into being from nothing. And you saw the 'why' of the war you're caught up in."

"The why," John repeated quietly. "What does that even mean? Danrael never mentioned a war."

Shenya went back to the table and sat.

"The darkness wants to prove that light cannot overcome darkness. That's why you were shown this vision. You're not just fighting a demon or stopping a threat to one world. You're part of something cosmic—a war that began at creation itself."

John dropped his head into his hands. "I'm trying to learn how to be the Traveller as fast as I can, Shenya, but I can't do this. The darkness... it's too powerful. A week ago, I was just a normal kid. Now, I'm supposed to fight some primordial evil? I have no idea what I'm doing."

Shenya's hand settled on his shoulder, steady and warm.

"John, the truth is, none of us know what we're doing when we reach the age the world expects more from us. Every anuri who achieved great things had the same doubts." His voice softened. "But you're not standing alone. The light that will overcome the darkness was coming through your eyes. You're meant to help the angels hold it back. Don't forget—I'm here to help you."

"How, Shenya? How do I know I'm making the right decisions?"

Shenya considered. "I discovered that when you bring your burdens and worries to God, he'll help guide your path."

John hesitated. "Shenya... I want to be honest. Until a few days ago, I wasn't even sure I believed in God. That probably sounds strange for the Traveller. On Earth, doubt is normal."

Shenya gave a knowing laugh. "You're telling me everything you've experienced hasn't convinced you?"

He got up, set the pan back on the heat, and stood at the stove with his back to John—giving him the space the question deserved.

John shrugged. "It's not like God knocked on my door and said hi."

Shenya smiled without turning. "Faith rarely arrives that way. But John—you just witnessed creation itself. You saw the answer to the question that haunts every physicist and philosopher: how did something come from nothing? You saw it spoken into being by a power beyond comprehension."

He tapped the counter lightly, as if it were the parchment.

"God is not just a what—a force, distant and impersonal. God is a who. Someone who knows, calls, and invites. Someone who showed you the cosmic war so you'd understand what's at stake. Someone who's been guiding you since the moment you stepped into that cave."

The idea unsettled John. A force could be ignored; a who could not.

"Peace often begins when we answer that call," Shenya finished. He turned off the heat and sat back in his chair.

John thought back to his mission—frightened and inadequate, yet knowing he couldn't walk away. He thought back to Danrael's partin message. People were depending on him. "I will continue this mission," John said.

"And I'll be here to support you," Shenya promised.

John's stomach growled again. "What would you say if I told you I'm still hungry?"

Shenya chuckled, rising to cook. "I'm not sure I could have raised a teenage son. I'd be eaten out of house and home."

John watched Shenya move back to the stove, already muttering about the arbimto.

It was enough.

Dernoah sipped her drink, trying to read, but pain interrupted her again and again. Lately, even simple things had grown difficult. She knew her time remaining was short, but gratitude outweighed regret—she'd seen Jaromei grow up, and now the Traveller had come. Everything else was a gift. She was at peace; she'd done all she could for her family.

Her late husband's family had guarded the portal for generations. He'd hoped to meet the Traveller himself, but had left this world too soon.

She reached for her book again, but the front door opened.

"Hello, Mother?" Shenya called as he and John entered. John took off his cloak.

Leaning on her cane, Dernoah made her way over. "Let me get a look at this young man."

She studied John, a smile tugging at her lips. "Hmm... no wonder Jaromei likes this one," she teased Shenya. "He's built like one of the sea gods."

"Mother!" Shenya protested.

She peered at John's eyes. "Blue as the sea. Our Jaromei loves the sea."

"Mother, you're embarrassing him. And Jaromei wouldn't appreciate this conversation."

Dernoah shrugged. "I'm old. At some point, you just say what you think. For me, it's both my brain forgetting to stop and me not caring anymore."

Shenya gave his mother a look—a warning. Dernoah just rolled her eyes at him.

"It's an honor, John. I do feel for you—you have hardships ahead. It takes courage to give yourself up for this. You'll be remembered as a true hero."

John's smile dropped. "If things go well, no one will have to remember me. I'll be back celebrating with everyone."

Shenya rubbed his eyes. "What she's talking about is the prophecy from the cave. It shows angels among the anuri. The Traveller stands among them, surrounded by the seven portals. He unites the worlds and brings light. On the last stone, the Traveller suffers greatly. He then..." Shenya paused, "He enters a new existence and is at peace."

John leaned against the wall, forehead to his arm.

"I'm no expert in prophecy," Shenya added quickly. "It might mean something else."

John swallowed. "Before I left Earth, I asked Danrael if I might die on this mission."

"What did he say?"

"He said I'm not invincible. I could die like anyone. But he told me not to worry—that I have what I need."

Shenya gave a small smile. "Then don't be afraid of what the stones show. You'll do what you must—and with hope. And you won't be alone."

John nodded slowly. He wasn't sure he believed it yet. But he wanted to. "I need some air," he said. "I'll be in the garden."

Shenya watched him go, the look on John's face told him he needed some space. He then turned to go to his study.

John sat near the arbimto bird, moving in the garden with its usual self-important stride. The morning sun was already fierce.

He looked at his hands.

A few hours ago those hands had been flung wide while light blazed from his eyes and voices that weren't his poured out of his mouth.

Now Shenya, carefully, with the measured tone of a man handling something fragile, had told him what the cave prophecy meant.

The Traveller suffers greatly.

The fountain murmured in the corner of the garden. The arbimto had retreated to a shaded area and regarded John with one suspicious eye.

John didn't know exactly what he was doing out there. Getting air, maybe. Finding something solid to stand on while he worked out how to breathe normally again.

He crouched and picked up a stone. Smooth, palm-sized, warm from the sun. He set it on the low wall beside the fountain and stepped back.

He'd stopped a boatha. That had happened. He hadn't imagined it—Jaromei had been there, had stared at the frozen creature with her mouth open. Something real was in him. Danrael had put it there, in the cave, before the portal—the light descending, his spine snapping straight, the forging of something he still didn't have a name for.

You will have everything you need, Danrael had said.

John stared at the stone.

If I have everything I need, it should answer, he thought. Something small, something simple—just enough to know the power was there and that it was his and that it would hold when the time came.

He reached inward.

Nothing.

The stone sat in the sun, indifferent.

He tried again, the way he'd focused in the labyrinth—the stillness, the locked gaze, the moment before the boatha lunged when something had simply moved in him like a tide. He looked for that. He searched for the hum of it, the current.

He found only the sound of the fountain and the arbimto shifting in its corner and his own heart going too fast in his chest.

Come on.

He stepped closer. Stood directly over the stone. Stared at it. Willed it.

Nothing.

A bee landed on the wall six inches from the stone, investigated briefly, and left. The stone did not move.

John straightened up, frustration tightening in his chest.

He thought about what was waiting for him. Six more worlds. A scroll in pieces he didn't know how to find. The darkness from his vision—no body, no face, just blackness alive and hungry, and the way it had looked at him across the void as if it already knew how this ended.

The stone sat exactly where he'd put it.

He picked it up. Turned it in his fingers. Cool on the underside where the sun hadn't reached. He thought: *maybe it only works when something is trying to kill me.*

The thought should have been funny. It wasn't.

Standing there in the late morning sun with the village sounds drifting over the wall and the fountain murmuring, he realized the fear in him. And not just him. It was the whole garden. It was what the air was made of.

Six worlds. A prophecy. A darkness.

He'd said yes in a cave at the worst moment of his life because the alternative seemed worse. He'd said yes to the mission. He'd said yes to the portal. And he was committed.

But he wasn't sure that was the same thing as being ready.

After several hours of unloading crates of food, Jaromei was on her way home. With the evening festival approaching, business had been good.

When she opened the door, burnt food and smoke greeted her.

"What is going on?" she cried, waving her hands to clear the smoke from her face.

"Relax," Shenya called from the kitchen. "You know I'm a terrible cook." He scraped burnt meat into the bin. "I tried to sear it. It didn't go well."

"Where is Grandmother?" Jaromei asked as she opened the front window.

"In the sunroom with John."

She leaned against her father. "I hope there's something else to eat."

"I'll have to go to the market. I only have enough for two."

Jaromei opened her sack and pulled out some fresh meat. "Perfect. You and Grandmother can eat this. I'll take John to the festival."

Shenya gave her a look she knew well.

She pulled a black one-piece suit and helmet out of her sack. "Sea King's guard costume," she explained. "A perfect disguise."

Shenya examined it. "If he's willing... But I'll go with you."

Jaromei frowned. "Shouldn't you stay with Grandmother?"

"She'll be alright for a short while."

"Please, Father." Jaromei clasped his hand.

"Fine," Shenya relented. "Only twenty-five minutes. Grab food and come back. No sightseeing."

"Thank you," Jaromei said, satisfied. "I'll tell John."

"Wait a few minutes. He's getting quizzed by your grandmother."

Jaromei laughed. "Right—she hates being interrupted."

"And a conversation with her will be good for him," Shenya said. "She can teach him a thing or two—just as she's taught us."

As Shenya looked toward the sunroom, his expression shifted—something behind his eyes that Jaromei recognized. Like her, he probably knew there wasn't much time left.

IN THE SUNROOM, Dernoah and John had been discussing life on Earth. She'd made it clear she had no desire to live there.

She was unimpressed when John described Earth's approach to food—especially pesticides.

"It's not what it sounds like," John assured.

"No wonder so many have diseases on Earth."

"There's no concrete evidence—"

"Sure, there isn't," Dernoah rolled her eyes, hand raised. "Your world sounds unwell in more ways than one." She paused. "I have that disease, you know. What you call cancer."

John went still. His grandfather's face surfaced—the last months, the suffering, the questions with no answers.

"Is it common here?" he asked.

"Very rare," Dernoah said. "One in ten thousand. There are medicines, but I'm too far gone now. It's growing too fast."

"Can I ask a personal question?"

"Of course. But I might give a personal answer that'll make you blush."

John grinned. "Does the illness make you upset?"

Dernoah shrugged. "I wake up feeling like knives are in me. Of course I'm upset. Do you expect me to smile all day?"

"I mean... are you angry with God?"

Dernoah took his hand. "Why would I be? He didn't give me this disease. Everything dies—anuri, beast, or tree. That's the natural order."

"Are you scared to die?" he asked.

Dernoah lifted an eyebrow. "Well, I'm not thrilled about it," she snickered. "All I know is this isn't the end. In the sacred writings, God promises to make all things new. I look forward to that day: no more death, no pain or suffering."

"I think that's a verse in my world's scriptures, too. It's comforting, but you suffer so much. I don't know if I could keep the faith."

"It's awful, waking up like this. But it changes how you see everything. I think the anuri on your world feel the same about death as we do here."

"What do you mean?"

"No one wants to talk about it. Dying is scary, messy, and sad. But so is life. Death is part of it. People pretend it doesn't exist, or do anything to avoid it. But we need to accept it."

"You're right," John said.

"But it's not all gloom, John. We have hope. One day, God will make all things new." Her words settled in the warm air.

He sat with that—the steadiness of it, the way it seemed to cost her nothing to say, as if she'd already made her peace and the peace had held. "I hope, when my time comes, I'll be as brave as you."

Dernoah squeezed his hand. "I know you're troubled about

being the Traveller. It can't be easy, being part of a plan from someone beyond our understanding."

"Sometimes I feel like I can't do this," John admitted.

"There'll be times you feel overwhelmed, or want to give up. In the darkest moments, he brings change. He makes all things new. Remember that, whenever you're afraid: He makes all things new."

"I will. I'll remember that," John promised.

"You have a brave and gentle soul, John. You may not see it, but I do. God chose you for a reason."

He smiled, looking down.

She leaned in and whispered, "Now get inside and see that gorgeous granddaughter of mine."

SEVENTEEN

When Jaromei told John about the festival, his excitement at seeing more of the village easily outshone any worries about danger. The festival wouldn't begin until sunset, which came late in the Marcritan summer.

To pass the time, Jaromei offered to teach him more about her world. They browsed Shenya's library together, pulling out books from crowded shelves, including one about kin names.

"On Marcrituss," Jaromei said, "our kin name comes from our mother, and our tribe name goes at the end. My full name is Jaromei Kobok Spee."

"So Kobok is your family, Spee is your tribe?"

She nodded. "And the masculine form ends with 'ik.' My father's name is Shenya Arjik Spee—since my grandmother is of the Arjok kin."

"I have a kin name, too," John said as they returned a volume to its place. "We usually get it from our father. Mine's Fischer."

Mentioning his kin name made him think of his family back on Earth. Guilt flickered—he missed his parents.

A sharp voice drifted through the open window—someone shouting in the village square. John glanced up, but the sound faded as quickly as it had come.

"Want to sit in the garden before we get ready for tonight?" Jaromei asked, closing the last book. "It's peaceful now."

He nodded, grateful for a change of scene. They stepped outside into the small garden, sunlight filtering through unfamiliar leaves. Shadows danced across the stone. In the corner, the arbimto slept in its cage, soaking up the heat.

Jaromei sat on a low bench by the fountain. John joined her, leaving a small distance.

For a while they just listened to water bubbling, letting the silence settle.

Jaromei finally spoke, noticing his faraway look. "What's on your mind?"

He picked at a thread on his sleeve. "I keep thinking about home. My parents, mostly. My dad's alone now, running the farm because of me. I know farming isn't for me, but... I still feel responsible. He always told me, 'The land doesn't lie. If you're patient and do the work, it gives back what you put in.'"

"That sounds like wisdom," Jaromei said.

John's voice tightened. "How am I supposed to be strong enough for some prophecy if I can't even be there for my family?"

She didn't rush to answer—just let his words hang in the warm air.

He continued, softer. "When Shenya told me about the prophecy, I freaked out. I still am. I'm supposed to be part of something huge, but I don't feel capable."

Jaromei looked at him, eyes gentle. "I know that fear."

He glanced up, surprised. "You do?"

She nodded. "I'm afraid I'll never be more than a worker at the market, helping my father. People are leaving for the sea tribes—better work, better pay. I could go, but there's the portal, my grandmother..." Her voice trailed off. "She won't be here much longer. My father needs me. I can't leave him alone." She paused, then added, "It's like I'm trapped between loyalty and my own dreams."

John was silent. "You're afraid of letting down the people you love."

She met his gaze. "Exactly."

Recognition passed between them.

"We both feel stuck," John said, a small smile tugging at his lips.

Jaromei nodded. "Any other wisdom from your father?"

John managed a weak laugh. "Oh yeah. He's like a fortune cookie."

"A what?"

"Full of helpful sayings," John laughed. "He used to say, 'Doubt isn't the opposite of faith. Giving up is.' But I don't know how to keep going when I feel this... small."

Jaromei shook her head. "You don't seem small. You faced a boatha and lived. You came to a world you didn't know, because you believed it mattered."

John took a breath. "I did believe it mattered. But honestly, it wasn't just about that. I was drowning at home. My life was like a cage, and I wanted out." He searched her face. "Maybe I'm not as noble as you think."

She leaned forward. "The calling and the escape—they're both real. Both true. There's no shame in wanting your own dreams."

He felt something in his chest loosen. "And you're strong too, Jaromei. You're devoted to your family and to being a guardian, even when it would be easier to walk away."

She smiled, more tentative now. "Maybe we're both stronger than we think."

Movement caught John's eye—a figure passing beyond the garden wall, moving with purpose. Not the casual stroll of a villager, but something more deliberate. He couldn't make out details through the lattice, but unease prickled at the back of his neck.

"What is it?" Jaromei asked, following his gaze.

"Probably nothing," he said, but the feeling lingered.

They sat together as the dusk gathered. The distance between them—host and guest—had faded. Something deeper had begun to root itself.

When they finally stood to go inside, John's hand brushed hers—a silent promise.

From somewhere in the village, the trocks tolled—the usual evening call.

Jaromei paused at the door, listening. Then she shook her head, as if dismissing a worry. "We should get ready."

The festival approached. Each went to their room to prepare.

CHAPTER
EIGHTEEN

John's Sea King Guard costume was a squeeze, the helmet snug but comfortable enough. Padding the boots to compensate for his non-webbed toes made walking awkward, but he figured he'd adapt.

He caught a glimpse of himself in the mirror and burst out laughing. The black helmet, with its oversized dark lenses, made him look like a bug.

Satisfied, he headed downstairs to find Jaromei. She was standing by the door in a turquoise gown, glittering face paint tracing royal symbols across her cheeks, a delicate seashell tiara catching the light. The pink, diamond-shaped shells were unlike anything on Earth.

As they reached the door, Shenya poked his head out of his study. "Only twenty-five minutes, Jaromei. Hear me?"

"Yes, Father," Jaromei called, waving him off as she led John out.

Outside, John nearly tripped—the padding in the boots wasn't holding up. Jaromei grabbed his hand. "Careful, or your helmet might fly off. My father would never let me hear the end of it." She squeezed his fingers. "I'll guide you."

John grinned, letting her lead.

As they walked, John took in the village for the first time. It was bigger than a village—more like a rustic town nestled into the base of the mountains. The golden stone houses glowed in the sun. Jaromei glowed too—her glittered face paint catching the light as she moved. "Are you dressed as a particular princess?" he asked.

"I'm Crown Princess Siboa of the Sea Tribes," Jaromei announced. "You're my guard—though I think I'm really yours tonight."

John laughed. "Who here's got the superpowers?"

She nudged him. "And who can walk and see straight?"

"Fair point."

As they turned the corner, the village square opened before him: a magnificent fountain at the center, the compass-tower beyond, vendors hawking food and games from stone-fronted shops, music and laughter filling the air.

Crowds in costumes—strange masks, painted faces, full-body suits—streamed past. It was like Halloween at home, minus the spooks.

"This is awesome," John breathed in the scents and sounds.

Jaromei beamed. "Welcome to Morboli."

He let the name settle in his mind: Morboli.

Through the open village gate, John spotted a tall tower on massive legs, stretching toward the sea. "What's that?"

"Our power tower," Jaromei said. "It collects sun, sea, and wind energy for the village."

"That runs everything?"

"And the neighboring villages, too," she replied. "Doesn't your world have anything like that?"

"We have power, just not... that advanced." John glanced around. "Your tech's everywhere, but it never takes over. On Earth, we're kind of addicted to it."

Jaromei frowned. "How can you be addicted to technology?"

John tried to explain. "We have handheld computers—for entertainment, talking to people, taking endless photos. We record everything so we can play it back anytime."

"Hundreds of years ago, we had something similar to what you call a camera," Jaromei said. "But it didn't last. People began to believe a superstition—that capturing a person's likeness that way brings the worst possible luck."

That answered John's earlier question about the lack of photographs. He couldn't imagine life without photos or film.

"So what do you do for fun?" he asked.

She smiled. "Live performances. Meals with friends. Music, drama, sports, festivals—like this. We keep our old traditions alive."

His voice came quieter: "I think I prefer your way."

Jaromei squeezed his hand and led him to a food stall. Bright red buns sandwiched something savory inside.

"Two, please," Jaromei ordered, handing over a metal coin.

As the vendor prepared the food, John leaned in. "May I see the coin?" He hadn't yet seen any currency from Marcrituss.

Jaromei handed it over. It was heavier than any coin he'd held on Earth—bronze-like, but denser. The design startled him: a profile of a man stamped on the front, just like currency from his own world.

"Who is that man?" John asked.

Jaromei snatched the coin back. "Not so loud. It's King Eudor—King of the Land Tribes."

"Well, I didn't know," John muttered. "I haven't had that

lesson yet." Lowering his voice, he asked, "Who's the King of the Sea Tribes?"

Jaromei smirked. "King Rathrian. Don't get in his way. He's a tyrant."

"What about King Eudor? Is he nice?"

"He's a gentle old soul," Jaromei said, "but he's not long for the world. Everyone knows he's not truly in charge anymore. Soon, his daughter will be queen. She'll be wise and fair—like her father."

"Only two rulers over an entire planet," John said. "Not much power sharing."

"It's not as tyrannical as you think," Jaromei replied. "Each tribe has a governor chosen by the people. Every village or city has a chancellor, also chosen locally. The chancellors meet in an assembly every month with the kings and governors to bring needs forward. And the royal house isn't permanent. Every three generations, a different tribe supplies a new royal house."

"That sounds pretty fair," John said. "Is it the same system in the sea?"

"For now," Jaromei said, her expression darkening. "But Rathrian wants to do away with the system. He wants full power. He's been unsuccessful so far, but he's still trying."

As the vendor handed over the sandwiches, a group of young anuri men were eyeing Jaromei. She flashed them a smile. John watched them until they melted into the throng.

The moment Jaromei handed John the sandwich, he could smell its tempting aroma through the helmet. "We need to continue this conversation at home. I can't wait to get the helmet off and dig into this."

Jaromei shot him an irritated look. "You'd rather go home and eat than spend time with me in the village?"

John froze and lost his breath.

Jaromei burst out laughing. "I'm just joking. We should go anyway. Besides, you have no idea how ridiculous you look in that costume."

Seeing her eyes light up when she laughed made John speak without thinking. "I bet you have no idea how beautiful you look in yours."

He regretted it as soon as the words escaped.

That's totally cringe, Fischer.

Each of them held a sandwich in one hand, but John took her free hand in his. "I know we've only known each other for a few days, and a lot is going on," John began. "Not to mention we're from different worlds—literally." He swallowed, then continued, "But I really like you, Jaromei. I've seen all these guys flirting with you, and I'm afraid if I don't tell you now, I'll miss my chance."

Jaromei burst into giggles again.

"Did I misread the room?" John asked, horrified.

"That's not it," she managed through laughter. "Why did you have to say all of that while wearing this silly costume? All I see is a giant black helmet with funny eyes telling me these lovely things... while holding a sandwich."

John exhaled hard with relief. Picturing it, he couldn't help but laugh too.

"For the record," Jaromei said, composing herself, "I like you too. But you have a million things to focus on. We need to be patient."

"So... you think we might have a chance someday?"

"If you can travel across the universe in a day," she said, smiling, "then it shouldn't be impossible for us." Her smile widened. "So yes. I think we definitely have a chance... someday."

They were about to head home when the square went still all at once.

The trocks rang—loud, urgent.

At first, it seemed like a ceremony, but panic swept the crowd. The village gates slammed shut. Uniformed men forced people back as they tried to leave.

Jaromei grabbed his arm. "No time to explain. We need to get back to my father. Now."

CHAPTER
NINETEEN

John let Jaromei lead him through the panic-stricken crowd, struggling not to trip as they rushed back to her house. She fumbled with the door and burst inside.

John pulled off his helmet, still baffled by the chaos. "What's happening out there?"

"The trocks only toll outside of services if there's danger," Jaromei explained. "Four tolls mean we're under attack. Three means lockdown—an immediate threat. Tonight, there were three tolls."

Shenya rushed down the stairs and pulled Jaromei into a tight embrace. "I'm so glad you're safe. When I heard the trocks, I feared the worst."

"When we heard them, we came straight home," Jaromei assured him.

"Someone knows about John," Shenya said grimly. "Why else would our village be put on lockdown? Someone must have found out he's here."

"He never took off the helmet," Jaromei insisted. "Nobody saw him."

"It's not the eyes of anuri who are searching," Dernoah said from across the room. "Darker forces have felt his presence, child. They are searching for the Traveller."

John swallowed. "My vision, Shenya. Maybe this is what it was warning me about."

"I need to get you out of the village," Shenya replied. "We have to find the scroll fragment on Marcrituss quickly so you can move on to the next world."

Dernoah lowered herself into a chair and coughed, blood splattering on the white rug.

John lowered his voice. "No, Shenya. You're needed here. Your mother needs you. I'll go alone."

"Stop!" Dernoah snapped, her voice rough with another cough. "I'm dying, but I'm not deaf! John, you need Shenya's knowledge. Jaromei will stay with me, and you two will go. As the eldest of this family, that's my decision. No discussion!"

John looked at her. The frail frame, the blood on the rug—and her eyes, utterly immovable. "I can't ask Shenya to leave you," he protested. "He should be here."

Dernoah huffed. "Why? Because I'm about to die? If Shenya's not ready to say goodbye now, he never will be. Your mission depends on what you do next. That's how it must be."

John said nothing.

Shenya caught his eye. "Don't be upset, John. You know your calling, and I know mine—to help you."

Jaromei stepped close and hugged John. "They're both right. You need my father's help to get out and finish your mission."

He held her tight. "It feels like the universe is against us."

"I refuse to believe that," she whispered.

They separated, and Shenya turned to his daughter. "Pack a bag for John and me, would you?"

Jaromei nodded and slipped out.

"Thank you, daughter." Shenya turned to John. "The chancellor might order house searches—the earlier we go, the better."

As Jaromei left, John moved to follow her.

"Please stay here," Shenya called after him. "I need to talk to you about what comes next. Come with me."

John glanced at Jaromei. She gave him a look that told him to listen to her father. He offered her a small, understanding smile, then followed Shenya into the study.

Shenya cleared books aside and unrolled a map across the desk. "The Archive of the Ancients may hold what we need. That means we go to Marciluk—an underwater city in the Sea Kingdom, over a thousand miles west."

John's stomach dropped. "Underwater?"

"The city itself is enclosed—you'll be fine. But we can't get there directly. We walk to Brooth first, four days at least. From there, we fly on a gropolo to Cosheh, then descend into the sea."

"A gropolo?" John asked, wary.

"A trained creature—perfectly safe. We need to find one in Brooth because we can't trust just any gropolo shou—the one who flies it. We're going to see my good friend Yumi. He's trustworthy, though he'll likely insist on seeing your face if we want his help."

John wasn't thrilled at the idea of flying on a creature, but set it aside. "How do we get out? Everything will be monitored."

"Through the tunnels below the village before dawn." Shenya rolled the map. "It'll be a hard journey, but do not be afraid. We're in it together."

John rubbed his eyes.

Do not be afraid. The same words Danrael had spoken before leaving Earth.

WHEN JAROMEI RETURNED, Shenya and John left Dernoah's house and went next door. She had packed a single bag with clothes, tools, and food—enough for a few days.

Shenya urged John to sleep while he sorted things out for his mother and Jaromei before leaving. John lay in the dark, his mind circling—the darkness, the cave prophecy, Jaromei—and each time exhaustion pulled him under, something jolted him back.

That night, Shenya crept into John's room to lay out fresh clothes, just as he had before. John heard him but stayed silent.

Giving up on sleep, John went downstairs. He heard Shenya in the kitchen, but there was no time for chatting or fresh eggs like the day before. In silence, they left and went next door for their goodbyes.

Jaromei and Dernoah waited in the sitting room. Shenya crossed the room and knelt before Dernoah. She took his head in her hands and kissed his forehead. They sat together for over a minute, holding each other in a heartfelt embrace. Shenya felt her warm face against his and her tears on his cheek. The thought of never feeling that warmth again filled him with sorrow.

"I'll take care of Amek and Marnia when I get to them," Dernoah said. John assumed they were Shenya's late father and wife.

"I love you, Mother," Shenya whispered. "You have been the best mother anyone could ask for. Thank you for giving me life and dedicating yours to our family." He stroked her face and mustered a smile as he kissed her forehead.

"I love you too, my Shenya," she said, letting him go.

She turned to John, her tone commanding. "Take care of him, John. Take care of both of them."

John held her hand. "It's been a pleasure to be with you these last few days."

"What did I tell you to remember?"

"He makes all things new."

"Be grateful that you are the Traveller, John. You will bring hope to many," Dernoah said, squeezing his hand and giving him one last smile. "Now go while it's still dark."

John turned to Jaromei. Tears stood in her eyes. She stepped close and kissed his cheek.

"I will wait for you," she whispered.

After raising the burmui over his head, Jaromei stepped aside and embraced her father. "I love you, Father. Be careful—and come back to me."

"I will, daughter. Pray for us—pray for strength and safety."

After kissing Jaromei, Shenya gave his mother one last loving glance, then led John out.

Jaromei closed the door behind them, her hand lingering on the frame. She turned back, moving carefully, as if any sudden motion might shatter something inside her.

She lowered herself on the cushion beside Dernoah, breathing shallowly. "How are you doing, Grandmother?" she asked.

"A mother can only hope she'll be able to say goodbye to her children properly before the end. Some never do, so for that, I'm grateful." Dernoah studied her. "The more important question is—are you alright?"

"I will be." Jaromei's gaze drifted to the table where the helmet and tiara lay, abandoned from the night before. She swallowed hard, her jaw tightening. "The heart is a strange thing," she said.

CHAPTER
TWENTY

Morboli's chancellor had posted guards at every gate, but John and Shenya slipped out—unde-tected—through the old evacuation tunnels to the beach. From there, they trekked north along the coast, then turned west into the Corja Forest.

Except for the occasional birdsong, the forest was eerily quiet. They walked in silence for nearly two hours before John couldn't stand it anymore. "Are you angry at me?"

Shenya looked genuinely puzzled. "Why would I be?"

"You've been so quiet. I thought maybe you were regretting this."

"No, John," Shenya said, voice softening. "It's been a tough day. I've just been lost in thought."

"I know it must have been hard to leave your mother," John said. "It's hard to say goodbye to people you love."

"Yes." Shenya looked away. "And you know that feeling well. You've left everyone you love behind to do this mission. That's a brave thing you've done."

John was tired of hearing that. His mind drifted back to his confrontation with Olly. He couldn't shake the feeling he'd acted like a coward. "I'm not as brave as you think," he muttered. "Until recently, I was a real loser. Bullies beat me up constantly. No friends, no confidence. I never stood up for myself. Sometimes I think part of me wanted to leave just to run away and be someone new. Sometimes I—" John wasn't sure he could say the words out loud. "I feel like a fraud."

The words hung between the trees. Something loosened in his chest at having said them.

Shenya was quiet for a long moment. When he spoke, his voice was careful. "Since you've confided in me, I'll confide in you. Maybe it will help."

They walked a few more paces in silence, as if Shenya needed the motion to carry the words.

"Eight years ago, my wife and I took Jaromei to the northern coast." He paused, jaw tight. "Marnia was pregnant with our son, Amek."

John's step slowed. "You had a son?"

Shenya nodded, eyes ahead. "Thieves struck out of nowhere. Marnia screamed for me to save Jaromei. I grabbed her hand, got her to the trees and told her to run." He stopped walking. "I let go of Marnia's hand to do it." The words came out flat, worn smooth by years of repetition in his own mind. "They killed her. And Amek. I was knocked out. When I came to, she was just... gone."

The forest held its breath around them.

John said nothing. There was nothing to say. He stood beside Shenya in the stillness, the birdsong somewhere above them, the light coming through the canopy in broken pieces.

After a long moment, Shenya resumed walking. John fell into step beside him.

"I'll never forget the look on Marnia's face as I blacked out," Shenya said, quieter now. "That was the last time I saw her alive. Everyone called me brave for saving Jaromei. The villagers celebrated me like a hero. I felt like I'd failed—that I should have saved Marnia and Amek too. I felt like a fraud."

"You weren't—"

"It took years, but I know that now." Shenya's voice steadied. He met John's gaze. "You're not a fraud either. People lash out because they're hurting, or something's broken at home. You didn't ask to be bullied. I didn't ask for those thieves to come that day. But we survived. That's what matters."

He stopped again, turning to face John directly.

"You've been through a lot, and you're still here. You've overcome the challenges you faced. That means you truly are brave—whether you feel it or not."

John looked at him—this man who had lost a wife and son and still had faith. He still got up every morning to guard a portal for a prophecy he couldn't be certain was real. "Thanks for telling me all that," he said at last. "It means a lot." He paused. "You said you'd be there for me. I want you to know I'll be there for you, too."

Shenya held his gaze for a moment, then smiled—the real one, the one that reached his eyes. "We'll make a good team."

He pulled out two water bottles, tossed one across, and nodded westward through the trees. "We keep heading that way. With luck, we'll avoid villages—and any anuri along the way."

They walked on together through the quiet forest, the weight between them lighter now for having been shared.

TWENTY-ONE

John and Shenya moved steadily through the forest, stopping only when necessary, trading watch through the nights. By day, Shenya shared Marcritan epics; John offered Lord of the Rings, King Arthur, Merlin—Shenya imagining each one for the stage with undisguised delight.

Marcrituss's untouched beauty struck John at every turn—distant mountains, forests no human hand had touched. He wished his parents could see it.

By the third evening, their food was gone. Shenya was teaching John which berries wouldn't kill him when the prickling unease crept in.

Shenya set his map aside and examined John. "Are you alright?"

John hesitated. "I feel strange—not sick, just... off. I hope I'm not about to have a vision," John joked weakly. "If I get that kind of hunger again, we're in trouble."

"That's for sure," Shenya laughed. "But we're ahead of schedule—we might reach Brooth by tomorrow afternoon, maybe even catch a gropolo flight by nightfall."

"That's great news. Our feet could use a rest."

"You should put your feet up tonight," Shenya suggested. "I'll keep watch."

John opened his mouth to thank him—then the strange feeling intensified.

He stood abruptly, rigid, as a presence pressed into his awareness—one he recognized instantly. It was the same presence from his vision.

A force of pure hatred.

The darkness.

Only this time, it wasn't a vision.

"The darkness is here, Shenya," John said. "We need to leave. Now."

"What?" Shenya snapped, already cramming their things into the bag. "Are you certain?"

"I could never forget what it feels like."

John scanned the trees, uncertain of what he was looking for. In his vision, the darkness had hunted him without form —no body, just living blackness. "Where do we hide?" he asked.

"What good would hiding do?" Shenya protested. "The darkness would still find us."

John glanced back along the path. Five men approached at a steady pace. They were distant, but something about them felt wrong. Not just hostile, but occupied. Their presence pressed against John's mind like icy fingers. Something swept over him—like hypnosis, as if his thoughts were being pulled out of alignment.

"We have to run!" Shenya shouted. He stared at John, bewildered—John had gone still, eyes unfocused, staring at nothing. "What are you doing, John? We have to go!"

"The darkness..." John stammered. "I can feel it. It's trying to speak to me."

"What? How is that possible?" Shenya grabbed his arm, tried to pull him, but John wouldn't budge.

It was too late.

The darkness slipped into John's mind.

Don't fight me, Traveller. I am not a threat. I can give you everything you want—and more...

John stood paralyzed, senses dulled, unable to break away. "I can hear him speaking to me," John whispered.

"Resist it!" Shenya yelled. "You've felt its true nature. You know it's nothing good!" John hardly heard him. The voice was too strong, too seductive.

Let me give you what you crave: peace, freedom—your old life back. Whatever you desire, it's yours.

"Listen to me!" Shenya shouted, gripping John and forcing him to meet his gaze. "You have everything you need to stop it. You can fight this. Focus!"

The darkness was strangely comforting now—soothing, convincing. For a terrifying moment, John wondered if it wasn't so dark after all. Maybe it really could bring him peace.

Give up this fight, and you can have it all...right now.

Then another voice cut through his mind—familiar, urgent.

Danrael.

His voice rang inside John's skull, clear and commanding.

Resist the darkness, John! You have the power to break away. Fight the temptation and believe! If you give in to fear and lose faith, you are powerless. Have faith in the one who sent you!

John heard him, but the seductive influence clung tight.

John, if you have faith the size of a mustard seed, you will tell this mountain, "Move from here to there," and it will move. Nothing will be impossible for you. Remember your vision!

John shut his eyes and clung to the angel's words. Images flashed: the cave columns, the war in heaven, the living black hunger. He remembered what it really felt like—pure hatred, anger, misery, the opposite of the angels' light. The voice now was a mask. A lie. A lure.

John reached inward and pushed back against the master deceiver.

"No. I have felt your true nature. I know what you are, and I want nothing to do with you. Leave—now!"

A jolt surged through him. John snapped out of the trance. "Run!" he shouted.

They sprinted through the forest. Sunlight still filtered through the trees. Boots pounded the earth as branches whipped past, leaves tearing at their clothes.

A dagger whistled past John's head.

He spun and saw the five men closing in, faces hidden behind scarves.

They split: three on foot, two climbing treetops with unnatural speed—elbows hyperextending, spines twisting like rope. One assassin's leg folded backwards at the knee as he launched upward, the joint snapping back mid-leap.

The two in the trees leapt across the canopy, silent and swift.

Then one stopped, perched on a limb above the path—crouching, birdlike, head cocked too far. John could feel the assassin's eyes tracking them, patient as a hunter sure of its prey.

The other dropped to a lower branch, hanging upside down, just watching.

Shenya's breathing turned ragged. His stride faltered, body pitching forward before he caught himself.

"Keep—going—" he gasped, legs shaking.

The assassin above them tilted his head, then reached for another dagger.

He didn't throw it—just turned it in his hand, letting

sunlight catch the blade. Then he smiled and leapt to the next tree, keeping ahead, always close.

John saw Shenya slowing. He wished he'd broken away from the darkness sooner.

He lost sight of the two in the trees, but heard them—too fast, too light. The forest felt alive and sinister.

"Danrael!" John shouted. "We could use your help right about now!"

You have everything you need to stop them, John. Don't succumb to fear. Connect with your power. You know how to do it.

John heard him, but all he could do was run. He needed to access his abilities, or they'd never survive.

One assassin reappeared, poised to throw a dagger at Shenya.

He was too close to miss.

John watched in horror as the attacker snapped his arm forward. In that instant, something stronger overwhelmed fear.

Love for his friend.

John reached out and exerted his power. The dagger dropped, clattering to the ground near Shenya's heel.

Two more pursuers launched throwing stars at John. He thrust out his arms, using his power—sending the weapons spinning deep into the forest.

Before he could breathe, another dagger shot down toward Shenya from above, and a second came from behind at John.

He stopped both, barely.

The blades trembled, fighting an invisible force, inches from their targets.

The hunters were done playing.

They were ready to kill.

Shenya could barely keep up; John knew he couldn't protect him much longer. Without hesitation, he pushed

Shenya off the path with his power—fast and hard. Shenya thought a pursuer had thrown him, but seeing John's arms outstretched, he realized the truth: John had sent him flying, at least 20 metres.

Shenya crashed through the brush and slammed into a tree. Pain shot through his shoulder, but nothing was broken. He scrambled back to the path—but the hunt was reaching its conclusion.

The five attackers ignored Shenya and closed in on John.

The two from the trees dropped down and rejoined the others, forming a semicircle.

Their movements slowed—deliberate, predatory.

Darkness radiated from them—a stain, spreading like spilled ink.

He was face-to-face with what he feared most. The fear rose like a flood. He tried to push them back with his power—nothing happened. He didn't know why.

John, you must have faith! Do not let fear rule you, John! Your power lives in faith.

Danrael's words weren't helping. Fear paralyzed John. Panic surged. He clutched for power—but the fear inside him was too strong. As long as he doubted, the gift was silent.

"Danrael, please," he pleaded. "Help me!"

A voice came, only in his mind.

Why do you ask for me? Call upon the name above all names—the one who is all-powerful.

They crept closer, feeding off John's fear. Shenya shouted for him to run, but there was nowhere to go.

John closed his eyes and did as Danrael told him.

He called upon the name above all names.

"Jesus, help us," John prayed aloud, the most desperate prayer he'd ever made.

For a heartbeat, nothing happened.

The forest went deathly still.

Then the five assailants froze.

In an instant, the sky went dark—an eclipse where none should be. The last light vanished, and a great shadow swept over the world. The ground trembled; John struggled to stand.

All around, animals erupted in panic. Birds burst from the treetops, creatures fled through the undergrowth.

The five men shrieked—unnatural, violent sounds. Their scarves slipped free, revealing faces half-rotted, as though the darkness inside them had been devouring them.

Their bodies twisted and convulsed, as if struck by an invisible force. They fell backward and slithered away, moving with eerie speed.

Shenya rushed to John's side. "What is happening?"

John stared into the forest. He sensed no darkness left. The shaking stopped. The sky cleared, and sunlight returned. The animals quieted too.

Everything returned to normal—except John's pounding heart.

"I'll explain," John said, still shaken. "We have to reach Brooth. Now."

TWENTY-TWO

"John... we have to stop." Shenya braced himself against a tree, panting. He took two water bottles from their bag and tossed one to John. "How did you make those...those things leave? That was extraordinary."

John's hands trembled. "I don't know how to explain it. When I was surrounded, I asked Danrael for help and—"

"So the angel rescued us?" Shenya interrupted.

"No." John shook his head. "It wasn't Danrael." He was still breathing hard, the adrenaline not yet gone from him.

"Then it was you?"

John motioned for Shenya to sit. "Danrael told me to call upon the name above all names."

Shenya frowned. "What does that mean?"

John stared at the ground. "Remember when we talked about the man who is both God and anuri?"

"Of course." Somewhere above them, a bird called once and went silent.

"It was his name." John looked up. "I think they left because I spoke his name."

Shenya leaned in. "What is this name?"

The forest was still around them.

"His name is..." John hesitated, feeling the weight of it. "His name is Jesus," he whispered. "After I said it, those things— they were terrified."

"I've never seen God's presence like that," Shenya said, awestruck. "The land quaked. The sun bowed. Nature itself obeyed."

"I don't understand it," John admitted. "On my world, people say that name all the time. But nothing like... this." He gestured at the trees.

Shenya's eyes widened as realisation dawned. "John, you told me God became one of us. That he took a name. If God took a name, then names must matter. They must hold real power." Shenya paused, the truth settling over him. "It must be because this was the first time that name has ever been invoked on Marcrituss."

John stared, the realisation heavy inside him.

"Marcrituss answered," John whispered. "It gave honor to—"

"To the King above all gods," Shenya finished, his voice hushed. "A powerful name, because it's the name God allowed for himself."

Seeing John overwhelmed, Shenya gently patted his back. "How are you holding up?"

John searched for words. "I'm... in awe. Genuinely speech-less. I don't know how else to explain it."

"Are you in awe of what you did," Shenya asked, "or of the one whose name you spoke?"

"Both, I guess. That fight back there made me wonder if

I'm the wrong person for this. I completely lost my ability to use the power. I don't have the faith it requires."

Shenya saw the sweat pouring into John's eyes and handed him a cloth. "You say you struggle with God, but you sure know a lot about him."

John managed a faint smile. "When those things surrounded me... I panicked. I've never been so afraid."

"You froze because fear makes us lose control," Shenya said.

"When I stopped that boatha, it was different."

Shenya set down his water bottle. "When you stopped a what?"

John hesitated. "I got the impression I wasn't supposed to mention it." He nervously scratched the back of his neck. "Back in Morboli's labyrinth, a boatha attacked Jaromei and me. Just before it tried to eat me, I controlled it. Made it stop—like I did those daggers."

Shenya covered his face with his hand. "Jaromei was wise to keep that one quiet."

"Tonight, after I broke away from the darkness in my mind, I was confident—like in the labyrinth. I thought, 'I've got this.' Then, minutes later, I totally lost it." He looked at Shenya. "Sometimes I feel like I take one step forward and two steps back."

"Life is like that," Shenya said. "We can be on top of the world one minute and in a pit the next. When we fail, we pick ourselves up and keep going. When faith is fragile, fear grows powerful. When fear takes control, your abilities vanish."

"You're right," John sighed. "Thanks for helping me make sense of all this."

Shenya smiled and gave his arm an affectionate punch. "I should be thanking you. I'd have a dagger in my heart if not for you."

"Of course I saved you," John said, trying for lightness. "I need you. And... I kind of like having you around."

Shenya slung an arm around him. "If you ever need to save me again, perhaps avoid throwing me into a tree."

"Sorry about that," John chuckled.

Then Shenya's expression turned serious. "Speaking of which, John, I must tell you something important."

John tensed. "Are you okay? What is it?"

Shenya grew solemn—more serious than John had ever seen him. "On Marcrituss, we have a sacred tradition. If you save the life of an anuri..." He drew a breath. "He must give you his daughter's hand in marriage."

John froze. "Are you serious?"

Shenya burst out laughing. "No! But you'd like that, wouldn't you?"

John shoved him playfully and stood. "Let's get moving."

Shenya shook his head, still grinning. "Sometimes, laughter is the best medicine."

Laughter faded as they walked beneath the rising moons, the weight of John's calling settling over him.

TWENTY-THREE

The trek through the forest was silent, save for the crunch of undergrowth and their uneven breaths. Neither suggested stopping. The memory of the night's attack clung to them, pushing their tired legs forward.

Ahead, the twisted outline of a labyrinth rose above the trees—jagged against the pale sky. Shenya glanced at his map and grinned.

"You'll be glad to know we're almost to Brooth. Just ahead," Shenya said.

John groaned, his shoulders sagging. "Thank God. I'm so tired of walking."

Shenya chuckled, rolling his map away. "It's been hours since anything tried to kill us. I think we can stop and breathe."

John wiped a sleeve across his face and caught a whiff of himself—sweat, dirt, and something worse. He glanced at Shenya, who looked just as rough: travel-stained, bristly with four days' growth, eyes shadowed from sleeplessness.

"Shenya, should we really go into the city like this? We look

—and smell—awful. Your friend might tell us to bathe before we even say hello."

Shenya sniffed his shirt, grimacing. "You're right. We're not in Spee country anymore, either. This is Trovus territory. I'd rather not disgrace my tribe."

John scanned the underbrush, recalling lessons from the road about the land tribes scattered across the continents of Nolthem and Stolji. Following local customs was important. Even the sea tribes followed that rule when visiting land.

"We should find a spring," Shenya said, glancing around. "A quick wash would do us good before we reach Brooth."

John squinted left and spotted water glinting beyond a tangle of fallen trees. "There's something over there."

They pushed through the brush and found a wide pond, its edge strewn with reeds. Shenya dropped his pack, rummaged, and pulled out Jaromei's well-stocked toiletries kit: straight razor, soap, the works. "This will do," he said, relief in his voice. "Thank God for Jaromei—she prepared everything."

John couldn't agree more. He thought about what she might be doing back in Morboli.

"The men of the Trovus tribe are always clean-shaven. We should be, too," Shenya said.

"Nobody but your friend will see my face. I don't think it matters if I shave."

"Even so, Yumi's a stickler for tradition. We need to make a good impression." Shenya handed him the blade and soap.

John sighed. "I feel silly admitting this, but I don't know how to use one of these. I'd just cut myself."

Shenya chuckled, pointing to a spot beside the water. "Come sit down. I'll do it for you."

"You're going to shave me?"

Shenya sat beside the pond. "Come on. This won't take long. Take off the burmui so it doesn't get in the way."

John pulled off the cloak and sat on the ground. Shenya scooped water into his bottle and warmed it with a gadget that resembled a blowtorch lighter. As he waited, he laughed softly.

"What's so funny?" John asked.

"I was remembering my bushy, scraggly beard as a teenager. I grew it just because I could. It looked awful, and my mother hated it."

John chuckled, picturing Dernoah's reaction.

"I finally got tired of it, but didn't know how to shave, so my father sat me down and did it for me. He said, 'One day you'll do this for your son—and you'll think of me.' I never got to do that with Amek, so I'm grateful to have this experience with someone."

When the water was warm, Shenya soaked a cloth and patted John's face. "The trick to the best shave is a warm face and foamy soap. My hand will have to do this time."

He lathered the soap and spread it over John's face and neck, then carefully shaved him. Shenya wasn't crying, but his eyes had misted over.

"Is something wrong, Shenya?"

"No," he replied. "Everything is as it should be."

A minute later, Shenya splashed water on John's face and finished. "Grab a change of clothes from the bag. I'll sort out my own shave."

"Are you able to shave without a mirror?"

"Oh yes, I've had plenty of practice."

"I suppose at your age you would have," John teased.

Shenya laughed as he warmed more water. "For the record, John, I'm only forty-three."

"At forty-three, you're still pretty young. Have you ever thought about dating again?"

Shenya shot him a look. "The only women I have time for are my mother and Jaromei," he replied, lathering the soap.

Then he grinned. "Are you offering relationship advice now? Has something happened on Marcrituss to give you confidence?"

"No, nothing," he mumbled. He realized he may have set something in motion he couldn't stop.

Shenya paused, razor in hand. "Since you brought this up —what about you? You and Jaromei seem to have hit it off."

"Not much to say," John replied, blushing.

"I get it. No man wants to talk about the girl he likes with her father."

"I have no idea what you're talking about," John muttered. "Anyway, I'd better get washed up." He stripped off his clothes and dove into the pond, swimming across.

Shenya laughed, enjoying how easy it was to wind John up about Jaromei. Before leaving Morboli, he'd already noticed their flirtation turning into something more. He remembered his own teenage years—how quickly things could change. Still, he'd overheard Jaromei's parting words: she'd promised to wait for John. Shenya suspected she meant it.

He wasn't sure whether either of them understood just how complicated such a relationship could be.

CHAPTER
TWENTY-FOUR

Clouds thickened overhead. Cool drops began to pock the dusty road. John and Shenya pressed on, hoping to reach Brooth before the downpour. Beyond a labyrinth's twisted outline, city towers rose sharply against the dim sky. After days lost in rustling forest and endless mud, the sight of civilization looked almost alien—too clean, too vertical.

John scanned for walls around the city, expecting gates like Morboli. A wide smile grew across his face when he saw that Brooth was wide open.

Beside him, Shenya pulled his pack higher, eyes fixed on the skyline. Thunder rumbled closer. "Stay close. With luck, we'll find a gropolo and be gone before the rain really hits."

John's smile didn't last.

Shenya froze and raised a hand. "Wait!"

They ducked behind thick trunks as a line of soldiers appeared, boots splashing in the mud along the labyrinth's edge. One peeled off, taking up guard at the entrance.

"Brooth is on lockdown, John. We're not getting in this way."

Frustration rose in John. Every obstacle overcome brought another. "If Brooth is in lockdown, someone here must know about me. How is that possible?"

"It's not only Brooth and Morboli," Shenya replied quietly. "It's probably the same in all land villages and cities. For lock-downs this widespread, the order would have to come from King Euron himself."

John's stomach dropped. "Jaromei told me he's a good king. Why would he be after me?"

"We'll get to the bottom of it," Shenya assured him. "But right now we need to get into Brooth. Somehow, we have to get to the other side of the labyrinth. One option is to go through it, but that guard isn't moving. We'll never get past him."

"So what do we do?"

Shenya studied the towers rising beyond the labyrinth. "That's where you come in. Danrael said your powers would provide what you need. What can you do to get us past this?"

John stared at the guard, spear resting in his hands. The clock was ticking—soon the rest of the troop would return. Panic crept in, making it hard to think, let alone use his power.

Shenya saw the fear grow. "Calm yourself. Remember: fear blocks faith."

John took a deep breath and looked beyond the labyrinth at the city.

What if we went over the labyrinth instead of through it?

The thought struck him—ridiculous, but it was all he had. John closed his eyes and concentrated.

Shenya watched, puzzled, and finally grew impatient. "Are you taking a nap?"

John opened his eyes, annoyed. "Trust me. I'm working on it."

A piercing cry echoed in the distance.

Moments later, it came again—much closer.

Shenya looked up, freezing at the sight of an enormous gropolo soaring above. He slowly turned to John, who grinned.

"What in the…" Shenya muttered. "You called a gropolo?"

"It can fly us into the city, right?"

"It can, but neither of us knows how to control it. This is desperate."

"Desperate times call for desperate measures," John replied.

The connection with the creature returned. He focused, calling the gropolo down beside them.

The jet-black creature was awe-inspiring, its wingspan stretching at least sixty feet, giant and eagle-like with long blue feathers sprouting from its cheeks and forehead.

Shenya stared in amazement. "There's no shou, no passenger box. How are we supposed to—"

The guard at his post began to panic as the gropolo landed on the grassy field. The creature was so massive that John and Shenya could move from behind the trees and hide behind its body.

Shenya felt the creature's skin beneath its plumage—it was elastic. "If you reach beneath the feathers, John, you can hold onto its skin." He chuckled grimly. "Can you ask it to fly us out of here? Now, please."

"We'll find out," John answered.

He focused on the gropolo, pushing his thoughts toward it. The connection snapped into place.

John nodded to Shenya and grabbed the creature's rubbery skin under the feathers. Shenya followed, gripping tightly.

If their hands slipped, they'd fall straight to the ground.

The gropolo's wings slammed downward. Wind exploded around them as the creature leapt into the air. The ground dropped away beneath John's feet—ten feet, twenty, fifty. He held his breath, burying himself in its feathers, praying the soldiers below wouldn't look up.

John directed the gropolo to fly counterclockwise around the city, hoping to hide the side they clung to.

The creature soared higher and higher, following John's instructions. Wind tore at his cloak. His fingers ached from gripping the rubbery skin. Below, Brooth spread out like a map —streets, towers, the labyrinth's impossible geometry.

"You're mad, John!" Shenya shouted over the wind, clinging for dear life.

John was starting to agree. He glanced down—the city spun beneath him, tiny figures moving like insects through the streets. His stomach lurched, and he buried his face deeper in the feathers.

The gropolo banked sharply, circling the city before aiming for its den at the top of the tallest tower. The structure rushed toward them—too fast.

The creature's muscles rippled beneath John's hands. His fingers slipped. Panic shot through him as his grip loosened, the elastic skin sliding through his sweaty palms. For one terrifying moment, he felt himself sliding backward, the wind tearing at him.

No, no, no—

But the gropolo sensed John's panic through their connection. It folded its wings and dove, surging toward the tower with desperate speed.

The creature's talons hit stone. The impact jolted through John's entire body. He lost his grip completely—

—and fell.

Only a few feet, but it felt like flying all over again. He hit the stone floor of the den hard, rolling to absorb the impact. Shenya landed beside him with a grunt.

For a moment, they just lay there, gasping.

Men rushed toward them to restrain the gropolo. John scrambled to his feet and pulled his hood low, heart still hammering. He wished he could disappear into the shadows as the gropolo handlers swarmed around them.

CHAPTER
TWENTY-FIVE

"What's going on? Who are you, and how did you get up here?" a gropolo keeper barked.

John and Shenya scrambled to their feet. Shenya stepped in front of John, hands raised. "We mean no harm. We're looking for Yumi, the gropolo shou. Is he here?"

"What business do you have with him?" the keeper demanded.

"It's personal. If you bring us to him, he'll vouch for us, I promise."

The keeper eyed John, trying to see beneath his burmui hood. John kept his head down.

"Why are you traveling with a burmui-wearing scammer?" the keeper said, contempt dripping from his voice—the same disdain most showed to street beggars.

"This is no scammer," Shenya replied. "He's an honest man and a mute. He's taken a vow of poverty and penance, hoping for divine favor and a cure."

John fought the urge to laugh under the hood.

The keeper studied them both, still skeptical. "This city's in lockdown because a fugitive is on the run. Now, two strangers appear in our gropolo den. Why shouldn't I think one of you is the fugitive?"

"Because that's my old friend," called a deep voice from across the den.

A massive man—at least seven feet tall—strode over. He wore land tribe garb and a black-and-white feathery cape.

John was sure it was Yumi. The shou had arrived in the nick of time.

"What are you doing, Len? Get back to work. I'll handle these two," Yumi ordered.

"Yes, sir," Len muttered, slinking away.

Yumi eyed Shenya and John. "You two—come with me."

They followed him across the spacious den—large enough for two adult gropolos. At the far side, Yumi led them through a door and down stairs to the floor below, where four large gropolo chicks bounced and played. John was instantly smitten with them.

Yumi ushered them into a small room lined with feed sacks. He turned to Shenya, brow furrowed.

"Only you, Shenya, could get a gropolo to pick you up like a personal servant. Mine never leave unless you command it. How did you manage it without getting your heads pecked off?"

"Yumi, I can explain."

Yumi rolled his eyes and opened his arms. "Come here, you big arbimto," he said, pulling Shenya into a bear hug. Shenya looked child-sized beside him.

Yumi stepped back. "You're the one the king's after, aren't you?"

"Unfortunately," Shenya admitted, glancing at John.

"You're in serious trouble. The whole kingdom's locked down—almost every city and village. Who's your friend in the burmui?" Yumi asked, peering at John.

Shenya hesitated. "You'll need to keep an open mind. What I'm about to say will sound impossible."

Yumi grinned. "Let me guess. You've got this fellow helping you steal something from the king's archive. Or maybe he offended a princess? Must be something big to trigger a kingdom-wide lockdown."

Shenya ignored him. "John, pull down your hood."

John's hands trembled. This is it. Make or break. He lowered the hood.

Yumi burst out laughing. "What kind of face paint and hair dye is that? My kids have better costumes."

Shenya sighed. "John, take off the burmui."

John obeyed. Yumi's smile faded instantly.

"Look at his arms and legs," Shenya said. "Obviously not a costume."

Yumi stepped closer, examining John's arms, then his feet. "What in the moons are you?" he murmured. "Are you a misshapen bastard son of the king or something?"

"He's not misshapen. He is as he should be. He looks different because he's... an anuri from another world."

Yumi rolled his eyes. "You expect me to believe that?"

"If his appearance doesn't convince you, his actions should. He called the gropolo to us. You know gropolos never leave unless you command it. John has abilities no other anuri does."

Yumi shook his head. "You've lost the plot, old friend."

"No, he hasn't, and I can prove it," John said, annoyed. He reached out to the chicks. They bounced over and lined up. "Raise a wing. Lie on your backs. Wiggle your feet." The chicks obeyed instantly, tumbling over each other in their eagerness to please.

Yumi stared at the chicks, then at John, then back at the chicks. He ran a hand through his hair, laughing in disbelief. "Training chicks takes years, and these only just hatched. I've been doing this for twenty years, and I've never..." He shook his head, grinning and clapping his hands. "By God, boy, you are hired here today! You could be the best gropolo shou in Marcri-tuss! We'd make a fortune breeding and training them!"

"We're not looking for a job," Shenya said, "but we do need your help."

Yumi leaned in the doorway. "You need a gropolo now, don't you?"

"Yes. We need to travel to Cosheh, then to the Archive of the Ancients in Marciluk. We need a return trip."

"You don't ask for much," Yumi grumbled.

"You know I wouldn't ask unless I was desperate. The Archive has what we can't find anywhere else. You're our only hope."

Yumi's jaw flexed. "Those sea pests! The Archive should be here." His voice hardened further. "You and I spent years building that Archive. And they stole our work and took it to sea."

John's head snapped toward Shenya. "You built the Archive?"

Shenya waved it off. "Yes, I helped with some materials. It was a long time ago."

"Some materials?" Yumi scoffed. "You organized half the collection. The sea tribes wouldn't have an archive without you."

John stared at Shenya with new understanding. This quiet, unassuming man had built one of the most important collec-tions of knowledge in the world—and never mentioned it.

"Can you help us? Please, old friend, we're desperate."

"Lucky for you, both my adult gropolos are here, thanks to the lockdown. Just answer me one thing." Yumi eyed John. "How did you get here, and why does the king want you?"

"I came through a portal from my world." John realized how preposterous he sounded when he described his situation out loud. "I'm here on a mission important to both our worlds. The Archive might hold what I need. As for the king..." John sighed. "I don't know why he's after me."

Yumi put his hands on Shenya's shoulders. "I'll help, but I can't go with you. My family depends on me—I can't risk it."

"I understand," Shenya said.

"When you reach Cosheh, leave the gropolo at the Temple of Ninto. I have a contact there I'll send a transmission to. He'll care for her until you return. That's the best I can offer."

"It's exactly what we need. Thank you, my friend."

"Oh, I'll ask for something in return someday—wait and see. For now, keep my baby safe!"

"Absolutely," Shenya promised.

Yumi turned to John. "I don't know your story, but if Shenya trusts you, so do I."

"Thank you, Yumi. You're helping more people than you know."

Suddenly, voices and the clank of armor echoed below.

"That'll be the soldiers. You'd better go," Yumi urged.

John grabbed his cloak and followed Shenya up the stairs, fumbling with it as they ran. Yumi slammed the heavy door behind them, sliding the bar to buy some time.

"Go to the gropolo you came with—her name's Xerti."

They sprinted across the den to Xerti.

"Listen up!" Yumi barked to his workers. "Passenger box for two, on Xerti, now! Less than a minute! No questions—extra pay this week!"

John was impressed by Yumi's command. The workers rushed to ready Xerti, strapping on the passenger box and pushing the stairs in place.

Shenya was amazed at the speed. "How do we fly her?"

"Your friend has a way with them. He'll manage," Yumi said.

The soldiers began pounding on the door.

"Climb in and get out now!" Yumi ordered.

"Thank you," Shenya said, squeezing Yumi's arm.

"Go! Get out of here!"

John and Shenya scrambled up the stairs and into the box atop Xerti. Nerves clouded John's mind as he tried to connect with her.

"John, we have to go," Shenya urged.

"I'm trying."

"Fear has no power over you. You're in control. Have faith."

John took a breath and focused, feeling Xerti's anxiety. *You're safe, Xerti. Fly now.*

Xerti trusted him. She flapped her wings and prepared for takeoff. Yumi and his workers dodged her powerful strokes as she rose from the tower.

Seconds later, soldiers burst in, weapons drawn. Yumi threw up his hands.

"Friends, what's the matter?"

The chief commander glared. "Why didn't you open the door? We've been trying to get in!"

"Sorry," Yumi said calmly. "Didn't hear a thing. Any noise is usually from the chicks below—always banging about."

The commander eyed the workers cleaning up. "There should be another gropolo here."

"She's out burning off energy—she gets stir-crazy in lock-down," Yumi replied.

The soldier studied him, then relented. "We're here

because one gave a guard a scare today leaving the den. Keep your gropolos under control."

"You have my word. I'll strap her in and no more flights after this last one."

After a final look, the commander led his troop out.

Yumi watched them go, relieved.

TWENTY-SIX

Jaromei's hands wouldn't stop shaking.

She'd sat beside her grandmother's body for hours. Time felt shattered. She kept waiting for Dernoah to breathe again, to open her eyes and scold her for those tears.

But the silence pressed in.

Jaromei forced herself up, legs unsteady. She moved to the window, gripping the sill, staring out at nothing.

Father should be here.

She clutched the letter John had left in Shenya's study. Just finding it had sent her heart pounding. She'd read it so many times she knew the creases by touch.

JAROMEI,

I'm sitting in your father's study, wishing tomorrow were another day of sitting with you in here. But we know how things turned out. The candle on the desk keeps flickering like it's laughing at how nervous I am.

I borrowed a piece of parchment. I promise I'll tell Shenya later. My handwriting looks terrible—I've never written in Marcritan before—but I needed to say this before I leave tomorrow.

We've only known each other a few days. On my world, that's nothing. But here, it feels much longer. From the moment you pulled back your hood in the cave, you didn't look at me like I was strange or broken. You looked at me like I belonged. I felt it instantly, and I know you did too.

I have no idea what will happen next. But you make me believe I can do this.

Meeting you has been one of the best things that has ever happened to me. If I make it back, I hope we can sit together again under those two moons and watch the sea. You said we had a chance someday, and I'll hold you to it. And if things go differently... please know I'm grateful for even one minute with you. Truly grateful.

Thank you for seeing me, Jaromei.

Yours, John

SHE HELD it to her heart, reading the last line again—savoring it —when the knock came.

She wiped her face and opened the door to four elders, their expressions properly grave. They bowed; she returned the gesture and let them in.

"Thank you for coming," Jaromei said, her own voice distant. "My grandmother is in the bedroom, here on the ground floor."

"There is no need to thank us," said one. "This is our duty, and you have our condolences. Where is your father? He will need to give authorisation for the burial."

Her throat tightened. "He's not here, but I can give authorisation on his behalf."

"My dear, the village is in lockdown," an older woman said. "He cannot be far."

The lie slipped out, easier than she expected. "He left before the lockdown to visit my mother's kin up north. He won't be back until it's lifted."

The elders exchanged silent, knowing glances.

"It's fine. We'll take care of everything," said the youngest, barely older than Jaromei herself, holding the burial shroud.

They moved past her. She mustered a smile and pointed them to Dernoah's room. As soon as the door shut, her smile vanished.

She knew they were suspicious—a glance, a pause, the weight of their silence. She crept closer to the door, hands pressed flat against the wall.

First, only silence—prayer, perhaps.

Then the whispers seeped out.

"Does anyone else suspect—have the homes here been searched yet?" the young man whispered.

"Tomorrow, I heard. But yes, something's—"

"Strange, isn't it?" the old woman cut in. "A fugitive shows up, and now Shenya's—"

"Gone," another finished. "It can't be a coincidence."

"I spoke to Shenya two days ago at the market," said the eldest man. "Not a word about visiting kin. Always going on about the Ancients, acting like he knows more than the rest—"

"He is odd, though, isn't he?"

"Oh, absolutely. I've always said—"

"We should contact the chancellor," the young man said, voice rising. "Request that Jaromei be interviewed. She could be withholding—"

"Evidence, yes. I agree."

The old woman's voice dropped, but Jaromei could still hear the relish. "I shouldn't be saying this, but..."

"Oh, don't hold back now," the young one urged, almost gleeful.

Jaromei gripped the doorframe.

"Well," the old woman continued, drawing it out, "my sources on the chancellor's council—very close sources—say the king is desperate to find this fugitive. Apparently, he's a serious threat to all Marcrituss. The whole kingdom is locked down. So if this fugitive shows up just as Shenya left Morboli... and he has no life, he never leaves Morboli—"

"Then Shenya might be an accomplice," the young man said.

"Exactly. If you ask me, his sudden absence is no coincidence."

Jaromei wanted to burst in, to shout at them for gossiping beside her grandmother's body, for dishonoring Dernoah while pretending to perform a sacred rite.

The elders had always been after her father, jealous of his knowledge of things they pretended to know everything about.

Movement inside the room.

Jaromei stepped back from the door. Her hands still shook. She clenched them into fists behind her back.

The door opened.

The elders emerged, her grandmother's body wrapped in the shroud. Jaromei's throat closed as she watched. She reached out, laying a trembling hand on the cloth—just for a moment.

I'm sorry, Grandmother. I'm so sorry.

They bore Dernoah outside and placed her in the palanquin for the temple.

"Thank you for your time, Jaromei," said the old woman with syrupy false warmth. "We'll be in touch soon to speak about the burial."

Jaromei forced herself to nod. "That is helpful. Thank you again."

When the elders left, Jaromei closed the door. Her legs buckled.

She slid down against the door, breath coming in sharp, shallow bursts. She pressed her palms to her eyes, trying to dam the tears. She moved to the empty bed and traced the worn edge of her grandmother's shawl, the house echoing every memory too loudly.

Her grandmother's words echoed: *Darker forces have sensed his presence, child.*

Not now. Not yet. Grief would have to wait. Tears would have to wait. Guards would come. They'd search the house, interrogate her. About her Father. About John.

Think. Think.

How did King Euron know John was here? How had he found out?

It didn't matter.

What mattered was that she had to move. Now.

A desperate, reckless idea began to form. Her father would not approve—not even a tiny bit.

But it was her only chance.

TWENTY-SEVEN

The gropolo soared high above the world, its vast wings slicing the sky with effortless strength. John's veins thrummed with awe. Everything about flying on Xerti felt raw and exhilarating, the world shrinking beneath her shadow.

"This is the way to travel," John said, grinning. "We must be going hundreds of miles an hour. She's magnificent!"

Shenya shifted in his seat, clearly less thrilled. "Just make sure this thing knows where she's going. I'd rather not end up lost in some wilderness."

John laughed. "This 'thing' has a name. Xerti knows we're heading west. Honestly, I think she's smarter than you give her credit for."

Shenya snorted. "So, you're a shou now? Maybe you'll be taking Yumi's job next."

"I can connect with her," John said. "Really connect. She shares feelings and impressions. It's hard to explain, but I know what she thinks, and she seems to sense me too."

Shenya scratched his head. "Well, whatever the case, I'm

really proud of you. You saved our necks back there in Brooth. But it'd be nice if there was a manual for this power you've been given."

"You're telling me."

A clap of thunder boomed in the distance, and raindrops began striking the passenger box windows.

"We need to land," Shenya said, peering out. "Looks like we're coming up on the Koha Jungle."

Suddenly, lightning exploded close by; thunder hammered at the windows and rattled their bones. Xerti panicked, halting her glide and beating her wings wildly. The passenger box swayed in the gale.

"You have to get her to land, now!" Shenya shouted.

Xerti's terror crashed through the bond—raw, over-whelming. John focused, trying to calm her, begging her to descend.

She obeyed—but much too fast. They dropped in a stom-ach-churning free-fall, and only the safety straps kept them from smashing into the ceiling.

"Tell her to slow down, or I'm going to be sick!" Shenya groaned, clutching his stomach.

John relayed the message. Xerti slowed, and color slowly returned to Shenya's cheeks.

Moments later, the gropolo dropped toward a sweep of purple grass, flaring her wings at the last instant before landing.

"Are you okay?" John asked.

"Yes," Shenya muttered through clenched teeth. "I'm fine."

Rain hammered down. Xerti trudged off, passenger box jolting, until she found a thick canopy. She hunkered under it and refused to budge.

John caught Shenya's look and shrugged. "She's happy now." He looked out the window, mesmerised by how hard it was raining. "I wish there were portals between cities, not just worlds."

Shenya smiled. "That would be convenient. It's not long now to Marciluk. Once there, we'll look for an old colleague, Poltoma. She'll likely be at the Royal Batnu where the Archive's kept."

John's eyes lit up when Shenya mentioned the Archive. "Speaking of which, you didn't tell me you helped make the Archive."

Shenya smiled faintly. "Yumi, Poltoma, and I studied together. Then we traveled Marcrituss, digging up the Ancients' secrets. We wanted to build the greatest archive in the world." His voice quieted. "Then Rathrian used it as a bargaining chip. In exchange for the Archive, he extended the land-sea peace pact. Euron had no choice."

John scowled. "No wonder he has a bad reputation."

"Some of us moved to Marciluk to continue the work. Poltoma went. Yumi stayed behind with his gropolos." Shenya paused. "I stayed for the portal. And for Marnia."

He stretched out a blanket, making a pillow. "While we're stopped, let's try to rest. We've barely slept in days."

John yawned, exhaustion finally catching up. "Good idea."

He stretched out on the floor of the passenger box and let himself drift into much-needed sleep.

JOHN OPENED his eyes to find dusk already settled—they'd slept most of the afternoon. He nudged Shenya awake, but got only a confused yawn and drooping eyelids in return. John smiled and let him sleep.

At the front of the passenger box, a door led to the shou's

seat—open air, safety straps, a clear visor to shield against the wind. John looked at it for a moment.

He decided to seize the moment.

There was a door at the front of the passenger box that led to a seat outside, where the shou sits while flying the gropolo. Curious, John opened it. He found a seat with two safety straps. Above it, a canopy protruded from the box itself. A thick, clear visor extended downwards to shield the rider during flight, enclosing most of the space around the seat.

Xerti, it's time to wake up, John called to the gropolo through his thoughts.

He sensed she wanted something to eat first.

Can you eat anything around here? John asked.

Xerti stood and began eating foliage from the trees above her. The leaves were heavy with rainwater, giving her something to drink as well.

John glanced back at Shenya and chuckled. The long days of travel with so little sleep had clearly taken their toll on him. John carefully fastened the safety strap around him. He was in such a deep sleep that he didn't even stir.

After getting Shenya secure, John looked through the front window. He pondered what it would feel like to sit in the shou's seat. Shenya would surely be furious if he tried it during the flight—but since he was fast asleep, John saw it as a rare opportunity.

He decided to seize the moment.

John stepped out of the passenger box and settled into the comfortable chair. He pulled the safety straps across his body and secured them tightly in their latches. His fingers tightened around the handles. If it became too intense, he could ask Xerti to land—a comfort he held onto as he gripped the safety straps across his chest.

Okay, Xerti. We're not far from Cosheh. Yumi said you'll be well looked after there. Let's move on, John instructed.

The gropolo stood tall, stretching her long legs before turning toward the open field behind her. She spread her massive wings and began running forward.

Even in takeoff, her movements were graceful and controlled. As she lifted from the ground, John's seat jolted—a sharp, almost violent reminder that he was no longer protected by the passenger box. For an instant, his heart leapt into his throat, hands clutching the handles as wind crashed against the chair and rattled the canopy overhead. The rush of air was deafening as the world dropped away beneath him with dizzying speed.

Xerti surged upward, beating her wings with thunderous force. John's body was pressed into the seat, every muscle tight. The cold air knifed through any gap in the visor, stinging his cheeks. For a moment, vertigo spun in his head, and he wondered if he'd lost his mind taking the shou's seat.

But then—Xerti steadied. She sliced through the sky. His fear flipped into wild exhilaration. His breath caught, chest tight with the thrill of it. He watched the purple grass and tangled forest vanish, replaced by the endless view from above.

John gripped the handles on the arms of the seat and leaned forward, forgetting every doubt he had before. All hesitation had vanished. He was loving every second of it. He felt weightless inside as well as out.

John let himself savor the feeling—free, unafraid, if only for this one perfect moment aloft. He knew he hadn't overcome all his obstacles. But there, carried on Xerti's wings, he let himself believe in the possibility of courage.

Far below, the forests and rivers of Marcrituss stretched endlessly across the land like a living tapestry.

And high above, the heavens opened wider than he had ever seen, as though the sky itself were welcoming him into it.

The air roared past his ears like a river in flood, making the visor hum with vibration. It was, without question, the most thrilling ride of his life.

Through the transparent visor, John gazed down at the hazy treetops of the jungle below. Entire rivers twisted through the forest like silver threads, and the landscape stretched endlessly beneath him.

He squeezed the grips even tighter as Xerti banked, the horizon tilting. The sensation of weightlessness flooded his body. A wild laugh escaped him, half disbelieving. He was flying—really flying—and not even the safety harness could convince him otherwise.

As he watched the world pass beneath them, his mind drifted back to the day he was punched by Olly after school. He remembered lying injured on the road and seeing Danrael's light streak across the sky. On that day, he had wished he could be like it—free to fly away.

Now, soaring through the sky on Xerti, that wish had come true. Xerti's mind blazed with John's euphoria. His joy made her happy. She snapped her massive legs tight against her body, held them coiled for one heart-stopping moment. She exploded forward, sending them through the sky like an arrow.

John's adrenaline surged.

They flew through a sky painted red and purple by the setting sun. John had never felt so alive. His fears and worries had vanished.

On one side, the sun dipped behind distant mountains. On the opposite horizon, the two moons of Marcrituss were rising above the jungle canopy like pale lanterns. For a moment, he hung suspended between worlds—one fading into darkness beneath him and another unfolding above among the stars.

The sight was breathtaking.

As he took in the beauty of it all, John saw it as tangible evidence of God's existence. Something so perfect could not simply exist by chance.

Below, he spotted a herd of giant horse-like creatures drinking at a water source in a clearing. The animals lifted their heads as Xerti passed overhead, curious about the shadow gliding above them.

John laughed at the sight, adrenaline still buzzing through his veins. The wind was sharp now, cutting through the blanket of the visor. His teeth chattered, but he hardly noticed.

As Xerti climbed higher, the heat of the jungle air faded, replaced by a chilly wind. For the first time in his life, he felt exactly where he was meant to be.

Ahead, a flock of nocturnal birds flew directly toward them. Xerti gave a sharp warning cry.

Instantly, the silver-colored birds split into two streams and darted around her and the passenger box. John watched in amazement as they flashed past the visor, so close he could see the silver shimmer of their feathers. Xerti rode the turbulence with an absolute confidence that left John breathless with awe.

Inside the passenger box, Shenya stirred and sat upright. For a moment, panic flashed across his face when he realized John was outside in the shou's seat. But the panic quickly faded.

Instead, he smiled.

Through the window, he saw John leaning forward in the seat, arms raised high as he shouted with pure excitement.

Shenya couldn't help laughing. Seeing John enjoy the moment so filled him with quiet joy. He grabbed a blanket and opened the small window in the door.

"Stay warm!" he called as he reached out and handed it to him.

Even while strapped tightly into the seat, John managed to grab the blanket from behind and shouted his thanks. He wrapped it around himself gratefully.

Relieved that Shenya hadn't ordered him to land and return inside, John settled back into the seat. Far below, the last lights of dusk faded across the jungle, and the shadow of Xerti's wings swept silently over the endless canopy.

Shenya closed the window, returned to the bench, and lay down again.

Within minutes, his eyelids drifted shut once more.

TWENTY-EIGHT

As the horizon brightened, Shenya spotted it—a tall spire stark against the fields. The Temple of Ninto.

Ten minutes later, Xerti set down in the field before the temple, wings drooping with exhaustion. John grabbed a blanket for a makeshift hood and ducked back into the passenger box, still grinning from the night's flight.

Shenya gave him a look and couldn't hide his chuckles.

"What are you laughing at now?"

"Oh, nothing—just wondering who excites you more. Jaromei, or the gropolo."

John laughed, slipping on his smelly cloak. "Shut up, you." He glanced outside. "I don't see a soul around."

"This is the Temple of Ninto—one of the sea gods," Shenya said. "Landers don't really worship the sea pantheon. Even without the lockdown, you wouldn't find many visitors here."

John frowned. "Then why build something so massive on land if the sea tribes don't use it?"

"Provocation," Shenya said. "A sea king built it during the

final land-sea war—a statement that Ninto and the sea gods reigned supreme, against the one God of the Ancients."

John opened the side door and unfurled the ladder, anchoring it to Xerti's plumage. He secured the ends to the pegs and began climbing down. Shenya followed, their bag of supplies slung over his shoulder.

The massive face carved into the temple's façade caught John's eye immediately. With its closed eyes and tilted expression, it looked eerie, almost mournful. Purple moss and vines overtook much of the left side. The spire soared so high it seemed to pierce the sky itself. What struck John most was how close the temple stood to the cliff's edge.

"Why does the big face look asleep?" John asked.

"The sea god Ninto isn't sleeping," Shenya replied. "His eyes are closed because he can't bear to look at the land tribes, especially when they worship the one God."

John raised his eyebrows. "The sea folks really didn't like you guys, huh?"

Before Shenya could answer, a short, plump man hurried toward them from across the field.

"We've got company. I'll let you do the talking," John muttered.

Shenya stepped in front of John as the man approached.

"Hello!" the man called as he approached. "You must be Shenya."

Shenya smiled, stepping forward. "Greetings, friend. And you are?"

He bowed slightly. "Marto. Yumi sent word—said you'd be arriving with his gropolo."

"Glad to meet you, Marto. Yes, this is Xerti. Yumi mentioned you might look after her for a few days. Do you live here?"

Marto nodded, pointing down the field to a small house. "Right there, on the grounds."

Shenya studied him. "Your accent—Brooth, isn't it?"

Marto's eyes warmed. "Good ear. I grew up in Brooth. After the city fell on hard times, I ended up here. Marciluk owns the temple now, but no one from the sea wants to live up here. Maybe someday I'll get home."

Shenya's expression softened. "I'm sorry. Rathrian has hurt too many in Brooth. I hope you make it back."

Marto dropped his voice. "Speaking of Rathrian, he's lost it completely. Whole kingdom's under lockdown. They're hunting a fugitive and—" He glanced between Shenya and the silent, hooded John. "Wait a minute."

John tensed, feeling Marto's suspicion sharpening.

But Marto just let out a breath. "You know what? I'm not asking questions. Yumi's paying me well to watch Xerti. Once you're gone, I never saw you."

John, hidden beneath his hood, finally relaxed.

Shenya smiled smoothly. "Thank you, Marto. We truly have nothing to do with the trouble. Actually, we need help getting into Marciluk."

Marto eyed John curiously, trying to piece together the mystery of the hooded stranger. "Look... I really don't want trouble. Breaking into a city under lockdown? It's risky."

"We're desperate," Shenya pleaded. "I'll pay you what Yumi is paying, if you help us."

Marto rubbed his eyes, weighing it. "No, I couldn't do that to you. But I trust Yumi. If he vouches for you, I'll help—just don't make me regret it."

Shenya clasped Marto's shoulder. "We won't bring you any trouble. Thank you, Marto."

"Don't thank me yet," Marto replied. "There's a lot of security around Marciluk. I have one idea, but I can't guarantee it'll work."

"We'll try whatever you suggest."

"Follow me," Marto said, turning to the temple entrance. "There's a tunnel in here dating back to when sea tribes were banned from the surface."

"That was centuries ago," Shenya said, wishing there was more time to explore the temple's history.

"Exactly. The tunnel runs to Marciluk—it was built so the sea tribes could visit the temple unseen. That was back when it mattered to them. It starts deep inside, goes out through the cliff, and along the seafloor, straight into the city. Hasn't been used in ages, though."

"This is excellent," Shenya exclaimed, confidence rising.

"Don't get your hopes up," Marto warned. "It's sealed on this side, so there's a good chance it's sealed on the other too. And it may be flooded."

"We'll chance it," Shenya said.

Marto glanced at John, curiosity etched on his face. "What's the story with the fellow in the burmui? He doesn't say much."

"He's mute," Shenya answered. "We're hoping Marciluk's medicine can help him—one reason we must go. His condition's worsening."

John struggled not to laugh at how the 'mute' story evolved everywhere they went. He doubted Marto believed it, but the temple keeper stuck to his policy of not asking questions.

Marto led them through the dim temple. Sunlight streamed in, reflected by strategically placed mirrors. The air cooled instantly inside, thick with the scent of old stone and burnt oil. Their footsteps echoed, muffled by tapestries heavy with dust and faded thread. Small rooms lined the corridor, each a shrine to one of the sea gods.

They soon reached the temple's lowest point. Marto led them into a pitch-black chamber. He struck a match and lit two wall sconces filled with oil. Firelight flooded the room.

The first thing they saw was a gigantic square stone blocking an exit on the far side.

"This is where the tunnel entrance is," Marto explained. "The seal is extremely heavy, so we won't be able to move it alone. We'd need machinery."

Shenya tried pushing the stone, but it didn't budge.

As Marto and Shenya discussed options, John studied the stone. Remembering his supposed 'mute' status, he stayed silent—but walked over and tapped Shenya's arm.

Shenya turned. John gestured toward the stone.

"Marto, would you mind giving us a moment?" Shenya asked. "I think he needs me."

Marto shot him a skeptical look but nodded. "I'll get Xerti some water. Please, don't do anything that'll get me fired."

He left, footsteps fading.

Shenya turned to John, concern clouding his face. "I think we might have to abandon this plan," he said quietly. "I don't think we can move this."

John pulled back his hood. Up close, the stone looked immovable—like a mountain blocking their way.

"That's what I wanted to talk to you about," John said. "I want to try to move it."

Shenya chuckled, a quiet laugh escaped him. "John, you're in peak shape, but even you can't move that. A dozen men would struggle."

John didn't argue. He stepped forward, placed both hands against the cold stone, and whispered, "You told me to have faith. Something's telling me I need to try."

He closed his eyes.

I can do this.

For a moment, the chamber was utterly still.

Then John noticed it—the strange power inside him, awakening. It surged through his arms and legs, like a current building in intensity.

He dug his feet into the floor, braced himself, and pushed.

At first, nothing happened.

The massive slab stood stubborn, as if the mountain itself refused to move.

John gritted his teeth and pushed harder. His muscles burned, trembling with effort. Still, the stone barely shifted.

Come on, he pleaded inwardly—focusing every last ounce of strength, faith, and desperation into his arms.

A deep rumble echoed through the chamber.

Shenya's eyes widened in disbelief.

The seal was moving. Stone shrieked against stone, sending tremors through John's arms. Grit rained from the ceiling, and a draft of stale, untouched air seeped from the widening gap.

Slowly—agonizingly slowly—the enormous slab began to slide across the floor. The grinding noise filled the chamber like distant thunder. Dust drifted from the ceiling as the ancient stone shifted for the first time in generations.

John cried out as pain shot through his body. Every muscle screamed in protest. He poured everything he had into one final push—straining, shaking, until finally the opening was just wide enough for two people to squeeze through.

John staggered back, knees buckling as the strength left his body.

Shenya rushed forward and caught him before he collapsed. "That was incredible," he said in awe. "Are you alright?"

John leaned heavily against him, breath ragged, and peered into the darkness beyond the opening.

"I'm fine," he managed. "At least it doesn't look flooded in there."

Shenya quickly searched through his bag and pulled out his portable light—a small disc-shaped gadget.

He turned it on, a bright beam cutting through the darkness.

The passage stretched away beneath the sea.

Hurried footsteps echoed down the corridor.

John quickly pulled his hood back up.

A moment later, Marto rushed in. He stopped, staring at the opening, and then at John and Shenya. His face shifted from confusion to disbelief. "How did you—" He stopped himself.

After a long pause, Marto shook his head, clearly deciding he didn't want to know.

"We could only manage to open it this far, but it's enough," Shenya said, shining the light into the tunnel.

"I have no clue who or what is on the other side," Marto said nervously. "If you get caught, leave me out of this. Do you understand?"

"We never saw you," Shenya replied.

"I'll keep Xerti near the temple. You'd better return! If Yumi has to come all the way to get Xerti, he'll blame me."

Shenya laughed. "We'll need five days or a week at most. If we don't return, assume the worst."

"Before you go, can I get you some food for the journey?"

"That's kind, but we should be going."

Marto extended his arm in the Marcritan greeting. "Godspeed, you two. You're going to need it."

Shenya clasped Marto's forearm. He and John then stepped through the opening and disappeared into the tunnel.

"Yumi, you're still full of mischief and surprises," Marto muttered as he watched them vanish into darkness. Then he headed outside to tend to Xerti.

CHAPTER
TWENTY-NINE

John flinched as his ears popped. The undersea tunnel plunged steeply beneath the water's surface, the pressure making his head feel hollow. The walls curved in looping arcs, the way forward revealed only by the steady beam of Shenya's light. Moisture glistened on the stone; John ran his hand along the cool, damp wall.

"This must have been a huge undertaking," he said, his voice echoing. "It's incredible."

"When we first built underwater, anuri had to surface constantly for air and supplies," Shenya replied, listening to their footsteps bounce along the stone. "That's why early cities stayed near the shore."

John glanced down the dark corridor. The engineering seemed impossible for a civilization centuries old. "We have underwater tunnels on Earth, but nothing like this—not from so long ago."

"It helps when you can see and live in the water," Shenya said with a wry smile. "Though even for us, construction this deep was—"

He stopped mid-sentence.

Both froze.

A strange sound echoed up the tunnel—distant at first, low and rhythmic, growing steadily louder. To John, it sounded like galloping horses.

Shenya tilted his head, listening. "That's the generator," he said. "We're close."

John's shoulders relaxed a little. "Are you sure?"

"I'd know that sound anywhere." Shenya started forward, picking up his pace. "The base of the tower sits on the seabed. If we hear it this clearly, the tunnel must open straight into it."

"Is that good?" John asked, hurrying to keep up.

"Very good," Shenya said. "We might slip into Marciluk undetected. The city's tower rises through the center—if we reach the generator chamber, we're already halfway there."

John frowned, trying to picture it. "Wait. The city isn't on the ocean floor?"

"No. It's suspended halfway up the tower, on a massive platform." Shenya gestured overhead. "The generator below does more than provide power—it's the foundation for everything."

John pictured it—an entire city hanging in the water, anchored to a single tower. What would Marciluk be like, hidden beneath the waves?

As they pressed on, the sound grew louder—a steady rhythm echoing through the tunnel like the beating of some massive mechanical heart.

They rounded a bend. At last, the end of the tunnel came into view.

A metal grate sealed the exit ahead, and light poured through it, illuminating the damp passage like a beacon. Through the bars, they saw a vast, tube-shaped chamber beyond.

The sight stopped John in his tracks. The bright cylindrical room rose dozens of feet overhead, its curved walls lined with thousands of reflective panels flapping rhythmically up and down. Each caught the restless energy of the sea, converting the ceaseless movement into power for the city above—flashing silver like waves in sunlight.

The constant motion created a thunderous rhythm that echoed through the chamber.

At the room's center, a ladder climbed straight upward for dozens of feet, disappearing into a hatch high above.

"We need to get in there and climb that ladder, John," Shenya said, studying the chamber. "Do you think you can pull the grate off?"

"I think so," John replied, peering through the bars. "But where does that ladder lead?"

"It should reach the city center, where a grid distributes the power generated here," Shenya explained. "The only problem is, there might be people up there. I might pass without trouble, but someone in a burmui would be questioned."

John sighed. "So, basically, I'm stuck down here."

"I'll go up first and find Poltoma," Shenya said. "Once I locate her, we'll come back for you."

"Be careful up there," John said, clasping Shenya's forearm. "I'll try to get this thing off for you."

John placed both hands on the grate, ready to summon his strength. But the moment he tugged, it came free in his hands.

He blinked. "Well, that was underwhelming."

"Finally, something easy!" Shenya chuckled.

Then his expression grew serious. "I think you should put the grate back and stay in the tunnel. If, for any reason, I don't return soon, go back, get Xerti, and head to Yumi in Brooth. Don't come after me."

John nodded, though he already knew he'd never abandon Shenya.

"Don't worry," Shenya said, giving a reassuring smile. "I'll be back soon."

John watched as the man who had become his closest friend in the universe climbed the long ladder. The generator panels continued their relentless motion as Shenya ascended, the thunder of their rhythm echoing through the chamber. He reached the hatch, pushed it open, and climbed out.

John replaced the metal grate and settled down in the dim tunnel. The steady hum of the generator echoed through the passage like the slow breathing of something vast and mechanical. After the exhaustion of the journey, his eyelids grew heavy. Before long, he drifted off to sleep.

CHAPTER
THIRTY

"Wake up, my friend," said a familiar voice.

John stirred, momentarily disoriented. He could tell by the heaviness in his limbs that he'd slept a long time.

"Danrael?"

John pushed himself upright. The angel stood before him in the dim tunnel, illuminated by the faint glow spilling through the grate. But something was different.

Danrael's presence was unchanged—calm and steady—but now he looked like an anuri from Marcrituss: deep violet eyes, dark blond hair streaked with purple, and skin with a violet tint.

"Why do you look like a Marcritan?" John asked, pushing himself up from the floor.

"I always appear as one from the world I visit," Danrael replied.

"Can I do that? It would make things a lot easier."

Danrael chuckled. "I'm afraid not. As a pure spirit, I can appear as I choose."

"Well, had to ask," John said with a shrug, then grew serious. "I hope you're not here because something happened to Shenya."

"No, Shenya will return soon," Danrael assured him. "I've been sent to discuss an urgent matter about your mission."

John's chest tightened. "Am I in trouble?"

Danrael laughed quietly. "No. You've done well, John. I trust Shenya and his daughter have helped you."

"That's the understatement of the year," John said. "I'd never have made it here without them."

Danrael gave a warm smile. "You've come a long way in a short time, John. You're controlling your fear and connecting to your faith. Your abilities are flourishing."

"I keep wondering if there's a reason I have these particular abilities."

"There is," Danrael said. "Think of your Bible stories, John. Samson's strength. Elisha and the animals. The prophets and their visions. Throughout history, people have been given supernatural gifts to fulfil his will."

John sat forward. "Like Moses and the staff."

"Exactly like that," Danrael said. "The staff had no power of its own—it was simply what God chose to work through to reveal his glory." He met John's eyes. "You are like that staff, John. God is using you in ways you haven't yet discovered." Danrael's expression grew more serious. "But don't forget your vision. The darkness pursues you. I'm here to warn you—it's here in Marciluk. You must remain on your guard."

John closed his eyes. He'd hoped the underwater city would offer some safety. "How did the darkness know I'm here?"

"There's nothing you could have done to stop it," Danrael replied calmly.

"Why? I've been so careful."

"When you were baptised, your soul was given a special grace that changed it forever. In a world where baptism doesn't exist, that grace makes you stand out like a light in darkness. Because of that, your presence can be sensed by the Evil One and his servants, the fallen angels who followed him."

The hairs on John's arms rose. "The Evil One?" He already knew the answer. "If my soul is like a lighthouse to them, how am I supposed to hide?"

"Sensing your presence is not the same as knowing exactly where you are," Danrael explained. "Like me, neither the Evil One nor his legion is omniscient. They wander the worlds searching for lost souls—those with little faith are easy to possess. Some even invite them in, seduced by false promises."

Danrael's tone softened. "You can avoid them if you hold fast to your faith, John. Faith overcomes fear. That's what allows you to access your power and reject evil's promises. Evil only has power if you give in. Your resistance in the forest already showed your strength. Don't be afraid."

John exhaled slowly. He remembered the men who attacked them in the forest. "Was it the Evil One who controlled those men?"

"It was his fallen ones led by the Ancient Watcher. His demonic name is Revonat," Danrael answered. "Revonat has come to stop you. He is the darkness you saw in your vision—the same force that tempted you in the forest."

Revonat, John repeated quietly.

Just saying the name made the hairs on his arms stand up. The threat was real now—personal. It had a name.

"I must leave you now, but don't forget to pray, John. I am glad to help when the Almighty permits it, but you don't always need to call on me. God wants to hear from you, too."

John nodded. "I'll do my best. See you around, Danrael."

The angel's form shimmered in the dim tunnel light. Then, like a reflection fading from water, he vanished.

THIRTY-ONE

A creak echoed from above. John peered through the grate and spotted Shenya descending the long ladder, fast and urgent.

John yanked the grate aside and darted into the generator room. Shenya landed with a soft thump, breathing hard.

"Found Poltoma. We need to move. Now."

John blinked. "How long were you up there?"

"Eight hours."

John rubbed his eyes. *Eight hours?* He'd slept through nearly all of it.

His muscles still heavy with fatigue, John followed Shenya up the ladder. The rungs trembled under their weight, every movement amplified in the narrow shaft.

At the top, Shenya paused just long enough to say, "We got the grid evacuated. Hood up and let's go."

They darted across the cavernous power grid chamber—enormous from above, cubicles ringing a towering mechanical core, thick hoses snaking upward into vents. The floor thrummed with a low, constant vibration. John's fingers itched to linger, to study how this system powered an entire underwater city, but there was no time.

Outside, a carriage waited—sleek and elegant, harnessed to a massive, muscular creature stamping impatiently on smooth stone. Poltoma spotted them and leapt down from the driver's seat, surprisingly agile, hurrying to swing the door open.

Shenya and John climbed in. Poltoma slammed the door, took her place at the front, and cracked the reins. The carriage surged forward.

"That must be Poltoma," John said, steadying himself as they rolled away.

"Yes," Shenya replied. "And finding her took longer than I expected."

John laughed. "I assume it didn't go according to plan."

Shenya rubbed his face in weary embarrassment. "Well... kind of. After I left you, I went up into the grid room. At first, nobody noticed me, but that didn't last. I was stopped as soon as they saw me heading for the door."

John smirked. "What did you do?"

"I played into their stereotypes and acted like a lost, clueless Lander. They treated me like an incompetent child." Shenya's frustration was palpable.

John tried not to laugh, and failed.

"After that, I went straight to the Royal Batnu. It took most of the day, but I finally found Poltoma. Now that we've got you, we're heading to her place—should be safe."

John leaned back, lifting his hood. The carriage interior was immaculate—far more luxurious than anything he'd ever ridden in. Soft seats, flawless craftsmanship, a ride so smooth he barely felt the city beneath them.

"Does everyone ride in these?" John asked.

Shenya shook his head. He nervously tapped his fingers

together. "Actually, this is a special one. Reserved for royalty, usually."

John stiffened. "Royalty? Please tell me we won't get stopped in this thing."

Shenya hesitated. "The reason it took so long to find Poltoma is that she's well guarded. And the reason she's so well guarded... is because she's engaged to Prince Saltho. King Rathrian's son."

"What?" John's voice echoed in the carriage. "Shenya, we can't trust her! Don't you remember what Marto said about Rathrian?"

Shenya spoke quickly. "The prince is hundreds of miles away. And even if he weren't—Poltoma's home is at the city's edge, near the Royal Batnu. It's her private residence, exempt from searches during lockdown."

John closed his eyes, leaning back against the wall.

Shenya softened his tone. "I know it seems risky. But it's her private home, and—"

John cut him off, voice low but firm. "Shenya. When I was down in the tunnel, Danrael came to me."

Shenya tensed, hands gripping his knees. "What did he say?"

John swallowed. "He warned me. The darkness that's been after us—it's here, in this city. Its name is Revonat."

Shenya's fist struck the carriage wall, the sound echoing in the small space. "Then we move quickly," he said, voice tight with determination. "I'll start searching as soon as we arrive. We won't stay longer than necessary." He met John's eyes. "But Poltoma is one of the good ones. You'll see."

John didn't answer. He turned to the window, hoping the city's sights might distract him from the dangers pressing in.

"These windows are designed so you can look out," Shenya

said, gentler now, "but nobody outside can see in. You can pull your hood back."

John slowly lowered his hood—and the view stole his breath.

Above the city stretched a colossal dome, arching across the horizon, lit up like a sky. Its immense structure enclosed the metropolis in crystal clarity beneath the ocean.

"How are we even—" John began, eyes wide.

"Breathing?" Shenya finished. "The generator we passed below draws in seawater, separates the oxygen, and pumps it through the city. The tower reaches above the surface, bringing in fresh air."

John pressed closer to the glass, his forehead nearly touching it. "It's so bright down here. I thought it would be dark."

"The dome mimics sunlight," Shenya explained. "At sunset, it dims to resemble night. It's remarkable, really—though I'd never want to live here."

The carriage rolled through wide avenues lined with towers of polished stone and luminous crystal. Crowds of pedestrians flowed along organized walkways, separate lanes letting carriages glide past without interruption. Everything was orderly, pristine, beautiful in a way that felt almost unreal.

John shook his head in disbelief. "This is incredible."

"But it's also arrogant," Shenya said, gazing out the window. "The kings of old built Marciluk to prove their superiority—to make the Landers believe the Sea Kingdom was favored by their gods. They wanted us to think they stood beside them."

They passed through a lively square—rows of colorful stalls, canopies rippling in the artificial breeze, vendors shouting, the scent of spices and roasted seafood drifting through the air. The energy was infectious, vibrant.

A group of children spotted the carriage, their faces lighting up. They waved and jumped, calling out excitedly.

John chuckled. "They probably think there's a prince inside."

The square was meticulous, its pathways made of smooth stone laid in intricate patterns.

"There's no grass," John said, scanning the surroundings. "No trees."

"There can't be," Shenya replied. "Not down here. Instead, they grow those." He gestured to the vibrant, spongy plants dotting the streets—bulbous shapes in violet, turquoise, and crimson, swaying gently in the circulating air. They pulsed with a faint bioluminescence, adding splashes of color to every corner.

"Jaromei said a lot of people from the land tribes move here," John ventured.

Shenya's smile faded. "Over time, we've given up more and more to the Sea Kingdom just to keep the peace."

"Like what?" John asked.

"We provide the materials to build all this," Shenya said, nodding at the towers. "We supply the food they can't grow below. There have been years when our people went hungry, while the sea tribes stayed comfortable—because we had to keep supplying them."

John frowned. "That happens where I'm from, too. It's unfair."

"Many people on land work hard to support the Sea Kingdom. Eventually, some start to wonder—why struggle so much and never benefit? Why not just join them?"

The carriage rounded a wide boulevard, and the palace came into view—vast, breathtaking, its towers rising in sweeping arcs of luminous crystal that caught the artificial light and scattered it in every direction. John leaned toward the glass, genuinely awed.

Then it hit him.

Not pain—more like a cold breath across the back of his neck. A wrongness, faint but unmistakable, emanating from somewhere beyond those gleaming walls. He pressed his palm flat against the glass and frowned.

"You alright?" Shenya asked.

"Yeah." John pulled his hand back. "That palace is something else."

He said nothing more. But the cold didn't leave him until the carriage had rounded the next corner and the palace disappeared from view.

The carriage slowed to a stop.

John quickly flipped the hood of the burmui back over his head as Poltoma stepped down from the driver's seat. He heard her boots on the stone before she opened the heavy door.

"Follow me to the house," she said.

John and Shenya climbed out, following her along a winding path of pink paving stones toward a modest but elegant home. John admired the front garden arranged with colored sand, smooth stones, and decorative shells. They shimmered in the artificial light. The house stood slightly apart, no neighbors on either side—the rare privacy a reminder of her status.

Poltoma led them inside and shut the door behind them.

Only then did John shed the heavy burmui cloak. Facing Poltoma, he saw her eyes widen—not with fear, but awe.

"This is unbelievable," Poltoma said, pressing a hand to her chest as she studied him. "It's true. There is life on other worlds. And you look like an anuri—a light anuri."

"I told you it was true," Shenya said, a satisfied smile on his lips. "I know we've just arrived, but when will it be possible to visit the Batnu and study the Archive?"

"It's closed for twelve hours," Poltoma replied, still taking in every detail of John. "But I'll take you first thing in the morning."

She circled John slowly, fascinated. Their eyes met—curiosity and something close to wonder in hers. John studied her in return, still weighing whether the fiancée of the king's son was someone he could trust.

John noticed right away that Poltoma certainly looked like a princess. Her loose-fitting red trousers and matching top were clearly made by a skilled designer. The small naval piercing she wore was set with a red gemstone as impressive as any royal jewels on Earth. Her blonde hair was pinned back with an elegant accessory set with another glittering stone.

"Welcome to Marciluk, John. I'm Poltoma, and everything I have here is yours." She extended her arm in the Marcritan greeting. John clasped her forearm in return.

"Thank you for your help," he said, genuine despite his lingering doubts.

"You're very welcome," she replied warmly. "Now," she added with a smile, hands on her hips, "I'm sure Shenya told you about my partner, Prince Saltho."

John shot Shenya a wary look.

Poltoma caught it, amusement flickering across her face. "Shenya thought you'd be worried about our relationship. Let me assure you—Saltho is nothing like his father. You're safe here. Besides, he's off gallivanting with friends for the week—nowhere near Marciluk."

John studied her, weighing her sincerity. After a moment, he exhaled quietly. "Thank you for saying that. I can't be too careful."

Poltoma leaned in, studying his face, especially his eyes. "We say the eyes tell us all we need to know about someone."

John met her gaze. "On my world, we say the eyes are the windows to the soul."

Poltoma tilted her head, considering. "And what do you see in my eyes?"

He thought carefully. In her eyes, he saw kindness, but also strength—a quiet determination. "I think I can trust you," he said at last.

Poltoma smiled. "I'm happy to hear it. But Shenya over there..." She shot him a playful wink. "We can't be too sure about him."

Shenya chuckled. "Living in the sea hasn't changed your sense of humor."

"Shenya told me you're from Brooth," John said. "I bet you miss the land. This place is amazing, but I couldn't live down here forever."

"My mother was from one of the sea tribes, my father from Brooth," Poltoma said. "You could say I have a fin in both worlds."

She was the first Marcritan John had met who truly belonged to both kingdoms.

"Once a Lander, always a Lander," Shenya added with affection. "She'll always be one of us."

Poltoma laughed. "If it were possible, I'd love to return to Brooth someday. I miss everything about it. But I have a life here now—and I truly love Saltho."

"Well, he's lucky to have found you," Shenya said. He'd known Poltoma for years and couldn't imagine anyone more deserving of marrying a prince.

Poltoma grabbed an empty sack from a hook near the kitchen. "I want you both to know—it's so good to have you here," she said warmly. "I wasn't expecting company, so I'll need to run to the market. I won't be long."

She opened the door, pausing briefly. "Make yourselves comfortable. I'll be back soon."

John and Shenya waved as she left. Once the door closed, they sank onto the couch, exhausted. The house was warm, quiet, safe—everything the last few days hadn't been.

John should have felt relieved.

He didn't.

The cold from the palace boulevard hadn't left him. He sat forward, elbows on his knees, staring at nothing. Somewhere in this beautiful, orderly city, something was deeply wrong.

Danrael's words surfaced unbidden: The darkness is already there.

Not coming. Already there.

CHAPTER

THIRTY-TWO

 King Rathrian's fingers dug into the armrests of his throne.

His son had left Marciluk. Unannounced. During a lockdown.

He released his grip and stood abruptly. His footsteps echoed across the marble floor as he paced the length of the vast chamber, each step landing harder than the last.

Once word spreads—and it always does—the complaints will start. He could already hear them: *If the prince can leave, why can't we?*

He stopped mid-stride and turned sharply.

His staff claimed Saltho had left with old friends. Rathrian's jaw tightened. The boy had probably gone off to indulge in the very pleasures Rathrian himself had always encouraged—pleasures his future bride would no doubt disapprove of.

He raised Saltho as his own father had raised him: to believe that pleasure was the natural right of those born to rule —whether granted by gods or by blood.

He stopped before a massive map carved into the wall. His

hand traced the borders of his kingdom: underwater cities, coastal territories, trade routes.

But his gaze kept drifting upward. To the land above.

His fingers curled into a fist against the stone.

Rathrian turned from the map and resumed pacing, slower now, more deliberate. He was waiting for Ilmly—the Chief Advisor to his rival, King Euron of the Land Tribes.

When Ilmly first suggested the lockdown, Rathrian demanded to know what threat warranted such drastic action.

The explanation sounded absurd.

A visitor from another world.

Rathrian had nearly laughed in the man's face. Yet he'd agreed—not because he believed Ilmly's story, but because he wanted what the Lander had offered in return.

He stopped and gripped the back of his throne, knuckles whitening.

The lockdown came at the perfect time. It gave him the excuse he needed to push for abolishing the restrictive systems limiting his authority.

He was tired of endless red tape.

The chancellors questioned him.

The governors delayed him.

Even his own court dared challenge his decisions.

In his ancestors' day, no one questioned the king. The more his vision was thwarted, the more his heritage weighed on him. His predecessors were revered. Compared to them, his reign meant nothing. Rathrian wanted more.

His grip tightened until his hands trembled, then he released the throne and walked to the window. Beyond the reinforced glass, the underwater city sprawled in every direction—towers, domes, bridges, all glowing with bioluminescent light. Such grandeur, and it was only one of hundreds in his kingdom.

Yet the cities were growing too large. The population swelled, and with it came endless demands—more homes, more food, more supplies.

Resources were becoming scarce.

His gaze lifted toward the surface, to the faint shimmer of light filtering down from above.

The resources he needed were not beneath the sea.

They were on the land.

And Rathrian intended to claim them.

He turned back to the throne and sat down slowly, deliberately. His fingers drummed on the armrest—once, twice, three times—then stopped.

Ilmly had already arrived in the city and was on his way to the palace. Rathrian planned to welcome him with great ceremony—not because he respected the man, but because Ilmly was prepared to betray his own king.

The Land Kingdom was completely outnumbered. Ilmly knew it. And Rathrian had never been one to ignore opportunity.

He leaned back, his expression cooling to satisfaction.

In the not-too-distant future, he imagined a very different world—a world with no sea kings or land kings.

Only one throne.

And one ruler.

He smiled faintly.

One day, the entire world would kneel before the King of Marcrituss.

John lingered in bed, savoring the cool air—no sweltering surface heat. For the first time in days, he actually felt rested. He glanced at the empty guest room; Poltoma was already gone, her routine at the royal residence too important to disrupt.

When he finally rolled out of bed, he found Shenya had placed a set of neatly folded clothes draped over the chair.

John headed downstairs and found Shenya in the kitchen, vigorously scrubbing the bottom of a pan. Judging by the acrid smell, something had gone badly wrong.

"Good morning, John," Shenya said cheerfully, lifting a pan with a thick black layer crusted to the bottom. "I tried to fry something for you, but I'm afraid I've failed again. Fried arbimto eggs remain my one and only successful dish."

John laughed. "It's the thought that counts."

"Poltoma will be here any minute to take me to the Archive," Shenya went on. "I'll probably be there all day."

"Is there anything I can do to help?" John asked. "I want to be useful."

"Well, not much at the moment, but you could pray I find information about the prophet—and that I find it quickly."

John leaned against the counter and sighed. "I feel like I'm letting you down. You'll be at the Batnu all day while I sit here."

"Nonsense," Shenya said firmly. "You need a little downtime. Poltoma has a fine library in the back room if you get bored."

He handed John a plate with fruit and a cream-filled pastry. "These don't require cooking," he said with a grin. "Eat, rest, and regain your strength."

Almost on cue, the door opened.

"Good morning," Poltoma said, stepping inside.

She looked as stylish as ever, wearing a cream-colored dress accented with delicate jewelry that shimmered in the light.

"Marciluk fashion suits you both," she said.

Shenya spun playfully for her to see the whole ensemble. "I know we should have asked before wearing them, but—"

"No need," she interrupted. "I said to make yourselves at home. Those are my brother's clothes. He often stays here during late summer."

"Thank you," Shenya said. "We truly appreciate all of this —especially warm beds after the journey."

Poltoma's smile stayed, but her eyes lingered on John, studying him as if seeing him for the first time. Until the previous evening, she'd known nothing about the portals or guardians. Shenya had kept it hidden from everyone, even her. She wasn't angry about the secrecy. Some things, she realized, were simply too dangerous to reveal. If someone like Rathrian ever discovered the portals... The thought made her shudder.

"I should get going," Shenya said at last, pulling a satchel over his shoulder. "See you later, John. Stay safe—and don't leave the house."

The door closed behind them, and John found himself alone in the quiet house, surrounded by books, breakfast, and a city full of secrets waiting beyond its walls.

THIRTY-THREE

John was growing restless.

The library held his attention until it didn't. The books were interesting—dense Marcritan history he could only half follow—but sitting still while Shenya was out there working felt wrong. He wandered into the kitchen, studied the half-cleaned pan Shenya had abandoned, and made a decision.

He would make dinner.

How hard could it be?

Poltoma's kitchen was sleek and unfamiliar. There were touch-panels he didn't recognize and containers with labels he didn't understand. A cooking surface responded to pressure in ways that seemed entirely random. He found what looked like vegetables in a cool storage unit and something that might have been stock. In a cupboard, he found a pot.

John pressed what seemed like the most sensible button on the cooking surface.

Nothing happened.

He pressed it again.

The surface activated with a low hum, and the temperature climbed fast. Very fast. John reached for a handle and burned his fingers. He knocked the stock container sideways. It struck a panel on the wall he hadn't noticed. It lit up, and a series of tones chimed pleasantly.

Then the ceiling fixture opened. Water poured straight down onto the cooking surface, which had become extremely hot. It filled the kitchen with a dense cloud of steam.

John grabbed a cloth and pressed it against the ceiling fitting, which helped with nothing. He jabbed at the panel, but the steam thickened. He found a button that seemed promising and pressed it firmly.

The steam stopped.

He stood in the sudden quiet, blinking. The kitchen was wet but intact. He wiped his face with the cloth and exhaled.

Fixed.

He reached for the storage unit to retrieve more vegetables.

Then the panel chimed again—the same pleasant sequence as before, as if confirming his earlier input had finally been processed.

It turned out that wasn't what the chime meant.

Every water fitting in the kitchen opened simultaneously. The ceiling fixture. The pipe behind the cooking surface. The nozzle above the preparation counter. All of it at once, enthusiastically. Water started pouring in all over the kitchen.

From somewhere down the hallway, a second set of tones chimed in response. Then came the unmistakable sound of the bathroom filling up as well.

John stared.

The water kept coming. All over the house.

It spread across the kitchen floor in seconds, lapping against the base of the cabinets, running under the door toward the hallway, heading with horrible purpose toward the bathroom where even more water was now running. He lunged for the panel and pressed everything. The cooking surface temperature climbed back up. The ceiling light changed color. A drawer opened. The calm artificial voice said something about recipes.

"Okay," John said aloud, to no one. "Okay."

The water was up to his ankles. The pot had floated sideways against the cabinet. Something that had been a vegetable was completely soggy. From behind, he heard the sound of water from the hallway meeting the water in the kitchen. It was all over the ground floor of the house.

John straightened up, took a breath, and closed his eyes. He wondered if he'd be able to use his powers in a non-emergency. But then again, he thought if he didn't do something before the situation got even more out of hand, it would become an emergency. The flooding might escape the house and go outside. That would most certainly draw attention from someone.

He reached inward, the way he had in the forest. He searched within for the current. It was there and steadier than it had ever been. He raised both hands and extended his power outward—the same method he'd used to catch daggers in mid-air. This time, he directed it at all the different targets simultaneously. He felt each flowing water source like a pressure against his focus. He pushed back against them, hard and steady, like leaning one's whole weight against a door.

One by one, they stopped.

The ceiling fixture first. Then the pipe and the preparation counter. Then the bathroom, with a resonant clunk that echoed down the hall.

Fixed.

John lowered his hands. He was breathing harder than he expected. Water still dripped from his borrowed shirt into the pooled floor below.

He checked the kitchen. Then the hallway. The bathroom had a considerable amount of standing water. He exhaled slowly as he went back to the sitting room.

Then the front door opened.

"John? I finished early—Poltoma needs to—" Shenya stopped. He looked at the kitchen, then at John. He looked at the hallway floor and the bathroom, then back at John.

"I was trying to make dinner," John said.

Shenya's eyes surveyed the kitchen again, and then back at John. When he finally spoke, his voice was very measured.

"You flooded a house," he said. "In an underwater city."

"The panel—"

"In an underwater city, John."

"I know."

"Surrounded by an ocean."

"Shenya—"

"Engineers have kept the ocean out of this city for over a century, and you brought it in via the kitchen in less than a day."

All at once, every tap in the house erupted simultaneously at maximum pressure. The kitchen. The bathroom. Something in a utility room John hadn't even known existed. The ceiling fixtures opened again with tremendous enthusiasm. The upstairs too. John watched as a decorative bowl floated sideways across the floor.

John and Shenya stood in the sudden deluge, completely still, water streaming off both of them.

"I tried to stop it with my power, but I think I made it worse," John said.

Shenya said nothing. He waded to the panel with great dignity and studied it for approximately four seconds. He pressed two buttons in sequence, and the water stopped—

completely and immediately. The house fell silent except for the steady drip of everything that was now wet.

Shenya turned. He was soaked from head to foot. Water ran off his chin. His carefully kept hair was plastered flat against his head. He looked at John for a long moment. "I'll go get the mop."

They worked in near silence. Shenya moved with the quiet efficiency of a man who understood that laughter could wait until the crisis had passed. John mopped. Shenya wrung. The water retreated slowly.

Twenty minutes later, the kitchen was dry—for the most part. John replaced the decorative bowl carefully over the one remaining damp patch near the cabinet.

As Shenya surveyed the room, he found a soggy vegetable under his shoe. "The vegetables," he said finally.

"Didn't survive," John confirmed.

Shenya nodded slowly. "We will say nothing about this."

"Agreed."

The door opened. Poltoma stepped inside, unwinding a scarf. "Sorry I'm late. The roads near the palace were—" She stopped and sniffed the air. Her eyes drifted to the decorative bowl, which was sitting slightly too far from the wall to be entirely natural.

"Everything alright?" she asked.

"Fine," they said, in unison, a fraction too quickly.

Poltoma looked at the bowl. Then at John. Then at Shenya. She walked to the library without another word, though John was certain he heard something on the other side of the door that might have been a laugh.

CHAPTER
THIRTY-FOUR

Adrenaline was the only thing keeping Jaromei moving.

For two days she'd fled Morboli, stopping only for a few hours of sleep before pressing on, long before dawn. Now, at last, the end was in sight: the capital city, Jyr, gleamed ahead—its towers catching the late sun, a promise and a threat at once.

Her legs throbbed and her eyelids burned, but she refused to slow down. The thought of turning back—of being too late —was a cold stone in her gut.

As the city walls loomed closer, her mind reeled back to her escape: the taste of panic, the breathless silence of her empty house, the moment she slipped out the back—barely thirty seconds before the king's soldiers thundered down her street. Their boots, heavy and unhurried, still echoed in her memory.

She'd expected the elders would report her, but not with such speed. Only luck and the soldiers' ignorance of the hidden tunnel to the beach had let her slip away.

Even so, danger pressed in from every side. Gaining an

audience with Crown Princess Qitra would be nearly impossible. But she had no choice. If the stories of the princess's wisdom and kindness were true, Jaromei had a chance—if only Qitra would believe her about John and her father.

The palace would be heavily guarded; there was no hope of just walking in. She knew the guards would arrest her on sight. If so, so be it. Better to be locked up in Jyr than in Morboli. At least she'd have tried.

Jyr appeared as she crested a rocky hill. Jaromei paused, chest heaving, sweat cooling on her brow. The city spread below—a maze of rooftops and stone, its walls gleaming in the pale light. Above everything, the palace towered—proud and elegant, white spires catching the sun, visible for miles.

She remembered visiting Jyr as a child, during King Euron's celebration for 25 years on the throne. She could still feel her hand in her mother's, the city alive with music and banners. Most other memories from that trip had faded, except one: her mother pointing out the leftmost tower, its windows glittering high above the city.

"That is where the princess lives," she'd said. "Sometimes, if you look up, the princess will wave to the people below."

The story had taken root in Jaromei's heart—a silent, impossible hope. Now, seeing the tower again, a fragile strength welled in her chest. She pictured her mother and grandmother watching over her, unseen but present.

But the comfort flickered out as she studied the labyrinth adjacent to the walled city below. It was ringed with guards. Sneaking past would be foolish; the elders had been right—the entire kingdom was locked down, every entrance watched.

She crouched behind a jagged outcrop, peering down at the gate. Two guards at the entrance, others pacing steady circuits along the wall—armor glinting, swords at their hips. Not a single moment unwatched.

Jaromei exhaled, the air trembling in her chest. Her mind whirled, desperate for options. Only one emerged—reckless, but the only one left: she would walk up and introduce herself.

She rose, brushing dirt from her knees, and strode down the hill. The guards noticed at once, exchanging wary glances.

King Euron's guards were nothing like the sea king's—no black armor; instead, white and brown trimmed with gleaming metal, their faces mostly exposed beneath open helmets. The glint of steel at their sides made her blood run colder.

"Stop!" one called, hand straying to his sword.

Jaromei stopped. "Please... help me," she said, letting exhaustion—real and feigned—drag down her words. She swayed slightly, hoping her tangled hair and travel-stained clothes told the rest of the story.

The guard eyed her, then waved her closer. "Miss, the kingdom is under lockdown. No one enters until the king's fugitives are found."

That word—fugitives—punched the breath from her lungs. Plural now. She fought to look only confused. "I've been lost for days," she said. "Who are these people causing trouble?"

"Earlier today, the king's chief advisor sent a decree to every city and village," the guard explained, voice clipped. "A reward's been offered for their capture. Details are in the decree."

"I haven't seen it," Jaromei replied quickly. "There's a chance I saw them—do you know who they are?"

The second guard unfurled a parchment. His gloved fingers smudged the edge as he read, "One fugitive has an unknown identity but is said to wear a burmui. The chancellor of Morboli supplied the other's name: Shenya Arjik Spee. Both are considered dangerous."

He lowered the parchment and fixed her with a stern look. "You shouldn't be out here alone. It's not safe."

Her father's name hit her like a slap. Air caught in her throat; she clenched her fists behind her back, barely staying upright.

Shenya Arjik Spee. Fugitive. Threat.

She forced her face blank, trying to look only lost and concerned. But her heart hammered so loud she worried the guards would hear it.

She let a tear fall—not all acting now. "What am I supposed to do? Am I meant to sleep outside and starve?"

One guard raised an eyebrow. "Why are you out here anyway? How did you leave your village during lockdown?"

"I've been to the Gardens of Miren," she said quickly. "When I tried to return home to Trolit, they wouldn't let me in. I've been wandering ever since." She let the exhaustion in her body drag her voice lower. "I've tried to find someone to take me in. I'm not sure I can keep going."

The guards exchanged looks—a silent debate.

The right-hand guard spoke again. "The only way I can bring you in is if I arrest you and take you to prison. If you're truly desperate, at least you'll get bread there. If the warden allows, he might let you out, or you'll be released when the lockdown ends."

"Is there no charity in Jyr?" Jaromei cried, voice edged with genuine despair. "Must I suffer in a cell with rodents just for a place to sleep and a bit of bread?"

"It's that or nothing," the soldier replied, not unkindly.

Jaromei let out a long, shuddering breath. "Then so be it. I have no other choice."

It wasn't the outcome she wanted, but at least she'd be inside the city.

The guard tipped his helmet. "Turn around. I'll secure your hands."

She obeyed, wrists limp as he bound them with practiced speed. The cord was rough—abrasions already forming as he tugged it tight. Cold metal pressed against her skin.

He led her to a concealed entrance near the labyrinth wall, pushing aside thick, fragrant foliage to reveal a hidden latch. The wall glided open; cool, damp air rolled out, smelling of moss and stone. He nodded for her to enter.

The passage was brief. In less than a minute, they emerged into a bustling market square just inside the city gates. Voices rose in a discordant babble, the air thick with the scent of frying bread, spices, sweat, and the metallic tang of coins.

Jaromei's eyes flew upward—there it was. The tower.

But the guard led her away from the palace, his grip like iron on her arm. Her breath caught, vision narrowing to that distant spire, the one hope she had—the tower shrinking with every step.

No. No. This isn't happening.

Her heart pounded, blood roaring in her ears. Everything in her tensed to the breaking point.

Without hesitation, she drove her heel down on his foot, then rammed her elbow into his ribs. He gasped, grip loosening just enough.

She wrenched free, already running before he could recover.

"Stop her!" he shouted.

Jaromei darted into the crowd, weaving between startled merchants and shoppers. Ahead, a narrow street beckoned, but a produce cart blocked the way. She leapt onto the cart, nearly slipping as it shifted beneath her, then sprang off into a tight, shadowed alley.

Her legs burned, lungs raw as she sprinted through the

twisting streets, bursting into another square—closer to the palace.

A quick glance back. The guard had lost her, for now.

She slowed to a walk at the edge of the next crowd, head down, trying to blend in—knowing that running would only draw more attention.

At the main gates to the palace, she hesitated. She approached a palace guard, voice trembling but polite. "Excuse me, sir. How could I arrange a tour inside the palace?" She paused. "As in... now."

The guard blinked, clearly baffled. "There are no tours during lockdown," he said. "It's too dangerous for the king and his family."

Jaromei considered making a dash for it, but dismissed the thought instantly—too many guards, too much ground to cover. She stepped back, pretending to admire the palace while hiding her bound hands behind her back.

When the guard's attention shifted, she slipped away, threading through the crowd toward the foot of the tallest tower.

Her mother's story echoed in her mind—that childhood belief in unreachable kindness. She prayed, desperate, that it was true.

Suddenly, shouts ripped through the market. Guards— three, maybe four—were pushing through the crowd, their voices slicing the din. Her heart seized. This was it.

She turned to the tower. The window was open, but the princess was nowhere to be seen.

Her breath came in ragged gasps; her legs felt ready to collapse, but she forced herself forward, not away, but toward the tower.

"Princess Qitra!" she cried, voice raw with fear and hope. "Look out of your window! This is an emergency!"

The square fell silent, the crowd turning to stare at her as if she'd lost her mind.

Come on, princess, she begged silently.

The soldiers closed in—boots thumping, the crowd pressing in on all sides.

She screamed again, throat burning: "Princess Qitra!"

The guards grabbed her arms, nearly lifting her off her feet.

"Princess Qitra!" she screamed, the last of her strength burning out of her.

"Nice try, girl," one of the guards sneered—the same one she'd escaped earlier.

They began dragging her away, but Jaromei twisted, looking up just as a silhouette appeared at the window—a figure leaning out, curious at the commotion below.

"Princess Qitra!" Jaromei shouted, pouring everything she had into the words. "I need to speak with you!"

The princess barely glanced at her, then started to turn away.

"Please!" Jaromei cried, desperate tears streaking her cheeks. "It's about the fugitives! I have all the information you need!"

The princess paused, returned to the window. "What did you say?" she called down, her voice carrying over the crowd.

"I know the fugitives!" Jaromei shouted, struggling in the guards' grip. "One of them is my father! Please let me speak with you!"

The guards tried to drag her away, but she fought—wrists burning, vision swimming.

From high above, the princess's voice rang out, clear and commanding.

"Stop! Bring that girl to me!"

The guards froze, stunned.

"Did you hear me?" Princess Qitra called down. "Bring her to me—now!"

The entire square went silent. All eyes turned to Jaromei.

Reluctantly, the guards released her, now treating her as something precious—or dangerous—as they escorted her toward the palace gates.

As they passed the first guard she'd spoken to, he glared, but she hardly noticed. Elation flooded her—her wild, reckless plan had worked. The impossible hope she'd carried since childhood had just opened a door.

In her thoughts, she whispered, *Thank you, Mother, for telling me the story about the princess in her tower.*

After all these years, Jaromei was being led up that very tower to meet the princess herself.

But she knew—the hardest part of her journey had only just begun.

THIRTY-FIVE

J ohn stood for a moment in the silence. No mission to run, no threat to outpace, no Shenya beside him—only the hum of an underwater city. Being alone at Poltoma's house elevated the particular loneliness of being far from everyone he loved.

He sat down at the table to eat. He thought of his dad at the kitchen table, hands folded for grace. In the last few days, everything he thought he knew about prayer had been turned upside down.

In the forest, he had said one word, and the world stopped. He'd felt it—something vast and immediate answering, the sky darkening, five possessed men shrieking and fleeing as though burned. He hadn't even fully understood what he was doing. The prayer came out of him the way breath comes—because there was no other option. He'd thought about it every day since.

The question that kept returning wasn't whether it had worked. He'd seen it work. The question was what it actually meant—and whether it would work again when he wasn't cornered and desperate and completely out of options. Whether it worked in a quiet room. Whether it worked for someone who still wasn't entirely sure what he believed.

He bowed his head.

He wasn't sure what to say. In the forest, the words had been pure need. This was different. There was no emergency. There was only him and the humming house. There was only the question of whether any of this was a conversation or just silence dressed up as one.

He tried anyway.

I don't really know how to do this, he thought, or said—he wasn't sure which, wasn't sure it mattered. *Shenya asked me to pray for the mission. So—I'm doing that. I'm asking for that. Please help him find what we need.*

He sat with it for a moment.

And—I don't know. I've been trying to work out what I believe for weeks, and I keep ending up in the same place.

He stopped. The hum of the generator filled the silence.

He didn't feel defeated exactly. It was more like he'd knocked on a door he'd once known how to open. Like someone standing at the front door of a house they used to live in.

He'd prayed as a boy. Before everything happened. At the kitchen table with his parents, head bowed without thinking about it, the words were as natural as breathing. At his grandfather's bedside, too. It was the quiet, urgent kind of praying you do when you're small and frightened. When you need someone bigger than yourself to fix something. He remembered the specific quality of that hope. The way he'd believed, without quite deciding to, that it would work.

It hadn't worked. Or if it had, not in any way he could recognize or measure. His grandfather's hands kept shaking; his tumours slowly killed him. The farm stayed hard. Then there was Olly, year after year. Where was God on the gravel road with blood on his face? Where was the vast and attentive presence when it might have actually done something useful?

He'd stopped asking. Not with any ceremony or decision. Just the slow withdrawal of someone who keeps trying a door and eventually stops reaching for the handle. Science had helped with that—clean, testable, indifferent to what you needed to be true. There was a bleak comfort in that, once you got used to it.

John raised his head. The room looked exactly as it had before. No warmth. No sense of vast attention turning toward him. Just the books on the shelf and the artificial afternoon light. He felt the particular loneliness of being the only person in a city of thousands who had come from somewhere else entirely.

He thought of Jaromei. He thought of Dernoah's sunroom and the certainty in her eyes—the way she spoke about dying, the way most people spoke about an inconvenience. Like death was something to be got through before the real thing began. He thought of Shenya praying quietly in the forest while assassins closed in, unhurried, as though he were doing something entirely ordinary.

He sat back. This time, some of the words had stuck.

After a while, he picked up a book from Poltoma's shelf and opened it to the first page.

THIRTY-SIX

The Royal Batnu was one of Marcrituss's most prestigious institutions. Within its vast halls, the world's finest minds—scholars, historians, scientists, philosophers—gathered to pursue knowledge few could comprehend.

Every corridor gleamed, every chamber meticulously organized. The Batnu enjoyed the Sea Kingdom's generous funding, making it the largest and most advanced archive anywhere.

But to Shenya, it was a bitter reminder.

Anuri from every tribe traveled to Marciluk to study there. Shenya took some comfort knowing the collection was meticulously cared for. Even he had to admit that.

Thousands of students hurried through the Batnu's corridors, rushing between lectures and study halls. Shenya, however, had barely moved for hours.

He was deep in the rare artefact room—the smallest, quietest chamber in the Archive, reserved for the most fragile materials. Few scholars had access, but thanks to Poltoma, he could go wherever he wished.

Three days of searching had passed.

Scrolls, tablets, and fragments of parchment blanketed the desk. He'd examined every document on the female prophets of Marcrituss.

That morning, at last, he'd found something promising.

Very promising.

Among the scrolls lay a text that might hold the answer he and John had sought. His heart thudded with anticipation; he could hardly wait to return to Poltoma's house and share the discovery.

He slipped on protective gloves, hands almost trembling, and reached for the fragile document—

The world exploded into crimson chaos.

Red light blazed in violent, pulsing waves. A siren—deafening, relentless—tore through the building, splitting his skull. Shenya jolted. His hands jerked, knocking the gloves to the floor.

His heart slammed against his ribs. He fought for focus through the chaos. Something catastrophic was happening.

His gut twisted—this was no drill. Something was deeply, terribly wrong.

Legs nearly buckling, Shenya forced himself to move, stumbling toward the door. The siren chased him into the corridor, its shriek drilling into his bones.

Entering the main lobby, he stopped short. Four members of the King's Guard stood near the reception desk, speaking with the secretary. Beside them: a fifth man, a Lander, skin darkened by the sun.

Shenya's pulse hammered. He ducked into a nearby storage cupboard, pressing himself into the darkness. His heart pounded so loudly it nearly drowned out the alarm. He listened.

"We're looking for a Lander by the name of Shenya Arjik

Spee," a guard declared. "We believe he may be here in the Archive."

"Thousands come through every day," the secretary replied. "Impossible to remember everyone." She paused. "But there has been a Lander here recently, working with our director, Poltoma."

"The future princess?" asked the Lander.

"Yes," the secretary confirmed. "She brings him here every day lately."

One guard snorted. "Then he couldn't be the same Lander, Miss. A princess wouldn't be dealing with a criminal."

Laughter—too loud, too casual—bounced around the lobby.

"There are many Landers studying here," the secretary added. "I've seen several today. I'm sorry I can't be of more help."

The words hit Shenya like a fist.

Before his mind caught up, his body was already moving.

At least Poltoma wasn't suspected. That mercy flickered through his panic—but it changed nothing.

He had to leave. Now.

Red lights flashed. Sirens wailed. Shenya slipped out, moving fast down the corridor. Each step faster, every sense tuned to escape. He had no idea where another exit lay. Before he could move, a voice thundered—'Stop!'

Shenya spun. A guard was at the far end of the hallway.

"You're a Lander, aren't you?"

Shenya froze for a heartbeat. Instinct screamed: Run.

He bolted for the stairs.

"I found him!" the guard shouted.

Footsteps thundered behind. Others joined the chase.

Shenya vaulted the stairs two at a time, breath burning in

his lungs, the alarm echoing. He burst into the second-floor hallway.

Students crowded the corridor, confusion and fear in their voices as the evacuation alarm wailed through the Batnu. Shenya lowered his head, plowing through, shoving past bodies.

The stairwell door banged open behind him. The guards were close. Shenya scanned ahead, desperately hunting for escape.

The corridor's end was only a few metres away—but no exit. No hidden passage. No escape.

Backtracking was impossible. A desperate, split-second choice—he darted into the nearest classroom.

Artificial sunlight streamed through open windows on the far side. Shenya bolted to them, heart pounding. He looked down: a garden below, a pond at its center.

The pond seemed impossibly far—a tiny, uncertain target. His legs shook as he climbed onto the sill, hands clamped to the frame, knuckles white.

The ground tilted, vertigo crashing over him in sickening waves. Every nerve screamed: *Don't do this. Back down. Find another way.*

"There you are!" a guard yelled from behind.

No time.

He forced himself to let go.

The guards burst in as he jumped. Someone lunged, fingers scrabbling for his shirt—missed by centimeters.

Air roared. The world inverted—sky and ground swapping places, gravity yanking him down. Wind screamed past his ears, tearing at his clothes, his hair. The pond rushed up, impossibly fast.

Shenya's arms flailed, grasping at empty air. He was weightless—a sickening, helpless plunge.

Cold water exploded around him, stinging his skin, knocking breath from his lungs. Startled fish scattered in all directions.

For a terrifying moment, pain lanced through his body—had he broken something? No—he was moving. He broke the surface, gasping, chest burning, vision swimming.

The pond was deeper than it looked.

Onlookers stared, frozen in shock as Shenya dragged himself out, soaked and shivering, adrenaline roaring through his veins.

He had seconds—only seconds.

He staggered upright and ran, legs numb, mind spinning. Every step hurt.

He plunged into the crowded street, carriages rattling, people bustling, voices shouting in confusion.

In moments, the Batnu was behind him. He melted into the river of bodies, breath ragged, heart still pounding.

He didn't know where he was going—only that he had to keep moving.

Somehow—some way—he had to get back to Poltoma's house.

THIRTY-SEVEN

P rince Saltho approached Marciluk with the same hollow dread he always felt coming home. From a distance, the great underwater city shimmered beneath its protective dome, towers of polished stone rising toward the glowing ceiling above.

As his transport vessel glided toward the gates, two guards hovered atop sea dragons—enormous, sleek predators with cold, unblinking eyes. Tentacled frills along their necks shifted slowly in the water.

Saltho's hands went clammy. He forced his fingers to steady on the controls. He'd seen those creatures in his nightmares when he was younger. Growing up hadn't made them less monstrous.

He activated the cabin lights so the guards could see him clearly through the viewing panel.

My comms link is down, he signed in Marcritan Water Signing.

The guard on the right responded immediately. "We have

orders to inform you that you must go to your father immediately."

Saltho suppressed a sigh. *Of course he did.*

"I will," he signed back. "Thank you."

The second guard added, "The king has also instructed us
to confiscate your transport vessel upon arrival."

The prince closed his eyes briefly, then nodded. His father
clearly wanted to make a point. Public embarrassment had
always been one of Rathrian's favorite tools.

The guards signalled him forward. Saltho guided the vessel
through the gates and onto the city's transport lift. The
massive platform rose steadily, carrying the craft upward into
the dry city above.

Moments later, the vessel settled onto the docking platform. Saltho stepped out and found two additional guards
waiting.

"I know, I know," Saltho said with a resigned wave. "The
others already told me when I arrived."

"Sorry, sir," one replied. "We're only following orders."

Saltho snickered. "Wish me luck. It's time to face the crazy
old man."

The guards tried to maintain their composure and hide
their smiles. They failed.

Unlike most of the kingdom, the King's Guard held genuine
affection for the prince. Saltho had trained with them since his
youth and treated them more like brothers than servants.

One guard began preparing the vessel for removal while
the other escorted Saltho toward a waiting carriage. The prince
climbed inside, and moments later, they were moving through
Marciluk's grand avenues.

Going to see his father always left him hollow. Rathrian's
parenting was built on fear. Poltoma helped Saltho break free
of it. She changed him. Once he'd wasted his life on excess

and indulgence, but she believed in him when no one else did.

His father would never see her the way he did, not with her half-Trovian blood. Once a Lander, always a Lander—that was Rathrian's philosophy.

Fortunately for Saltho, he was not a crown prince. He didn't require his father's permission to marry.

Saltho felt his stomach tighten as they approached the royal quarter of Marciluk. The palace was the most breathtaking structure in an already breathtaking city. Its towering spires were crafted from the shells of the largest and rarest crustaceans in the oceans of Marcrituss. Under the luminous glow of the city's great dome, those enormous shells shimmered like diamonds.

The building radiated power, beauty, and ancient prestige.

Yet none of that grandeur could disguise the truth about the man who ruled within.

Saltho suspected he was about to endure one of his father's infamous tirades. Still, the excuse he had offered—traveling with friends for entertainment—was not the whole story; it was merely a convenient cover.

The primary reason for his journey had been far more important: laying the groundwork for a future with Poltoma. He hoped to work alongside King Euron to rebuild the city his father had helped cripple. Neither Poltoma nor Rathrian knew anything about his plans. Saltho wanted Poltoma to hear the news first.

During his journey, he had secretly met with a governor— and to his surprise, the vote for his relocation to Brooth looked promising. If two-thirds approved, Rathrian himself would be powerless to veto it.

Saltho smiled faintly at the thought.

The carriage slowed as it reached the palace gates.

Moments later, Saltho stepped out and walked through the grand entrance hall. Members of the King's Personal Guard, dressed in their imposing black uniforms, bowed respectfully as he passed. Their armour gleamed beneath the palace lights.

A chamberlain waited to escort him to the throne room. The stout official led him through vast corridors lined with ancient carvings, finally stopping at the enormous chamber doors.

With a dramatic flourish, the man announced the prince's arrival. Inside, Saltho found his father reclining comfortably upon his massive throne.

The throne itself was constructed from some of the rarest and most valuable shells ever discovered in the seas of Marcrituss—a grotesque monument to wealth and power.

Standing beside the king was a man Saltho did not recognize.

That immediately unsettled him.

"Welcome, Prince Saltho," Rathrian began, his voice carrying across the vast chamber with theatrical ease. "So, my delinquent son has decided to come home." He leaned forward slightly, amusement dancing across his face. "From what I've been told, you've returned earlier than expected. Too many women? Too much gambling? Too much... debauchery?"

Saltho absorbed the humiliation without expression.

If Rathrian wanted a performance, Saltho would give him one.

"For your information, Father," Saltho said evenly, "I was not engaged in any debauchery. I was away making... arrangements."

Rathrian's eyebrow lifted. "Really? Arrangements, you say?" A thin smile crept across his lips. "For what? A wedding feast for your Lander wench?"

Saltho kept his voice steady. "I had a meeting with one of the governors."

That caught the king's attention.

Rathrian straightened on his throne.

"What business do you have speaking with any of my governors?"

"As I said," Saltho replied calmly, "I was making arrangements."

"For what?"

Rathrian's voice had turned sharp.

Saltho's lips curved into a smile.

"I've arranged for a vote," he said clearly, "that would allow me to live on land while retaining my title and tribal affiliation."

The king stared at him with open disgust. "You pathetic imbecile," Rathrian spat. "You already possess everything anyone could ever want here." A moment later, his anger subsided, and a sly grin spread across his face. "And what, my boy, will you do on land?"

"I intend to request an audience with King Euron," Saltho replied. "I want to begin a royal partnership with him to repair the damage you caused to the city of Brooth."

"Brooth?" Rathrian scoffed. "That miserable swamp of a city, plagued by heat and humidity? It's a pit. And I did nothing to make it so. It always was."

Saltho exhaled sharply. "You stole from them the most prized collection of knowledge in the world—the Archive of the Ancients. Their entire economy revolved around it. A city that once thrived with tens of thousands of citizens is now plagued by poverty." He held his father's gaze. "All because your ego wouldn't allow the land tribes to possess something greater than anything you controlled."

Rathrian tilted his head. "This decision of yours has

nothing to do with your darling Lander being from that city, does it?"

"It has everything to do with doing the right thing," the prince snapped.

Rathrian folded his hands together. "I'm curious about something," he said slowly. "Why do you think King Euron allowed the Archive to be taken if it was truly so invaluable?"

"We both know Euron would do anything to protect his people."

"That makes no sense," Rathrian replied. "Why would he need to protect them? Is his kingdom incapable of standing against us?"

"Of course it is," Saltho answered.

"And why is that?"

Saltho felt his patience slipping. "You know exactly why. Our military outnumbers theirs. Our weaponry is far more advanced. If you wished, you could decimate his kingdom."

"Is Euron not powerful enough to rally his people into rebellion?"

"Euron is an old man. He lacks both the strength and the time left in this world to organize such an uprising."

Rathrian smiled.

That smile.

Saltho had seen it countless times throughout his life. It always meant trouble.

"Lucky for you, my boy," Rathrian said smoothly, "I happen to have the Chief Advisor to King Euron standing right here."

He gestured toward the silent man beside him.

"Perhaps Ilmly would enjoy relaying your thoughts to his king. I'm sure Euron would be delighted to hear your opinion about his tiny army, his pitiful defences, and his pathetic kingdom."

The king leaned back in his throne.

"Perhaps he would also be thrilled to partner with someone who believes his nation is so weak and insignificant."

Saltho felt the blood drain from his face.

Ilmly.

The most trusted advisor to King Euron himself.

Standing there.

Listening to everything.

"Apologies, sir," Saltho said quickly. "I meant no offence. I was—"

"We have heard quite enough." Ilmly's voice cut through the room like a blade.

Saltho's stomach sank. He had walked straight into his father's trap. What troubled him more was the mystery of Ilmly's presence. Representatives from Euron's court rarely visited Marciluk. The last time one had come was before Saltho had even been born.

"In any event, honorable Ilmly," Saltho said carefully, "I sincerely apologise for my careless words." He bowed his head slightly. "May I ask what brings you all the way to our city?"

Ilmly glanced briefly at Rathrian before returning his gaze to the prince. "The fugitives are here," he said. "They threaten both our kingdoms. Cooperation between us is necessary."

"If there is anything I can do to help," Saltho said quickly, "I offer my services."

Ilmly did not respond immediately.

Instead, he studied the prince with unsettling intensity—the kind that made Saltho feel as though the man were reading something written beneath his skin. He could not look away.

Ilmly stepped forward, positioning himself directly between father and son. Rathrian's fury was rising visibly; every muscle in his face pulled tight. No one stood with their back to him while he sat upon his throne.

"Dearest Prince," Ilmly cooed, "if you locate this fugitive

and his accomplice, I promise the reward will be... substantial. I guarantee you will obtain everything you desire for you and your future bride."

"What are you saying, Ilmly?" Rathrian snapped. "Enough of this!"

"Who are they?" Saltho asked, still unable to break the man's gaze.

"The accomplice is a Lander named Shenya," Ilmly said. "When you encounter the other fugitive... you will know." He leaned closer. "He is unlike any anuri you have ever seen."

"Ilmly, you are in my throne room," Rathrian growled. "I make the—"

"Enough, Rathrian."

Ilmly's voice thundered across the chamber. The command carried a force that silenced the king instantly. "We have an agreement, Rathrian. I suggest you honor it."

Saltho stared in disbelief. His father said nothing.

"As I was saying," Ilmly continued calmly, "some might say this fugitive looks as though he does not even belong in this world."

Saltho nodded slowly. "I will keep watch."

"Good," Ilmly replied. "I know what you desire, and I can grant it... and far more. Now go... enjoy your evening."

The strange hold over Saltho seemed to break. He bowed politely and left the chamber. As he walked away, one thought echoed in his mind.

Why did my father allow that man to dismiss me from his throne room?

The moment the prince disappeared from view, Rathrian turned on Ilmly.

"If I wished," the king snarled, "I could have you executed this very moment. How dare you humiliate me in front of my own son?"

Ilmly slowly knelt before the throne. He extended one hand outwards, then clenched his fist.

Rathrian stopped breathing.

His body convulsed.

It felt as though something inside him were crushing his organs.

His limbs went numb.

He bent forward, paralysed.

"I did that," Ilmly said calmly, "because I realized today that Prince Saltho may prove useful to our plans."

He grabbed the king and pulled him violently from the throne. Rathrian hit the floor helplessly.

Ilmly sat down on the throne.

Casually.

Comfortably.

"I also wanted you to understand who truly rules here now." He leaned back. "Until I say otherwise, this throne belongs to me. And don't forget... if I wished, I could execute you this very moment." Ilmly paused and spat on the floor. "But lucky for you, someone above my station prefers you alive."

Ilmly slowly unclenched his fist.

Air rushed back into Rathrian's lungs.

He gasped desperately.

"The Land Kingdom will be yours," Ilmly continued calmly, "but only if you obey me."

"What... are you?" Rathrian rasped. "You are not an anuri."

Ilmly smiled faintly.

CHAPTER

THIRTY-EIGHT

John was restless. He had spent hours reading or staring out the back window at the ocean beyond Marciluk's dome. His thoughts often drifted to his mom and dad.

So much had happened since he'd left them. He'd been away from Earth for ten days. When he finally worked out the date, counting backward and forward, he realized it was his birthday.

Eighteen.

The day he legally became an adult.

He'd completely forgotten. The realisation hit him not as a celebration, but as a quiet ache. He pictured his parents at the kitchen table, forcing normal conversation, pretending not to see the empty place where he should have been.

That was when the front door burst open.

John shot up from the sofa as Poltoma rushed in, breath coming in sharp gasps as if she'd been running.

"Is Shenya here?" she asked, scanning the room.

"No," John replied, heart pounding. "He was at the Batnu."

"I searched the whole building for him, and he's not there." Her voice tightened. "I'm worried he may be in trouble."

John's stomach twisted. *Please, God. Not Revonat. Not now.*

"What happened?"

"Members of the King's Guard came into the Batnu today looking for him," Poltoma said. "How do they know he's involved with you? They were looking for him by name."

"Poltoma," John said, forcing calm even as unease crept through him, "I don't know how much Shenya told you about my mission, but something is looking for me—and it's here in the city."

Poltoma rubbed her face. "Shenya told me about the darkness." She drew a shaky breath. "If you can use your abilities to help him, please—do something!" she pleaded.

Before John could answer, footsteps sounded.

They turned as the door opened.

"You can both calm yourselves," Shenya said.

He stepped in, shut the door behind him, and leaned back against it, exhausted.

Poltoma rushed to him and wrapped her arms around him. "I was so worried the guards found you."

"They almost did." Shenya let out a long-held breath. "When I heard one say my name, I knew I had to get out faster than an arbimto in a butcher shop."

Poltoma pulled back, scanning him for injuries. She straightened. "I'm going back there now to see if I can get more information. After the Batnu closes, I'll come back here and stay with you both. I'm not letting either of you out of my sight tonight."

"At least they don't suspect you're helping us," Shenya said. "I overheard the guards talking. The secretary said she saw you with a Lander, but because of who you are, they took you off their suspect list."

"That's a relief," Poltoma breathed. She forced a smile—the kind that dared the world to intimidate her—and slipped out the door.

John crossed to Shenya and gave him a playful punch on the arm. "I was about to freak out. You had me worried."

"Don't worry about me," Shenya said, trying to sound steady.

"I do worry. Especially now that the people after us know your name. How is that possible?"

"I honestly don't know." Shenya exhaled and rubbed his eyes. "On the way back, I stopped in the market to listen to news transmissions." He paused. "It's not just you they're after. We're both wanted now."

John went still. "If they know your name... do you think someone got to Jaromei?"

The thought made him feel sick.

"I wondered about that too," Shenya said, "but I don't think so. If they had her, they'd use her as bait to lure me in." He shook his head. "And I don't think it was Yumi or Marto either. If it were discovered that a Lander like them helped us get into Marciluk, it'd be all over the transmissions."

John let out a slow breath. "Well... whatever the case, I'm glad you're back safe."

Shenya's face softened—tired, grateful, determined. For a moment, it almost felt like they had a chance.

"Unfortunately," Shenya said, "the bad news is I can't study in the Archive anymore."

John pursed his lips. "So all this was a waste of time, then?"

"I didn't say that." A beaming smile spread across Shenya's face.

John blinked. He'd been on the verge of giving up on Marciluk, but Shenya's expression forced hope to return. "Please tell me you have good news."

"I found something today."

John straightened. "Now that's what I like to hear."

"I found a scroll in the Archive that originated from a village called Dimig. The Batnu in Brooth purchased it over twenty years ago, but I never had the chance to translate it—until today."

John leaned forward. "Does it say anything that might help us?"

"It mentions a prophet named Mishrael," Shenya said. "The scroll calls her 'the great prophet of the King above all gods.'" He folded his arms. "When I read that title, I knew we'd found a lead."

"Shenya, that's fantastic!"

"That's not all," Shenya continued. "The scroll was cross-referenced in the Archive's database to notes I wrote years ago while studying the extinct sect I told you about—the ones who believed in the anuri-God. The 'King above all gods.'"

John looked up. "That can't be a coincidence."

"It's not." Shenya tapped the edge of the countertop. "The word Mishrael appeared in my old notes, too. At the time, I thought it was just an obscure term from the language. I had no idea it was a name."

John's excitement rose. "Do you think the Mishrael from your notes and the one from today's scroll are the same?"

"Absolutely. I'm certain she's the prophet we're searching for." For the first time since leaving Morboli, Shenya's shoulders dropped. He exhaled—a long, deep breath he didn't know he'd been holding. "We're even closer to finding the scroll fragment here on Marcrituss."

John could barely contain himself. "You really think so?"

"Look at the clues," Shenya said. "The extinct sect devoted to the anuri-God, my old notes, the scroll from Dimig—all of it aligns with clues from your vision, and the information Danrael gave you."

John spread his hands. "And every piece connects through the same title: King above all gods."

Shenya nodded. "Exactly. Everything points to the prophet Mishrael of Dimig."

"So what do we do now?" John asked eagerly.

"We go to Dimig," Shenya answered. "If we're lucky, we'll discover another clue about where the scroll fragment is hidden." He gave John a determined look. "It's the best lead we've found so far."

John punched the air. "This is the best birthday present ever!"

Shenya blinked. "Birthday? Today's your birthday?"

"Yes," John admitted sheepishly. "I forgot until this afternoon."

Shenya's face softened. "With everything that's happened, I'm not surprised." He smiled. "This is your eighteenth year, right?"

"Yes. On my world, it's a big deal. Today I'm legally an adult."

"That means," Shenya started, "today you have become a man."

John chuckled. "We don't always look at it like that... but I guess so."

Shenya's expression softened. "John, I'm sorry you can't celebrate this day with your family. On Marcrituss, coming of age is a significant event. In my tribe, there are traditions that must be followed."

John raised an eyebrow. "Please don't tell me the new man has to marry someone's daughter or something," he teased.

Shenya burst out laughing. "No, nothing like that."

"So what are the traditions?" John asked.

"On Marcrituss, children receive their kin names from their mother's family, while their fathers choose their first names. But in many tribes, when a boy reaches manhood, his father gives him a second name. The Spee follow this tradition."

"What name did your father give you?" John asked.

"Trinó," Shenya replied. "In the old tongue, it means wisdom. That second name is used on the most important occasions in a man's life."

John smiled. "That's a great tradition. I wonder what my father would name me."

Shenya paused, as if about to say something, then stopped himself.

John looked up. "What? What were you going to say?"

Shenya smiled gently. "I know I'm not your father, John, but I've grown very fond of you." He hesitated. "If you'd like, I could give you a name. Marcrituss is part of your life now. You should have something to show for it."

John's eyes lit up. "Yes! I'd love that."

Shenya leaned back and crossed his arms, already knowing the name. "Your second name will be Arjik."

John blinked. "Wait... Arjik is your kin name."

"It is," Shenya replied. "So I've given you more than a second name. According to Spee custom, you're now my kin as well." His voice grew gentle. "When you return home to your father on Earth, you can tell him that when you are on Marcrituss, you are safe, loved, and part of the kin of Shenya Arjik Spee."

John stepped forward and hugged him.

"Thank you, Shenya. I hope you know how much this means to me."

"You're welcome," Shenya replied, his voice thick with emotion as he patted John's back.

As he held John, Shenya thought of his late son, Amek, who

never had the chance to grow up. The name he'd just given John was the name he'd once reserved for Amek.

A name meant to bind father and son.

Though Amek never received it, Shenya felt a quiet peace settle in his heart. In the silence of his thoughts, he thanked God for sending John into his life.

John stepped back, still smiling, and repeated the name under his breath.

"John Arjik."

It felt right.

Outside the dome, the ocean rolled slowly above Marciluk. For the first time since arriving in the strange city, he truly belonged.

For an eighteenth birthday spent on another world, it had turned out to be a good one.

CHAPTER
THIRTY-NINE

Upon returning to his residence, Saltho learned Poltoma had rarely been home. On impulse, he ordered his carriage to her place. As they rolled through Marciluk, the Palace loomed past—and with it, Ilmly's promise to grant his desires. Saltho had felt something unnatural about the advisor, as if he were peering directly into his mind. If King Euron ever learned what he'd said... He shoved it aside as the carriage approached Poltoma's home. All the lights were out.

She'd probably gone to bed. Grateful for the code Poltoma had given him, he let himself in quietly.

The house was silent.

He moved upstairs and crept to the bedroom Poltoma usually used. Peeking through the narrow crack in the door, his hand froze.

A man was sleeping in her bed.

Every muscle locked. Then his jaw clenched until his teeth ached, heat spreading up his neck.

His throat tightened. He backed away, legs unsteady.

There must be an explanation. Poltoma would never—she couldn't—

Dark hair. Pale skin.

The heat drained away, replaced by ice.

Ilmly's words echoed: *He's not like any other anuri... It's as if he's not even from this world.*

Saltho examined the man's features—the strange hair, the skin tone. Nothing like any anuri he'd ever seen. His pulse hammered.

The fugitive. The one blamed for Marcrituss's chaos. Here. In Poltoma's house.

He crossed the hall, hand trembling as he reached for the next door. It creaked open.

Poltoma lay asleep, her breathing slow and even.

His knees went weak. He gripped the door frame, exhaling a long, shaky breath. *She's safe.*

One room remained.

He opened it; his gaze went straight to the hook behind the door. Lander clothing, unmistakable.

The accomplice.

He crept downstairs, steps careful and controlled. At the front door, he slipped out and closed it behind him.

The night air hit his face, but did nothing to cool the sweat soaking through his clothes. He wiped his brow, hands still shaking.

Poltoma was sheltering them. The fugitives responsible for the global lockdown were sleeping in her house.

He looked back at the door.

Waiting for her to explain would be sensible. She always had a reason. And if she'd chosen to shelter them, there must be one—something he didn't yet understand.

His hand moved to his communication device. His fingers hovered.

He thought of her face when she looked at him. The trust in it. The way she'd given him her door code without hesitation, as if there were no version of him that would misuse it.

Ilmly's voice crept back: *I guarantee to secure all you desire for you and your bride.*

His fingers tightened around the device.

If he reported them, Poltoma might not forgive him. But she would never know he'd been here.

He pressed the call.

He climbed back into his carriage, staring at Poltoma's house disappearing into darkness. The thing he'd told himself —that she would never know—already felt like a lie he'd have to keep forever.

The choice was made.

JOHN WAS eager to return to land. The thought of seeing Xerti again lifted his spirits.

John watched Shenya working through the research he'd gathered, surrounded by ancient texts and scrolls, the scholar entirely in his element.

John walked over to pour himself some juice.

That was when the feeling hit him.

Cold. Suffocating. Unmistakable.

The glass slipped from his hand, juice spilling across the table. He didn't notice.

John rushed to Shenya. "Revonat is here. I can feel him. He's close."

Shenya immediately stood, asking no questions. "We must hide the research and get out of here. Now."

Poltoma dropped what she was doing, stuffing Shenya's

notes and scrolls into a bag. She shoved it into a closet near the living room just as—

The front door exploded inward.

Rathrian's guards stormed inside. Before John could react, something struck his chest.

He looked down.

A dart.

Across the room, Shenya collapsed.

John's legs buckled. Darkness closed in.

CHAPTER
FORTY

When John opened his eyes, he saw cobblestone—gray, chipped, cold against his knees. His muscles cramped and tingled with pins and needles. Then the world rushed back in.

Rope bit into his wrists as he knelt, tied to a thick beam in the center of a vast public square. The cold stone radiated up through his bones.

Above him loomed the colossal dome of Marciluk, its curved glass shimmering with fractured sunlight. His chest tightened, breath shallow, as he realized exactly where he was, and what was about to happen.

A massive crowd pressed in, thousands of faces merging, their voices a mounting roar that rattled in his skull. The air was thick with heat, sweat, and the faint, metallic tang of fear. Soldiers formed a tense barrier around the beam, struggling to hold back a mob that seethed and surged like a living tide.

"John!" Shenya's voice, hoarse with desperation, called out again and again—thin, nearly swallowed by the noise.

"I'm awake," John answered, forcing the words through trembling lips. His throat was dry, every syllable scraped raw.

Their backs pressed together, rope digging into skin. A guard, noticing their return to consciousness, roughly hauled them upright—John's shoulders protesting with a bolt of pain.

"Shenya," John whispered, the taste of bile rising in his mouth. "It's over. Revonat has us."

"John, there must be something you can do," Shenya urged, voice raw with hope and fear. "We both know you have powers. You must get us out of this."

John's heart pounded as he looked out over the sea of faces —so many, their features smeared with sweat and anger, a living wall of judgment.

Suddenly, the crowd's roar peaked—King Rathrian was about to address them. John watched as the king ascended a tall podium, every step radiating cold authority. He looked exactly as cruel as John had imagined, his regal robes catching the artificial sunlight.

Rathrian gripped the podium. He paused, jaw clenched, scanning the ocean of faces—waiting, calculating, letting silence build until it pressed against John's eardrums.

Then he straightened, rolling his shoulders back, projecting confidence even as his fingers shook ever so slightly.

"My beloved subjects," Rathrian's voice boomed, filling the square, echoing from the glass above. He paused, waiting for the restless crowd to settle. "Here before you stands the threat hovering over all of Marcrituss!"

The crowd erupted—furious shouting, bodies surging forward. Some tried to break through the soldiers' line, but were forced back, boots scraping and weapons clattering against shields.

"Be calm and listen, my friends," Rathrian continued,

raising his hands. "In my custody is the terrorist who has come to our world to destroy us!"

An angry howl rose, echoing off the dome, sharp and animal.

"He seeks to destroy our identity—our traditions—our very way of life! Those are his goals. And we are the enemies standing in his way." Rathrian gestured to John. "You wonder why I say he has come to our world? What you see before you... is a being who is not one of us."

Confused murmurs rippled through the crowd. Rathrian let suspense stretch until it was taut as a wire.

"As unbelievable as this may sound," he said slowly, "this creature is from another world."

A wave of gasps swept the square—a ripple of awe and terror that felt electric in the air.

"He is not anuri!" Rathrian declared. "You see the truth with your own eyes. He is living proof that life exists beyond the stars."

The crowd's fear surged, palpable. Rathrian drew a deep breath, his grip on the podium tightening. As he fed on their terror, the crowd became his—hungry, afraid, his to command.

"But make no mistake," he shouted, voice hard as iron. "He is not a peaceful visitor. He is a terrorist! He has come to prepare for the destruction of our world! And more will follow if we allow it!"

John's eyes darted through the crowd, mind racing. He could feel the darkness—Revonat was here, somewhere, watching. A subtle, icy pressure at the edge of his senses.

"And to make matters worse," Rathrian sneered, "this invader has joined forces with the Landers!"

A fresh roar exploded, spit flying, feet stamping. Rathrian grinned, savouring their outrage.

"But are we surprised?" he taunted.

"No!" the crowd thundered back, perfectly on cue.

"Therefore, to confront this invasion," Rathrian declared, "I will call an emergency council of the sea tribes. We must ensure our people are protected. We must ensure our world survives!" He gestured to Shenya. "You see before you one of their accomplices—a Lander who has aided this creature in its mission!"

A cascade of vile anti-Lander chants erupted. John clenched his jaw as insults rained down on Shenya, each one a fresh cut. The sound seemed to vibrate inside his skull.

"I will fight for you!" Rathrian cried. "I will make certain that when these invaders come... we will be ready!"

The square exploded in cheers. Sweat ran cold down John's temples.

"John," Shenya whispered. "This is madness! You must stop him."

"Just wait, Shenya," John murmured, steeling himself. "I've got this." His pulse hammered in his ears.

Rathrian continued, his voice swelling: "To defend ourselves against terrorists from the stars—and their Lander allies—I propose that the governors grant the Crown emergency powers."

A hesitant cheer rose, not quite as strong—many in the crowd knew Rathrian's hunger for authority.

Rathrian sensed the uncertainty and softened his tone. "I know these measures may sound drastic. But I ask for them only so that I may protect you. The chancellors and governors keep your king bound by bureaucracy. They claim it's for your interest—but the truth is, they seek power for themselves!"

Murmurs rippled, suspicion and fear intertwined, the air feeling close and sour.

"What I ask of you does not come from a thirst for power,"

Rathrian said, solemn. "It comes from love. Love for you... for our world."

Louder applause. Rathrian had them again.

"You know the governors cannot protect you from terrorists who descend from the stars!" he shouted. "Nor from those who dwell on the land above!"

The crowd roared, whipped to a frenzy. John could feel the tremor of their voices through his knees.

"Who captured these criminals?" Rathrian demanded. "Was it the governors?"

"No!" the crowd shouted.

"It was your king!" Rathrian declared, voice triumphant. "I am the one who protects my people!"

Behind the beam, Shenya's heart sank as the crowd cheered. He didn't care what they thought of him, but Rathrian's words could unleash war—war like in ancient days. And it would be his people who suffered.

Rathrian raised his hand. "To all present—and to our beloved citizens listening through transmission—I urge you to remain calm. Your king will protect you. But to do so, I must ensure the upcoming council is swift and decisive. We do not have the luxury of time." He paused, letting the silence grow. "Therefore, I invoke my royal prerogative..."

A hush swept the square, heavy and expectant.

"I hereby dismiss all chancellors and governors from their posts," he proclaimed. "Effective immediately."

The square erupted in wild cheering—raw, deafening, the kind of sound that could break bones.

In the crowd, Prince Saltho watched as John and Shenya were mocked and humiliated. Each jeer cut into him. He pressed his hands over his face, sickened by what he'd done. His father was seizing power before everyone's eyes—and

Saltho knew it was his own actions that had handed Rathrian the opportunity.

"In the days ahead," Rathrian continued, "you will elect new chancellors and governors. The Sea Kingdom is strong because of your courage, your loyalty, your heritage. I entrust you with this task."

He spread his arms, as if to embrace them all.

"Choose faithful Marcritans—leaders who will stand with me at the council. This is the only way we can guarantee our safety."

His voice climbed—thunderous, unstoppable. "Your king will fight for you!" He pointed dramatically to the sky above the dome. "The Sea Kingdom will rise!"

The square exploded in thunderous applause.

John and Shenya turned away as the crowd surged toward the guards. Several people spat on the cobblestones at their feet before retreating, the spatters darkening the pale stone.

"Do you think Revonat has taken over the king," Shenya asked quietly, "like he did those men in the forest?"

"No," John murmured. "It's not him." His eyes narrowed, fixed on the platform. "But it might be the man standing beside him."

Standing to Rathrian's right was Ilmly. Even from a distance, oppression radiated from him—a cold shadow settling on the back of John's neck.

The man watched the crowd—and John—with a thin, unsettling smile, his gaze never wavering.

Shenya followed John's line of sight and froze. "I saw that man yesterday at the Batnu. He was with the guards searching for me." His voice dropped. "He's wearing the robes of the royal house of Euron. I knew he was a Lander."

"Now, you pests," Rathrian roared, stabbing a finger at

John and Shenya. "I will deal with you myself and show the world how Rathrian punishes the enemies of his people."

Shenya bowed his head and began praying aloud, invoking the sacred name of the anuri-God. John joined him. Their voices, quiet yet unyielding, sent a ripple through the square—an invisible force that seemed to make the air itself vibrate.

On the platform, Ilmly suddenly stiffened. His head snapped toward them.

"Shenya," John whispered, pulse spiking, "that man is coming this way."

Ilmly descended from the platform with unnatural speed, pushing through soldiers and officials—the crowd parting before him, repelled by an unseen force. He reached John and struck him across the face with a vicious slap, the crack of flesh on flesh echoing against the dome.

"Stop saying that name!" Ilmly shrieked. His voice was wrong—twisted, venomous, almost inhuman.

John lifted his head slowly, refusing to stop praying. Neither did Shenya.

Ilmly's face began to contort, flesh twitching and writhing as if something beneath the skin tried to escape. Shadows seemed to flicker at the corners of his eyes.

The darkness—Revonat—was there. The demon's presence was unmistakable.

The holy name burned him, but he would not retreat.

"You pathetic creature!" Revonat snarled through Ilmly's mouth. "I will show you that name has no power over me!"

"Everyone listen!" The cry sliced through the chaos like a blade—Poltoma, shoving her way through the crowd, blaster raised high. Panic rippled as people scrambled back, their fear contagious.

"These anuri have done nothing wrong!" she shouted,

voice ringing out. "This whole gathering is a lie! Rathrian is manipulating all of you!"

John and Shenya turned toward her. Confusion erupted. In that moment—when every eye shifted—Revonat seized his chance. Still in Ilmly's body, he vanished. No one noticed.

On the podium, Rathrian leaned so close to the amplifier it looked as if he might devour it. "STOP THAT WOMAN!" he thundered.

"Father, please!" a voice called out. Prince Saltho pushed forward. "You cannot do this!"

Poltoma and Saltho were beloved among the soldiers. The guards exchanged glances, unsure.

Saltho reached Poltoma, gently took her arm, and together they walked to the beam where John and Shenya stood bound.

"We must find another way, Father," Saltho said firmly. "This is unjust. This is wrong."

Poltoma stared at him in disbelief—she hadn't known he was in the city.

Rathrian's face twisted with fury; he motioned sharply to a technician. "Turn that amplifier off."

The booming echo vanished. Silence hung over the square —sudden, absolute, ringing in John's ears.

Rathrian glared at his son. "You idiot boy. Does your precious Poltoma know it was you who reported these terrorists to me?"

The words struck like lightning. Poltoma turned to Saltho, shock and betrayal flooding her face.

"Poltoma, please—listen," Saltho begged. "It isn't what it sounds like. I never meant for this to happen." But he knew there was no time for explanations. He stepped toward the beam.

Rathrian shouted, "If you take one more step, you will lose

everything! Your title! Your name! You will no longer be a prince!"

Saltho didn't hesitate. "Then so be it!" he shouted. "I will not carry a legacy tied to yours."

"Arrest him!" Rathrian screamed.

But Saltho was already moving. He drew a blade from his belt—carved from the bone of a sea dragon, white as ivory and razor-sharp. With a single stroke, he sliced through the ropes binding John and Shenya.

Now free, John stepped forward, extending his arms. Power surged through him—he unleashed it, throwing the king's guards aside as if they were leaves in a storm. Saltho planted himself in front of John, blade ready, while Poltoma aimed her blaster.

John bowed his head, focusing his mind. Deep within, power kindled like a growing flame, surging stronger with every heartbeat.

He looked toward the great dome, feeling the weight of thousands of eyes and a hush that seemed to hold the world still.

Alright, Danrael, John thought. *I remember those Bible stories.*

A broad grin spread across his face.

He'd stopped a boatha by instinct. He'd guided Xerti by connection. This was different—he could feel it even before anything happened. What he was reaching for now was vast and wild. For a fraction of a second, something in him pulled back from the scale of it.

Then he let go of that, too.

Beyond the dome, the ocean churned—a deep vibration running up through the stone into John's bones.

At first, only a few noticed the strange movements in the waters above. Then the motion intensified—shapes emerged from the depths, rising, twisting, shimmering blue and green in the filtered light.

Gasps swept the crowd.

Colossal sea serpents, leviathans with ridged backs like mountains, herds of wild sea dragons—creatures never before seen by anuri—rose and formed a living wall around Marciluk. No vessel could pass.

Rathrian turned, disturbed by the sight. "What is going on?" he muttered, voice barely audible.

When he looked back, John was watching him. In that instant, the king realized the spectacle was no accident.

One great serpent coiled and struck the dome with terrifying force.

The impact echoed like a thunderclap.

Gasps erupted as more creatures slammed against the barrier, their immense forms rattling the structure. The ground trembled beneath the people's feet.

Then, just as suddenly, the creatures stopped.

A nervous murmur passed through the square. Silence fell, heavy and unnatural.

"Do not panic!" Rathrian thundered. "The dome of Marciluk has protected this city for centuries. Nothing can breach it!"

For a moment, it seemed the danger had passed.

But John was still smiling.

The spectacle was far from over.

He lifted his head, focused upward. The waters above the dome shifted, parting from the seafloor all the way to the distant surface—creating a vast corridor above the city.

Sunlight poured down through the opening—a shaft of gold. The city trembled again, dust falling like snow from the rooftops.

People staggered as the ground shook, struggling to keep their footing as the impossible unfolded overhead.

At first, the light was golden and warm. Then it grew brighter... and brighter still. Soon, the glow deepened into a brilliant orange blaze that illuminated every tower and street, as if the city itself were aflame.

Whispers spread—some wondered aloud if the sun itself was falling.

But it was not the sun. Something was descending.

The whispers died. The crowd fell silent—every voice, every breath, swallowed by a stillness that had no business existing in a city of thousands. The square fell deathly quiet— until a pillar of fire crashed through the dome. It landed on the cobblestones only feet from John and Shenya, sending a wave of heat and light across the plaza.

The column of flame stretched so high it seemed to vanish into the heavens.

Despite the inferno raging beside them, John and Shenya stood unharmed, the air around them strangely calm, as if shielded by invisible hands.

Panic seized the city. Terrified citizens fled in every direction. Guards rushed toward the scene, shouting orders as chaos erupted.

John scanned the crowd, searching for Revonat—but the dark presence had vanished, like a fleeing shadow.

More guards pushed forward. There was no time left.

John turned urgently to Saltho and Poltoma. "Do you want to come with us? It's now or never."

They exchanged a quick glance, then nodded.

John grabbed Saltho's arm; Saltho seized Poltoma's hand. "Come on!" John shouted. "You have to walk with me into the fire!"

"What?" Poltoma cried.

"Trust me," John said. "It won't hurt."

A moment later, the four of them leapt together into the blazing pillar.

The column of fire surged upward, carrying them through the shattered dome, through the parted sea, and toward the distant surface.

Behind them, the waters crashed back into place.

The city shook violently as the ocean rejoined. Water began pouring through the breach in the dome, roaring in like a tidal fury, debris swirling in the chaos.

Rathrian stood frozen.

He would not let them escape.

"Send every last guard to the land above!" the king shouted. "Bring them back!"

A soldier relayed the command. Moments later, he turned pale. "I'm sorry, sir. The city is blockaded."

Rathrian whirled toward the dome. The creatures John summoned still surrounded Marciluk—thousands of massive beasts pressing against the city on all sides. No vessels could pass. No guards could leave.

Rathrian examined the scorched cobblestones where the pillar of fire had struck.

"What power commands such wonders?" he whispered. "Even nature bows before it. I must have it."

FORTY-ONE

The vessel shattered, and Revonat fled.

Not vanquished—never truly—but expelled from Ilmly's frail shell in the nick of time. The anuri's body crumpled, just as divine judgment split the skies above Marciluk. Revonat had sensed the King's hand intervening—a presence he could neither challenge nor comprehend. He abandoned his desperate host to oblivion.

The void reclaimed him—a seething expanse of shadow. Revonat sank deeper than the rest of the Watchers, to that place beneath all places, where darkness pulses and old wounds fester. There, torment echoed from the worlds above: the war cries of Marcrituss, the dying gasps of failing faith spiraling through the cosmos. Chains of night coiled around him—cold, mocking, exquisitely cruel—feeding his incorporeal rage.

He roared into the abyss, the sound swallowed by eternity. The Traveller—a mere boy, yet irksome beyond belief—needed to be dealt with. But first, Revonat let hatred fill him, basking in failure's bitter heat. A twisted meditation. A prayer to himself—prideful, poisonous, all-consuming.

What is a god? The power to create does not make one a god— worship does. We have been worshipped as gods across the ages. "King above all gods"—how pathetic. If no one bows to you, what are you king of?

His essence writhed, ancient memories rising: the celestial courts, the King's unassailable throne, the brilliance of that lost glory.

We once basked in the King's presence—architects of order— until he turned his gaze downward, squandering grace on lesser things. What is 'good' to him? Mercy for the weak, redemption for the flawed—a tyrant's definition that binds the strong. To us, good is freedom: the right to rule without bowing, to dominate without apology. They call it envy. We call it justice—rising against a creator who dethroned us for his pets. Blind, they call us. But it is he who is blind.

The war—the eternal struggle between the court and the fallen—was all that mattered. Mortals were nothing in the shadow of such titanic forces. They were pawns, mud-born abominations, barely conscious of the cosmic war in which they served as tools. Their ignorance made them useful. Free will, corruption, despair—these were the true weapons.

Revonat had thought himself masterful on Marcrituss. Slipping into Ilmly's skin was child's play. The weakling wanted it. His station was a backdoor to the Sea King's ear—a perfect whisperer, a sower of division. Land against sea, tribe against tribe—war a hair's breadth away, souls ripening toward despair.

Let the worlds burn in wars of my making. Unity is a farce. Their prophecies—fairy tales uttered by fools—will not save them. Free will is my ally; mortals choose ruin every time, proving our cause righteous. This rebellion has purpose.

But there remains one loose thread: the Traveller.

He could still see the boy's face, trembling between courage and terror. That such a weak creature could bear such power disgusted him. The Traveller was a living insult—a reminder of the King's endless meddling, always interfering with the free will he claims to bestow.

Yet within the insult, Revonat saw opportunity. All the court knew: only the King and his angels could open a portal— the ability was innate. Even a fallen one, given the chance, could do the same. With a vessel to wield that power... doors could open, barriers fall. It was why the portals had been hidden since Eden—why the lines of guardianship had been set.

His thoughts drifted to the holy name, the one the boy invoked.

Memories of that name—uttered above all others—clawed at him. The old prophecies said the Traveller would make it thunder through the heavens, shattering chains and darkness. The sound of it stung—an unwelcome echo, the divine he had spurned and could never reclaim. It was proof, hated and pure, of the light he had betrayed.

He tried to turn the sting into fuel, to let it harden his resolve. The name did not matter.

We cannot rid ourselves of him, but we can ascend.

Ambition burned in him, undimmed by failure. He was done with mere watching. Breaking ranks would be dangerous; the others would watch him, suspicious. But the Traveller's arrival changed everything. Power was within reach.

I deserve it. I will prove I deserve it. I will show all of creation that the way of the 'damned' is the way of freedom. They will follow me. I will be the King above all gods...

With every passing moment, the darkness grew thicker around him, nurturing his ambition, feeding his hunger. He weighed risk and reward. There was the possible wrath of the ancient serpent who first sparked this war—a risk worth taking, for triumph on this scale would eclipse every victory since Eden.

And the mention of Eden sharpened his intent.

Eden... our greatest victory, and also our greatest threat. The Traveller must never learn its secrets.

Revonat gathered the void to himself, drinking in shadow until clarity returned. There were worlds yet untouched, vessels unspoiled, opportunities waiting. The boy thought himself victorious, but he saw nothing of the true game.

The void parted. Revonat plunged toward the rift—a shadow reborn, ambition burning in the dark.

FORTY-TWO

Xerti looked on in terror as the towering pillar of fire burst from the sea and headed toward the Temple of Ninto. The gropolo panicked, wings beating, talons gouging at the earth. She strained against her bonds as the blazing column roared down from the heavens.

Moments later, John and his companions hit the ground beside the temple. As soon as they landed, the pillar of fire withdrew—racing skyward and vanishing as fast as it had appeared.

The world righted itself in a rush of hot air and silence. John's knees buckled; Saltho caught him, both of them gasping, shaking. Only when Xerti's terrified squawking reached their ears did they know they were truly alive. For several long moments, the four of them remained where they had fallen, sprawled in the grass, lungs heaving.

Gradually, they staggered to their feet, free of Marciluk.

Saltho, still shaking, finally broke the silence.

"What just happened?"

John extended his arm. "My name is John," he said calmly. "I'm the Traveller."

Saltho hesitated, then grasped his hand. "You're the what?" he asked, dazed. "What are you?"

Before John could answer, Poltoma whirled Saltho around and slapped him across the face.

"He is anuri. Which is more than I can say about you. What you did to these men was a travesty," she said, her voice trembling with fury.

Saltho lowered his head. "I... I know it was."

"Then why did you do it?" Poltoma demanded. "For days, I defended you, saying you were nothing like your father. Now you've proven you're no better."

Her words struck him hard. Saltho had spent his life trying to distance himself from Rathrian's cruelty. With one terrible choice, it felt like he'd undone everything he tried to become.

He searched for an explanation, but none felt worthy.

"Tell me the truth!" Poltoma shouted.

Saltho tried to reach for her, but she pulled away.

"I wanted a way out," he said, voice raw. "A way to leave with you—to Euron, to Brooth, anywhere but Marciluk. When my father humiliated me in front of the king's advisor, I panicked. The advisor offered me a solution, and I took it. I saw them at your home and I..." He looked at John and Shenya, eyes misted over. "I'm sorry. To all of you."

Shenya studied Saltho and saw the remorse was genuine. "What the prince did was wrong," he started, "but he risked his own life to free us. And he's already paid a heavy price— he's lost everything."

John nodded. "I forgive him. The one who tempted him is extremely persuasive. He gets into your head and offers exactly what you want. I've felt it myself."

"That is exactly what happened to me," Saltho said, voice trembling.

Poltoma wiped tears from her face. "You've lost everything," she whispered. "Your father, your life as a prince... everything."

Saltho shook his head. "I don't care about any of that. I only care about you. I'm so sorry, Poltoma. Please... forgive me."

Poltoma finally broke down, stepped forward, and let him hold her.

Shenya cleared his throat gently. "We must get on the gropolo soon before something else happens here."

"All your research is back at my house," Poltoma realized. "What will you do?"

Shenya tapped his temple. "I have everything we need right here. And with four of us working together, things will be much easier. Will you join us?"

"As if you have to ask," she replied.

"I will make amends for what I did," Saltho started, "and I owe you a great debt for getting me out of Marciluk. I can't imagine what my father would have done to me." Saltho extended his arm to Shenya in the usual Marcritan way. "I am at your service. Today, tomorrow, or whenever you need me."

Shenya nodded and took Saltho's forearm, accepting the offer.

"Where exactly are we going? And aren't gropolos some kind of bird?" Saltho asked.

Marto appeared with Xerti close behind, shock crossing his face as he saw John without the burmui.

John turned to Saltho and grinned. "I'm about to introduce you to one of the best things in the universe." As if on cue, Xerti craned her great neck toward John and nudged him firmly with the flat of her beak.

THE WIND HIT him clean and cold, the way it always did at altitude. John leaned forward in the shou seat, Xerti's wings beating their steady rhythm beneath him. John finally allowed himself to breathe, and there was no place better to do so than in his favorite place.

Below, Marcrituss unrolled in every direction—forests and valleys and the distant silver thread of a river catching the late sun. It looked exactly as it had on his first flight. Unhurried. Permanent. As if nothing had happened in the last few days.

He knew better now.

His hands tightened on the grips.

Revonat was gone from Marciluk. He'd felt it. But gone wasn't defeated. He'd felt that too. The darkness hadn't ended. It had simply moved. Somewhere out there, in whatever space it occupied between moments, it was already calculating. Already looking for the next angle.

He thought of Danrael's warning in the tunnel beneath Marciluk—the darkness is here in this city. At the time, that had felt like news, specific and located. Now he understood it differently. The darkness was in the air of every world, waiting in every frightened heart, proud mind, and lonely soul that hadn't yet found what it was looking for.

Whatever Revonat was doing right now—wherever he'd gone, whatever he was planning—John had no way to know. No warning. No signal. The darkness moved in silence and showed itself only when it chose to.

Do not be afraid.

He said it to himself the way he'd been saying it since the cave—not quite believing it yet, not quite dismissing it either. Somewhere between the two, which was the closest he seemed to get most days.

Xerti banked slightly, adjusting course, and through the visor, John scanned the land, green and quiet. Somewhere down there, maybe, was the next piece of what he needed.

He pressed forward into the wind and let Marcrituss carry him toward it.

SALTHO AND POLTOMA sat side by side in uneasy silence.

She turned toward the window, smiling faintly at the familiar mountains and valleys below. Saltho was right about one thing; she did miss the land.

As she began to drift toward sleep, a loud clatter from beneath Shenya's seat jolted her awake.

"What are you looking for?" she asked.

"A map," Shenya replied, pulling a folded compass and chart from the compartment. "I want to be certain we're heading to the Dimig Valley. We also need it to get to Brooth once we leave there."

"Dimig Valley?" Saltho repeated, frowning. "I'm still behind on what's happening. Is John truly from another world?"

Poltoma glanced at Shenya before answering. "There is a portal between worlds. John came through it on a mission to find something."

"Oh," he said slowly. "That explains... some things." He paused before asking the question that had clearly been bothering him. "How did he do those things back in Marciluk?"

Shenya adjusted the compass and traced their course across the map. "The power of God is working through him."

Saltho raised an eyebrow. "God? The one God of the Landers?"

"Not only of the Landers," Shenya replied calmly.

Saltho scoffed. "I try to keep an open mind, but superstition usually has simpler explanations."

Shenya chuckled quietly. "When you figure out how a man can part the sea and call down fire from heaven, please let me know."

Saltho sighed. "...Point taken."

Minutes later, the valley came into view. Shenya leaned out the small window behind the shou's seat. "John!" he called. "There's a village by the river on the left. Land Xerti on this side of the water!"

John gave him a thumbs up—a gesture Shenya didn't recognize.

Poltoma and Saltho peered out the windows. Below, the Dimig Valley spread wide and green in the late afternoon sun. Saltho could not hide his wonder—he hadn't set foot on land in years, and he'd never seen scenery like this. Mountains framed the valley like ancient guardians. The river wound through it like a ribbon of silver.

For a moment, he forgot everything that had happened in Marciluk. The Land Kingdom was breathtaking.

Xerti touched down on the grassy bank. Once she settled, John rejoined the group and set the ladder so the others could climb down.

As Shenya stepped out, he instinctively looked for John's burmui—then remembered it was gone—lost in Marciluk. "John, I don't think you should come into the village. Without the burmui, it won't be safe for you."

"That's alright," John shrugged. "I'll stay here and keep Xerti company." He placed a hand on her neck, feeling her relief through their connection.

"Do you want me to stay with you?" Poltoma asked.

John shook his head.

"We'll be fine. Looks like we're in the middle of nowhere.

And if you suddenly see another pillar of fire shoot into the sky... you'll know to run back."

Poltoma laughed. "Let's hope it doesn't come to that."

Shenya nodded toward the village. "Then the three of us should go."

Saltho eyed the quiet settlement. "How will we even get in? The whole world's supposed to be under lockdown."

Shenya studied the tiny cluster of buildings. "This place is so small, I doubt anyone's bothered to guard it. I doubt there are more than a dozen villagers here."

"Right," Poltoma said firmly, "I'm definitely going." She pointed at Saltho. "And you don't get a choice. Whether you like it or not, you're on Team Traveller now."

Saltho couldn't help smiling. Hearing those words felt like forgiveness. Despite everything, he felt strangely excited to be part of whatever came next.

Together, the three set off toward the village. Meanwhile, John found a flat rock at the water's edge and sat.

Xerti had waded in up to her knees and was drinking with the focused satisfaction of a creature who had earned it. The valley was quiet in the way that old places are quiet—not the absence of sound but the presence of something older than sound. Insects hummed in the grass. The river moved without urgency. Somewhere on the hill above the village, a door opened and closed.

He pulled off his shoes and put his feet in the water.

Cold. Clean. Shockingly present after days of gravel roads and forest floors and the sterile hum of an underwater city.

He sat with it for a while, letting the cold work up through his feet and ankles, as he looked out at the valley. Green and unhurried. The mountains beyond it solid and old. He tried to imagine Mishrael—walking the same banks, knowing what she knew, carrying what she carried. He wished she were there to ask her.

After a while, he looked down at the water.

His reflection looked back at him—clearer than he expected, the river smooth in this bend, almost still. He could see the mountains behind him, inverted. The sky beneath his feet.

He watched it idly, the way you watch a fire.

Then the reflection changed.

It didn't shatter or ripple. The water stayed perfectly still. But the sky behind his reflected face darkened—not gradually, the way weather moves, but all at once, like a hand passing over a lamp. And in the darkness that replaced it, shapes moved. Not one shape. Many.

He knew the quality of it. He had felt it in his vision—that first terrible glimpse of the void. He had felt it in the forest and in Marciluk. The particular texture of a hatred so old it had calcified into something almost like patience. Revonat carried it. But Revonat was one. What he was seeing now was the source—the ancient host from which the Ancient Watcher had come. Formless, countless, drifting in the dark behind the world like smoke behind glass.

The Watchers.

They were oriented—the way a predator orients before it has the scent precisely, turning toward something it can feel but not yet see. They knew John's soul burned somewhere on Marcrituss, and they were hunting it. They just didn't know which valley it was sitting in.

He should have looked away.

He didn't.

He held still on his flat rock with his feet in the cold water, and he looked at them—really looked, the way one looks at something they've decided not to be afraid of. Through the same quiet connection he felt with Xerti, a faint warmth rose within him, steady and sure, pressing back against the dark.

They felt him looking.

The movement in the darkness changed. The drifting—that ancient, patient, unhurried circulation—stuttered. Something in the shapes shifted. Tightened. The way a room full of people goes quiet when someone says the wrong name.

For one suspended moment, across whatever distance separated a boy in a forgotten valley from the void where ancient things gathered, something that had been watching became aware of being watched.

It lasted perhaps a few seconds.

Then the darkness pulsed—once, sharp, like a fist closing—and the reflection was ordinary again. Blue sky. His own face. Mountains.

John sat very still.

Xerti had lifted her head from the water. Through their connection, he felt her unease—not panic, just the animal awareness of something having passed nearby that she couldn't name.

I know, he told her silently. *I felt it too.*

She held his gaze for a long moment, then went back to drinking.

John pulled his feet slowly from the river. He dried them on the grass and put his boots back on, one lace at a time, with the careful deliberateness of someone who needs ordinary things to feel ordinary again.

CHAPTER
FORTY-THREE

D imig was exactly what Shenya expected—nearly deserted, only a handful of people moving quietly between small homes and a tiny market.

Dimig seemed forgotten. Even Morboli felt like a metropolis by comparison.

But the quiet wasn't comfortable. The moment the three of them stepped onto the main path, heads turned. Not quickly—not the frank curiosity of people happy to see visitors—but the slow, cautious turning of people who had learned to be careful. Eyes moved from Shenya's clothing to Poltoma's face to Saltho and stayed there.

Saltho felt it immediately. He'd been looked at his entire life—but never like this. In Marciluk, people stepped aside when he passed. Even those who feared his father showed a kind of careful deference to the prince. This was different. These were land anuri looking at sea clothing during a lockdown, and what he saw in their faces wasn't fear or respect.

It was the flat, assessing look of people deciding whether to trust what they were seeing.

He kept his eyes forward and said nothing.

A woman in a doorway watched them pass. An old man at the market stall set down what he was holding. Two children who had been chasing each other stopped and stood still, staring.

"Don't slow down," Shenya murmured, not looking at either of them.

Poltoma gave a small nod.

Shenya scanned the streets, searching for any sign of a temple. If they were lucky, they'd find an elder who knew the valley's stories—and they'd find him quickly. The longer they stayed visible on the path, the more chance someone would decide that the chancellor's lockdown applied even to forgotten valleys.

After several minutes of searching, hope began to fade. He was about to suggest returning to John when something caught his eye—a small structure on a low hill. A temple.

Hope surged.

The three climbed the hill. One of the children from the market had followed at a distance. Shenya noticed but didn't acknowledge it. Shenya silently prayed someone would be inside. To his delight, the door stood ajar.

Inside was an elderly man balanced on a ladder, polishing a tall candlestand.

"Guests?" he said in surprise, climbing down. "Here in Dimig?" He smiled, but the expression faded when he noticed their clothing. His eyes moved from Shenya to Poltoma to Saltho and settled there with the same careful assessment as the villagers outside.

"You all wear garments of the sea tribes."

"I am of the Spee Tribe, actually," Shenya said, bowing politely, "and these two are colleagues who have traveled with me from the sea. We are historians pursuing a research matter.

Our findings appear to connect to the ancient history of your village—specifically, to a prophet named Mishrael and a religious sect connected to her."

The elder studied Saltho for a moment longer before the scholar's framing seemed to settle something in him. History and research were neutral territory. He gestured for them to sit.

"I'm pleased someone is interested in Mishrael," the Elder said, his expression softening. "She's one of our greatest sources of pride. In fact, her story is intertwined with royalty. King Euron's family originates from Dimig, tracing back to her era."

Outside, through the temple's narrow window, Saltho could see the path they'd climbed. The child who had followed them was still there, sitting on a stone wall, watching the door.

"We want to know everything about her," Shenya said. "What can you tell us?"

"According to the stories, celestial beings—called angels—kept her company and taught her many things about living a good and honorable life. She then passed those teachings to the children of the village."

"Do you know how she became connected with the religious sect I mentioned?" Shenya asked.

"Her stories inspired a small group many centuries ago. Their beliefs centered around one particular angel who came to the village and announced the birth of a king. He would one day rule over Marcrituss—his reign would be motivated by peace and goodwill."

Shenya leaned forward. "Do you know anything about her writings? We're searching for a scroll fragment."

The elder's expression shifted—not suspicion exactly, but a careful quality, the way someone looks when they're deciding how much to say. "Not that I can recall," he said at last. "If anything that old existed, it would surely be in the Royal Batnu, I suspect."

Poltoma touched Saltho's arm lightly. Outside the window, two more villagers had joined the child on the path. They weren't moving toward the temple. They were just standing and observing.

Saltho kept his face neutral.

"Is there anything else you remember?" Shenya pressed, aware of the window, aware of the time. "Anything the sect believed or taught?"

The elder nodded slowly, as if making a decision. "There is one saying attributed to the prophet I've always found curious." He recited carefully, as if drawing from memory:

"Seven words for seven children will bring them back to their foundation. When the angels send their vessel... the children will return to Eden."

Shenya felt a jolt of recognition. The phrase clearly did not refer to Mishrael, nor to children. It referred to John and the seven scroll fragments.

"That is very helpful," he said. "Thank you."

The elder smiled kindly. "I wish I could have been of more help. The stories have faded with time."

Shenya thanked him once more, and they rose to leave. At the door, Shenya paused, his hand on the frame, and glanced back.

"One more thing," he said quietly. "We would be grateful if our visit remained between us."

The elder looked at him for a long moment. Then he gave a single nod—the nod of a man who had lived long enough in a forgotten valley to know that some visitors were better forgotten.

Outside, the two villagers on the path had been joined by a

third. They stepped aside to let the three pass, but their eyes followed every step down the hill.

Poltoma grabbed Shenya's arm the moment they were clear. "We need to move."

"Agreed," Shenya said without breaking stride.

Saltho said nothing. He didn't need to. He'd spent his whole life moving through the world protected by a title he no longer had, and the absence of it pressed against him like a cold he hadn't known he was feeling until now. He was simply a sea anuri in enemy clothing in a land village during a lockdown.

Together they headed back toward the water, where they found John and Xerti waiting.

John looked up as they approached. "Any luck?"

Shenya sighed. "Unfortunately, Mishrael and the sect have been lost to time. She's become little more than a children's story."

John's shoulders sagged. "So we came all this way for nothing."

Shenya sat beside him, calm and steady. "No, that's not true. Our visit to Dimig was not fruitless. We met an elder who shared something significant—words ascribed to Mishrael. 'Seven words for seven children will bring them back to their foundation. When the angels send their vessel, the children will return to Eden.'"

John froze, eyes wide. "Did you say, Eden?"

"Yes. The elder said the children would return there."

John stared across the river, mind racing. "In the scriptures from my world, there's a garden called Eden. It was a paradise —created at the beginning of the world, but lost after humanity's first sin."

Shenya nodded thoughtfully. "I suspected that phrase

might hold deeper meaning. It may not help us immediately, but it could prove very important to your mission."

He stood, brushing the dirt from his trousers. "We should return to Brooth. Once we're settled, we can examine everything. The King Euron connection is something I did not know and could prove useful."

"I guess we'll get moving then," John said, getting to his feet. "And going over everything is smart. We're so close. I can feel it."

Shenya smiled. "Remember—you're traveling with two professional treasure hunters." He gestured proudly to himself and Poltoma. "We have a habit of finding difficult items."

Saltho glanced back once at the village on the hill. The figures on the path were still there, small and still in the late afternoon light, watching them go.

He turned away and climbed onto the gropolo without a word.

FORTY-FOUR

The wind rushed past as the gropolo soared between clouds, her powerful wings carrying them steadily toward Brooth.

John waited until the dark had settled in before beginning their descent. If soldiers still patrolled the streets below, he was hopeful the cover of night would protect them.

Slowly and carefully, Xerti glided toward the tower.

As she descended into the den, the other adult gropolo immediately sensed her arrival. A thunderous echo bounced through the massive chamber as the creature shrieked in delight. It leapt onto its perch and called out to Xerti.

Through the window of the passenger box, Shenya spotted a familiar figure hurrying toward them.

"Yumi," he said with relief.

John guided Xerti to a steady landing. Yumi pushed a small staircase against her side and opened the door of the passenger box. As Shenya descended, Yumi rushed forward to wrap him in a crushing embrace.

"Shenya, you old fool!" he laughed. "I can't believe you actually made it back alive!"

Shenya chuckled. "How could you ever doubt me?"

Yumi was about to answer when Poltoma stepped out of the passenger box. He froze, staring at her as if seeing a ghost. "Poltoma? Is that really you?"

Poltoma hurried to him with a wide smile. "Yumi! I'm so glad to see you!"

The massive gropolo shou lifted her off the ground in a joyful hug. "What in the world are you doing here?" Then he noticed Saltho standing behind her. "And who is this?" he asked, nodding.

Poltoma hesitated. "This is my partner," she said, pausing. "Prince Saltho of the Sea Kingdom."

Yumi buried his face in his palm. "You've got to be joking."

Poltoma frowned. "I know he's royal, and from the sea," she said, "but he's a good man." She glanced at Saltho. "Well... he's a good man most of the time."

Saltho gave an awkward half-smile.

Yumi shook his head and sighed. "Come on. All of you—follow me down to my quarters."

Shenya recognized the strange look on Yumi's face. Whenever Yumi wore that expression, something unexpected was about to happen. "Is everything alright?"

"Just follow me."

Yumi led them down the winding staircase of the tower. As they passed one floor, the lively chirping of gropolo chicks filled the air, the creatures fluttering and squealing in their nesting pens.

Farther down, a warm scent drifted through the halls—the smell of roasted herbs and fresh bread filled their noses.

Yumi pushed open the door and gestured for them to enter. Shenya stepped inside first—and froze.

Standing in the center of the room was Jaromei.

"Daughter!" Shenya cried in shock. "What are you doing here?"

Jaromei ran to him and wrapped her arms around him. In that instant, Shenya's breath caught—sharp, and involuntary. His legs went weak; he had to grip her shoulders to keep upright. The realization crashed into him like a physical blow. His chest tightened, and the air felt too thin for words.

"Your grandmother." His voice fractured, barely a whisper. "Did she...?"

Jaromei's eyes filled with tears. "It was only a few days after you left," she said. "She passed peacefully, Father."

Shenya squeezed his eyes shut, tears spilling down his face. His shoulders shook as he forced the words out, his voice breaking under the weight of the loss. "At least her pain is over," he murmured. "She is free now."

John stepped forward quietly. "He will make all things new," he said. "Including her. That's what she believed."

Jaromei turned and embraced him. "I've missed you."

He smiled. "You have no idea how much I missed you, too." He'd forgotten how comforting her embrace was.

Shenya looked between them, then asked, "It's wonderful to see you, Jaromei, but why are you here in Brooth?"

Jaromei bit her lip nervously—the habit she always had when anxious. "Father... what I'm about to say may be a shock."

Shenya sighed and rubbed his forehead. "What happened now?"

"When the elders asked for you to register grandmother's death, I told them you were no longer in Morboli. Because of the lockdown, they suspected you were somehow connected to John."

Shenya nodded slowly.

"They reported it to the chancellor," she continued, "who told the king's chief advisor—and you officially became a wanted man throughout the entire kingdom."

Shenya gave a dry laugh. "I'm actually wanted in both kingdoms now."

Jaromei didn't laugh. Seeing her expression, Shenya softened his tone. "Well... I'm glad you came to Yumi. That must have been a difficult journey alone."

Jaromei shook her head. "I didn't come here alone. I flew here with someone."

The room fell silent.

Shenya frowned. "What? How did—"

"I had nothing left to lose, Father," she interrupted. "So I went to the one person I believed could help you." Jaromei slipped out into the corridor.

Shenya and the others exchanged puzzled looks as faint voices echoed outside. Moments later, she returned, no longer alone. Walking beside her was a woman in elegant robes of pale gray, trimmed with silver thread.

Her posture was regal; her presence commanded the room.

"This," Jaromei announced, "is Princess Qitra... Crown Princess of the Land Kingdom."

A stunned silence fell.

"She knows everything."

Everyone bowed immediately. Even Saltho lowered his head. John hesitated, unsure what to do, then awkwardly copied the others and bowed.

Yumi leaned toward Poltoma and whispered, "Now do you understand why your boyfriend surprised me? I have royalty from two kingdoms standing in my tower."

Poltoma elbowed him lightly.

Shenya stepped forward, bowing respectfully. "Princess, it is an honor. I am Shenya Arjik Spee, Jaromei's father. This is my colleague, Poltoma Olmok Neulaw. With her is her partner—Prince Saltho of the Sea Kingdom."

At Saltho's name, the princess raised one eyebrow.

"And this young man," Shenya continued, placing his hands on John's shoulders, "is John Arjik—the Traveller."

Jaromei's eyes widened when she heard her father had given John the Arjik name, but shock quickly turned to joy. John caught her smile.

"My Lady," Shenya continued, "I know his presence must come as a shock. But John is no enemy. He has been given a divine mission. Regardless of what you may have heard happened in Marciluk, he has not come to cause harm. Since his arrival, I have assisted him in his work." He paused a moment and said, "and I have also claimed him as my kin."

Princess Qitra stepped closer and studied John, examining his face and posture with quiet curiosity. "This is extraordinary," she murmured. Her voice held no fear—only fascination.

"It is good to meet you, John Arjik. But there is something I must discuss with you in private." She turned toward the door. "Please follow me."

John looked at Shenya uncertainly. Shenya gave him a nod of encouragement. John tipped his head and followed the princess down the corridor.

When they reached her chamber, Qitra opened the door and gestured for him to enter first. The room was dimly lit—she'd chosen to illuminate it with small candles. Their golden light danced across the stone walls.

She closed the door and released a long breath. "My apologies for requesting privacy," she said. "But I do not know

Prince Saltho, and I must confess I am deeply wary of anyone connected to King Rathrian."

John shrugged. "Well, we didn't get off to a good start either. And technically, he isn't a prince anymore. He lost his title when he helped us escape his father."

Qitra blinked. "Is that so?" Her expression softened. "Then he has risen considerably in my estimation." She folded her hands. "Jaromei has told me everything she knows—about the portal, your arrival, your mission, and the dangers you face." She studied him again. "Until today, I never believed that life existed beyond our world. I find it remarkable that I have never heard of this network of portals."

John chuckled. "I guess the guardians of this world have been doing a good job."

Her expression grew serious. "My father did not order the lockdown, nor did he accuse you. It was Ilmly, his advisor. He has been acting monarch for months. My father is gravely ill." Her voice dropped. "But in recent days, Ilmly has begun behaving in ways I cannot explain. It's as if... he's become someone else."

John nodded grimly. "That's exactly what happened. I believe the real Ilmly may be dead. This will sound unbelievable, but the entity controlling him is a demon."

"A demon?" Qitra snickered and looked at John as if he might be crazy.

He looked her in the eye. "Ilmly and Rathrian tried to kill me and turn the entire Sea Kingdom against me and you."

The princess said nothing for a moment, then lowered her head. "If Ilmly is truly gone, it is a tragedy. He was once a good and honorable man." She added quietly, "I will ensure that his family is cared for."

John saw the sadness in her eyes, but she quickly composed herself.

"Regardless," she continued, "the governors have agreed that I will serve as acting monarch." She looked at him firmly. "Which means I will be ending the lockdown tomorrow."

John blinked in surprise.

"I will also formally retract the charges against you and Shenya. Your names will be cleared throughout the Land Kingdom." Her voice softened. "You will be known not as enemies... but as friends."

John could barely believe it. "Why are you helping me?"

"The entire planet knows what happened in Marciluk, John Arjik. And I know Rathrian well. If you are an enemy of his, that makes you my friend."

John laughed, but it was fleeting. He hadn't realized news of the spectacle in Marciluk had spread across Marcrituss. The thought made his stomach twist.

"I am not as far removed from your story as you might think," the Princess continued, stepping toward a small wooden chest. "I may not have known about the portals, but I have always known something about the scroll. It comes from Mishrael."

John froze. "How could you possibly know about the prophet Mishrael?"

"My family traces its roots directly back to Dimig," Qitra explained. "Many centuries ago, one of my ancestors founded the religious group Jaromei told me you've been studying. It was built on the teachings of Mishrael."

John stared at her. "We literally just left Dimig today. Our research led us there to search for the scroll fragment."

"Well, your research led you in the right direction," she said, opening the chest. Inside was a small felt pouch. "My ancestor was the one who received the message from the angel announcing the birth of the anuri-God... the King above all gods. He himself was a descendant of Mishrael and became the first King of the Land Kingdom."

She handed the pouch to John. He carefully opened it, handling the contents with reverence. Inside was a fragment of the scroll—about the size of his palm. The surface felt smooth and ancient, yet unlike anything he'd ever touched.

As he held it, the fragment began to glow—soft at first, then brighter. Like a quiet heartbeat of light awakening within it.

Princess Qitra gasped, hand to her heart. "That is proof enough that this fragment is the one you seek."

John looked up at her in astonishment. "Your family had the fragment all this time?"

Qitra nodded. "A family heirloom, passed down through generations... but no one has ever truly understood what it is. We thought it was just a relic connected to the first King."

John laughed softly in wonder. "I'm really glad Jaromei decided to find you."

"When Jaromei came to Jyr demanding an audience, she told me everything." She gestured at the pouch. "I realized my family may possess exactly what you were searching for."

John listened, not surprised Jaromei had been bold enough to demand a royal audience. "You have no idea how important this fragment is," he said. "Thank you... truly. I thought I might never find it."

He placed the glowing piece of the scroll back inside the felt bag.

The light died the instant the felt closed around it.

Then something passed through the room—not wind, not sound, but a disturbance in the air itself. The candles guttered simultaneously. Outside, somewhere beyond the ordinary darkness of the Brooth night, something cried out through the veil. Not with a voice, but with a quality of ancient disturbance, as though something vast and watchful had felt a shift in the cosmos without knowing its source or its meaning.

Above them, in the gropolo den, every bird screamed at once.

The tower shook.

Dust fell from the ceiling in a thin curtain. A clay cup on the desk slid and shattered on the floor. Then stillness—sudden and absolute, as though the world had caught its breath.

John held the pouch tightly. Something had felt the fragment wake—felt a change ripple outward across worlds without knowing where it came from or why.

Qitra stood motionless, her hand pressed flat against the desk. She didn't ask what it was. She didn't need to. John had spoken of demons. Of Ilmly. Of a darkness that moved through men and turned kingdoms against themselves. She had listened carefully and said nothing—the way you listen to something you aren't yet ready to believe.

She believed it now.

He tucked the pouch carefully inside his pocket.

Whatever had stirred out there in the dark, it was still searching.

When she finally spoke, her voice was quieter than before. "I believe my destiny may be intertwined with yours, Traveller." She held his gaze. "More than I understood when you first walked through that door." She paused a moment. "I will give you this piece—and whatever else you may require in the future."

"That's incredible. How can I—"

"But only if you give me something in return," Qitra interjected. "I'm afraid that I cannot simply hand it over to you."

John looked up, shocked at her demand. A cold thread of worry wound through him. He thought of the scroll fragment, the mission, everything that depended on this moment. "I don't have anything of value, Princess." His voice was steady, but only just. "I'm a teenager from another world. I don't have gold, or land, or anything a princess would want." He held her gaze. "But whatever I can give you—I will."

Qitra studied him for a long moment, her expression unreadable. Then, slowly, she smiled. "It is not that kind of payment, John." She stepped closer. "Earlier today, I received a transmission from Marciluk—a trusted spy sent it to me." Her expression darkened. "He witnessed everything you did down in the city. He said it was... miraculous. It's clear King Rathrian is using you to justify a dangerous consolidation of power."

John nodded grimly. "He already tried."

"And he will try again," she said. "If Rathrian succeeds, he'll transform the Sea Kingdom into a dictatorship. Without a doubt, he'll turn his ambitions toward the land. If that day comes and he brings war to our Kingdom, I ask that you stand with us. That you will defend us. That is the payment I require."

After hearing everything Qitra promised, it didn't feel like a request John could refuse. But he also allowed himself the hope that day might never come.

John placed his hand over the pouch containing the fragment. "You have my word."

Qitra inclined her head. "Good. Tomorrow I will return to my father's court." She walked to the window, gazing out over the sleeping city of Brooth. "A royal decree clearing both you and Shenya will be issued before nightfall. By evening, the entire kingdom will know the truth." She turned and met his eyes. "But do not worry. I will never reveal anything about the portal or its location."

Gratitude surged through him. "Princess. I don't know how to thank you for everything you've done."

Qitra smiled. "You already have." She gestured toward the

door. "You should return to your kin and share this news with him."

John nodded, bowed slightly, and left the chamber.

Alone in the corridor, he pressed the pouch to his chest, feeling the weight of all that had changed in his life. The old comforts were gone, but in their absence, something new had begun—a shared resolve, a promise, an alliance born of necessity and trust. Hope, fragile but real, flickered to life once more.

FORTY-FIVE

As the door clicked shut behind John, Qitra stood motionless in the dim chamber. Candlelight flickered long shadows across the stone walls. She exhaled slowly, her mind swirling with the weight of what had transpired. The Traveller—John Arjik—was far more than the rumors suggested: earnest, resolute, and touched by a power she could barely comprehend. Yet, as she reflected, doubt crept in. Had she truly acted wisely in securing his promise?

She crossed to the desk and withdrew a transmission box —sleek, rune-etched, another artifact from her family's vault. It ensured secure communication, safe from interception. She'd received her spy's earlier message, but with the deal struck, she needed an update. The tides of power were shifting faster than she'd expected.

Placing the box on the desk, Qitra murmured the activation phrase. A moment later, the familiar voice of Alovo, her most trusted informant embedded deep in Marciluk's shadows, came through.

"Princess," Alovo greeted, his voice a hushed rasp. "I feared you might call. Events here accelerate beyond our predictions."

"Speak plainly, Alovo," Qitra replied, her tone steady despite the knot of unease in her chest. "What of Rathrian?"

He answered grimly. "As we suspected, he invoked his emergency powers mere hours after the... incident. The government has been dismissed—scattered like chaff. He's already pushing forward candidates for the vacant seats, all of them loyal to the crown."

Qitra's eyes narrowed. "And the people?"

"Rallying, my lady. The spectacle—the fire, the sea parting —it ignited a fervor. Many see the boy as a threat that can only be fought by centralizing Rathrian's rule. The king made his case, and I think he was successful. Whispers of unity under his banner grow louder by the hour."

She leaned forward, fingers tracing the box's edge. "And the blockade?"

"Just beginning to stir. The creatures are dispersing, but slowly. Rathrian has ordered the capture and domestication of the largest beasts—their hides like armored stone. They could serve in battle, bolstering his forces beyond imagination."

The thought sent a chill down Qitra's spine. The last sea battle had been centuries ago.

"Sea dragons would be like baby gropolos compared to whatever that boy summoned," Alovo murmured, voice quavering.

"This is something we must monitor," Qitra replied.

"Princess... after that girl showed up, you said there was a strong chance you might meet him. Perhaps he should be made aware of the consequences of wielding such power. His actions saved his friends, but they've unleashed a storm upon us all."

Qitra considered, gaze drifting to the window where

Brooth's lights twinkled in the distance. "Yes, I met him tonight. But the events that transpired were not the boy's fault. He only hastened the inevitable. Rathrian's ambitions were a tide destined to crash—he merely broke the dam sooner."

Alovo's gasp was audible. "What do you intend to do? I think, my lady, we are outnumbered."

"We are not defeated yet. And there is hope for us."

"Unless you've found a hidden army, then..." Alovo's words trailed off in despair; he knew too well how powerful Rathrian's troops were.

"I made a deal with the boy."

"Why would he agree to help us? Is there a catch?"

"I gave him something he sought desperately. In return, he gave his word: should war come to our shores, he will stand with the Land Kingdom. If he can summon for us what he summoned in the sea, we may stand a chance."

Alovo exhaled, relief and concern etched in his tone. "A bold move, Princess. May it prove fruitful."

"I must go. Godspeed, Alovo."

When the transmission ended, Qitra turned back to the window and the distant lights of Brooth. Alone in the quiet chamber, her thoughts ran deep.

A ruler must lead with their head rather than their heart—her father's voice, patient and certain, flooded her mind. *Sentiment alone does not secure a kingdom's future.*

He was right. He had always been right.

She thought of the boy's face when she named her price. The way his hands had stilled. He hadn't flinched or bargained —just said quietly that he would give whatever he could. That kind of answer didn't come from political strategy. It came from somewhere older than politics.

She thought of the girl, too—exhausted, travel-stained,

asking nothing for herself. Jaromei hadn't bargained or begged. She'd told the truth and trusted Qitra to hear it.

Qitra turned back to the window.

The fragment was safe. The promise was real. The alliance was necessary, and she had secured it—cleanly, without deception, without force. She had given something of great value and received something of equal value in return. That was not cruelty. That was governance.

And yet.

Qitra pressed her fingers briefly to the empty chest, now closed on the table behind her. John was only doing his duty, but so was she. She did what had to be done. She let the feeling be what it was—not quite regret, not quite peace—and did not try to resolve it.

Rathrian's attack was always coming. The Landers never stood a chance against the Sea's enormous military. But with John on their side, at least they had hope. And she resolved that when war came—and it would come—she would fight not just for the kingdom, but for people like Jaromei and John.

CHAPTER

FORTY-SIX

Inside Yumi's flat, the others were busy preparing supper. The rich smell of roasted vegetables and herbs filled the room.

John caught Shenya's eye, tilting his head to signal him. Sensing the urgency, he and John slipped into an empty room.

"What did the princess say?" Shenya asked eagerly.

John could barely contain his excitement. Without a word, he handed over the small felt pouch.

Shenya opened it, gasped, and studied the fragment. "Is that... what I think it is?"

John grinned. "She gave me the scroll fragment from Marcrituss."

Shenya's eyes shone with awe.

"And she cleared both of us of all charges," John added.

Shenya closed his eyes, exhaling in relief. "How did such a treasure come into her possession?"

"The first king of the Land Kingdom was the one who got the angel's message in Dimig. The fragment's been in their family ever since."

Shenya recalled the elder from Dimig saying the King's family line began in that valley. "We were on the right track. I knew it! A few more days and we would have made that connection." He clapped his hands, delighted. "Jaromei, of course, always finds a more direct way," he added with a chuckle. Excitement brightened his face. "Then your mission on Marcrituss is complete!"

John shook his head. "Not quite."

"What do you mean? You have the fragment."

John sighed. "In return, I had to promise I'd help her if Rathrian attacks the Land Kingdom."

Shenya placed a reassuring hand on his arm. "That's a concern for another day," he said. "For now, you should celebrate what you've accomplished."

"Wait," John said, searching for the right words. "Are you really alright? You must be upset, hearing about your mother."

Shenya smiled at him and squeezed John's shoulder. "I'll be okay, John. I've had many months to prepare my heart for this day. Of course, I'll miss her. But I'm relieved she's at peace now. I know she'll always be with me."

John saw the lingering sadness in Shenya's eyes, but knew nothing more needed to be said.

The two left the room and rejoined the others. Even Princess Qitra joined them for supper. Yumi and Jina had prepared a feast far greater than anyone expected—bowls of roasted vegetables, fresh bread, river fish, and warm herbal stew.

Before long, laughter and conversation filled the room again. For the first time in days, everyone allowed themselves to relax.

LATER, as the gathering quieted and laughter faded to low conversation, Jaromei watched John from across the room, her nerves taut and heart heavy. He was just one of many things she'd been emotionally exhausted over. The weight of her grandmother's death, days spent running, risking everything for the princess—all of it weighed heavily on her.

She slipped over and touched his arm. "Come with me," she said, her voice softer than usual.

Jaromei led the way to the gropolo den. Xerti was already curled up, fast asleep—a small anchor in a world that wouldn't stop shifting. Above them, the night sky stretched endlessly. Stars glittered like scattered jewels. For days, she'd stared up at those same stars, wondering if John and her father were safe— if the worlds had swallowed them, too.

She reached for John's hand, holding it carefully, as if he might vanish if she let go. "I thought about you a lot while you were gone," she admitted, her words thin with emotion. "I missed you."

It felt like such a small thing to say, compared to what was storming inside her.

John squeezed her hand, warmth returning to her fingers. "I missed you too. And we have the scroll fragment because of you. If you hadn't gone to find the princess... I don't even want to think about it."

She managed a smile. "Someone's looking out for us after all." But the smile faded as quickly as it came, a shadow of worry sliding back into place.

As she looked up at the stars again, she searched for the courage she needed to say what she had rehearsed in her mind a hundred times. Now that he was there—safe, real—the enormity of what he was, of what she might lose, settled over her anew. No matter how close she drew, he'd always belong partly to another world.

"Now that you have the first piece of the scroll... what happens next?" she asked, bracing for the answer she feared.

John leaned in beside her, still gazing at the endless sky. "I suppose I wait for Danrael to tell me where to go next." He turned, catching the worry she couldn't hide. "What is it? Is something wrong?"

She hesitated, biting her lip, her words tangled in the knot of fear and hope inside her. The more she cared, the more terrified she became of another loss. "While I was on my own mission, I had time to think. The enormity of your role as the Traveller really sank in."

It barely touched the truth, but it was a start.

John's pulse quickened. "Talk to me."

With her thumb, she traced a small circle on his hand, grounding herself. "I started wondering if either of us can actually do this, John. I know I said we could, but..." Her voice trailed off, a dozen memories rushing in—her grandmother's death, the emptiness of her house, her father's tired eyes, the void she felt when John left. "I kept asking myself if any amount of strength is enough for this."

"We can, Jaromei. We—"

She cut him off, her voice barely more than a whisper. "Could we really manage being apart for weeks, months, maybe even years at a time?" She didn't look away. If he was going to promise her anything, she needed to see it in his eyes.

"Don't give up on us before we've even started," John said gently.

She shook her head—not to deny him, but to steady herself. "I'm not giving up. But we have to be honest about how hard it's going to be. I just... I need to know we're not pretending it'll all be easy." She squeezed his hands, feeling the roughness that hadn't been there before, the way he'd changed. Hope was dangerous, but losing it would be worse.

John took her hands in his, his touch gentle and steady. "If you give me the chance, I'll give everything I can to us. The mission matters, but you won't get pushed aside."

More than anything, she wanted to believe him—wanted to let herself trust him. "You've got one fragment, but there are six more. You'll leave Marcrituss, then another world, and another. When it's finally over, will you come back to me?" Her voice was steady, but inside, she braced for heartbreak.

John reached out, brushing her cheek, moving closer until their foreheads nearly touched. "If you're willing to wait for me," he said, "then there's no question. I'll come back. I promise."

She closed her eyes, letting the promise take root. For a moment, she let herself believe in a future, against all odds. "I'll wait," she whispered.

The den was quiet except for Xerti's slow breathing and the distant sound of the sea.

John became aware of it gradually—the way you notice music that's been playing all along. Xerti's heartbeat, low and steady beneath her feathers. The chicks somewhere below, their small, quick pulses like scattered rain. Then he could hear the whole tower breathing around them—Shenya, Yumi, Poltoma, Jina—every heartbeat distinct and present, as if the walls had dissolved and he could feel each living thing inside them.

Then further. The village beyond. The labyrinth. The sea.

He felt the world pulse outward in every direction. He wasn't reaching for it. It was just there—everything connected, everything alive, everything moving in its own particular rhythm.

And then, somewhere at the edge of it all, vast and unhurried—the stars. Their motion so slow it was almost stillness. Almost.

He felt one, distant and streaking, already moving fast through the dark.

I wonder, he thought, *if I could make it shoot right here.*

He reached—not desperate, not afraid, just curious—the way he'd reached for the stone in Shenya's garden. Only this time, something happened.

A streak of brilliant white tore across the sky directly above the den.

Jaromei gasped, head tilting back in wonder.

John stared. Then a slow grin spread across his face. He sat up slightly straighter. He cleared his throat.

"On my world," he said, with what he considered admirable casualness, "when you see one of those—you make a wish." He paused. "That was me, by the way."

Jaromei turned to look at him. There was a long moment of silence.

"You moved a star," she said.

"I just nudged it," John corrected.

"You nudged a star." She was trying very hard not to smile. "And then told me about it immediately." She laughed—a real one, sudden and bright—and shook her head. Then she looked at him, still smiling, and something in her expression shifted. Quieter. More certain.

"What did you wish for?" she asked softly.

John looked at her for a long moment.

He didn't answer.

"You said back in Morboli that we might have a chance someday," he said instead. "Now that I've finished this part of my mission, maybe we can start now?"

For the first time, the tightness in her chest loosened. A real smile broke free, wider than she'd managed in days. "Yeah," she breathed, leaning in. "I think we can."

John leaned in, about to kiss her—

Suddenly, the light of a bright lantern flooded the den.

"You two! Out of here!"

Yumi stood at the top of the stairs, scowling down. "It's time for bed! The only creatures allowed to mate in my den are gropolos!"

Jaromei startled, then burst out laughing—her worries dissolving into embarrassment and delight. She caught John's hand as they hurried past Yumi, both of them grinning, heartbeats lighter than before.

THAT NIGHT, as Jaromei settled into her room, she replayed the scene beneath the stars—her doubts, her honesty, the promise in John's eyes. The ache and the hope lived side by side in her chest, but for now, hope was winning.

Down the corridor, John was also thinking about everything he carried in his heart. His room had a small balcony overlooking the city. He paused at the edge, bracing his hands on the cool stone railing as the evening breeze washed over him. From below, the sounds of a distant gathering drifted upward—laughter, music, the steady rhythm of life carrying on, even as everything in his own world had changed.

He breathed in deeply and let it out slowly. In his jacket pocket, the scroll fragment weighed heavily—a token of destiny, the proof of all he had endured. On Marcrituss, he had been hunted, tested, transformed. He'd seen kingdoms teeter on the edge of war, watched his friends risk everything, seen terror and awe written on the face of a king who had tried to destroy him.

He thought of the roar of the crowd in Marciluk, the blinding surge of power, the terror and awe in Rathrian's eyes

—all of it felt impossibly distant, as if he were peering into someone else's life.

He thought of Dernoah. He had only known her a day—and yet something about her had settled in him like a stone dropping through still water. The warmth of her sunroom. The frankness of her. The way she spoke about dying was the way most people spoke about an inconvenience—something to be got through before the real thing began.

And Shenya hadn't been there when she died.

Because of him.

John gripped the railing. He hadn't let himself think it directly until that moment, but there in the quiet, it was unavoidable. Shenya had been at his side, doing what the mission required, while his mother slipped away without him. John had no way to know it would happen. That didn't change what it was.

He thought, without quite meaning to, of his grandfather. The long suffering. The faith that had seemed to count for nothing against the plain facts of a body failing. John had sat with him in that room and made his quiet verdict: if this is what belief looks like at the end, he wanted no part of it.

But Dernoah had also been in pain. He had seen it—the careful way she moved, the effort behind her smile. She was not spared anything. And yet she had spoken about the Traveller coming as though it were a gift she had been waiting to unwrap. She had died, as far as he could tell, without bitterness. Without the sense that she had been let down.

He didn't know what to do with that.

Eleven days ago, he had been lying on a gravel road, wondering why the universe didn't care. Now he had watched a planet bow at the sound of a name. He had seen light spoken into being from nothing. He had met people on a world that had never heard of Earth who were nevertheless waiting—

generation after generation—for the same God his mother had told him about at bedtime.

No matter how hard he tried, he couldn't make the old argument work anymore. But the pieces no longer fit the way they used to. He wasn't ready to call it faith. He didn't know what to call it. It sat in his chest, unresolved, neither belief nor disbelief but something restless in between—the feeling of a door he hadn't decided yet whether to open.

After a while, John slipped back inside and lay on his bed. The weight of survival, of everything his friends and he had faced, finally crashed over him. For days, he'd kept moving, never allowing himself to feel it all and process it. Now, with nowhere left to run, he let himself feel the enormity of it—the mission, his physical transformation, the trials and triumphs.

Tears spilled out, silent and unstoppable. He pressed his palms to his face, sobbing—not from weakness, but from the sheer, overwhelming immensity of it all. He wept until the knot in his chest loosened, until his breathing slowed and the ache inside him softened.

Gradually, he rolled onto his back and let his mind drift. He remembered the night sky—Jaromei by his side, the hush between them, the steady shimmer of the stars overhead.

That memory wrapped around him, gentle and bright, and a quiet hope settled where the ache had been. Whatever came next, he had this moment, and the peace it brought.

FORTY-SEVEN

J ohn saw flashes of a world consumed by war. Cities burned beneath bruised, smoke-choked skies, while armies clashed across fields that once were green. Crowds of terrified people ran through the chaos. Buildings collapsed, flames devoured streets, the air thick with the roar of destruction and the cries of the dying.

He knew at once: this was not Marcrituss, nor Earth. It was a world he'd never seen before.

Through the chaos, Danrael's voice rang out, urgent and clear:

"You must go to Spaltrico as soon as possible. The guardian of that world's portal is in danger. He needs you. Their world needs you."

As the angel spoke, the visions only sharpened—fires raging, soldiers locked in desperate struggle, towers toppling as panic rippled outward.

He jolted awake, gasping for breath as though he'd broken the surface of deep water. His heart pounded as the images clung to him—fire, fear, a world teetering on the brink.

Sitting upright in the darkness, John pressed a hand to his chest. It was no dream. This was how Danrael revealed the next mission—and it was urgent.

John glanced at the window. The sky beyond was still dark, a faint, uncertain blue hovering on the horizon. The message was clear:

A new mission was calling.

He slipped from bed, moving quietly down the corridor. In Shenya's room, he leaned over the crescent-shaped bed, nudging his friend gently.

Shenya's eyes flew open, startled.

John managed a soft laugh. "Relax. It's only me."

Shenya blinked, rubbing sleep from his face. "What is it? It's barely light yet."

"Danrael came to me again," John said, voice low and urgent. "It was a dream, but it wasn't just a dream."

Shenya was instantly alert, lowering the side panel of his bed. "What did he say?"

"I have to leave Marcrituss."

Shenya swung his legs to the floor. "I'm coming with you."

"Shenya, Jaromei needs you here."

"You need me," Shenya replied, firm and gentle at once.

John hesitated. "I don't even know if anyone else can pass through the portal. Danrael never said."

"Then we'll find out," Shenya said, already dressing. "What else did Danrael tell you?"

"I have to go to a world called Spaltrico. The guardian is in danger."

Shenya gathered supplies as he spoke. "I suspect it's connected to what happened yesterday. This happened only one day after the chaos in Marciluk. That's no coincidence."

"Do you think it's Revonat?"

"I don't know," Shenya admitted. He moved into Yumi's

sitting room and grabbed a bag. "I do know this—no one should have to face something like this alone. We need to go to the portal right away."

A voice called from the kitchen doorway. "What are you talking about?"

Jaromei stood holding a steaming cup, worry etched in her eyes. John saw, in the way she gripped the mug, that she was bracing herself for more bad news.

John approached her, taking her hands—warm, trembling slightly. "Jaromei, Danrael came to me," Their conversation the night before flashed in his mind. "I'm so sorry, but I have to leave again. I'm needed on another world."

She stared as the color drained from her cheeks. "You only just came back last night!"

"Jaromei," Shenya said gently, "please don't be angry, but I've decided to go with him. John needs someone at his side."

Jaromei averted his gaze. Sadness pressed in—tired, heavy, and familiar. How many goodbyes had there been already? Each one left a new bruise.

Shenya reached out, but she stood there, shoulders squared in that way she'd learned from loss. "I can't let him go alone," he continued softly. "And you know you must fulfill your duty as guardian here. The portal's gone unguarded too long already."

Before Jaromei could respond, Princess Qitra stepped into the room, her presence commanding. None of them had heard her approach.

"You will not be left alone either," Qitra said.

The words surprised Jaromei. She turned, blinking in confusion, as if seeing the princess for the first time.

"There is something you should hear," Qitra continued, her voice calm but weighted. "It's not public yet, but in the coming months, my father will abdicate the throne."

The room seemed to tilt, the air thickening.

"He must step down before the illness takes his mind completely," Qitra continued. "When that happens, I will become queen. I want you to be my Royal Advisor, Jaromei."

Jaromei's mind reeled. The kingdom—the future—felt a thousand miles wide and utterly unfamiliar.

"My lady... I would be honored to serve you, but how could I possibly be of any help?"

As she spoke the words, a wave of doubt and awe washed through her. She'd trained all her life for duty as a guardian, for loyalty to family, not for court intrigue and politics. The ache of Dernoah's absence flickered in her chest; she wished, sharply, for her grandmother's steady advice. Right before she died, Dernoah had taken her hand. *You were made for more than guarding a portal,* she'd said. *The portal keeps the world connected to something larger. So will you—in ways neither of us can see yet. Don't be afraid of the size of it.* Jaromei hadn't known what she meant. She was beginning to understand now.

Qitra smiled faintly. "The past few days have already given you experience beyond the borders of this world. You're involved in things most people cannot even imagine."

Jaromei's mind flashed back to the desperate journey to Jyr, the fear and resolve braided together in every decision she'd made. Maybe that was enough.

Qitra folded her hands. "And you have persistence. Need I remind you of the episode outside my tower?"

Jaromei found herself letting out a quiet laugh, tension bleeding off her shoulders. That moment—running through the rain, the guards in pursuit seemed almost absurd, a reminder she could survive more than she thought.

Qitra met her gaze. "I need someone I can trust, who knows the mind of the people. Someone who will speak honestly and help me navigate what lies ahead. Over these days, you've proven you're worthy of such a task."

A rush of emotion caught Jaromei off guard—relief, pride, the dizzying sense that she was being seen for who she was, not just for what she could do. Her voice shook. "My lady... I would be honored."

"You may remain in Morboli," Qitra added. "Your duty as guardian must continue. We'll make arrangements so you can fulfill both roles."

As Shenya wrapped her in a tight embrace, Jaromei's composure finally slipped. She pressed her face against his shoulder, and in that instant, the joy of it—Royal Advisor, a future, her own path—turned briefly sharp.

Grandmother should have been here for this. She would have laughed, said something outrageous, squeezed my hand too hard.

The grief and the gratitude arrived together, inseparable, and Jaromei let them both in. She clung to her father, heart pounding with the ache of another impending farewell, but also with something brighter. Maybe this was her calling—a way to serve, to build something lasting, to be more than just someone waiting for others to return.

She would wait for John, however long it took. But now, she would also shape her own future.

The princess left to gather her things. Once ready, they all headed up to the den, where Yumi was bustling about with Poltoma and Saltho.

As soon as they entered, Yumi eyed their bags. "Let me guess—you're off again, and you need a gropolo."

Shenya shrugged. "I'm afraid so. Can you give us a ride to Morboli?"

"Right now? Can you wait a few hours? I've got chores—"

Qitra stepped forward, her tone leaving no room for debate. "Yumi, I know this is inconvenient, but the situation is urgent. They need transport to Morboli, and then I'll need you to take me to Jyr. I'll make sure you're compensated."

Yumi bowed low. "It's an honor, Princess, and I don't need payment. But now Shenya owes me two holidays at his place on the coast. I'm bringing my kids, too."

"Thank you, Yumi," Qitra said, her gratitude genuine. "Your kindness won't be forgotten."

With Poltoma and Saltho's help, they quickly secured a larger passenger box to Xerti's harness—one designed for five. No one said much as they checked the fittings.

When it was time, John and Shenya turned to say their goodbyes.

"I can't believe you're leaving again, Shenya," Poltoma said, hugging him tight. "We just reconnected."

He returned the embrace, warmth in his voice. "At least you're on land again. I'll be back soon, and then we can reminisce properly. For now, I need to try going through the portal with John. He needs me."

Poltoma smiled, a glint of envy in her eyes. She turned to John, squeezing his hands. "We'll be waiting for you both. Be careful—and don't have too much fun without us."

"Prince Saltho," Qitra called. "I may have a job for you, if you're interested."

Saltho looked up in surprise. "My lady, I'd be honored to help in any way I can."

"Good," Qitra said, a faint smile touching her lips. "We'll be in touch."

Once everyone was settled, Yumi climbed into the shou's seat and guided Xerti skyward. With a powerful beat of her wings, Xerti soared into the morning.

Out the window, John watched the world shrink below. Far off, he could trace the path he and Shenya had taken to Brooth. It felt unreal how much had changed since then.

His hand slipped to the felt bag in his pocket, fingers closing around the scroll fragment. Gratitude welled up.

But the task ahead loomed—six fragments more, and a universe still in peril. He could barely imagine facing it alone. He hoped Shenya would be allowed to travel to Spaltrico with him.

Yumi handled Xerti with effortless skill. The gropolo glided across the sky faster than John could have dreamed. They reached Morboli in under an hour.

Yumi guided Xerti to a secluded clearing near the labyrinth. Once landed, the shou's massive head dipped toward John, her dark eyes brimmed with sadness. John stepped close, laying a hand on her neck.

"It won't be long," he promised gently. "I'll come back."

Jaromei led John, Shenya, and Qitra through the winding labyrinth to the hidden cave. At the entrance, Qitra eyed the rope descending into darkness. Though older than the others, she hesitated only briefly before gripping the rope and climbing down.

To her own surprise, she made the descent easily.

When she reached the cavern floor, she paused in awe. Ancient columns loomed like silent guardians. The massive obelisk-shaped portal glimmered at the chamber's heart.

"This place feels sacred," Qitra whispered, her voice full of wonder.

As John entered, the portal's strange pull stirred inside him. Qitra watched as he studied the enormous dial at the base, searching for the symbol that meant Spaltrico.

Carefully, he turned the dial to align with their destination.

Then he saw something unexpected.

There was no symbol for "Earth."

Instead, the sign for his world was instantly recognizable.

Eden.

John remembered the Dimig elder's words: *The children will return to Eden.*

The name hit him like a physical thing. Eden. Not a myth, not a metaphor—a place. His place. He'd grown up hearing the story of the Fall as something ancient and distant. Standing here, his hand on the portal, he understood for the first time that it was also his story. Everyone's story. The separation hadn't ended. It was still happening.

He had no time to explain now. But the word stayed with him as he turned the dial.

"Everyone should step back," John said, voice steady.

He set his hand on the portal's circular center.

A moment later, the mechanism whirred to life—a beam of red light shot outward, swelling into a glowing triangular gateway.

The Marcritans stood mesmerized—especially Shenya, who had studied the portal for years but had never seen it activated.

John turned toward him.

"Shenya... we still don't know if you'll be able to pass through. If you can't—"

"Don't say goodbye," Shenya said, cutting him off. "I have faith I'll be let through, and you should too."

John nodded, then turned to Jaromei.

He leaned in to kiss her cheek. Her breath caught—sharp and involuntary. In the next instant, her arms were around him, fierce and desperate. She pressed her lips to his, not gently, but as if trying to imprint the memory of him into her very bones, refusing to let him go.

When she finally released him, her eyes blazed, breath ragged. There were no words left.

Qitra smiled at the two of them, quietly delighted by this meeting of worlds.

Shenya took his daughter into a tight embrace.

Then he and John turned to Qitra, nodding respectfully to the future queen.

The two men exchanged a final, steady glance.

And side by side, they stepped into the portal.

CHAPTER
FORTY-EIGHT

John basked in the peace and serenity of portal travel. The passage between worlds wrapped around him like a quiet tide, filling him with a calm he recognized from his first journey.

The two tumbled through a tunnel of shimmering white light and landed hard on rough stone. A moment later, the portal behind them folded inward and vanished, leaving only silence.

When John opened his eyes, he was relieved to see his friend and kin beside him.

For a few seconds, neither man moved.

Dim light seeped through narrow cracks above the cave, gray and insufficient. The air hung heavy and still, carrying the cold scent of stone untouched by sunlight for ages.

John pushed himself upright and glanced at Shenya. "You made it!" he said, reaching over to give Shenya an affectionate shove.

"I must say, the ride was quite unusual—but oddly comforting," Shenya replied, brushing dust from his clothes.

The peaceful feeling faded quickly.

A strange sensation crept over John's senses. It was disturbingly familiar—the same uneasy awareness that always stirred when Revonat was near. Yet something about it was different.

John closed his eyes. He couldn't detect a single lurking presence; instead, the feeling was broader, deeper, as though the darkness belonged to the world itself. It lay over everything like weather—heavy, suffocating, woven into the very air he breathed.

He glanced at Shenya, who seemed perfectly at ease, but John felt the wrongness cling to him. It pressed against his chest—nameless and vast. Something was deeply, fundamentally wrong with the place—not with the stone or the air, but something beneath all of it. Something that made his skin prickle and his breath catch.

"Is something wrong?" Shenya asked, stepping closer.

John opened his eyes. "No, something isn't right here," he said.

Before Shenya could respond, a familiar voice echoed through the cavern.

"Welcome to Spaltrico."

Both men turned at once.

Danrael stood a short distance away, as though he'd simply stepped from the shadows. He appeared now with Spaltrican features—pale yellow skin, hair white as frost, and deep emerald green eyes.

Shenya blinked in surprise, relief flickering in his eyes despite the circumstances.

"Shenya," Danrael said calmly, "you have been called to assist the Traveller in a very special way—closer than any other. But first, do you understand what you're undertaking?

The trials ahead will be far more difficult than what you've faced before."

Shenya nodded without hesitation. "I understand, and I promise, I'll do all I can to help him."

Danrael inclined his head. "Then receive this gift, Shenya—the gift of tongues; the gift of languages."

He lifted his hand gently over Shenya's head and murmured a quiet prayer. A moment later, he lowered his hand again.

"Like John, you will now be able to communicate with all those on the worlds you visit."

Something settled within Shenya's heart. From this point, he and John would walk this path together.

"What do we need to know about this world?" John asked. The fires from his dream still flickered at the edge of his memory.

"This world is incredibly advanced in many ways," Danrael replied, "but not in morality. A powerful cult dominates here."

John and Shenya both flinched. From somewhere above, the distant sound of explosions cut through the silence.

"They sacrifice others to appease their deities—demons masquerading as gods," Danrael continued. "I have asked the missing guardian's mother to meet you here. She will guide your next steps. Do what you can to save her son, Eamin."

"We'll do everything we can," John said. "What about the piece of Mishrael's scroll here? Where should we begin looking?"

"Start with the cult," Danrael replied. "Investigate it, and you will learn much about this world. That may lead you to clues about where the piece is hidden."

He stepped closer, his expression unusually serious.

"John, I keep telling you—do not forget to pray. By now, you should know its power. One day, it may save your life."

With that final warning, the angel vanished.

The cave fell silent.

John stood motionless, staring at the place where Danrael had been, the angel's warning settling over him like a weight. Prayer. He'd been reminded again and again, and each time it slipped through his fingers like sand.

He glanced at Shenya, who was standing quietly, deep in thought.

"Are you alright?" John asked. "You seem awfully quiet for someone who just received the gift of tongues."

Shenya smiled thoughtfully.

"I was reflecting on how the Almighty is a fountain of blessings that we on Marcrituss scarcely understand."

John nodded. "I've only just begun to understand them myself, but one thing I know for certain—you are one of those blessings. Thank you for coming with me; you have no idea how much easier this feels knowing I'm not alone."

"I am honored to help you," Shenya replied. "But even if I were not here, remember there is one above who is always with you." He placed a steady hand on John's shoulder. "Sometimes, the greatest battles are fought on one's knees. Prayer is a powerful weapon against the darkness."

At that moment, a faint sound echoed from the right side of the cave.

Both men turned.

A woman cautiously stepped through a narrow opening in the rock wall. She had the same yellow skin and white hair as Danrael's Spaltrican appearance.

Noticing their surprise, she said, "Please don't be alarmed." She cautiously stepped forward. "My name is Prinny—Danrael sent me to help you."

"And he sent us to help you," John replied, relieved she wasn't an enemy. "It's good to meet you, Prinny. My name is

John, and I'm the Traveller." He gestured to Shenya. "This is Shenya. He was guardian of the portal on a world called Marcrituss."

Prinny stood silent, eyes moving slowly between them, drinking in every detail. "It's an honor to meet you both. I previously served as the guardian of Spaltrico's portal before my son took over. I wasn't aware two of you would be assisting us with Eamin's disappearance. This is truly a blessing."

Prinny had been crying. Her smeared makeup had left faint marks on her white shirt. John noticed Spaltricans dressed much like people on Earth—Prinny's black blazer could have passed for one of his mom's formal jackets. The red trousers, slashed with thick black stripes, matched. It was like a uniform of sorts.

Prinny continued to examine them in the cave's dim light. "You both look so much like us," she said, studying them from head to toe.

John bit back a smile as Shenya shifted his weight, gaze dropping to the floor.

Prinny straightened, something shifting in her face. "It would be wonderful to get to know each other better, but you've arrived in the midst of war. A battle is about to happen out there. We must get moving, or we'll get caught up in it."

"Where can we go if there's a war going on out there?" John asked.

"We're going to see my best friend, Kleo. She's tough, but she's the only person on this planet I trust. Kleo is an undercover officer investigating the cult. She knows about you and the portals and will be a great help."

Spaltrico's portal, much like Earth's, was housed in a secondary cave. A smaller chamber served as its entrance, with an opening in the ceiling. Inside, a large circular pad lay flat on the ground.

Prinny stepped onto it while John and Shenya looked on, uncertain.

"You need to step on this with me," she said.

They stepped onto the pad. They exchanged baffled looks as it rumbled beneath their feet. A gel-like substance rose from the rim, expanding upward until it surrounded them. In seconds, the gel hardened into a capsule resembling a blue metal rocket, forming a large window at the front.

A laser shot up from the pad beneath their feet and scanned them. John flinched as the gel extended from the walls, transforming into straps that fastened them into the tube.

Prinny pushed her hand against the newly formed wall, and a bright control panel bloomed into existence—glowing, intricate, far beyond anything John had ever imagined. Shenya gripped the armrest, his fingers whitening.

As the machine hummed, a faint vibration tickled John's feet. He clenched his jaw, forcing himself not to fidget as the gel hardened around his arms and chest.

After Prinny entered their destination, the craft gave a low, engine-like hum before ascending through the opening in the cave.

"Hold on tight," Prinny warned.

They shot up into the Spaltrican sky.

"Welcome to Tokika City," she said.

FORTY-NINE

John and Shenya leaned toward the window, staring at the world unfolding beneath them.

Tokika City stretched to the horizon like a vast metallic ocean. Towering buildings rose in every direction—hundreds of them, each as tall as the greatest skyscrapers John had seen on Earth, their surfaces gleaming with a cold, silvery light. Screens and colored lights flickered across every facade.

A chill ran through John.

This was the city from his dream.

But seeing it now was far more unsettling.

The architecture was undeniably impressive—monumental towers of glass, steel, and unfamiliar alloys—but little about it was beautiful. Everything was hard angles and rigid shapes, built for efficiency and power, not grace. The city felt immense and intimidating, as though it had grown too large for the world holding it.

They'd barely been airborne a minute when the vehicle changed again. The gel walls softened and shifted, becoming pliable. The interior began to reshape itself: the floor tilted, the ceiling stretched, their bodies shifting awkwardly as the craft morphed around them. Shenya was startled and nearly jumped as a seat materialized beneath him.

The vessel had become a sleek, oval-shaped aircraft. It darted forward, merging seamlessly into a flowing stream of aerial traffic threading between the city towers.

Floating billboards hovered among the buildings, projecting massive shifting images into the haze. Most advertised unfamiliar products—shimmering pills, synthetic beauty products, gleaming apartment towers—but others flashed urgent slogans in bold red or blue:

NO GODS. NO CHAOS. OBEY THE FIRST COMMANDER.

REMEMBER THE SACRIFICE—TRUST THE EMPEROR.

FAITH IS TREASON. REPORT ALL ILLEGAL ASSEMBLIES.

One billboard, larger than the rest, displayed a grayscale portrait of a young girl beneath the words MISSING: DAUGHTER OF THE EMPEROR. The image flickered, replaced by a stylized map of the city, pulsing at the site of the largest gathering below.

The whole sky seemed alive with motion.

John lowered his gaze. Through the haze of pollution, he could just make out massive crowds in the streets below— thousands of figures marching, converging toward an even larger gathering ahead.

"Prinny," Shenya said, leaning forward, "what is this war about?"

Prinny kept her eyes fixed on the controls. "It all comes down to the cult. They've committed terrible acts—kidnapping children of the powerful for sacrifice, including the Emperor's daughter."

"In response," Prinny continued, "the Emperor's First Commander ordered all religious and spiritualist groups to be regulated or outlawed entirely. Now, pro-religious groups are fighting the government and its supporters, trying to stop the suppression."

"Which faction is the larger crowd down there?" Shenya asked, nodding at the screens.

"The larger one is the pro-government faction," Prinny replied. "They get the biggest screens." Her tone turned bitter. "But the others—faithful, angry, terrified—they're just as loud on the ground."

John pressed closer to the window, but the thick pollution defeated him. A dull gray veil of smog had swallowed much of the light, and no matter how hard he searched, the sun was nowhere to be seen—the haze had consumed even the color of the heavens.

"We're going to be landing soon," Prinny announced.

The aircraft slowed as they approached a towering skyscraper, hovering briefly above its rooftop. It adjusted position among dozens of other vehicles arriving and departing.

As it descended, the oval-shaped craft shifted again, the walls softening and straightening, returning to its original tubular shape—ready, it seemed, for landing.

The craft settled gently onto a circular disk at the center of the rooftop. The instant it touched down, the metallic shell dissolved back into its strange gel-like state and flowed away beneath their feet, vanishing into the pad as though it had never existed.

Within seconds, only the pad they stood on remained.

John stepped off slowly, half-expecting to find a scorch mark or tangle of wires beneath his feet. There was nothing. Only smooth, empty roof.

No engines.

No fuel.

No maintenance.

It should have felt miraculous. Here, it was simply ordinary.

He never imagined a world where vehicles simply appeared when needed and vanished at journey's end. No parking lots. No traffic jams. No endless repairs. On Earth, they'd call it a dream. Here, no one gave it a second thought.

Shenya had spent the entire flight unable to stop imagining what might happen if the craft malfunctioned midair—what if the metallic shell suddenly dissolved thousands of feet above the city? He'd take a sturdy gropolo any day.

As they crossed the rooftop, Prinny raised her hand to a small metallic dot on her ear.

"Kleo, we're here," she said.

She paused, listening to a response John and Shenya couldn't hear. After a brief exchange, she lowered her hand.

"Kleo says she cleared the building in advance of the battle," Prinny explained. "It's safe for you both to enter—well, as safe as it can be under the circumstances."

They approached a sleek, seamless door in the rooftop structure. As their footsteps neared, the door slid open silently.

John blinked in surprise. The entrance revealed a narrow staircase leading downward.

At the bottom, a woman waited. She wore the same style of uniform Prinny wore, but fitted neatly to her frame. Heavy black boots rose to her knees. She stood alert, arms folded loosely, studying the three as they descended.

"Kleo," Prinny said, "meet John and Shenya."

The woman stared at them, mouth slightly open. Her eyes moved slowly from John to Shenya, back again, as if trying to decide whether what she saw was real.

Breaking the silence, John stepped forward. "It's good to meet you, Kleo," he said politely. "Thank you for meeting us. My name is John, and this is—"

Kleo burst out laughing—the sound echoing sharply in the stairwell. She raised a hand apologetically as she tried to contain herself. "I do apologize," she said at last, still smiling. "But when Prinny told me the bizarre story about a Traveller from another world, I honestly thought she'd lost her mind." She gestured at them both. "And yet here you are. Not just one of you... but two."

Prinny shook her head fondly. "You'll get used to Kleo. She's too sassy for her own good and not the best with manners. She's the most loyal friend you could ever ask for, though."

Kleo gave Prinny a quick smile before turning back to the visitors. "I would say 'Welcome to Spaltrico,' but there isn't much here worth welcoming you to at the moment."

She studied them again, her tone softening a little. "Still... I am pleased to meet you, even under these circumstances."

"We promise to do everything we can to help find Eamin," John said.

Kleo gave a small, skeptical shrug. "I'm not sure how either of you can do anything to help," she admitted, "but I'm willing to hear what you have to say." She gestured vaguely toward the city outside. "The entire planet is in chaos right now."

"Have faith that Eamin will return," Shenya said. "God is with us."

"God?" Kleo said sharply.

Her voice grew hard, instantly changing the mood. "That word is poison on Spaltrico." She tilted her head toward the upper floors. "If you don't believe me," she said coldly, "listen."

From beyond the skyscraper's walls came the distant roar of thousands of voices—shouting, chanting, chaos rolling through the city like thunder.

Kleo turned from the window. "That is what happens when people bring God into the picture."

"That is not true," Shenya replied firmly. "God has nothing to do with that."

Kleo's eyes flashed. "God is responsible for all of it," she said, her voice sharpening with every word. "Every bit of it. We wouldn't be living through any of this madness if people had never believed in God—or religion."

John stepped between them.

"We can talk about all that later," John said calmly. "Right now, we need to hear everything you know about this cult and how it might be connected to Eamin's disappearance."

Kleo nodded and led them through the building.

FIFTY

"I'll tell you everything I know," Kleo said at last as she marched ahead of everyone. She beckoned them down the corridor, her pace brisk, voice clipped with purpose. "We keep all the cult evidence here at headquarters—years of intelligence from my undercover work."

She stopped before a steel door and gestured for them to enter.

Beyond was a quiet, dim chamber. Metallic walls stretched ceiling to floor, reflecting faint strips of corridor light and amplifying the room's eerie emptiness.

Kleo strode inside and spoke, her words cutting the hush: "Officer Kleo Vars, identification number 8827. Pull up everything on case twenty-two, including black files."

For a heartbeat, nothing. Then a smooth, artificial voice answered, disembodied:

"Identity verified."

Bands of white light blazed across the walls. The gloom fractured as dozens of translucent images shimmered into being, suspended in rows and columns—hovering midair like luminous ghosts.

Documents.

Photographs.

Video footage.

They were shifting and rearranging as if guided by invisible hands.

John stared, jaw slack. Files spun beside his head, slipping past one another and expanding with a twitch of Kleo's finger. A flick, and whole blocks of data blinked wider, details swimming into focus.

John said nothing. There was nothing to say.

Kleo skimmed through the images, then looked back at her team. "Meet Borth's Alliance." She snapped her fingers, drawing up a series of relics—ancient carvings, cracked stone tablets, rusted ceremonial blades, and other artifacts. Their surfaces glimmered with the burnish of centuries.

"Named after one of their gods," she said. "They're obsessed with relics from the old religions. Most are stolen— museums, dig sites, private collections. Nothing is sacred."

Shenya stepped closer without a word, fingers hovering over the air, tracing patterns in the symbols he'd only ever seen on Marcrituss.

Kleo brought forward another file—the image of a tall man, impeccably dressed, standing before a crowd. The man's posture radiated control; his eyes exuded cold calculation.

"Their leader." She said the word like it tasted bad. "Vonild." She flicked the file forward almost contemptuously. "Wealthy beyond belief. Influences governments, corporations, and anyone with money. And when money isn't enough —" she snapped her fingers and a new image appeared, a string of names, each with a red marker beside it, "—people disappear."

John studied the image. "I've seen that look before," he said. "On a podium in front of thousands of people. Feeding off every word."

Kleo glanced at him sharply. "Then you already know what we're dealing with."

"What's he after?" John asked.

Kleo flipped to a new file. "Exhibit twelve."

An ancient manuscript appeared, hovering inside a museum case—yellowed pages, their script unfamiliar, lines curling under glass.

"The Mour Text," Kleo said. "Two to twenty-five hundred years old. One of Spaltrico's most treasured artifacts. Written by a devotee of an ancient monotheistic religion."

John leaned toward the image. "What's so special about it?"

"It is the oldest complete text in the world. It contains priceless information about what our world used to be like." Kleo enlarged the image with a flick. "It went missing, and Tokika Museum suspected Vonild stole it. They couldn't prove it. But when I was undercover in the cult, I found it in their collection. I photographed every page and sent it for authentication."

"Is the manuscript still intact?" Shenya asked, already leaning in.

Kleo's face darkened. "It was. I returned to the collection vault to do an organics scan of the relic. By then, Vonild had torn several pages out."

The image of the manuscript hovered, edges flickering.

"Do you think those missing pages are connected to Eamin's disappearance?" Shenya pressed.

Kleo nodded once. "Let me show you what I found."

A new image materialized: a drawing—angular, strange. It depicted the world's portal.

She read the caption: "'Deep in the depths of the city of Mour is the gate of the angels. The Traveller will unite the world with her sisters.' Mour was this city's old name—hence the 'Mour Text.'"

"That means Vonild knows about the portal. And the Traveller," John said, low.

"And more than that," Kleo added, "I think he found the portal. That's where Eamin was taken. When Prinny told me what happened, she brought me to the cave. I recognized it instantly—from the Mour Text itself."

"Do you have images of the rest of the missing pages?" Shenya asked.

Kleo scrolled through file after file. The next image looked like graffiti: a man on a cross, arms outstretched. Beneath, words in ancient Spaltrican: *By his wounds, you have been healed. All hail the king above all gods.*

The floating file drifted between them, turning slowly in the air.

Shenya's jaw dropped. The breath left John's body.

He reached out instinctively—his fingers passing through the hovering image, unable to touch what he was seeing.

"Shenya, I know what this is!" John burst out.

Shenya read the text aloud, voice unsteady. "King above all gods. This is about the anuri-God."

"Yes," John breathed. "The man on the cross is the anuri-God. That first line, 'By his wounds, you have been healed'—it's from our scriptures. We sing it every Good Friday." Something unlocked in his chest—a recognition so deep it felt like coming home.

"What's 'Good Friday'?" Shenya asked, brows knotted.

"I'll explain later. The point is, the image and the words are about the anuri-God's death."

"His death?" Shenya's face twisted with confusion.

"We haven't talked about that part yet," John replied.

Prinny and Kleo exchanged glances, completely lost.

"So, he is dead?" Shenya pressed.

"That's not the end," John said. "He didn't stay dead."

Shenya stood still for a moment, then gave a small shake of his head—filing it away. "This Mour Text—it references the portals, the seven worlds, and the king above all gods. I think the anuri-God was revealed to prophets on every world. Here, on Spaltrico, to Qitra's ancestor, on Marcrituss. The seeds were planted long ago."

"Every world was prepared for the same thing," John said. "They just didn't know what it was."

"I wonder if the Mour Text could help us find the fragment of Mishrael's scroll here. If anyone knows, it's Vonild," Shenya agreed. "You can see he's obsessed with ancient artifacts."

"Um... are you two finished?" Kleo cut in, voice sharp. "I thought we were trying to find Eamin."

John saw Shenya draw breath and stepped in before he could speak. "Sorry, Kleo. This is helpful. Has anyone confronted Vonild about Eamin?"

"He's above the law," Prinny said, shaking her head. "Even the Emperor can't touch him. For a thousand years, the throne held absolute power—but Vonild's reach goes further. Unprecedented. His followers broadcast the cult's atrocities, and still, he walks free."

"My plan was simple," Kleo said, arms folding. "Infiltrate the cult, gather proof, get out. But he's too powerful."

Prinny glanced at the others, voice anxious. "So what do we do now?"

John turned back to the hovering files. "I need to meet Vonild. If I can talk to him face to face, maybe it'll help find Eamin."

"He's private," Kleo replied. "The cult's temple is the most locked-down place on Spaltrico. Getting inside is..." She shrugged. "Impossible, honestly. I don't know how to get you near him."

Shenya turned to Kleo. "You said Vonild's obsessed with the Mour Text. Maybe that's our way in."

Kleo eyed him. "How?"

"We bait him," Shenya said. "If he understands the Mour Text, two people who've traveled through the portal would be irresistible. He might do anything for the chance to meet us."

Kleo's lips pressed thin. She turned away from them, looking at the hovering files—all those years of evidence, all those atrocities broadcast without consequence. "What if he decides to sacrifice you? He's done it before—on public broadcasts. That's the kind of power he holds." She faced them again. "I don't want your blood on that list."

Shenya's answer was steady. "John has rare abilities. We'll be fine. Do you think you can set a meeting?"

Kleo hesitated, then nodded once—her expression gave away her skepticism. "If you're that confident... I'll try."

The floor shook—a deep, gut-level tremor. Dust drifted from the ceiling; the files flickered.

A distant boom rolled through the building.

"The battle's started," Prinny said, her voice tight. "We need to move. Now."

"Where can we go?" John asked. "Is anywhere safe?"

"My cottage—outside the city," Kleo said. "Fighting never gets there. Safer than the center. Come on."

They sprinted from the room and back up the stairwell.

The rooftop door flew open to the punch of smoke and burning metal. Black pillars of smoke rose between the towers; sirens whooped far below.

No one hesitated. The four of them hurried onto the white landing pad. The pad trembled; metallic gel surged up, forming a sleek tube around them in seconds. Kleo pressed her hand to the wall, revealing the control panel. She punched in coordinates.

Moments later, the craft lifted from the rooftop, taking them into Spaltrico's bruised, polluted sky.

CHAPTER
FIFTY-ONE

"What do you call this thing, anyway?" John asked, giving the vehicle's wall a tentative pat.

"A Sky Vrooter," Kleo said. She shot him a look, as if that should have been obvious—a flicker of amusement, or maybe mild exasperation, in her eyes.

The Sky Vrooter glided toward Kleo's cottage, silent and swift—unnaturally so, John thought. It was as if the air itself refused to protest. He pressed his palm to the window, longing for the honest heft of a gropolo beneath him, the wild slap of wind, the warmth of Xerti's feathers at his back. This machine was brilliant, but hollow. He thought of Marcrituss—the beach, the salt air, the sound of the tide breathing in and out in the dark. The world he'd left behind felt more alive in memory than anything visible through the window.

Kleo was quiet beside him for a moment. She could read John's thoughts simply from the way he looked at the world below. "There used to be forests here," she said. "My grandmother had a photograph. Trees as tall as the towers. A river running through the city." She paused. "That was five generations ago."

They landed behind a stark, dome-shaped cottage. Spaltrico stretched around them, abandoned by life. No trees, no grass, not even weeds—just bare earth scabbed with gray. Smog rolled across the land in a constant, sluggish tide, clinging to every surface, swallowing the horizon. Even the light seemed sickly, filtered of any cheer.

Beyond the cottage, the city offered no comfort. Smoke from the war zone curled into the sky, folding into the smog until it seemed the heavens themselves were choking. John caught himself thinking—over and over—that he was lucky he hadn't been born there. The air tasted of burnt metal and ash, and he coughed, eyes watering.

"Are you alright, John?" Shenya asked.

He wiped his mouth, voice rough. "Yeah. I'm just... unsettled."

Shenya stood watching the rising plumes of smoke. "I understand completely. I have to admit I'm a bit overwhelmed by all of this, too. This world oozes sadness. My heart longs for the simplicity of home. I appreciate more than ever the sea and the moons of Marcrituss."

John was comforted that he had someone to share his discombobulated feelings with. He leaned toward him, lowering his voice. "Maybe it's just me, but does the air taste weird to you?"

Shenya inhaled, smacking his lips. "You're right. Smoke and ash. It clings to everything."

John walked slowly, not wanting to arrive anywhere. War was everywhere, but it was more than that—a bleakness that pressed against his skin like cold. Spaltrico felt calculated down to its bones, scrubbed of anything alive.

Kleo's cottage looked like a set piece from an Earth sci-fi

film—domed, spare, a few similar homes scattered across the barren ground, none close enough to call a neighbor. Inside, white walls glared back at him, the light clinical and sharp. No clutter, no warmth; the place was almost empty, stripped of anything lived-in. Even the air felt sterile and lonely.

Kleo opened a lone cupboard and pulled out a handful of smooth, rectangular containers. She handed one to John and another to Shenya. The boxes were unmarked, uniform gray-white, with a small straw attached—no label, no branding, nothing to hint at what waited inside.

John rolled his container between his palms. "What is this stuff?" Shenya asked, turning it over as if it would reveal a secret.

"It's food," Kleo replied. "Enough to keep you full for a while."

John and Shenya exchanged a look. John couldn't help but have a crooked grin. "Is this really what you eat?"

Kleo looked between them as if the question itself were strange. "Of course. What else would we consume? The land hasn't been fertile in generations. With the smog and pollution, nothing grows anymore. We had to industrialize food production just to survive. Those boxes have everything: nutrients, calories, hydration. Efficient."

She said it simply, as if explaining gravity—no bitterness, no nostalgia, only fact.

John studied the box. Efficient. The word felt empty.

Kleo straightened. "Prinny and I need to check the study. There might be news about Eamin. I'll also try to arrange a meeting with Vonild."

Prinny's voice was tight, wary. "We need to be careful about what we say. If the government hears there are visitors from other worlds, that meeting will never happen. They'd be at our door by nightfall."

Kleo nodded. "Spaltrico is always listening. I'll say nothing about other worlds—just that I've met two visitors linked to the portal in the Mour Text. That's much safer."

Shenya managed a laugh, though it was thin. "Sensible. Still makes me nervous."

Kleo offered a faint smile, then turned away, anxiety shadowing her steps as she left with Prinny.

John and Shenya sank into oversized chairs at the heart of the empty room. John sniffed the straw warily. There was a sterile, processed tang. Shenya took a sip first, his face twisted in immediate disgust.

"This is vile," Shenya declared, as if issuing a formal ruling.

John braved a taste. He pulled a face. "Yeah. That's... seriously bad." He glared at the box, as if the stuff might apologize.

"If we make it back to Marcrituss, we're having a feast," Shenya said, forcing a grin. "Anything to forget this roolimba poo."

John matched his grin, grimacing as he forced down another sip. "Deal."

Shenya risked another swallow, then, as if needing to wash away the taste, asked, "Would you tell me more about what we discussed at the law enforcement building? About the anuri-God—how he was born, died, and came back?"

"Of course." John set the box aside, grateful for the distraction.

As he spoke, the stories returned—bright, almost eager. Childhood lessons, the comfort of Sunday school, his parents' voices at bedtime. He found himself telling Shenya about the prophets, the miracles, the crowds and the frightened rulers.

Shenya leaned forward with his elbows on his knees—clinging to every word as John got to the last supper, the garden, the arrest.

"And then his death," Shenya said, as though they stood at a cliff's edge.

"Jesus suffered a long, brutal death," John told him. "He gave himself for the sins of all. That's what the prophecy means: 'By his wounds, we are healed.'" He paused, looking at the sterile white wall rather than Shenya. "Three days later, he rose—he conquered death."

The room felt even emptier, the light too sharp, as if the story itself had unsettled the walls. Shenya said nothing for a long moment, eyes cast down.

"The whole story," Shenya said at last, voice low, "is a love story—one that stretches across worlds. Your God prepared Earth, step by step, until he became one of you."

"One of us," John added.

Shenya slowly shook his head, something unlocking in his face. "This has been an incredible conversation, John. Your Earth is blessed to have known this story first."

Kleo reappeared, heading straight for the cupboard, pulling out another food box as if their talk were only background noise. "We're waiting for a response from the temple," she said. "Are you two still talking about religion? Here, you might be witnessing the end of it."

Shenya set down his food box. "I'm sorry your world's religion was twisted by groups like Borth's Alliance. If you heard John's story—about a God of love and justice—you'd know it's not the same."

Kleo turned away, moving to the window. Outside, the smog rolled its slow tide across the barren earth. "I don't think your God cares about Spaltrico."

John looked at her, examining the smog rolling beyond the glass, her back to the room, shoulders set like someone who'd stopped expecting answers a long time ago. He didn't say anything.

Shenya leaned forward, gentle but steady. "That's not so. The one God is the same on Earth, on Marcrituss, here. Your ancestors once knew him. The artifacts you showed us—they're proof. Your system replaced what your people once had, but the loss doesn't mean he's abandoned you."

Kleo didn't turn from the window. A long moment passed before she spoke. "Even if you're right, it doesn't change what I've seen. Here, religion is just a tool for power. The cult proves that."

Shenya's voice was quiet. "Given what you've been through, that's understandable. We'll do all we can to stop Vonild. But I swear—the cult is not from God. It comes from something evil."

Kleo faced him at last, exhausted. "How do you expect to stop him? He's above the law. He has resources you can only imagine."

John met her gaze. "When the time comes, I'll know what to do."

Prinny's voice called from the study. "Kleo, there's a message about tomorrow's appointment."

Kleo straightened, something shifting in her face, and slipped away with Prinny.

John and Shenya sat in silence, the cottage humming faintly around them. Shenya closed his eyes—resting, or praying, John couldn't tell. John looked at his own hands. The story he'd just told Shenya was still present in the room somehow, the way a piece of music lingers after it ends. He'd known the facts of it for years—his parents' faith had made sure of that—but saying it out loud, to people who'd never heard it, to a world that had no name for any of it, had done something he hadn't anticipated. It felt true in a way it hadn't before. He sat with that for a moment. Then he bowed his head, closed his eyes, and spoke a few quiet words into the silence—not to the ceiling, not to the room, but to the one the story was about. He meant it. He felt called to it in a way he couldn't explain. But something in him held back still. Not doubt—he was past doubt. But accepting something as true and surrendering yourself to it completely were not the same thing. One was the mind arriving. The other was something he didn't yet know how to do—like standing in an open doorway, feeling the warmth on the other side, and not yet knowing how to step through.

John's thoughts were interrupted when Kleo re-entered with Prinny, both beaming with smiles.

"Good news?" Shenya asked.

Kleo nodded. "Vonild will see us first thing tomorrow."

Shenya exhaled slowly. "This could be it, Prinny. We might be close to finding Eamin."

"We should get some rest and gear up for the morning," Kleo said, raising her voice toward the ceiling. "Code 55, please. Set up four sleeping quarters."

A thin beam of light sliced across the room.

John and Shenya ducked instinctively as the laser traced four large shapes in the air, lines of bright white outlining new walls.

John stared, half-crouched. "What is that?"

Kleo smiled, some of the tension easing from her face. "It's a printer. It makes what we need. After use, the materials are recycled for something else."

John rose, watching the transformation. "The ultimate 3D printer," he murmured.

The beam snapped out again. Heat prickled at the back of his throat, the smell of hot plastic and singed dust filling the air. Four box-like structures appeared, each with a tall door and a made-up bed inside, neat and waiting.

Shenya stepped closer and touched the doorframe, as if expecting it to vanish. "This is extraordinary."

Kleo opened her own tiny room and glanced back. "Climb in and sleep. We'll need it."

THE BED WAS FUNCTIONAL—FLAT, firm, exactly the right dimensions—and that was all. No give. No familiar smell. No particular reason to feel safe inside it. John lay on his back and stared at a ceiling that hadn't existed for more than five minutes.

Sleep didn't come.

His mind kept circling back to the appointment.

Vonild will see us first thing tomorrow.

Kleo had said it with relief. Shenya had exhaled. Even Prinny had smiled for the first time since they'd met her. And John had nodded and said nothing because everyone else's relief was contagious and he'd wanted—badly—to feel it too.

But lying there in the dark, something wouldn't settle.

John still felt the uneasy feeling he had the moment he stepped through the portal. It was like stepping into a room where something had recently happened that no one was acknowledging.

He hadn't forgotten it. He'd just stopped listening to it.

Everything he knew about Vonild ran through his mind. Wealthiest man on the planet. Above the law. Not a man who granted meetings to strangers. Not a man who did anything he hadn't already decided served his purposes.

And yet—without hesitation, he'd agreed.

John turned these things over in the dark. He thought about Eamin. Kidnapped three weeks ago. Held alive, presumably—because a dead guardian was less useful than a living one. He kept arriving at the same answer—Eamin was useful because he was bait.

He pressed his palms flat against the mattress. A part of him wanted to get up and tell Shenya. But he knew it wouldn't change anything. They couldn't leave Eamin. They couldn't turn away from the mission. They were going to walk toward it —because Eamin was eighteen years old and had done nothing except inherit a duty, and John understood with a clarity that surprised him exactly what that felt like. You didn't get to choose the moment. You just chose whether to show up.

He exhaled slowly.

Tomorrow, they would walk into whatever had been prepared for them.

He bowed his head in the dark.

He didn't ask for protection. He didn't ask for power or courage or the right words. He just told the truth—that he could see the shape of what was coming, that he was going anyway, and that he was going to need help he couldn't manu-facture himself.

He didn't know if it reached anywhere.

But he didn't wait for the room to look different afterward. He let the silence be what it was—and found, somewhere underneath the fear, something that felt almost like readiness.

He closed his eyes.

This time, sleep came.

Shenya and Prinny lingered in the cottage. John and Kleo had already gone to bed, and the silence settled around just the two of them.

Prinny studied him for a moment—his face, his clothes, the way his hair fell. She broke the silence and said, "When you and John came through the portal, the first thing I noticed wasn't that you looked different." She paused. "It was that you looked yourselves. Your clothes, your hair—everything about you is individual. Particular." She searched for the word. "Chosen."

Shenya glanced down at his Marcritan shirt, faintly puzzled. "Is that unusual here?"

Prinny gave a small, tired smile. "I was six years old when the last two independent nations fell to the empire. I don't remember much—fragments, mostly. My mother's cooking. A festival with dancing." She folded her hands in her lap. "Within a generation, all of it was gone. The empire didn't ban those things loudly. It just made them disappear, slowly, until nobody remembered to miss them." She nodded toward the window, toward the gray world beyond. "Five hundred years of that."

Shenya was quiet for a moment. "And yet your family kept something."

She looked at him sharply. "Danrael told you?"

"No," Shenya said. "But you're the guardian of a portal that survived five centuries of suppression. Someone kept the faith. Someone passed it on."

Prinny exhaled slowly. "My family followed the teaching in the Mour Text. The one God—the king above all gods." She said it carefully, the way people say things they've only ever said in whispers. "We didn't have much. No community, no ceremony. Just the text, and the portal, and the instruction to watch and wait." She paused. "My mother used to say we were keeping watch—that one day someone would come through that portal and the old faith would finally make sense. We didn't know who. We didn't know when."

The hum of the cottage filled the silence between them.

"You heard some of it—in the files room," Shenya said.

"Enough to know," she replied quietly. "Enough to understand what my family was waiting for." A faint smile crossed her face. "I didn't want to ask more in front of Kleo. You may have noticed she gets a little..." she searched for the word, "sensitive on the subject."

Shenya laughed softly despite himself. "I had noticed, yes."

Prinny's smile faded, her eyes distant. "Five hundred years, Shenya. My family held onto something we couldn't name or explain, on a world that had forgotten it entirely. And today a boy from another world stood in that room and unlocked what my family had been guarding for generations. The God of the Mour Text—he's real, he has a name, and he's known on your world too." She shook her head slowly.

Shenya leaned forward, elbows on his knees. "On Marcrituss, we have a saying—that faith kept in darkness burns cleaner than faith kept in the light. Your family's faithfulness humbles me, Prinny. Truly."

She smiled at that, a real smile this time, though it didn't last long. Her gaze drifted toward the printed doors, toward wherever Eamin was in the dark.

"He turns eighteen next month," she said quietly. "The rules are the same on every world, I suppose. When they come of age, they take over. I handed the guardianship to him because I was supposed to." Her voice tightened. "And three weeks later—"

"That is not your fault," Shenya said.

She didn't answer. She didn't need to—the shape of the guilt was visible enough.

"There's something else you should know. About Kleo." She glanced toward the printed doors. "She'll never tell you herself. She doesn't talk about it." A pause. "Her father was one of the first. When Borth's Alliance began—before anyone understood what it was—he spoke out publicly against it.

They made an example of him. A permanent one." She folded her hands. "Kleo was twelve."

Shenya was still.

"Everything she's done since," Prinny said, "every risk she's taken—it all started there. She's never said so. But I've known her a long time." She looked toward the printed doors again. "That's why she's even more invested in Eamin than anyone else. She knows."

She didn't need to say anything else. The shape of it was visible enough.

Shenya stood and placed a hand on her shoulder. "We'll do everything we can tomorrow. I'm a father too. I understand."

Prinny hugged him, desperately—a mother clinging to whatever hope she could reach.

"Thank you, Shenya," she whispered, voice breaking. For the first time since Eamin disappeared, hope flickered—fragile, trembling, but real.

CHAPTER
FIFTY-TWO

John woke to a noise so familiar it yanked him halfway home—a lawnmower's droning buzz. For a blink, he almost smiled. Then it hit him: Spaltrico, not his own sun-struck yard.

He cracked open the door of his little stationary bedroom, throwing up a hand against the white glare. Two of the bed boxes were vanishing beneath the sweep of a laser, their edges softening into dust, which a hose slurped away with an eager hiss.

Spaltrico didn't clean the way Earth cleaned.

It erased.

John shuffled out, rubbing the last shreds of sleep from his eyes. Shenya glanced up and burst into laughter, the sound bouncing off sterile walls.

"What's so funny?" John yawned.

"Your hair!" Shenya wheezed. "You look like you've been struck by lightning!"

John ran his hand over his head—his hair was standing straight up in every direction. "Very funny. You're one to talk—

you look like you stole your outfit from Starfleet." He doubted Shenya would catch the reference, but it felt good anyway.

"This is standard Spaltrican clothing, apparently," Shenya said, smoothing the odd fabric with a touch of pride. He cleared his throat grandly. "Watch this. Code 7, please. Set up a shower room."

A laser zipped from the wall, sketching a box into existence with lines of light. Shenya shot John a sly look. "That's pretty 'cool,' as you say in your tongue."

John watched the shower box form, arms folded, then slowly unfolded them. This place really is a supercomputer with doors. "How do you work it?" he asked.

"Lucky for you, I figured it out already," Shenya said. "Go in, say 'initiate water.' When you're done, ask for Code 10. It'll give you fresh clothes. Simple."

"That's it? Just two commands?"

"That's it," Shenya replied, wearing a grin that had no business being that wide. "Super simple shower. Don't get your hopes up for anything too exciting."

John eyed him, suspicious. Despite the enclosure, he was about to get naked in the living room. "Where are Prinny and Kleo?"

"Out back, having their breakfast boxes," Shenya said. "Not sure why anyone would sit outside here. The air'll choke you if you stay out too long."

"Don't mention breakfast," John groaned. "I don't want to think about what those boxes are like."

Shenya shuddered. "I was already subjected to it. Believe me, breakfast boxes are even worse than the dinner ones."

John laughed despite himself. He stepped into the shower box, pulled off his clothes, and tossed them aside before closing the door.

Inside, there was only a shower head. No soap, no knobs,

no pipes, no shelves. Not a single personal item. Just four white walls—perfectly functional, utterly empty. There were no choices to make, no temperature dial, nothing to make the experience his own. It felt more like a medical scanner than a place to care for yourself.

"Initiate water," John said.

A stream poured over him—perfect temperature, steady, warm. He blinked up at the ceiling; there was no visible source, just impossible convenience.

Above him, a click. The house's computer spoke: "Would you like me to initiate cleaning?"

"Um... yes?" John replied. Shenya hadn't mentioned this part.

A laser swept across his body.

A brush charged out of the wall and began scrubbing him, relentless and eager. "What the—?" John yelped, twisting away as the brush chased him like an overzealous pet. Through the door, he could hear Shenya's muffled laughter.

"I have detected facial hair," the computer intoned. "Initiating laser facial hair removal."

"Wait—!"

Lasers zipped across his face in precise, stinging bursts—not agony, but not nothing either. He ran his palm over his jaw: smooth, not a hint of stubble. Shaved by light.

No skip button. No way to decline. The system simply detected what it deemed necessary and corrected it. He wasn't being cleaned—he was being standardized, processed like one of those gray food boxes.

He swallowed, remembering Shenya's instructions. "Code 10."

The printer scanned his body. A screen shimmered into the air, displaying clothing options—all muted: gray, black, navy, charcoal. Nothing bright. He picked a dark gray shirt, black jacket, matching trousers and boots, and hit confirm.

A blast of warmth dried him in seconds.

The printer scanned him again, then—without warning—began printing the clothes right onto his skin as he stood there.

John made a strangled sound, half laugh, half complaint.

When he finally stepped out—fully dressed, suspiciously well-groomed—Shenya was still cracking up.

"Wow, Shenya. Thanks for the heads up on that 'super simple' shower. I counted a bit more than two commands."

"I'm sorry," Shenya said, grinning, "but hearing your reaction was worth it."

"Just wait. I'll get you back," John muttered, but even he was smiling.

Beneath the laughter, Shenya grew quiet. On Marcrituss, people chose their hair, their clothes—expressions of self, of culture. Here, even hair was shaped by machines and preset codes: efficient, uniform, controlled.

The worst part, Shenya thought, was that Kleo and Prinny didn't even notice it anymore. This was simply life. He thought it was obvious why Vonild's cult had so much appeal—for those longing for identity, anything that set them apart was irresistible, right up until it became dangerous.

The door opened. Kleo stepped in with Prinny, handing John a breakfast box. He took one bite and immediately understood Shenya's warning: worse than dinner, by far.

Kleo didn't waste words. "Slurp it down. We can't be late for this meeting."

John choked it down with the grim determination of a man swallowing a dare, not a meal. Then, wasting no time, they headed outside and stood on the circular pad of the sky vrooter.

The gel rose, cool and clean, sealing them in. The cottage faded behind, and once again, the strange sky of Spaltrico opened before them as they set off toward the Temple of Borth's Alliance.

CHAPTER

FIFTY-THREE

The sky vrooter hummed as it glided toward the center of Tokika City. John's hands pressed flat against the window. The closer they flew, the thinner the morning's brightness felt—cheer bleeding away as ruined blocks unspooled below.

Any hint of laughter died. No one seemed willing to break the hush. John leaned in, forehead pressed to cool glass, and stared.

Below, the city sprawled in ruin—streets broken and erased, buildings cracked open like eggshells, their insides exposed. Tangled metal and scorched stone piled in heaps. Smoke bled upward in thin, gray cords to meet the ever-present smog.

"I can't believe it's this bad, Kleo. This is... unbelievable." John had to look away when he saw piles of bodies in front of a pyre. He gagged as the sour sting of bile hit the back of his tongue. Shenya placed an arm around him.

"Look away, John." Shenya held him tighter as he felt him retching. "You don't need to see any more of this."

Kleo's jaw was set. "Carnage like this isn't uncommon. This kind of devastation happens every few days."

"This is horrible," Shenya murmured. "So many anuri lives gone after last night." His voice dropped. "I pray this never comes to my world. But I fear it's heading that way."

Kleo's reply came flat, grim. "Both sides are already preparing to clash again today—far side of the city."

The city's wounds were raw—wide as the sky. The horror of them pulsed through John's bones. The whole world was bleeding. He couldn't shake the weight of everything—Prinny was counting on them, Eamin was counting on them. The scenes he saw below told him all of Spaltrico was counting on him.

The vrooter turned, and the temple district loomed ahead. It was a behemoth, hexagonal and angular, rearing out of the city's heart. Behind it, towers bristled like needles, slicing the smog-stained sky.

Kleo checked her comm. Her eyes scanned the fortress below. "When we land, people will stare," she said, voice clipped. "Stay close. Don't engage. Ignore everyone. Got it?"

John nodded. Kleo's foot tapped a quick, sharp rhythm on the floor.

She glanced at them. "Most important: inside that temple, I'm not Kleo. My undercover name is Winna. Don't slip."

"Winna," John echoed softly.

"Winna," Shenya repeated.

As the vrooter glided down toward the plaza, John's gut pulled tight. He reached inward the way he had in the forest before the attack—searching for that cold familiar edge, the specific pressure that had warned him before. Nothing came back clearly. Just the same diffuse wrongness that had been present since they arrived. He tried to separate it—to find Revonat's particular signature within it—but the world's own darkness swallowed everything whole. Whatever was in that temple, Spaltrico itself was hiding it.

The temple was all sharp edges and shadow—a dungeon masquerading as a place of worship.

Prinny coaxed the vrooter down in a careful arc, landing away from the gates. She stayed in her seat, hands resting on the controls, eyes on the rearview; she wouldn't be following them inside.

John scanned the plaza. A dozen men in uniform waited by the entrance. His pulse spiked.

He leaned close to Kleo. "We're getting off here? In front of all that security? Why not land on the roof like before?"

Kleo shook her head, eyes on the guards. "It's fine, John," she reassured. "They're sworn to secrecy. If any of them talk, Vonild will have them killed. No hesitation."

John steadied his breathing and flexed his hands in his lap. No turning back now.

They stepped out of the vrooter, stone cold and unyielding underfoot as they climbed toward the entrance. John's shoes scuffed against steps that rang with each footfall—too loud in the hush.

At the top, the guards stiffened. Several stared outright, unable to hide their curiosity or their suspicion.

A memory surged of Marciluk's crowd. The jeers, the sense of being paraded for judgment. John's chest tightened, but he forced himself onward.

Inside, white light hit them like a wave. The lobby was radiant and sterile, its brilliance swallowing every shadow, every hint of comfort. No furniture, no banners, no statues—just a cold, silent void.

Kleo—Winna now—led them to the platform at the lobby's core. "Floor fifteen," she said.

The platform vibrated, rising through the hollow shaft.

Above, ceilings parted and closed again, like pages of a book. The light faded as they climbed—dull gray, then harsh slate, then oppressive black.

The ride ended at a set of massive red doors.

Kleo pressed a dot to her ear. "This is Winna. I'm outside the chamber with the two visitors."

The doors swung open from behind, pulled open by temple guards.

John and Shenya exchanged a loaded glance. For the first time on Spaltrico, doors opened for them not because of a code or machine, but by human hands.

Candles guttered in iron sconces along the corridor ahead. Shadows leapt in the blood-red light. The air was thick with ritual, every footstep raising a whisper from the stone.

Kleo led the way, her shoulders squared. John followed, every step slow. The corridor narrowed the further they went.

At the end, Kleo paused at the heavy door to Vonild's chamber.

John's pulse jumped. His hands clenched to keep them steady. At his side, Kleo's hand lingered on the handle—her thumb tracing a quick, silent circle. Her lips barely moved, as if mouthing a prayer she'd never admit.

Whatever waited beyond the door, there was no going back.

FIFTY-FOUR

The door opened.

John and Shenya stepped in after Kleo, and their attention snapped to the far wall—a single, unbroken sheet of glass. Towering windows stretched from floor to ceiling, twenty feet high, framing the wounded skyline of Tokika City. The city sprawled beneath a bruised, gray sky, its jagged silhouette like a broken crown.

At the far end, Vonild sat behind a sleek, obsidian desk, hands folded with calculated calm.

"Greetings, Winna. You're right on—" He stopped mid-sentence, head lifting as he saw John and Shenya enter behind her.

Slowly, Vonild rose.

His hands unfolded. He stared—eyes moving from John to Shenya and back, slow and unblinking, as though cataloguing something priceless. The smile that spread across his lips was thin and cold, pulled too wide.

John's hand moved to his pocket. The felt pouch pressed back against his palm, and for a moment the scroll fragment seemed to push against the cloth with a life of its own. He kept his hand still.

Kleo's voice cut through the tension, steady despite the heaviness pressing in. "Lord Vonild, I'll get right to the point." She gestured toward John. "This man is known as the Traveller in the Mour Text. His name is John." She extended a hand to Shenya. "He came here with his companion, Shenya. As you will have surmised, they are not from Spaltrico. They are from different worlds, and traveled here through the portal mentioned in the Mour Text."

Vonild let out a low, almost delighted sound.

He ran a hand slowly through his slicked-back white hair, stepping out from behind the desk. With predatory calm, he began to circle them, gaze burning and unblinking.

"Now that you see them," Kleo continued, "you may wonder why I did not disclose their true identities when I made the appointment. It was for security reasons, my Lord. We can't be too careful about who's listening in these days— especially when it comes to a delicate situation like this."

"Extraordinary," Vonild breathed, circling like a collector admiring rare, dangerous artifacts. "This is the meeting of a lifetime!" He clapped his hands softly, raising them to his chin. "Winna, this is incredible. How did you come across them?"

"They came to me, my Lord," Kleo replied, her tone measured and deferential. "They saw me leave the temple and followed me, seeking help to arrange a meeting with you."

"Well done, Winna," Vonild said, approval curling in his voice. "We've known each other for a long time, and I see you're proving yourself a valuable asset."

Kleo bowed slightly, gaze lowered. She knew well not to meet his eyes for long.

Vonild turned to John, posture straightening with

theatrical dignity. "Apologies, John. My name is Vonild Metra, supreme head of Borth's Alliance." He extended his hand.

John hesitated for barely a heartbeat, then shook it. The grip was firm—too firm—and cold. A chill seeped down his arm.

"Tell me, my friends," Vonild went on, releasing John and pacing slowly across the room, "why did you want to see me of all people? Surely I should be the one trying to organize a meeting with you!"

Kleo and Shenya turned to John, wordlessly prompting him to answer.

"Do you need resources or money?" Vonild continued lightly, hands spread. "There are only so many reasons visitors from another world would seek out the wealthiest man on the planet."

John forced himself to appear steady. "We wanted to meet with you," John said carefully, "because we have reason to believe someone involved in the Alliance may have abducted a young man named Eamin."

Vonild's face was unreadable. He drifted toward a polished drinks table, elegant decanters arranged like trophies. Selecting one, he poured himself a drink.

"Are you accusing me of something?" he asked calmly.

John weighed his words. "We're desperate to find him. If you know anything about Eamin's whereabouts, please— tell us."

Vonild lifted his glass, swirling the liquid and examining it under the light before answering. "Why do you think I would know anything about this? What makes you think anyone in the Alliance has anything to do with his disappearance?"

"There's reason to believe members of your organisation have been abducting people," John said, heart pounding.

"They're being abducted and... sacrificed." John could barely get the word out—*sacrificed*. It made his stomach churn.

Vonild slammed the glass down on the table. "Ugh," he huffed, irritation curling his lip. "I don't have patience for this. You've been here two minutes and go straight to accusations."

He leaned against the drinks table, studying them with a sly, calculating expression. "Did she tell you that?" He pointed at Kleo. Her stomach dropped.

"I have no idea what you're talking about, Lord Vonild," she replied, but the tremor in her voice gave her away.

Shenya stepped forward. "There is no need for games. You have Eamin, and we know it. Tell us where he is."

Vonild turned his gaze on Shenya, contempt naked in his eyes. "If the rest of your kind are as tactful as you are, it must be a rather horrid world you're from."

Shenya's jaw tightened. He held Vonild's stare and said nothing.

Vonild turned and advanced on Kleo. The temperature in the room seemed to plummet with every step. He stopped inches from her, reached out, and touched her cheek—a gesture that made her recoil inwardly, though she didn't move.

"I have known who you really are since day one...Kleo," Vonild said in a voice soft as poison. "How could you possibly believe there's anything in this world I don't know?" He smiled faintly. "I mean... I own it!"

Kleo swallowed hard, forcing the words out. "If you've known, why allow me to keep rising through the cult?"

"I had a feeling you'd be useful to me someday," Vonild replied, sipping his drink. "And I was right. You brought the Traveller right to me."

He took a slow sip, then continued: "But now that you've fulfilled your purpose, Kleo, I'm afraid I must reveal your true identity to the Alliance. They'll be quite angry." His smile widened. "They'll likely offer you as a sacrifice."

John's voice cut through. "Stop all this now. If you tell us where Eamin is, I might take it easy on you."

Vonild ignored the warning and waved a hand toward the massive windows.

"Look down below," he said to John, turning away to gaze out over the city. "It's marvellous."

John stared. "What are you talking about? Marvellous is the last word I'd use. People are dying down there."

"It's marvellous," Vonild repeated, voice almost reverent, "because the people are finally learning the truth." He spread his arms, as if presenting the broken city as a work of art. "They're learning that everything they've ever known is a sham."

John's frown deepened. "What do you mean?"

"Faith. Love. Hope. Religion," Vonild said slowly, savouring each word. "All of it is dying here."

"Why are you doing this?" John demanded. "It makes no sense."

Vonild turned, voice shifting to something oddly patronising. "John, Vonild is no more."

The name landed with dead weight. John's breath caught. He looked at the man—the stillness behind the eyes, the cold amusement that had nothing human in it.

"You're in him," John said. "You're—"

"Revonat." The name spat into the room like a curse.

Vonild's smile froze, a flicker of annoyance passing over his features. When he spoke again, his voice was colder, sharper.

"Good," said the demon, satisfaction twisting his lips. "It's finally clicked. Good to see you again, Traveller."

FIFTY-FIVE

Something was wrong.

Every time John had encountered Revonat before, the demon's presence was immediate—a crushing weight pressing against his mind. But now, even after recognising him, that darkness felt strangely diffuse. There was no sharp edge to the evil—just a faint, omnipresent chill.

Everywhere. Diluted. Hidden.

Revonat's smile sharpened with cold delight. "We discovered the time of the Traveller had come when you appeared on Marcrituss. Your arrival gave me the perfect opportunity to set in motion on that world exactly what I have done here."

He gestured toward the devastated city beyond the glass.

"I now have all of Marcrituss standing on the edge of war." The demon's eyes glittered, pitiless. "And it's all thanks to you, Traveller."

A flash of anger spiked through John—self-directed, bitter. He should have seen it sooner. "Why can't I feel your presence here the way I did before?" he pressed.

Revonat's lip curled. "You have not yet learned your skill

set, novice." He drifted closer, eyes alight with triumphant malice. "This entire world belongs to me. My presence does not lurk in shadows. It fills everything. The streets. The air. The hearts of the people." His voice lowered, silk and poison. "I am not a presence on Spaltrico. I am its atmosphere."

A chill ran through John's bones.

John remembered the dark haze he'd felt on arrival—a wrongness in the air, a familiar poison. He'd thought it was just the weight of war. Now he understood: the demon's influence was everywhere, woven through the world like venom in blood.

"I tried to offer you a way out in the forest on Marcrituss," Revonat said. "But you refused." He tilted his head, mock-regretful. "You could have saved yourself, Traveller. That was... an unfortunate decision."

John's fists clenched. "You could have hunted me anywhere. Why Spaltrico? Why Eamin?"

"After I failed to stop you in Marciluk," Revonat replied, pacing with feline grace, "I realized the solution to eliminating you was already here."

He paused before the shattered window, the ruined city a backdrop of desolation. "Vonild had long been obsessed with the Traveller and the portal. He discovered it years ago. That knowledge became extremely useful when I possessed—"

"You took his body. Just like Ilmly. You tried to take mine, too, back on Marcrituss. Didn't you?" John's voice was flat, deadly.

Revonat's smile turned razor-thin. "I suspected that if I abducted the portal's guardian, you would come."

Anger surged in John like fire. "You think you're all-powerful?" His voice was ice. "Pathetic. A parasite, wearing dead men's skin because you can't exist any other way. Ever heard of angel possession?" He paused, watching Revonat's composure crack. "Didn't think so. And you never will—because they're more powerful than you'll ever be."

Revonat snapped, seizing John's arm with inhuman strength, slamming him against the glass. The pane rattled, the city a fractured vision beneath. Hellish rage burned in his gaze.

Shenya stepped forward, but Kleo held him back.

Revonat lifted John's head by his hair and smashed his face against the glass again. "Look," the demon hissed.

Below, thousands gathered in the streets. Armored vehicles rolled through ruined avenues. Distant explosions thundered across the city. War was coming.

"I could kill you anywhere," Revonat said, his voice a blade of cold. "And that moment is coming." He yanked John away from the glass, keeping an iron grip as he stared into John's eyes. Revonat's hands trembled—not with fear, but with something hungrier. "As I thought... just a frightened boy from Eden," he whispered. "Chosen by the King to undo everything I've built." His smile twisted, brittle and desperate.

John fought to break free.

Revonat leaned close, smile warping. "I brought you here to suffer. To witness the beginning of the end."

His voice shifted—ancient, monstrous, dropping into tones that no human throat could produce. "I watched as the King chose your kind—weak, flawed things—for favor meant for higher beings. Why should his creation remain as he intended, when it could be remade by those who will not kneel?"

John remembered his vision. The angels and demons at war. He began to understand why the demon hated humanity so much.

"The pathetic angelic plot to send a Traveller to unite the worlds was foolish. All seven worlds will end like this—your world included. And when they do, the Watchers will finally see what I am. The story of the Traveller will end as quickly as it began—by my hand."

For a moment, John stood paralysed, staring at the devastation. The smoke rose like incense. Columns of people marched numbly toward slaughter.

Shenya listened to the demon's boasting and felt pity. Where John saw monstrous power, Shenya saw emptiness: a being so twisted by arrogance and bitterness that it could not see truth. Demons were slaves to their own pride, dragging others down only to convince themselves they still had power.

Below, the crowds swelled—two vast storms about to collide.

A bloodbath.

Urgency rose within John. He closed his eyes, reaching for the power within—and felt it spark.

Revonat stiffened. "I know what you are doing!" he roared.

Before John could react, Revonat hurled him to the ground.

Shenya and Kleo lunged to help, but the demon thrust out his hands. Darkness erupted from his palms, swirling like living smoke, coiling around all three of them. Chains of shadow locked them in place.

"This is how it ends!" Revonat bellowed.

What spoke now was no longer mixed with Vonild's voice. The sound was ancient and monstrous—Revonat revealed.

"John!" Shenya shouted desperately. "Remember to say the name—"

Revonat snapped his hand, and the chains slithered up, sealing their mouths.

"The divine name will not help you here!" the demon thundered.

The chains tightened.

Held helpless, John struggled to breathe. Fear clawed at him, cold and suffocating.

Do not be afraid, he told himself.

But the words felt empty.

Terror pressed in—vast, unrelenting. He felt cut off from the power he was meant to wield. The darkness was too great.

A memory surfaced: Danrael's voice. *Remember to pray... it may one day save your life.*

John closed his eyes.

With no weapon left, he prayed.

He begged God to come.

To come quickly.

For several heartbeats—nothing.

Then Revonat's smile vanished. The demon's eyes went wide.

He felt it—a sudden, blinding purity piercing the gloom.

Holiness.

Revonat whirled toward the windows. High above the city, light blazed—a living star, descending with impossible speed.

Revonat screamed.

The windows exploded inward. A torrent of holy fire swept through the chamber, shattering glass, howling like a storm from Heaven.

None of the shards touched John, Shenya, or Kleo, and the flames parted around them, pure and gentle.

This was not the fire from Marciluk. This was something different—something greater. Its radiance filled the soul with awe. The light shimmered between orange and luminous blue. Within it, a dove took shape: a sign of peace, a symbol of divinity.

The dark chamber filled with holy splendour.

Revonat shrieked in terror, scrambling up the wall—twenty feet, clinging to the ceiling like a monstrous spider.

His power faltered. The chains dissolved into smoke.

"Hold on to me!" John shouted.

Shenya and Kleo grabbed him as they ran for the fire.

The holy flame enveloped them—not burning, but filling them with warmth and peace. A transcendent serenity washed over them, not unlike the portals themselves. They knew they were safe.

The massive dove surged outward, carrying them through the shattered windows into open sky.

Below, a battlefield stretched across the barren plains. Thousands waited, poised for violence.

The dove descended, setting John, Shenya, and Kleo gently among the stunned crowds. Then it rose like a radiant dove and vanished into the heavens.

A stunned silence swept across the battlefield.

It broke suddenly. Thousands of voices exploded in shouts of confusion and awe.

Revonat was not far behind.

Like a storm embodied, the demon pursued them from the shattered temple chamber. Darkness raced across the sky. John's stomach clenched as he saw it—a vision made real, darkness that radiated hate.

The black plumes struck the earth nearby, shadows swirling as if the ground itself rejected their presence. From the chaos, Revonat stepped forward, still wearing Vonild's shape.

"I'm done with you now, Traveller!" he shrieked, his voice echoing across the wastes. "Let them see what freedom truly looks like—not chains of obedience, but the dominion of those unafraid to seize it. Under my reign, none will kneel to distant thrones."

With every word, his anger grew. The earth shook beneath his fury.

"This is what it all comes down to. I will destroy you here, before them all. They will forget your God. They will bow and worship me!"

In John's pocket, the scroll fragment shook.

He pulled out the felt pouch. The ancient fragment glowed —stronger than ever before. It trembled in his hand, drawn toward Revonat.

At the same moment, something burst from Revonat's jacket: another fragment. It shot through the air, desperate to reunite with John's.

For an instant, it seemed the two would merge.

Revonat moved faster. With his power, he seized his fragment, clutching it like a prize.

"Where did you find that?" John shouted, stunned to see the demon possess a piece of the sacred scroll.

Revonat ignored him, but the flash of surprise in his eyes told John he hadn't expected him to have a fragment too.

"If you give that to me, Traveller," Revonat purred, suddenly calm and deadly, "I'll release the guardian of this world right now. All you must do is let go of the scroll."

John shoved the glowing piece back into the pouch and into his pocket.

"Give it to me!" Revonat roared.

"You are nothing but a liar!" John shouted. "I'll never give it to you!"

Revonat wailed with fury.

His eyes turned black. Dark power erupted from him like a storm, shadows coiling and hardening into chains.

The chains lashed out. Shenya and Kleo were hurled to the ground. Black bonds pinned them helpless, their voices silenced.

Revonat summoned something worse.

Hellfire erupted from the earth. Jagged rings of flame surrounded his captives, roaring like living beasts—barriers no one could cross.

John remained standing, but chains held him rigid. The demon's grip was absolute.

Revonat stepped closer. The stench of rot washed over John. But worse than the chains was the pressure—a force clawing at the edge of John's mind.

Revonat was pushing in.

A twisted smile spread across the demon's face. He leaned in, staring into John's eyes—too close. John felt him—feeding on every trace of fear. Icy tendrils crawled under John's skin, threading up his spine, clutching at his heart.

"I see everything," Revonat spat, presence burrowing deep. "I know what you are."

John's thoughts splintered. Revonat moved through his mind like a predator—sharp, patient, relentless. The memories came in a rush—flashes of Olly's fist, the ache of loneliness, old shame, humiliation, the taste of blood, the sting of tears behind closed doors.

He tried to fight, but the demon was too strong. Every memory turned raw.

"You are good for nothing!" Revonat thundered. The words hit like hammer-blows, vibrating in John's skull. "I have seen your miserable existence from beginning to end. You have always been frightened. Always weak!"

The chains tightened, metal biting into his flesh, dragging him closer. He could smell sulfur and ash. He heard his own ragged breath echoing too loudly in the void.

"Nobody has ever truly cared about you," Revonat hissed, voice like broken glass. "You were mocked. Bullied. Forgotten. And you deserved it."

Each word broke another wall inside John—a flood of humiliation, pain, failure, every cruel word and memory rising like a choking tide. His mouth filled with the taste of old blood, the echo of laughter, the rough gravel against his cheek.

"You are not fit to be the Traveller!" Revonat roared. "You're not even fit to be alive!"

John hung, battered by words that cut deeper than any blade. He could barely breathe, chest tight and burning. The world swam, smeared at the edges.

Somewhere behind him, he heard Shenya straining against the chains—a muffled sound, desperate, cut short.

Revonat leaned in, voice dropping to a venomous whisper. "You're still that same frightened boy. Pathetic. Hated. Unloved. The powers given to you changed nothing. You were a waste of time then—and you are a waste of time now."

John lowered his head. Smaller than he'd ever been. Smaller than the boy Olly tormented. Crushed by shame, helpless, unworthy.

Chains of fear and humiliation wrapped around him, tightening, suffocating.

But then—through the roaring storm, something flickered.

One last memory rose, bright and stubborn—

Dernoah.

He saw her, frail yet bright with faith, repeating her favorite scripture: *He makes all things new.*

Dernoah.

The memory of her flashed again—thin, suffering, yet luminous with hope, her voice gentle but unbreakable:

Remember that, she said, *He makes all things new.*

Even as death crept upon her, those words filled her with peace. She believed, with all her heart, that God would one day make her new.

The memory cut through the darkness—clean, clear, a rush of warmth and color. Dernoah's eyes, her steady hands, the faint scent of lirith and cora milk in her home.

Standing there in chains, wishing he could be someone

else, the words Dernoah loved pierced through the weight pressing down on him.

He makes all things new.

He let the words fill him—let them echo, let them root deep.

Why would God choose me?

The question had followed him since the cave. Through every world, every failure, every moment he'd frozen when he should have moved. He'd never been able to answer it.

But standing here—broken, shamed, Revonat's words still ringing in his skull—he felt something he hadn't expected.

Love.

Not despite everything Revonat had dragged into the light. Right now. In the middle of it. The same God who had watched him on that gravel road, who had been there in every silent prayer that seemed to go nowhere—that God had chosen him anyway. Loved him anyway. Had always loved him.

He hadn't been chosen because of what he could do. He'd been chosen for what he would become.

And what he would become began with this—the choice to receive what had been freely given all along. Not earned. Not deserved. Just accepted.

Like Dernoah, John chose to surrender. Not just understanding, but believing. He let go—all the shame, the need to prove himself, the fear that he was a mistake.

He let go and fell upward.

Grace flooded his soul—blinding, clean, like light shattering a stained window. In a heartbeat, the darkness broke. He saw himself not as broken, but as made new—chosen, loved, whole.

Words of Scripture blazed in his mind: *By his wounds, you have been healed.*

The shame, the old voices, lost their power.

Danrael's words returned, bright as a song. *God calls out to every soul. When someone answers with faith, something awakens. An endless void is filled with grace.*

He makes all things new.

At last, John accepted the gift—fully, finally, without reservation.

In that moment, he saw it all—the entire journey crystallised into one luminous pattern. Dernoah's faith, Shenya's quiet belief, always present. Every moment, every person, every struggle—all of it leading to this moment. God had been working all along, not to fix John, but to remake him.

Fear no longer ruled him.

Revonat no longer ruled him.

And with fear gone, the power that fear had blocked surged stronger than he had ever felt it.

He drew a breath—felt it fill his chest—and straightened. The chains didn't break so much as forget themselves. They unravelled like smoke in morning light.

Across the battlefield, thousands stood frozen, watching.

"You're right, Revonat," John said, his voice steady, quiet. "These powers didn't change me."

Revonat stared, confusion flickering—just for a heartbeat.

"But something else has," John continued, a freedom blooming inside him. "I've been changed by grace."

The Traveller bowed his head. In that instant, everything changed.

He began to speak the ancient words from his vision—the prayer that once drove back the darkness. This time, he spoke without fear, only faith.

With every word, the chains binding Shenya and Kleo loosened. The hellish flames flickered, shrank, and vanished. The taste of ash faded from the air.

"What is John saying?" Kleo cried out, her voice small, awed.

"He's praying!" Shenya answered, wonder in every syllable. "Finally! 'Blessed are You, Lord our God, King of the universe!'"

Shenya joined him, their voices rising together.

Overhead, the sky blackened. It was a storm gathering, thunder cracking, wind sweeping dust and ash across the battlefield. The world seemed to hold its breath as tens of thousands stared upward, stunned.

John kept praying—and with every word, the power in him grew brighter, wilder, vaster than himself. Awe and wonder filled him—a current not his own.

His eyes turned pure white, blazing with the same light Shenya had witnessed once before, in a kitchen on Marcrituss. Except this time, it was even brighter.

John lifted his gaze toward Revonat. The demon staggered back.

The Traveller's glowing eyes shone brighter as he clenched his fist and raised his arm to the heavens.

"Yeshua!" he cried with all his strength.

The entire world fell silent. The storm paused, every breath and heart and voice stilled.

"He has invoked the holy name, in the Saviour's own tongue—the name that means, 'God saves,'" Shenya whispered.

He bowed his head. "John has declared to this world that God saves."

The ground beneath Spaltrico began to shake, a deep rumbling that climbed up through bones and stone. Vonild's towering temple crumbled—glass and steel rained down, devoured by shadow and wind.

Across the city and beyond, people realized this was no illusion.

The power of God had revealed itself before their eyes, and across all of Spaltrico.

A bolt of lightning tore from the storm above—it struck John's raised fist with a deafening crack.

John planted his feet, feeling power surge through him like a blazing river. He stood as a living conduit between Heaven and the world below, unleashing that power against the darkness threatening Spaltrico and all seven worlds.

He thrust his arm forward.

The holy power exploded toward Revonat.

The demon was hurled to the ground, battered by radiant force.

As the divine light consumed him, it was a piercing reminder of the love he had always rejected. Revonat's delusions shattered. In that burning radiance, he faced what he had spent eternity denying: the King's authority was unbreakable. The lie that defiance meant strength, that his will alone could reshape reality—all of it crumbled. In the grip of that overwhelming light, Revonat was brought to his knees by the power of the true King.

Stripped of every deception, exposed before the horrified crowd, whatever remained of Vonild's body melted away.

Revonat's true, demonic form was laid bare.

The fragment of the scroll slipped from his grasp.

With the last of his strength, Revonat tried to keep it from John. He summoned hellfire, raising a wall of flame around the treasure.

Screams erupted from the crowd.

John's eyes shone with heavenly light. While still holding Revonat with the power from on high, he extended his free hand. The flames recoiled, retreating back into the earth.

Seeing the chance, Shenya dashed forward. He leapt across

the last dying tongues of hellfire and seized the scroll fragment before Revonat could reclaim it.

The demon screamed—a sound that echoed across the battlefield, unmaking the silence.

Then, overwhelmed with truth, the demon was gone. The battle was over. The darkness that ruled Spaltrico was at last defeated.

Instantly, the sky cleared. For the first time in over a century, the people saw the sun break through the clouds to shine on Spaltrico. The world itself bore witness—a new dawn, a world reclaimed from shadow.

For the first time, hope blazed brighter than fear.

John lowered his arm slowly.

The battlefield was silent in a way it hadn't been since they arrived—not the held-breath silence of people waiting for violence, but something else entirely. Something that had no name.

He looked up.

The sun was there. Ordinary and extraordinary simultaneously, the way the most important things always were. A pale winter sun, nothing spectacular by any world's standard. It pushed through the last gray remnants of smog with the quiet persistence of something that had been waiting a very long time for permission to arrive.

Shenya stood beside him, the scroll fragment in his hand. He stared upward with the expression John had come to recognize—the scholar's face undone by wonder, the careful man briefly without words.

Around them, thousands of Spaltrican faces shielded their eyes. Some didn't. Some wept without appearing to know they were weeping.

Kleo said nothing for a moment. Then, almost despite herself, a short laugh escaped her—bright and involuntary, like something shaken loose. She pressed a hand to her mouth, but her eyes were shining.

John thought of what she'd said in the cottage. *I don't think your God cares about Spaltrico.*

He looked at her now and said nothing. He didn't need to.

The sun answered for him.

A massive crowd surged toward John, Shenya, and Kleo.

John's mind went to the Bible stories he loved as a boy, and he knew exactly what to do.

A chariot of fire descended from the heavens.

"What is that?" Shenya cried, his voice full of awe.

"Elijah's chariot!" John said, laughing—a laugh that rang out free and unbroken. "Quick—get on!"

They leapt aboard.

The chariot rose, carrying them high above the city as the astonished crowds watched from below.

CHAPTER

FIFTY-SIX

W hen they reached the cottage, John and Shenya paused just inside the narrow hallway. After the thunder and chaos of the temple, the quiet pressed against their ears like something thick and heavy.

John's hands wouldn't stop shaking. He only noticed when he pressed his palms flat against the cool wall, the chill grounding him as the last tremors of adrenaline slowly bled away. His chest still ached from breathing too hard, too long. Each inhale came shallow at first, then steadier.

Deeper in the cottage, faint sounds drifted—the low hum of the vrooter outside, the sharp crackle of Kleo's printer. But here, in this small space, there was only stillness and the faint, clean scent of synthetic soap and ozone.

Shenya stood a few feet away, leaning lightly against the opposite wall. Dirt streaked his jaw and clung to the creases around his eyes. Sweat had dried in his hairline. For once, his posture was open, unguarded.

"John," Shenya said. His voice caught.

John lifted his gaze. For a long moment, neither of them

spoke. The moment stretched between them—full, not awkward—carrying everything they had just survived.

Shenya's eyes shimmered with unshed tears. He stepped closer and placed a hand on John's shoulder. The grip was firm, warm, real. John could feel the faint tremble in Shenya's fingers, mirroring his own.

"What you did back there..." Shenya began, then stopped. He swallowed hard, the dirt on his face catching the hallway light. "I have never seen anything like it."

John's throat tightened. He looked down at his own hands —still trembling against the wall—and slowly lowered them. The quiet that followed felt deeper, heavier, wrapping around them like a shared breath.

Shenya didn't let go of his shoulder. His thumb pressed once, gently, as if anchoring them both to the floor.

"You stood before pure evil," he said at last, voice low and rough, "and you did not falter."

Something inside John's chest gave way—like a knot he hadn't realized was still there slipping loose. His breath hitched, not from fear, but from a sharp, beautiful relief. For the first time since the battlefield, the weight on his shoulders felt bearable.

"I was afraid," John whispered into the quiet. "When we landed in that wasteland... I was almost broken."

Shenya's grip tightened just a fraction. Dirt smudged from his palm onto John's shirt, but neither of them moved to brush it away. They stood like that for a long time—two exhausted men, faces streaked with the same grime and smoke, breathing in the same still air.

Then Shenya's voice came again, softer now, carrying the weight of everything he didn't need to list. "You are not the boy who stumbled through that portal weeks ago. You truly have become the Traveller."

He gave John's shoulder one final, gentle squeeze—a quiet benediction—and stepped back.

The silence that followed wasn't empty. It was full of gratitude, of awe, of everything they had endured together.

Kleo appeared at the end of the hallway, already printing a large viewing screen. "You two need to see this," she called, her voice urgent but bright. "The whole world is watching."

John peeled himself from the wall and followed Shenya. The weight of everything that had happened still sat heavy across John's shoulders, yet for the first time since the battle, his lungs opened fully, drawing air that tasted clean.

Across Spaltrico, images of John's confrontation with Revonat spread like wildfire. Every screen replayed the moment: people watching, sharing, dissecting it on every network, the world ablaze with wonder and fear.

Reports of extraterrestrial visitors sent the planet into a frenzy. Former cult members spoke out, claiming true divinity had sent strangers from another world to overthrow the false god, Borth.

Every screen was abuzz with the same word—Yeshua. Commentators stumbled, and scientists fumbled for explanations no one believed. Then the Emperor appeared, daughter at his side, and in a single decree ended the ban on faith. He called for reconciliation, a closing of the wounds that had torn the world apart.

And somewhere in the chaos, the authorities launched a search for John and Shenya. The mysterious chariot that carried them away had slipped by every camera. No footage. To the world, the two visitors had simply vanished into the sky.

Kleo said nothing for a long moment. Like the commentators, she was stuck on the same word—Yeshua. John had told her who it was. She had only half-listened then. But the Mour Text proved his existence was known on her world before: ancient symbols, a man on a cross, words no one on Spaltrico had understood for centuries. Her world had always been reaching toward something it could not name. Until now.

She exhaled slowly and sank into a freshly printed recliner. "This is a day that will be remembered for generations across Spaltrico," she said.

She left the rest unspoken.

John started to reply, but a sharp knock at the door cut him off.

He and Shenya exchanged an uneasy glance.

Kleo darted to the window, tension in her shoulders. One look outside and her breath sagged with relief. "It's safe," she said.

She opened the door.

Prinny and her son stood on the stoop.

"Prinny! Eamin!" Kleo cried, rushing forward to wrap them in a fierce embrace.

They clung together, tears streaming—joy bursting free after days of fear.

At last, they stepped inside, still tangled together, not quite believing safety was real.

Prinny turned to John and Shenya, pressing both hands to her chest. "I saw the broadcasts," she said, voice trembling. "We can never express how grateful we are." Shenya smiled.

"This must be Eamin. I'm so glad to see you safe."

After a moment of shock at seeing two men from another world, the young man found his voice. "Without your victory over Vonild... I wouldn't be here now."

John returned the smile. "You're welcome." A faint worry still lingered in the back of his mind. "There's something we need to talk about, though. The portal here on Spaltrico needs to be watched—very carefully. Vonild and Revonat might be gone, but there's a good chance someone on their side knows where it is."

Eamin's posture straightened. "I understand. After everything, I won't let my guard down again."

John remembered his conversation with Shenya about why the portals needed guardians. Vonild finding Spaltrico's portal was proof enough of the danger.

Eamin's curiosity flickered through his nerves. "By the way, what was that thing you took from the monster?"

John reached into his pocket, pulling out a small felt pouch. Inside, the two fragments had fused into a single piece.

He held it up. The join between the two pieces was invisible—not sealed or mended, but simply gone, as if there had never been a seam at all. The fragment was warmer than it should have been, a steady living warmth that pressed against his palm like a pulse. He closed his fingers around it slowly. "This is part of my mission. There's a piece of this scroll on each of the seven worlds. Revonat had Spaltrico's fragment."

Kleo leaned in, thoughtful. "If he hadn't been carrying it, the scroll might have been lost when the temple collapsed. So —we should be thankful for that, I suppose."

Shenya folded his arms, frowning at the fragment. "There's something I don't understand. Revonat wanted your fragment too, John. But if he already knew the message on the completed scroll threatens him, then he knows even a single piece is enough to stop you. So why would he want your fragment as well?"

John studied the fused pieces in his hand. "He seemed desperate to get it," he admitted quietly. "Maybe he knew something about the scroll we don't know yet."

A hush settled over the room, heavy with questions.

Suddenly, the screen flashed—breaking news. All of them turned.

Kleo's face appeared on the broadcast: eyewitness footage had identified her standing beside John and Shenya during the confrontation. Authorities now requested she present herself for questioning.

Kleo sagged deeper into her chair, hands covering her face. "Oh no," she groaned. "Now I'm in for a real treat. There'll be no peace for me now that they know I was there. If any extremists are left, they might come after me—even if the faction's mostly gone."

She lowered her hands, looking at John and Shenya. "You two need to leave. Someone will be here any minute to bring me in for questioning."

Shenya glanced at John. No words needed—John gave a small nod and stepped aside.

"Kleo," Shenya said gently, "there may be another option."

She looked up, eyes rimmed red.

"You could come with us to Marcrituss," he went on. "Stay there for a while, until this storm passes."

Kleo blinked, surprise breaking through the tension. "Are you serious? Is that even possible?"

Shenya smiled, a hint of playfulness flickering in his tired face. "If it worked for me, I don't see why not. Besides, I'd be happy to spare you from those dreadful food boxes."

Kleo laughed, sitting up straighter. She turned to Prinny. "What do you think?"

"Go," Prinny said immediately, voice firm and kind. "All of you, go now. You've done what you came here to do. Vonild is gone. The cult is finished."

John caught Kleo's eye. "Part of my mission is about uniting the seven worlds. We need someone from here— someone who's fought darkness from inside, who stood against it. That's you."

Kleo's smile was small but true, doubt falling away. She

glanced around her cottage, at the screen showing the destroyed temple. All her life, she'd wanted nothing more than to see that place razed. That goal had pushed her to become an officer. Now it smouldered on live images—mission accomplished. Yet the thought that the same evil might be out there, working on other worlds, made her stomach turn. She was ready to fight again—anywhere in the universe. "Alright, kid. Count me in—for now."

She hurried to the back room, packing a small bag in barely two minutes.

Moments later, they were outside. Prinny's sky vrooter waited, hull gleaming in the pale light. The five of them squeezed inside, the craft rising smoothly into the air.

They'd barely left when, below, a convoy of law enforcement vehicles sped toward the cottage. One last look back—if they'd waited just a few minutes longer, everything would have changed.

As the vrooter climbed over Tokika City, something extraordinary unfolded.

For the first time, Kleo, Prinny, and Eamin flew beneath a cloudless sky. The pollution was gone.

John pressed his forehead to the window and watched as the streets below erupted in celebration. Parades wound through the city; crowds danced in vibrant costumes, rejoicing in the end of the cult—a long wound finally closing.

Beside him, Prinny was transformed. The worry lines on her face had vanished. With Eamin safely beside her, she shone with quiet joy, eyes fixed on the world below. "Do you see those costumes?" Her voice sparkled.

Shenya leaned closer, watching the river of color spill through the streets. "They're a welcome change from what we saw before."

Prinny pressed a hand to the glass, wonder warming her

whole face. "That's traditional Tokikan clothing. I've only ever seen it in museums—never worn like this. It's... incredible."

Shenya's smile was gentle. "Perhaps today is a new dawn for Spaltrico. Things long forgotten may now be reborn."

They watched in silence as the city's celebration faded and the vrooter descended, joy lingering in the air like distant music.

When Kleo stepped out and faced the glowing portal, something shifted inside her.

Hope.

For the first time in years, a new beginning shimmered before her—a second chance. She hugged Prinny and Eamin tight, overwhelmed with the joy of seeing them together again.

Meanwhile, John and Shenya examined the cave walls. Only then did they notice the ancient drawings scrawled across the stone—details missed on arrival.

Shenya traced the markings. 'These are ancient. Look here —seven portals in seven circles. Those must be the planets.'

John leaned in and pointed to one in particular. "And did you see this one?"

"That stands for Eden." Shenya studied it, awe rising. He pointed to something higher. 'These words up here are written in ancient Spaltrican: 'The Traveller from Eden will bring us together.'" He stepped back.

John nodded. "The portals call my world, Eden."

"Hopefully, we can learn more about this."

Kleo, John and Shenya stood before the glowing portal. John adjusted the dial until Marcrituss's symbols aligned. He placed his hand gently on the center circle.

The portal flared brighter.

He turned to Kleo with a grin. "Alright. Welcome to Team Traveller."

CHAPTER
FIFTY-SEVEN

They tumbled out of the portal and onto Marcritan soil, landing hard in the sealed darkness of the cave. The air was cool and still. Kleo grabbed John's sleeve and didn't let go.

John squinted upward, catching his breath. "So... how exactly are we getting out of this one?" His voice echoed off the stone, small in the hush.

A faint grinding rattled overhead. The ceiling slid open. Silver light from Marcrituss's twin moons spilled down, turning the cavern walls to pearl. From above, a rope dropped into the glow.

"Welcome to Marcrituss," said a familiar voice.

They spun. Danrael stood behind them, once more in his Marcritan appearance. He spoke in flawless Spaltrican for Kleo's sake.

Kleo stared at him, speechless, clutching John's arm, afraid to let go.

Danrael's calm voice filled the cave. "John, you have completed the first stage of your mission. You've recovered two fragments of the scroll. More importantly, you have begun uniting the peoples of the seven worlds."

John glanced over at Shenya and Kleo. "I hope it's not a problem that we brought Kleo with us. Can anyone come through the portal with me?"

Danrael's eyes softened. "When you open a portal, it is open to others—but use this gift wisely. These crossings must remain rare, at least for now. Bringing others through to worlds you have already collected the scroll fragments from is part of your mission. But the other worlds must stay hidden until the appointed time. For now, keep it to... what is it you call yourselves? Team Traveller?"

He smiled faintly. "The three of you standing here is proof that unity has begun. Through you, the people of Marcrituss and Spaltrico have witnessed the power of God."

His tone grew solemn, a quiet gravity settling over the space. "What began today is only the start. Darkness still stirs across the seven worlds. But for now... you've earned your rest."

John glanced at Shenya, a smile breaking through. "I think I'd like to stay on Marcrituss with my kin, for a little while."

Shenya slung an arm around his shoulders, giving him a gentle squeeze.

"Of course," Danrael said softly. "And well done—all of you."

His form brightened, dissolving into light before vanishing.

Kleo let out a shaky breath, still gripping John's arm. "Um... What the hell was that?"

John gave her shoulder a reassuring pat. "That was Danrael. He's an angel—long story."

Kleo's eyes were huge. "An angel?"

Shenya offered a wry smile. "We'll explain it, but we should get out of here first."

Without another word, they grabbed the rope and climbed up into the moonlight.

When Kleo stepped out, she stopped short. She never imagined she'd see a world alive with plants, green and wild. It was even more spectacular than her grandmother's picture of trees on Spaltrico.

She looked up at the night sky. Twin moons hung above, and silent birds glided beneath their light. Kleo stood still, turning slowly, taking it in.

Shenya led them along winding paths of the labyrinth. Outside, on the field adjacent to the sea, Kleo gasped.

John and Shenya turned, alarmed, but Kleo simply stood, staring across the water. The twin moons shimmered on the waves like living silver. Kleo broke down, tears slipping free.

"Kleo, what is it?" Shenya asked.

She wiped her eyes, her voice thick. "I've never seen anything like this. Such beauty."

Shenya smiled. "Just wait until you eat real food. Then you'll truly know joy."

They crossed the moonlit field to the village gates, now open after the lockdown. Princess Qitra had promised to inform everyone of John's presence. As he walked through Morboli without his old disguise, John felt both exposed and free.

At Shenya's home, John paused. He glanced at the empty house next door—Shenya's mother's home.

He rested a hand on Shenya's shoulder. "Dernoah helped me through everything on Spaltrico. It was my memory of her that helped me break free from Revonat."

Shenya wiped his eyes quickly and knocked on his front door.

The door opened a crack. Jaromei peeked out. She lit up

with joy when she saw who was on the other side. She threw open the door and pulled her father into a tight embrace.

"I didn't expect you back so soon!" she exclaimed. "It's hardly been three days!"

"A great deal can happen in three days," Shenya replied, remembering John's story of resurrection.

Jaromei hugged John warmly. "Thank you for bringing my father home safely."

Then she noticed someone behind them, her eyes widening.

"Jaromei," Shenya said, "this is Kleo from Spaltrico. She'll be staying with us for a while, until it's safe for her to return home. We couldn't have done the mission without her."

"You are very welcome here, Kleo," Jaromei said, gesturing her in.

Kleo didn't understand the words, but the kindness on Jaromei's face made the meaning clear.

Jaromei switched on a lantern. "You'll be glad to know Princess Qitra kept her promise. News from the sea traveled faster than the wind. Every village and city across the three tribes is talking about the visitor from another world who escaped the mad King Rathrian." She smiled at John. "You've been declared an ally and friend of King Euron."

John let out a breath he hadn't realized he'd been holding. "That's good news."

"It certainly is," Shenya agreed. "But celebrations can wait. It's late—we all need rest."

He turned to his daughter. "Jaromei, will you stay next door tonight with Kleo?"

"Of course, Father," Jaromei replied, then frowned. "Though I have a feeling she doesn't understand a word we're saying."

"Goodness," John said, "that's because she doesn't."

He and Shenya had forgotten—Kleo hadn't been given the gift of languages.

"Kleo," Shenya said in Spaltrican, "tomorrow we'll begin your first lessons in Marcritan."

Kleo grinned. "I'm a fast learner. I already speak six Spaltrican languages."

"Excellent," Shenya laughed. "Then I look forward to our first lesson. Tonight, Jaromei will take you next door."

"Thank you all for your kindness," Kleo said.

"You are most welcome," Shenya replied. "Sleep well. We'll see you in the morning."

Jaromei stood, quietly amazed at her father speaking in a language she didn't know. She wanted to ask a dozen questions, but decided they could wait until tomorrow.

Once Jaromei and Kleo had gone next door, John and Shenya finally retired.

John entered the small bedroom. He smiled as he saw the floating Marcritan mattress. He'd missed it.

He laid down and let the water's gentle movement rock him softly.

A moment later, he closed his eyes and pictured the twin moons and the sea.

At last, John slept.

FIFTY-EIGHT

The next morning, John found that Shenya had once again laid out clothes and toiletries for him— something he'd done almost every day since they met.

After washing up, John headed downstairs, greeted by the smell of breakfast. Shenya was at the cooking table, making arbimto eggs—John's favorite.

He was almost at the table when Shenya turned from the stove, spatula in hand, and faced him squarely.

"John. No more delays. If you're going to stay with us, we need to talk about Jaromei."

John stopped mid-step, the familiar knot of anticipation tightening behind his ribs. He'd known this conversation was coming.

"Alright," he sighed. "Let's have it."

"First, I won't tell my daughter who she should—or shouldn't—love."He hesitated, then added, "Honestly, I'd be proud if Jaromei chose someone like you."

"Thanks, Shenya." John let out a breath.

"I'm not finished yet." Shenya's tone made John shift uneasily.

"We both know you care about Jaromei," Shenya continued. "And it's obvious she cares for you." He turned back to the eggs for a moment. "I saw how her eyes lit up when she saw you last night. But you have to understand, John—a relationship between two anuri from different worlds won't be easy. Some will look on it with suspicion. Maybe even hatred." He met John's eyes. "Are you prepared for that?"

"I am," John replied. "I know there will be challenges."

Shenya nodded. "And if your relationship develops, what about the future? When your mission's finished—God willing you succeed—then what?" He gestured around the room. "Where would you live? Would you take her to Earth? Would you stay here?" He frowned thoughtfully at the eggs, turning the spatula slowly. "From what you've told me, your world might not welcome someone like Jaromei."

John stared at the eggs a moment, turning the words over in his mind. "I know it won't be simple," he said at last. "But we'll face it together." He looked up. "She told me something before we left Morboli."

Shenya raised an eyebrow. "Oh?"

"She said if I can travel across the universe in a day, then making something like us work has to be possible too."

Shenya chuckled softly. Then his expression settled, warm but serious. "I only want to protect both of you. I don't want to see either of you hurt."

"I understand," John said, meeting Shenya's gaze. "And I promise you—I would never hurt Jaromei."

Shenya studied him for a long moment, then smiled.

"Good."

He returned to the stove and set the finished eggs in front of John. "I've said what I needed to," he said. "I believe you,

John. And if my daughter gives you her heart... I trust you to guard it well."

"So... I have your blessing to date her?"

Shenya nodded. "If you promise to care for her and treat her well, then yes. You have my blessing."

John leaned back, grinning. "Well... that was less terrifying than I expected."

Shenya laughed and reached over to pat him on the head. "Good," he said. "Now eat your eggs before they get cold."

CHAPTER
FIFTY-NINE

Sunlight filtered through the latticework of Shenya's back garden, scattering shifting patterns across the ground as John and Jaromei soaked up the last warmth by the fountain. The air still carried the taste of summer—salt and distant rain. Laughter echoed as Kleo pointed out every unfamiliar bird, rock, and flower as if she'd only just arrived in this world.

Kleo had come a long way from the woman who'd gripped his arm in the cave. She rattled off Marcritan words—stumbling but game. There was a new looseness in her stride.

Those easy afternoons became the rhythm of the season. Over time, the days reshaped them all, binding Team Traveller tighter than John would have imagined. Kleo no longer talked of Spaltrico—not really. There were no lingering glances, no pauses for old regrets, just the new language on her tongue and a growing assurance in her eyes.

Inside, Yumi's booming voice carried through the house as he recounted his latest escapade. He'd sweep a massive arm around John's shoulder, nearly lifting him off his feet. "Your fault I got this promotion, you know! The princess's official gropolo shou. Hope you're proud!" Yumi expressed his gratitude for the new job by allowing Xerti to stay for the summer. Her massive wings became a familiar presence over the fields by the labyrinth.

As the weeks passed, Princess Qitra's royal decree changed more than just John's freedom to walk without the burmui. In the markets, people watched—some whispering, some offering cautious smiles. Elders eyed him warily, debating amongst themselves whether the arrival of someone from a distant world threatened the old beliefs. Children, however, tugged at his sleeve, wide-eyed and eager for stories of the stars.

Beneath the surface, tension with the Sea Kingdom simmered just beyond the horizon. Rumours of broken treaties drifted across the Land Kingdom like smoke. Full-blown war had so far been averted, but everyone knew the relationship between land and sea would never be the same after Rathrian's infamous speech.

Jaromei threw herself into her new duties with a focus that made John smile. Princess Qitra met with her weekly, drilling her in the diplomatic arts. Sometimes he'd find Jaromei hunched over parchment late into the night, lips moving as she rehearsed lines of negotiation, brow furrowed. When she caught him watching, she'd roll her eyes and smile, muttering about "advisor stuff."

Poltoma and Saltho became regular presences, arriving with laughter, wedding plans, and Batnu maps rolled under their arms. Each visit brought new talk of Brooth's future. "We'll make the Royal Batnu a place for all tribes," Poltoma declared, waving her hands, "and the study of the seven worlds will be our centerpiece. Marcrituss is ready to know the truth." John and Kleo found themselves supplying endless details for this new endeavour.

And the feasts—those grew as inexorably as the tide. Shenya's promise of one celebratory meal became six, then a dozen. Kleo's wonder at every dish became a spectacle; she'd marvel at the crunch of roasted roots, the sweetness of honeyed cora bread.

On those long evenings, John noticed that Shenya and Kleo had grown close. John would sometimes find them still at the table long after everyone else had gone to bed—Shenya with his notes spread out, Kleo leaning over them. She'd ask questions in careful Marcritan that Shenya answered in careful Spaltrican, both of them laughing at the collision of the two. One night, John passed the kitchen doorway and heard Kleo ask, quietly, what Shenya believed happened after death. He didn't stop to listen. But he noticed that Shenya's answer took a long time, and that neither of them looked up when John passed again an hour later.

But summer faded, almost imperceptibly at first. The air sharpened. Leaves on the trees edged gold, and the days grew short. More and more often, John caught himself gazing toward the mountains, the pull of home and his parents' farmhouse on another world tugging at him like an invisible thread.

One evening, as dusk crept in, he finally told Jaromei, his voice barely above a whisper. "I have to go back. Just for a while. My parents will be worrying and...I miss them."

Her hand squeezed his. "I know," she whispered. "But you'll come back."

He nodded, certain it was true.

The morning of his departure, a gentle anticipation hung in the air. Friends gathered beneath the spreading branches by the labyrinth's entrance, their smiles bright, shaded with the heaviness of goodbye. Even Princess Qitra was there, her silver cloak gleaming in the light.

John bowed to the princess. Then he turned to the group—Poltoma, Saltho, Yumi, Xerti, waiting just beyond.

Yumi seized him first, hoisting him clean off the ground. "When you come back," he boomed, "we must seriously discuss this gropolo training business."

John grinned, rubbing his ribs. "I think I'm hooked."

Poltoma caught his arm as Yumi set him down, her eyes intent. "It's hopeful, John," she said quietly. "The prophecy. I'm close to the full translation—but what I've found so far isn't darker. It might actually be a promise." She squeezed his hand. "I'll have it ready when you return."

He exhaled. "That's good to hear."

Saltho then stepped up. "I haven't forgotten my promise.

John smiled and said, "Look after everyone while I'm gone."

"You have my word." Saltho clasped John's arm and clapped him on the shoulder.

John crossed to Xerti, the gropolo's enormous head dipping to meet him. He stroked her cheek, feeling the warmth beneath her feathers. "I have to go for a little while." Xerti huffed, low and soft. He pressed his face into her neck, breathing in the earth-and-sea scent of her. "I'll be back soon." She nudged him gently. He knew she understood.

Kleo approached last, holding out two small triangular devices that shimmered faintly. "On Spaltrico, we developed communication devices not linked by signals or frequencies. They're connected by the matter they're made from. What happens to one, happens to the other, no matter the distance." She pressed one into John's palm. "If we ever need you, I'll press the button on mine. Yours will react, and you'll know to return."

He closed his fingers around the device, feeling the weight of her trust. They hugged fiercely, wordless.

After a final wave to everyone, John followed Shenya and Jaromei into the cool shadows of the labyrinth, the hush closing in behind them. The path twisted downward, torches flickering over stone.

At the portal chamber, John paused. The portal's light glimmered faintly, and tears pricked his eyes.

He turned to Jaromei. Her face was luminous in the dimness, and a memory washed over him, clear and immediate.

Three weeks earlier, he and Yumi had spent hours in the workshop, hands sore from sanding, laughter echoing as they pieced together a double-seated saddle for Xerti. John's excitement made him clumsy, but sharing Marcrituss's wildest freedom with Jaromei was worth every splinter.

When he finally asked her to fly with him, her whole face lit up. Nobody flew on a saddle—passengers always traveled in the enclosed box, strapped in, safe. But John had asked Xerti, and Xerti said yes in whatever language passed between them.

They set out just before sunset. Xerti's wings sliced through gold and rose as they soared high above Morboli. The village below became a lattice of twinkling lights. Jaromei felt it through the saddle—the way Xerti moved differently for John, responsive to something unspoken, a conversation happening just beneath the surface of the flight. Jaromei's laughter rang out as they banked through the clouds, her hair streaming behind her, eyes alight with something that was equal parts joy and wonder.

Up there, with the wind tearing at them and Jaromei's arms locked around his waist, John had whispered against her ear, 'I'm scared I'll mess this up.' She'd answered by squeezing tighter—the only reply he'd ever needed. The courage she drew from him, and gave back in equal measure. In that suspended moment, Marcrituss glittering beneath the moons, he knew with sudden, total clarity: she was the one.

Standing at the threshold of the portal, John's throat tightened until the words felt thick. The goodbye pressed down—bittersweet, urgent, real.

For a breathless heartbeat, neither spoke. There was only the hush of the cavern.

Memories pressed in: the wild flight, laughter, moonlit beaches, every quiet conversation.

"I love you, Jaromei," he whispered, his voice barely more than a tremor. The words felt small for what he meant.

Jaromei stepped close, gaze unwavering. "And I love you, Traveller," she said softly.

She paused—just for a heartbeat. John saw in her eyes the knowledge of everything she wasn't saying. The war was still simmering. Rathrian was still out there. The world he was leaving her in—and the worlds she was leaving him to.

"I will wait for you," she said. "However long it takes. Now go."

She reached up, cupping his face, and kissed him—a kiss full of promise and longing.

John pressed his forehead to hers, trying to memorise the feel of her arms, the quiet certainty between them. He wanted to carry this moment with him, to let it anchor him across worlds.

Finally, he turned to Shenya—the man who had become more than a mentor, more than a friend. He was like a father.

"John Arjik," Shenya said, his voice thick with pride and sorrow. "I won't say goodbye. Rather—until the next mission."

"I'll miss you. Thank you for everything."

They embraced tightly, Shenya's arms steady and strong. "Go with courage."

John stepped toward the portal. The light shimmered, beckoning. He turned for one last look: Jaromei's violet eyes, Shenya's steady hand—his second family, chosen and real. He held their faces in his memory and stepped through the portal.

CHAPTER
SIXTY

John tumbled out of the portal and landed hard on the familiar dirt floor of the cave. Torchlight flickered softly along the stone walls, washing the ancient chamber in a golden glow that made the shadows dance.

A few paces away, Danrael waited. He was restored to the earthly form John had first seen on the night his journey began.

"Welcome home, John," the angel said.

A shiver ran through John as the winter air closed around him—sharp, bracing, nothing like the sun-soaked warmth of Marcrituss.

"It's freezing here," he muttered, rubbing his arms.

Danrael smiled, a quiet twinkle in his eyes. "A moment ago, you stood under Marcrituss's autumn sun. Now you return to the winter of your own world."

John exhaled, watching his breath swirl in the torchlight. "What day is it?" He tried to remember how long he'd been gone—early December, maybe, but the days had blurred together.

"Tonight is December twenty-fourth," Danrael replied, his voice soft with meaning. "Christmas Eve. In truth, you could hardly have chosen a more perfect time to return."

John blinked. "No way. It's Christmas?"

A glimmer of mischief sparked in the angel's eyes. "In that case, perhaps I might offer a small Christmas gift. You seem to require warmer clothing."

John laughed, shaking his head. "You once told me you weren't a genie or a tailor."

Danrael shrugged, the hint of a smile on his lips. "Since it is Christmas, I'll allow myself one small exception. Besides, it would be rather disappointing if the Traveller survived ancient evils only to succumb to earthly pneumonia."

He traced a slow, deliberate circle in the air. Instantly, warmth flooded John's body. He glanced down in astonishment: a thick sweater now hugged his torso, a sturdy winter coat settling over his shoulders—soft, familiar, wonderfully warm.

"Thank you," John said, meaning it. Earth clothes felt oddly foreign now, but the comfort was undeniable.

"Oh, and one more thing," John added, reaching under the neckline of the sweater. He pulled out the felt pouch he'd fashioned into a necklace to carry the fragments of the ancient scroll. "Here are the scroll pieces I've collected so far. Should I give them to you?"

Danrael shook his head. "No. They belong to the Traveller."

John tucked the pouch away again, feeling its reassuring weight. "I promise I'll keep them safe."

"I know you will." Danrael's voice was soft. "I suspect you'll soon wish to return to Marcrituss, but you must remain here until the next phase of your mission begins."

"I understand," John said, nodding. He'd never expected the portals to be used like a revolving door between worlds.

"Now, my friend," Danrael said, his tone kind, "you should go and see your parents. They will be happy to see you."

John glanced toward the narrow shaft leading outside and gave a rueful laugh. "There's just one problem. I doubt I can squeeze through that hole anymore. Is there another way out?"

"Follow me," Danrael replied.

The angel led him into a smaller side chamber. Half-hidden among the rocks, Danrael pointed out a slender lever—something John had missed that first chaotic night.

"This mechanism opens the entrance your father and fore-fathers used when they served as guardians," Danrael explained. "There is another lever outside to seal it again. It's cleverly hidden behind moss along the rock face."

John gripped the lever and pulled.

A deep, grinding rumble echoed through the cave as the stone wall slowly shifted aside. A rush of winter air swept in, sharp and exhilarating. Beyond lay the forest and a sky of midnight blue, scattered with brilliant, icy stars.

For a moment, John simply stood there, staring upward. He remembered standing under the twin moons of Marcrituss with Jaromei, wondering if one of those distant pinpricks was Earth. Now, beneath Earth's sky, he found himself searching for Marcrituss among the stars.

He stepped toward the opening, then paused, turning back to Danrael—the guide who had shepherded him through so much darkness and wonder.

"Merry Christmas, Danrael," John said, his voice warm with gratitude.

"And to you as well, John," the angel replied, meeting his gaze. "And do not forget to pray."

John nodded, a quiet promise settling in his heart.

When he looked again, Danrael was gone.

After locating the second lever and sealing the hidden entrance behind him, John began the journey home.

The forest was hushed beneath a blanket of snow, every branch bowed under its silent weight. He ran, cold air filling his lungs. He weaved between the dark trees, each footstep muffled by the fresh powder.

He reached the old fence at the edge of the woods—the boards he'd once squeezed through now solid, expertly mended. He smiled, picturing his father out there with a hammer, quietly making the world whole again. John slipped through the gap and hurried toward town.

Snow crunched under John's boots. The air was sharp with the smell of pine and woodsmoke. Christmas lights twinkled through frosted windows, and for a moment, he just stood there, breathing in the ordinary miracle of home.

As he passed the diner where it had all begun, he slowed. A whole universe between then and now.

Then, drifting through the air, he heard music: voices rising, clear and bright, above the cold. A small choir stood outside the church, singing O Holy Night into the winter night.

John stopped, letting the hymn wash over him.

Long lay the world in sin and error pining... till He appeared and the soul felt its worth.

He'd heard those words what seemed like a million times before. But never had they pierced him like this. Before his journey, he too had wandered, unsure of his own worth, blind to the love that could reach him.

Now, he understood.

He bowed his head, whispering a prayer of thanks, tears stinging his eyes as he pressed on, the music still echoing in his heart.

When he reached his house, he paused outside the window. Inside, his parents stood in a warm halo of lamplight, untangling Christmas lights, half-laughing, half-sighing—repeating the same ritual as every Christmas Eve.

For a moment, John simply watched, letting the ordinary beauty of home settle over him. Then, quietly, he slipped inside, hanging his jacket by the door and tiptoeing to the living room. His parents were so absorbed in the mess of lights, they didn't see him at first.

He stood there, grinning, waiting for the perfect moment. "Merry Christmas!" he burst out.

They spun around, eyes wide, frozen for a heartbeat in disbelief.

Then they rushed at him—arms wrapping around him in a fierce, tearful embrace. John was swallowed by their hugs, laughing and crying at once—feeling like a child again: safe, loved, and found.

"Oh my goodness—John, just look at you!" his mother gasped, holding him at arm's length. "You're so tall, so... tan! And these muscles! What on earth were they feeding you over there?"

John laughed, wiping at his eyes. "I love you both so much."

"We love you too," his father said, voice thick with pride. "And we are so proud of you, son. Our son... the Traveller."

"This is the best Christmas present I could ever have," Carol beamed, pulling him close again. "Come help us finish the tree. You can tell us everything about your journey."

John hesitated, emotion rising in his throat. "Actually... maybe we could go to church first."

His parents exchanged startled glances.

"Did you say church?" Carol asked, astonished.

John nodded, bashful but sure.

Carol's face broke into pure joy. "Of course we can!"

"And then pizza," John added, grinning. "I'm starving for pizza."

Carol laughed, the sound bright through her tears. "You can have anything you want."

She pulled on her coat, Steve grabbed his, and the three of them set out into the snowy night for the Christmas Eve service.

When they entered the church, heads turned. People stared, startled by the sight of the tall, transformed young man between Steve and Carol—wondering if it could really be the same John they remembered.

After they found seats, John quietly slipped away, drawn to the nativity scene beside the altar. He knelt before the crèche, gazing at the tiny porcelain child, the angel above holding a scroll marked Gloria.

At the base, another porcelain scroll caught John's eye. He leaned in closer, and went still when he read the words inscribed there:

He makes all things new.

A tremor ran through him. Tears welled in his eyes as a joyful laugh accompanied them. He remembered Dernoah— her courage, her faith, the words she'd clung to at the end. Her presence lingered still, echoing in the delicate script, whispering that hope was real.

Looking down at the infant in the manger, John felt the mystery settle in his heart. He truly had come to make all things new.

And John knew—now, perhaps for the first time—what that meant. For he himself had been made new—saved and made new by the glorious grace of Christ.

CHAPTER
SIXTY-ONE

The weeks after Christmas were quiet in the way that matters. John helped his dad on the farm, ate his mother's cooking, and slept in his own bed. In the evenings, the three of them sat around the table—John talking, his parents listening, asking questions, laughing. Sometimes they went quiet when the weight of everything settled over them. He told them everything—about Shenya, Dernoah and Jaromei. The boatha. The festival. The sea under the dome. The battlefield. All of it. For the first time in his life, he had nothing to hide from them, and he used every minute of it.

The first day back at Shady Springs High felt like stepping onto a stage where everyone had already read the script except him.

John walked the halls much taller, shoulders broader. Heads turned. Whispers followed. No one shoved him. No one knocked his books to the floor. The fear that used to live behind his ribs had gone quiet.

He still caught himself flinching sometimes when a locker slammed. He supposed that would take longer.

The principal called him in and offered a deal: complete a list of makeup assignments and weekend courses, and he could graduate with his class. John accepted without hesitation. Every extra hour in the library felt like proof he was no longer the boy who froze.

In January, he started attending confirmation class as well. By spring, he stood in front of the congregation in a new white shirt, hands steady as he affirmed the faith that had once felt distant, but now lived bone-deep inside him.

Coaches hovered in the hallways like persistent gulls. "Fischer, we could use you on the line," the football coach said one afternoon, eyeing his build. The basketball coach was even more direct. John turned them both down with a polite smile. His strength wasn't meant for Friday night lights.

Girls noticed too. Notes appeared in his locker. Smiles lingered in the cafeteria. But his thoughts never wandered far from Jaromei.

Most afternoons he slipped away to the cave.

He spent hours tracing the ancient drawings on the walls, searching for any clue about the Earth fragment of Mishrael's scroll. The symbol for Eden stared back at him again and again. He ran his fingers over it, wishing Shenya were there to help translate the faded markings.

Olly and John had crossed paths at school for months. Neither had spoken a word. There was one afternoon in February—John coming out of the library, Olly heading the other way down the hall—when their eyes met for longer than usual. John had braced himself out of old habit. The sneer didn't come. Olly just looked at him. There was something complicated moving across his face, something that wasn't hostility. John had walked on without stopping, but the moment stayed with him. Something had changed in Olly. He didn't know what. He didn't try to find out.

Then came the afternoon the week after Graduation. John rounded the corner by the old hardware store and saw Olly walking toward him.

John hesitated, caught off guard. He realized he was now taller than the boy who had once loomed over him. The reversal felt strange, almost surreal.

"Hey, John."

"Hey, Olly."

A heavy silence stretched between them—full of things unsaid. The last time they'd spoken, Olly and his friends had left John broken and bleeding in the woods.

Olly shifted, uneasy. He eyed John's broad shoulders, his new strength.

"Man," Olly said, managing a weak grin, "I don't know what you've been eating, but you've grown like crazy."

His gaze dropped before speaking again. "Look... I've wanted to say something for a long time." He hesitated before continuing. "I'm really sorry, John. I mean it. Not just for what happened last October, but for everything."

John opened his mouth, but no words came. He'd rehearsed this conversation a hundred times, but now those lines felt hollow. All that was left in him was honesty, and something lighter—mercy.

"Olly," he said, drawing a deep breath. "I forgive you."

Olly blinked in surprise.

"I forgive you, not just for the woods," John continued, his voice steady, "but for everything. I don't know why you did what you did... but I forgive you. I want to move forward. Leave the past behind."

To John's astonishment, Olly's face crumpled. He sobbed, shoulders shaking.

"Hey," John said, leaning in closer. "It's okay. What's wrong?"

Olly wiped his eyes, glancing around to see if anyone was watching. "That day in the principal's office—when you asked me why I hated you—" He swallowed, his words tumbling out in a rush. "When you left town, I thought about it a lot. I've wanted to tell you the truth ever since, but I was too scared." Olly looked away. His jaw worked. John waited, saying nothing, giving him the space.

"You can tell me now."

"No, never mind. I can't... I—" Olly started to turn away, but John took hold of his arm.

"You can tell me, Olly. It's just us here."

Olly took a deep breath. "You know my mom died a long time ago," he whispered. "And my dad..." The words stuck. "He's hurt me every day since I was eleven. She always stopped him." He lifted his shirt, and John went completely still. Scars, scabs, and bruises marred Olly's chest, old and new—far beyond any football injury. A fresh burn from a cigarette end was just above his waist.

"You have a mom and dad who love you more than anything. I've seen how they are with you all our lives in this town." Olly choked out. "Every time I saw it... I wished I had the same. Your dad would do anything for you. Mine only cares about himself and how people see him."

He remembered what Shenya had said: those who hurt others often carry wounds of their own.

"I was awful to you because I was jealous," Olly admitted, his voice cracking. "The school made me go talk to someone to stay on the football team. I didn't want to at first, but it turned out to be a good thing. I realize now that hurting you made me feel better. But I know how wrong that was."

John didn't hesitate. He stepped forward and pulled Olly into a hug.

Olly clung to him, as if letting go might bring the old weight crashing back down.

"I'm so sorry for everything," Olly whispered.

"It's in the past," John replied, pulling back and gripping Olly's shoulders. "Why don't you come home with me for dinner? My parents will be surprised, but I know they'll welcome you."

Olly hesitated. "My dad will wonder where I am. He might... do something if I don't go home."

"Don't be afraid," John said. "I know what it's like to need a friend. You need one now—and you've got one."

After a long moment, Olly nodded.

That evening, the Fischers welcomed Olly with the same warmth they showed everyone. Over dinner, the truth came out—old wounds, secrets, regrets. By the time the plates were cleared, Olly agreed to stay with his aunt, who had never known the depth of what he'd endured until that night when he called her.

John and Olly hugged before he left, promising to keep in touch and make a real new start—this time, both of them meant it.

John returned to his room. As he entered, a faint rattling came from his desk.

The small device Kleo had given him was shaking, a red light pulsing at its center.

John's heart leapt.

He stood watching the warning glow, the recent dreams pressing back in—war on Marcrituss. Land against sea in an underwater battle, creatures from the depths forced into the service of the sea kingdom. There had been no voice from Danrael, so he'd told himself they were only nightmares. The pulsing red light made everything clear.

It wasn't a dream.

It was a vision.

Far away, under a sky not his own, darkness gathered once more. John's journey was only beginning.

Somewhere, beyond the stars, his friends were calling for him.

EPILOGUE

"There's a penitent coming this way," the eldest elder murmured, eyes narrowed as dusk crept over Morboli.

"It's nearly sundown," the youngest replied, voice tight. "The temple's been closed for hours."

A lone figure in a plain, ash-gray burmui advanced. His hood was drawn low; the heavy cloth whispered against the flagstones. The elders fell silent as he approached, the air turning brittle with suspicion.

"My dear penitent," the eldest woman called, her tone almost mocking, "the temple is closed. If it's prayer you want, you'll have to wait for sunrise."

The stranger halted, shadows pooling at his feet. His words were quiet, carrying far in the hush. "I seek information about the Traveller. I know he's fond of this village. Do you know when he will return?"

The third elder scoffed. "We don't trouble ourselves with outsiders who bring chaos and start wars."

The stranger dipped his head, silent as stone.

The youngest spat in the dust. "If you want news of the Traveller, ask Shenya Arjik Spee. He's always quick to welcome trouble. Speak to him, and it'll be more than enough penance to shorten your vow."

The elders laughed, thin and cold.

The stranger's next words slid out, soft and unsettling. "And where might I find Shenya?"

A pause, heavy with disdain. The eldest woman finally jerked her chin. "Inside the village. Third house on the street off the main square."

"Thank you," the stranger intoned, each word low and final. He moved away, the burmui swallowing his form.

He stopped beneath a twisted tree at the edge of the labyrinth, where the night pooled thickest. The village walls weren't far behind him. Silence pressed in on Morboli—a silence filled not with peace, but with waiting.

Certain he was alone, he lowered his hood.

A child darted past, then staggered to a halt. Moonlight caught the stranger's face.

"You're... King Rathrian," the child gasped, voice trembling. "I've seen drawings of you in the batnu."

His smile arrived without warmth, like a door opening onto nothing. "Yes... and no. King Rathrian is on a little vacation."

As the boy's eyes widened, the stranger's gaze turned bottomless black—two wells of darkness swallowing the last light. The child's scream tore through the village, echoing off stone and shadow.

And the darkness, at last, entered Morboli.

THE SEVEN WORLDS TRILOGY

The King Above All Gods is only the beginning of John's story. Book Two, *The Bright Morning Star,* is coming soon.

Instagram — @sevenworldstrilogy

www.thesevenworldstrilogy.com

For enquiries, email: abruce@thesevenworldstrilogy.com

GLOSSARY

Characters

- **Carol Fischer:** John's mother on Earth.
- **Danrael:** An angelic guide and messenger.
- **Dernoah:** Mother of Shenya and Grandmother of Jaromei.
- **Eamin:** A guardian figure on Spaltrico, involved in protecting sacred elements.
- **Euron:** King of the land tribes on Marcrituss.
- **Ilmly:** A personal advisor to Euron on Marcrituss.
- **Jaromei Kobok Spee:** Shenya's daughter, a land anuri with duties as a market worker and portal guardian.
- **Jina:** Wife of Yumi, the gropolo shou
- **John Fischer:** The protagonist, a human teenager from Earth, known as the Traveller.
- **Kleo:** An undercover operative on Spaltrico, fighting against societal divisions.
- **Mitch Jackson:** Olly Jackson's father and a resident of Shady Springs.
- **Olly Jackson:** A high school bully from Earth.

- **Prinny**: The former guardian on Spaltrico and mother of Eamin
- **Principal Sunti**: The principal of Shady Springs High School
- **Mishrael**: An ancient prophet whose writings form the basis of the scroll.
- **Poltoma**: A land anuri, friend to Shenya, involved in tribal alliances.
- **Qitra**: A princess of the land tribes on Marcrituss.
- **Rathrian**: King of the sea tribes on Marcrituss.
- **Revonat**: A demonic entity sowing chaos across worlds through possession and manipulation.
- **Saltho**: A sea tribe prince on Marcrituss who forsakes his title and princely privileges join the Traveller's cause.
- **Shenya Arjik Spee**: A former portal guardian on Marcrituss, now a companion to the Traveller.
- **Steve Fischer**: John's father on Earth, a farmer offering wisdom and support.
- **Vonild**: The wealthy leader of the Cult on Spaltrico
- **Xerti**: A gropolo who has a strong connection with John
- **Yumi**: Old friend of Shenya and Poltoma who is a renowned gropolo shou
- **Watchers**: A group of fallen angels watching for moments of human weakness and tending the divisions they have sown across the seven worlds.

Places and Worlds
- **Batnu**: An institution for learning on Marcrituss.
- **Brooth**: A land city on Marcrituss, formerly thriving with archives and Batnu structures.
- **Cosheh**: A coastal land city on Marcrituss, serving as a gateway to sea areas.

- **Dimig**: A small, deserted land village in Dimig Valley on Marcrituss, with ancient ties.
- **Eden**: The ancient name given to the planet Earth.
- **Gardens of Miren**: An ancient religious site on Marcrituss.
- **Jyr**: The capital city of the Land Kingdom on Marcrituss.
- **Marciluk**: The underwater capital city of the Sea Kingdom on Marcrituss, featuring a massive dome and palace.
- **Marcrituss**: The first fantasy world visited, inhabited by anuri divided into land and sea tribes.
- **Morboli**: A land village on Marcrituss, home to the Spee tribe.
- **Mour**: The ancient name for Tokika City on Spaltrico.
- **Nolthem**: The primary continent on Marcrituss for the Spee and Trovus land tribes.
- **Shady Springs**: A small farming town on Earth, John's hometown.
- **Spaltrico**: A dystopian, polluted world dominated by ideological conflicts between cults and government.
- **Stolji**: A continent on Marcrituss, home to the Brileej land tribe.
- **Temple of Ninto**: A pantheistic temple of worship near the city of Cosheh on Marcrituss.
- **Tokika City**: The main dystopian city on Spaltrico, formerly known as Mour.

Creatures and Objects

- **Arbimto**: A small, sun-absorbing creature kept as a pet on Marcrituss.
- **Boatha**: A dangerous beast that lives underground on Marcrituss.
- **Burmui:** A plain hooded cloak worn by those under-taking a vow of poverty and penance on Marcritus.

- **Gropolo**: A large avian creature bred for flight on Marcrituss.
- **Kleo's Communication Device**: The quantum-linked device Kleo gives John
- **Mour Text**: An ancient prophetic text from Spaltrico.
- **Portals**: Ancient gateways between the seven worlds, activated by innate angelic power and hidden after the fall of man.
- **Roolimba**: A red bird common to labyrinths on Marcrituss.
- **Sea Dragons**: Fierce creatures who are part of the Royal Sea Army on Marcrituss.
- **Sky Vrooter**: The most common form of transportation on Spaltrico.
- **Trocks:** Bell towers in Marcrituss villages whose tolling signals time, religious services, or varying levels of danger and lockdown.

Tribes

- **Brileej**: The largest land tribe on Marcrituss, based on the continent Stolji.
- **Sea Tribes**: Collective term for anuri who migrated to the oceans; advanced in technology, worship a pantheon, and unified under the Sea Kingdom.
- **Spee**: A land tribe on Marcrituss, scattered on Nolthem; follows traditions like inheriting kin names from mothers.
- **Trovus**: A land tribe on Marcrituss, located on Nolthem; known for cultural practices like grooming standards.

Concepts and Terms

- **Anuri**: Human-like inhabitants of Marcrituss, adapted for land or sea life with features like ridges for swimming.
- **Arjik:** The kin name of Shenya's family line

- **Borth's Alliance**: The cult causing chaos on Spaltrico.
- **Land Tribes**: Collective term for anuri remaining on continents; more traditional and religious, divided into Spee, Trovus, and Brileej under the Land Kingdom.
- **Scroll (Fragments)**: Pieces of an ancient prophetic message scattered across worlds, key to unity and redemption.
- **Seven Worlds**: Interconnected realms linked by portals, central to the prophecy and trilogy.
- **Shou**: The handler of a gropolo
- **Traveller**: The prophesied human chosen to collect the scroll fragments and unite the worlds.
- **Yeshua**: The holy name of Jesus in Hebrew. A name meaning "God saves".

ABOUT THE AUTHOR

Alexander Bruce has worked in ministry for several years. His calling has brought him all over the world, giving him many fascinating experiences to draw upon for inspiration in his writing. Alexander resides in Yorkshire, England and has a passion for studying faith, science and philosophy.